For Will Atkins
&
For Mary –

Whose yeses changed my life
in very different ways.

Should the wide world roll away
Leaving black terror
Limitless night,
Nor God, nor man, nor place to stand
Would be to me essential
If thou and thy white arms were there
And the fall to doom a long way.

Stephen Crane

Don't threaten me with love, baby.
Let's just go walking in the rain.

Billie Holiday

NO TAKE-BACKS

ONE

Look at this boy, thirteen years old, sitting on the edge of a bed. His feet do not touch the floor. He wears only white socks and underpants, his narrow frame otherwise bare. The socks droop loose from his feet like empty sacks. His bangs, kitchen-scissor trimmed by his mother, hang unevenly over his eyebrows. There's a scab on his lower lip, the result of an altercation with a bully at school, and his upper lip is chapped from constant nervous licking. His narrow shoulders are slumped, spine zippered up the middle of his pale, freckled back. He looks down at his lap. His hands rest there. In them, held in his cupped palms like some holy object, a small makeshift pistol.

His stepfather keeps his gun locked away somewhere, but the bullets he stores in his sock drawer. The boy, Sandy, found them by accident. He was poking around his mom and stepfather's bedroom looking for a few dimes. He wanted to see a movie and eat a bag of popcorn. Instead of loose change he found the bullets. They were in a small cardboard box. He took three. He thought he could get away with three, and so far he has.

It's been two weeks.

During the first several days Sandy carried the bullets with him everywhere, in the pocket of his wool school pants, and whenever he had a moment alone he took them out and examined them. He went to the bathroom at school several times and locked himself in one of the green-painted toilet stalls just so he could hold them and look at them. They felt heavier in his hand than they did in his pocket. They felt more substantial.

He imagined being able to shoot his stepfather. That would put an end to things. Then he wouldn't have to be afraid anymore, not in his own house. Then this man who pretended he could replace his dad would be gone. Then this man he hated, who clearly hated him, would be gone.

He had no intention of acting out his fantasy. Not at first. He'd had dozens of others and nothing had come of any of them. Not until last summer, anyway, when he'd imagined stabbing his stepfather to death, while taking his rage out on a cat. Later he felt bad about killing the little thing, but at the time he was simply thinking of this man he despised. He wasn't thinking at all. But even then he never came close to actually stabbing his stepfather. Even with a knife he felt weak and small. He still does. He feels like little more than a walking cringe.

Every time he comes home from school, every time he steps through the front door, his stomach is a terrible knot of dread. He walks straight to his bedroom, hoping his stepfather won't see him or hear him, hoping he can pass like a ghost. He hides there till dinnertime, doing homework and reading comics. At dinner he sits stiff, eats without speaking but for please and thank you, eats despite a sick stomach, and tries not to make noise when he chews. He certainly doesn't put his elbows on the table. Last time he did that his stepfather stuck a fork into the back of his hand. He heard Neil later tell his mother that he hadn't meant for it to break the skin. I was just trying to make a point, he said, and laughed at his accidental pun. But whatever his stepfather's intentions, Sandy was unable to use his hand for several days. The holes turned black and the skin surrounding them turned red, and his hand swelled up, and it ached so bad he couldn't even hold a pencil.

Soon he found himself wondering how he might get his hands on a gun. He looked for his stepfather's, but found nothing, not even a safe inside which it might be locked. He broke into two different houses down the street while he was supposed to be at school, but came up empty-handed yet again. He didn't know what to do. The fantasy, which had only begun to take form in reality, was about to blow apart again, like smoke on the wind.

Then it occurred to him that he could make a gun.

Last year his friend Nathan had found a shotgun shell, and they went into Nathan's garage and put it into his father's vise and hit it with the rounded end of a ball-peen hammer. It exploded, punched a dozen holes in the garage door, tore out chunks of wood. Great splinters hung off the front of the door, the circle of damage bigger than a dinner plate. It was great and terrifying. Nathan was grounded for a month and told he could no longer play with Sandy. His parents said Sandy was a bad influence. They said Sandy got him into trouble. It had been Nathan's idea, but that's the way it's always been with him.

He gets picked on by other kids at school. Teachers slap the back of his head when it was the boy next to him who was whispering. If he walks into a store he almost always gets yelled at by the proprietor. Sometimes for flipping through the comic books without buying, sometimes for no reason at all. Simply because he's there and looks like a good receptacle for rage. People don't like the look of him. Random people on the street will find excuses to yell at him – if he accidentally steps on their shoe, for instance, or bumps into them while running to school.

His stepfather is, of course, the worst of all.

Sandy's mother told him once that he was a lightning rod. Some people, she said, simply have faces other people want to kick the teeth out of. You're one of those people, Sandy, for whatever reason, so you've got to be tough. You've got to be careful and you've got to be tough.

But he's tired of being tough. And he isn't a lightning rod. He's a cup. Violence doesn't flow through him and safely into the ground; he's been filled up and is now overflowing with it. He feels it pouring out of him like a boiling liquid.

He knows he'll go to Hell. When he was eleven a preacher named Billy Graham came to town and did revival meetings in a big tent on Washington Boulevard. His mom took him to one of those meetings after dinner and he heard a lot of talk about Hell, talk that stuck with him, so he knows that's where he'll go, but he doesn't care. He can't live with his stepfather even one more day.

To make the gun, Sandy folded a roadmap until it could be used comfortably as a handle. It was already folded, it came that way, and it took only two more folds to get it to the right size. First he folded it lengthwise to get it the correct width. Then the other way. It was surprisingly sturdy as a handle. He put the antenna into the crease of the last fold and taped it into place. When he was done he couldn't pull the antenna away from the handle even if he wanted to.

After that he let it sit for a couple days. It was shaped something like a gun, and the bullets he took from his stepfather fit snugly into the barrel, but he couldn't think of a way to make it fire.

His problem was that his imagination was more dexterous than his fingers. Everything he thought of was far too complicated.

Then, while he was on the back side of Bunker Hill, shooting rocks at tin cans with a slingshot, he thought of the solution. He cut a rubber band and put it through a metal washer and taped each end of the rubber band to the gun's handle so that he could simply pull back on the metal washer and let go and it would snap against the back of the shell and the bullet would fire.

Bang.

He hit his knuckle the first two times he tried it, snapped the washer against bone, drawing blood on the second attempt, but on the third try it worked. The sound it made was not nearly as loud as he'd expected, not a bang but a small pop. The bullet put a hole in his bedroom floor and the spent shell shot out the back of the gun and thwacked against his right arm. His mother came in and asked him what was that noise I just heard, and he said I don't know, mom, and she said strange, could have sworn I heard something, and paused a moment in the doorway looking suspicious. He thought she must know, maybe she even smelled it on the air, but she said nothing. And after a moment she simply told him he needed to wash up for dinner, it would be ready in fifteen minutes. He said okay, and she turned and left.

His arm is still bruised, like someone poked him with a finger, but Sandy doesn't care. He managed to make a working gun, it didn't explode in his hand, and he has two bullets left. He plans to use one of them tonight – as soon as his stepfather comes home from the bar. He looks at the clock on his night table.

It looks back at him.

It says tick . . . tick . . . tick.

It's just past twelve o'clock in the morning. His mom works nights and won't be home for hours, so he has time. As long as Neil comes home from the bar early, as he often does, and drunk, as he always does, and as long as Sandy doesn't lose his nerve, he can do this. He knows he can.

He just waits till his stepfather is sleeping, walks up to him, points, and . . .

Yes.

TWO

Teddy Stuart looks across the felt-topped game table to the pimple-faced son of a bitch dealing cards. Dead black eyes and hollow cheeks. Face colorless but for the pink acne on his chin and forehead. Hair slicked into place with a week's worth of unwashed grease. Like all the dealers here he wears a white shirt with an arm garter, a waistcoat, and a black bowtie. Unlike most of the dealers this one's a mechanic. Teddy's sure of it. The little shit has busted him five times in a row on hands under fourteen, and that just wouldn't happen if the kid wasn't a mechanic.

There's nothing Teddy hates more than playing smart and losing anyway. He knows that's why they're called games of chance, but goddamn it, chance won't kick you in the balls five times in a row. Only people will do that: only people have hearts that black. Chance is merely indifferent.

He came out to Los Angeles to make a delivery for the Man, and instead of being allowed to blow off a little steam after a cross-country journey, Atlantic to Pacific, and the stressful handing over of a briefcase with more money in it than he's personally earned in the last ten years – though he's well paid – he's expected to sit across from this pimple-faced kid not much older than the turd he squeezed between his cheeks this morning while the little mother-fucker deals crooked hands with a straight face.

There are two other players at the table besides, one on either side of him.

Teddy exhales with a sigh and looks at his cards. A six of hearts and a seven of clubs. Red and black. Thirteen.

The lady to his right hit on seventeen and collected an eight of hearts, his eight of hearts. Stupid bitch keeps collecting cards meant for him.

'If you bust me again . . .'

He clenches his jaw and wipes at his mouth with the palm of his left hand. He closes his eyes, trying to keep himself calm. He opens his eyes and taps the table with a dirty, chewed-on fingernail.

The dealer puts down a nine of clubs.

'You son of a bitch,' Teddy says, reaching forward to grab the kid, wanting to pull him down by the collar, slam his smug face against the table. But the kid's fast – faster than Teddy, anyway. He pulls back, dodging the swipe, and next thing Teddy knows he has both barrels of a sawed-off shotgun pressed against his forehead, hello, looks like your brains might be leaving by the back door, and the two other players are on their feet, taking several steps back.

'I think it's time for you to leave, friend.'

'You cheating bastard, do you know who I am?'

'I don't care if your name is Jesus Humphrey Christ, you gotta leave.'

'You have no idea who you're fucking with.'

'Theodore Stuart, a numbers cruncher for James "the Man" Manning who thinks just because he works for someone with some pull, that means he has some pull hisself. Well, your boss don't have as much pull on this coast as you seem to think he does, and even if he did he don't have no pull with me, and even if he did have pull with me you ain't him. Far as I can tell, you're just a fat drunk who can count money okay, but can't seem to hold onto any hisself.' He licks his lips. 'Now, all this conversation is stimulating, I admit, but I got a job to do, which means you gotta leave. Get to it, friend.'

'Take the gun off me.'

Teddy knows the night is over, knows he must subtract himself from this situation, but something in him refuses to budge while the dealer has the gun on him. He will have this one small victory. He will walk out of here with a little dignity. He will not walk out of here with his shoulders slumped, with his gaze on the floor, watching his feet drag him into the night. He will not walk out of here hating himself. The kid will take the gun off him or Teddy will not move. Not an inch.

Not a goddamned inch.

'No.'

'Take the gun off me and I'll go.'

'You'll go anyway, friend. I'm the one at the trigger end of this weapon.'

Herb Boykin, this place's owner, wearing a well-tailored suit and a hand-painted tie, is staring at them from across the room. Teddy can see him over the kid's shoulder. Can see him rock back on his heels with his hands in his pockets. Can see him suck on an eyetooth. Can see him rock forward. Can see him walk toward them.

'What's going on here, Francis?' he says as he arrives.

'Mr Stuart's out past his bedtime.'

'You're making the other patrons nervous.'

'Tell em to relax. I only hit what I'm aiming at.' He says this without taking his eyes off Teddy. Then he says: 'Are you gonna leave, friend?'

'Take the gun off me.'

'Back away and it'll be off you.'

'Shotguns are less than – uh – discriminatory, Francis.'

'It's pushed against his forehead, sir. I ain't gonna miss.'

Teddy can feel tears welling in his eyes. Fifty years old and tears welling in his eyes over an altercation with a kid barely out of high school. But he refuses to lose this battle completely. He refuses to leave here humiliated. He blinks. His eyes sting. He knows they're reddening and knowing this makes him angry. How dare the kid do this to him. How *dare* he. He pushes his head against the barrel of the gun, making it hurt, wanting it to hurt, wanting to feel more anger and less humiliation.

'You gonna pull the trigger or put the gun away?' he says. 'Your choice.'

'Take the gun off him, Francis. Mr Stuart's leaving.'

The kid hesitates but finally does as he was told.

'That's right, boy,' Teddy says. 'Do what the boss man says.'

The kid twitches at being called boy and mumbles something about not being no spade. This is good. He's at least gotten under the kid's skin. It doesn't release the spring-pressure in his belly, the tension that wants to explode from within him, but it's good nonetheless. It's something.

He stands up and straightens his tie. He glances around the large room. Most everyone is looking at him, silent. He recognizes several of them, their white faces like signs showing him their amused shock. He feels tears wanting once more to well in his eyes, but refuses them, blinks them away.

'I'm sure it was a misunderstanding, Mr Stuart,' Herb Boykin says. 'I do think it's best if you leave for the night, but you're welcome back. You'll have fifty dollars in chips waiting for you at the counter.'

'I'm not coming back here, you stupid son of a bitch. What happened here wasn't a misunderstanding. Your dealer's a mechanic. A *cheat*. That's a reflection on you. You and your place. So fuck you. *Fuck* you.'

He hawks up a mouthful and spits it into Boykin's face. It runs down the man's cheek like frothed egg white.

Boykin removes a handkerchief and wipes it away. Then he looks past Teddy and nods. Teddy turns around in time to see a large Negro take two steps toward him while swinging a hefty enameled sap. A moment later everything goes bright, like looking into the sun. Then black.

There is no transition, just click, like a light being turned off.

THREE

1

Headlights flash briefly against Sandy's bedroom window as a vehicle turns onto the street. It rolls up the hill from the corner and pulls to a stop outside. The brakes squeal. The engine dies, turning over a last couple times slowly, winding down like a clockwork toy, then going silent. A car door squeaks open, slams shut. Footsteps approach the front door and the front door, after a jangling of keys, swings open. A moment later it closes. Then the sound of a deadbolt sliding into place. Keys being set down on the scratched surface of the table by the front door. Shoes being kicked off and dropping to the floor one after the other with a thud and a thud. Footsteps padding away. Water running in the kitchen. The pipes moaning. A glass being filled. Silence. A glass being set down on the counter. Creaking floorboards. The couch straining.

Then five minutes of silence. It rings loudly in Sandy's ears, like tinnitus.

Finally the snoring begins. His stepfather's asleep. Soon he'll be asleep forever.

Sandy pushes off the bed.

The carpet feels strange beneath his feet, coarse and unnatural and unpleasant. He sets down the gun to put clothes on. His stepfather's asleep; he's not going to look in on him and wonder what the hell he's doing dressed in the middle of the night. You up to no good again? What you been up to? You answer me, you little shit, don't just shrug with that blank-stupid look on your face. What you been up to? Why you dressed? His stepfather's asleep and Sandy wants to be clothed for what he's about to do.

Being unclothed makes him feel vulnerable.

After putting on a pair of pants and a T-shirt Sandy collects the bullets from a shoebox under his bed and puts one into his pocket. The other he puts into the back of his homemade gun. He walks to his bedroom door. He stands there for a long time – heart pounding, hands sweaty. He licks his lips.

His mind is chaos, thoughts coming at him from every direction. Don't do it, you have to do it. What if mom comes home? What if he wakes up? What if mom comes home? Don't do it. If he wakes up and sees you with the gun he'll take it from you and kill you with it. You have to do it, don't do it, just get undressed and get back into bed and go to sleep. Just get into bed and sleep. It's safer. What if he wakes up? Sometimes you have good dreams. If you go to sleep now maybe you'll have good dreams. Don't do it, don't do it, you have to do it, you've got to, you must, don't—

He steps into the hallway. He walks down its narrow length. The walls feel like they're pushing toward him. Then he's through the hallway and into the living room with the gun gripped in his fist. Gripped tight.

He's afraid.

But as he walks, a strange thing happens:

Picture a single-storey house with blue-painted wood siding covering the exterior walls and gray asphalt shingles lining the roof. Picture it standing in the dark of night, the windows bright yellow rectangles revealing every room to anyone who might wander by. A record player blares scratchy in the dining room, sounding as if the record's spinning the wrong way. On a radio in the front bedroom someone talks excitedly but incoherently, the consonants and vowels somehow failing to form words. In the kitchen a dog wails like an infant while in the hallway a baby barks madly.

This is Sandy's mind when he begins walking.

But with each step one room in the house of his mind goes dark. With each step one room goes silent. Each step is like a switch shutting off part of his brain until when he arrives before his stepfather his mind's quiet and dark and calm as the space between two heartbeats. Everything outside this moment is a dream. Everything outside this moment has ceased to exist.

There's only one window still lighted and Sandy, stand-ing on the sidewalk, can see himself through it, lifting a makeshift pistol and aiming it at his sleeping stepfather's left temple.

His stepfather: sprawled out on the couch, the old sagging couch with its itchy upholstery, one arm flopped over his fat belly, the other hanging down, knuckles on the carpet, palm open like he's expecting silver. Shallow nasal snores as he inhales through his nostrils are followed by quiet exhalations through his open mouth like wind through a canyon but distant.

Except for these sounds, silence.

All other noises have been erased. In their place, a strange calm.

But something's coming. Like a train you sense even before you can hear it, the vibrations on your skin, some-thing approaches.

It's happening. He doesn't even feel like he's doing it. It feels as though he's a mere puppet and someone else is con-trolling him. Someone else is pulling the strings, but it's happening, and soon it'll be finished.

Sandy watches himself raise the gun. Watches himself pull back on the washer. Watches the rubber band stretch. Watches the color change slightly, turning a lighter shade of beige as the rubber thins and grows taut.

He watches himself let it go.

There's nothing to it. The fingers separate by mere milli-meters and the metal washer jumps from between them.

The gun makes a muted popping sound. The empty shell shoots out the back of the gun and thwacks Sandy in the neck. His stepfather's head snaps to the right. Then he sits up, his stepfather sits up, wobbling drunkenly, reminding Sandy of a buoy on the water, bobbing . . . bobbing . . . bobbing.

With the sound of the shot Sandy seems to have been slammed back into himself, and now here he is again – hi, old friend, it's been too long – standing only feet from his stepfather, and his first thought is that it didn't work. The gun didn't work correctly. If it had worked correctly his stepfather would be dead. But he's not dead. He's sitting on the couch, he's lifting his head, he's looking at Sandy. He's saying, 'What – what happened?'

Blood trickles down the side of his face.

Sandy opens his mouth to respond, but there are no words.

2

He looks at his stepfather. His stepfather looks back. The gun hangs from Sandy's small fist. Blood trickles down the side of his stepfather's face. His left eye fills with blood. The hole in his temple is black. You could easily plug it with a pencil eraser. There you go, sir, all fixed up, see the girl at the front desk about the bill. His stepfather blinks. A tear of blood rolls down his cheek from his left eye.

He repeats his earlier question: 'What . . . happened?'

Sandy can only stare.

'Oh, God,' his stepfather says.

He leans forward, resting his arms on his knees, looking down at the carpet between his feet. His hair hangs in sweaty clumps. There's a bald spot at the crown of his head, a semi-circle of shiny skin about as big around as a silver dollar, and a red pimple just inside the hairline. Blood drips from the side of his face and onto his calf. Blood drips onto the carpet. He doesn't seem to notice.

'Fuck,' he says. 'I must've drunk more . . . more than I . . . more than I . . .'

He spits between his feet. A long string of saliva stretches almost a full foot before snapping and falling to the floor.

'I think I might be sick,' he says.

Sandy puts a second bullet into the gun, forcing himself to stay where he is and do this. His heart pounds in his chest and he wishes already, with it still unfinished, that he had listened to his doubts. He never should have done this.

He wants to turn and run. He could run away and never come back. If he did that he wouldn't have to finish this. He could just go away and live the life of a hobo and he would never have to see Neil again. He wouldn't have to finish this and he wouldn't have to see Neil either. That's what he should have done in the first place. Some older hobo would teach him about hobo life. Maybe that's where his real father is, riding the rail, looking for day-labor jobs, cooking beans over an open fire in a hobo camp somewhere. He might run into his real father. They would instantly recognize each other, and his father would say he was sorry for leaving, and he would teach him about hobo life, and he would tell him stories of his adventures. He could do that instead of this. He could do that and everything would be okay. Everything would be fine. Everything would be great.

He aims the gun with a shaky hand at the bald spot at the top of Neil's head. He closes his eyes. Neil's going to look up now and stop him.

Right now. Right now.

Sandy opens his eyes. The man still sits, sagging, looking down at a dark circle of spit on the carpet. Drool hangs from his face. He has a strange rotten-sweet smell to him, like a fruit bowl left on the table too long in the heat of summer. He always smells that way after he's been drinking. Sandy's come to associate that sweet smell of fermentation with violence, with getting hit.

Tears stream down his face.

'You shouldn't have been so mean,' he says.

His stepfather starts to look up at him now, too late, saying in a slurred voice, 'Wha—'

But that's all he ever manages.

FOUR

1

Teddy wakes up face-down in a parking lot. He rolls over, sits up, touches his face. There are bits of gravel imbedded there. He brushes them from his cheek and they fall to the ground.

At first he's possessed by confusion and a strange uncomprehending sadness, as if he'd awakened from a nightmare he could not quite remember – just vague unpleasant images and a sound like a gate swinging on a rusty hinge – but that soon gives way to anger as he remembers what happened, how he was humiliated.

He looks to his right and sees a black coupe looming over him. Reaches up and grabs the jutting door handle. Pulls himself to his feet, swaying there a moment unbalanced. Looks down at his clothes. His suit is ruined. It's covered in grime and dirt, one of his waistcoat's buttons is missing, and a pocket has torn loose.

His head throbs.

He touches his temple and feels the sharp sting of pain and a crust of dried blood.

That little pimple-faced son of a bitch.

Teddy's gonna make him sorry. The hell he won't. He'll not be made to feel this way by anyone. He's been through too much in the last ten years to take what he took tonight without giving some back.

He's been through far too much.

2

A decade ago Teddy was simply an accountant in Jersey City. He had, over the years, developed a reputation as someone who could and would massage numbers when necessary, and that occasionally brought those with less than fully legal interests to his office. But these were small-time guys. Greek deli owners who wanted their taxes to reflect a mere fraction of their income, cops who skimmed drugs from busts to resell on the street and wanted a way to invest the money without raising eyebrows, that sort of thing. He'd never expected the Man to walk through the finger-smudged front door of his small rented office. But that was what happened. He walked in and sat down across from Teddy and crossed his not insubstantial arms in front of him after scratching his fat rippled neck like an overstuffed sausage skin and said, 'I think we can probably do a little business, you and me.'

At first Teddy simply handled taxes for a couple of the Man's legitimate businesses – a car dealership in Newark, a stationery store in Hoboken that maybe saw more cash filter through its till than was strictly legitimate. Sometimes the numbers by themselves wouldn't say exactly what you wanted them to say. But Teddy was adept at algebraic ventriloquism, could make numbers say whatever he wanted them to say, and he thought nothing of the Man's requests.

And, as will happen, when the requests got more extreme Teddy found himself going along with them, telling himself it's not that big a deal, not much worse than anything I've already done, and now a decade later he's doing things he never would have agreed to during that first meeting.

Teddy climbed down that ladder same as anyone would: one rung at a time.

Now he knows as much about the Man's business affairs as the Man himself, which means, of course, that there's no way to sever ties with him. The only thing that can end their relationship at this point is death, either Teddy's or the Man's.

But Teddy knows which is likelier.

3

Despite the stories he'd heard about the Man's ruthlessness, Teddy went a very long time before seeing that side of him. The Man was quiet. You had to lean toward him to hear what he was saying. And his voice was gentle when he spoke, as if soothing a frightened animal. When he talked it was because he had something specific to say and once it was said he stopped working his jaw. He could, at times, seem almost shy. But the stories Teddy heard about him suggested a monster, someone who'd snap your legs for the smallest offense, who'd put a hatchet into your skull if he even suspected something more serious, who'd put your corpse on the hood of your mother's car if you expired without first apologizing for what he thought you'd done. And then, when he was finished, he'd wash his hands of blood and go to his favorite steakhouse, sit at his corner booth (always held for him, no matter how busy the place got) and have himself an English-cut prime rib slathered in horseradish, a baked potato fully dressed, two orders of creamed spinach, two slices of apple pie with melted cheese on top, and finally a glass of scotch. Then, if it was the weekend and he wasn't staying in his apartment in the city, he'd head home to Shrewsbury and sleep like a baby in his large comfortable bed, warmed by the body of his faithful wife, who seemed to be the only person on the East Coast who had no idea what he did for a living, how he paid for their four-thousand-square-foot house and their frequent vacations.

At first Teddy was certain the stories that surrounded the Man were simply part of the mythology that built up around him during his twenty – now thirty – years in business. One could not do the kind of work the Man did without being hard, of course, but Teddy found the stories which surrounded him impossible to believe. These were things no human was capable of.

But things have changed since Teddy first heard those stories. He is, for one thing, no longer certain the Man is strictly human.

In the years since Teddy first started hearing stories about the Man he's witnessed horrors beyond anything Goya could have imagined, and without having to close his eyes or paint them into existence. He knows now that if the stories he heard aren't true, other stories like them are. And worse.

But despite what he's witnessed, despite what he's experienced, he's still only an accountant. A corrupt accountant, sure. He massages numbers, he helps launder dirty money, he delivers and explains the terms of briefcase loans to people whose names end up in obituary pages. But his hands to now have remained bloodless.

Yet there's a part of him that believes he's learned important lessons in detached violence. So he believes he knows what he's getting into as he removes the knife from his coat pocket, as he thumbs it open, as he stands in the shadows of night to await the kid. He's wrong about what he is capable of, of course, wrong about his ability to remain detached from what he's doing, but he can't know that.

Otherwise he wouldn't do what he does.

4

He stands in the dark parking lot with a knife gripped in his fist and watches the red-painted metal back door. The knife was a birthday gift from his ex-wife. He's been carrying it for years. He frequently has to deal with dangerous people, hard people, people who view weakness as an invitation, people whose first instinct is destruction, and while he's never cut anyone he has on more than one occasion used the blade to bluff his way out of a situation. He might have knelt before the toilet later, covered in sweat, entire body shaking, but he got through.

One thing about working for the Man: people who have something against him but are afraid to take him on directly will make themselves feel tough by coming after you instead. It's what happened tonight. He's sure of it.

He thinks about how the kid embarrassed him. He thinks about how the kid made him feel stupid and weak. He refuses to be seen as stupid and weak. He refuses to *be* stupid and weak. A man is defined by his actions in difficult situations. If someone walks on you and you lie there, you're a rug. You're made to be walked on. Soon others will see the footprints on your back and know it too. It's how a path is made. No, if someone tries to walk on you, you stop them. You stop them dead. You're no rug and you will not be stepped on.

Teddy waits a long time.

There are false alarms. A drunk fellow stumbling to his car. Someone taking out a bag of trash to throw into a bin in the alley. A stray dog. Occasionally while he waits the tide of anger and humiliation goes out and he thinks about leaving, about simply driving away, and if he were to do that things would turn out differently, not only for him but for many people – because his actions and the actions of a small boy named Sanford Duncan fifteen miles away will affect the lives of several people whom they will never meet – but every time he considers absenting himself, driving back to his hotel and getting some sleep, he thinks again about what happened in there, and the tide of emotion comes flooding back.

Eventually when the red door opens it's the kid.

Teddy refuses to think of him by his name. He can have no name, for things with names deserve to live. To Teddy he's simply the kid.

The kid reaches into his pocket and removes his wallet. He pulls a narrow cigarette from within and puts it between his lips. He lights the cigarette with a match. He pinches it between finger and thumb and takes a deep drag, holding it in for some time before releasing a wave of smoke and jagged coughs.

The scent comes to Teddy on the breeze. The kid's smoking a reefer.

Teddy stands in the shadows at the back of the parking lot and lets him smoke it. He watches him while he smokes it. That greasy forehead. Those patches of acne. Again and again that son of a bitch shamelessly dealt him crooked hands. Then humiliated Teddy for calling him out on it. The little shit. The worthless little—

His face gets hot. A saltwater sting in the eye.

He steps out of the shadows and walks with great purpose across the black asphalt toward the kid. His steps are long and solid. Tears stream down his face.

As Teddy nears him the kid looks up while simultaneously hiding the reefer behind his back and saying, 'It's not what you—' But then he recognizes Teddy and goes silent. When next he speaks his tone has changed. '*You*,' he says.

'Yes, me, you dismissive son of a bitch. You goddamn piece of—'

He swings the blade in an uncontrolled arc. The kid sees it coming and turns away. The blade slices through the back left shoulder of his shirt. At first it seems as though Teddy missed the person beneath. The fabric simply hangs in two pieces from the shoulder like a pair of sails on a windless day. Then the blood begins to flow. The pain must arrive with it, because Teddy watches it slap a grimace onto the kid's face. The kid grabs at the bleeding spot and his eyes go wide and glistening, and for a moment, three ticks of the clock, four at most, there's some chance that Teddy will be able to stop himself from going any further. Pity envelopes him. He recognizes the pain on the kid's face so wholly it could be his own. He almost steps back and disappears into the shadows with an apology falling from his tongue.

But then the kid's pained expression turns into a scowl.

'You fat fuck,' he says. 'You have no idea what hell you just walked into.'

The kid reaches down to his boot.

Teddy knows he can't let him get to it. The kid has a weapon there. A single-shot pistol. A knife. Something. Whatever it is, one thing's clear. Teddy's begun something he must finish. He swings the blade at the reaching arm and puts a deep gash into it. A sheet of blood pours from within. Then he swings again and the face opens up, the left cheek, revealing white bone, the Halloween skeleton beneath. Then he swings again, the throat opens with a clogged-drain gurgle, and he finds himself standing over this motionless thing which a moment ago was moving, which a moment ago was human.

There's nothing left in Teddy now but sorry. All the rage and humiliation which were in him as he approached the kid and swung for the first time have vanished. It seems so long ago that he began this. Could it really have been less than a minute ago that he took that first step? He feels like a different person from the one who was standing at the back of the parking lot with bad intentions.

Who was that guy?

5

He drops the bloodied knife. It rattles against the asphalt before going still beside the kid's dead body. He reaches down and touches the kid's face and says the kid's name. 'Francis,' he says. 'Francis, are you . . . are you okay?'

But of course he's not okay, and he'll never be okay again.

Teddy looks down at his hand. There's blood on it, a lot of blood. There's less on his coat sleeve, a few scattered droplets. It looks black beneath the light of the three-quarter moon. His mother told him once that you had to scrub bloodstains with soap and cold water right away if you hoped to get them out. This after he'd been punched in the nose on his way home from school, punched and had his hard-rock candy stolen. He'd bled down the front of his shirt, but his mom had managed to get the stains out, scrubbing them in the washtub. He liked to wear that shirt afterwards because it made it seem like the punch in the face had never happened. If it happened, where was the blood?

But some stains neither cold water nor hot can remove.

He turns away from the body and the blood pooling beneath it. If he were thinking clearly he'd pick up the knife, walk to his car, and drive back to the hotel, where he could clean himself up, discard his bloody clothes, and go to the bar freshened up and ready to chat with someone who might be willing to give him an alibi, some drunkard with no concept of time, yes, officer, he was drinking with me all night. But he's not thinking clearly. The detached violence he thought he was capable of he was not. The violence was angry and scared and the scene bears witness to that.

He leaves the knife where it lies.

He walks with jerky, robotic steps, like a man suffering advanced syphilis, vertebrae welded together; walks across the parking lot, down the alley, toward Sunset Boulevard. He stands near the street and watches cars go by. Then he sits. Several more cars pass him. Streaks of color: green blue black. Then one does not pass by. It slows and pulls up in front of him. At first he can't see it clearly, the headlights blinding him. Then it stops and he sees that it's a Los Angeles County Sheriff's car. A deputy sits behind the wheel, a young man with light brown hair and an Errol Flynn mustache. He looks down at Teddy and asks him, is everything all right.

'I think I just killed someone,' Teddy says. He looks down once more at his hand. 'Can you – can you tell him I'm sorry?'

FIVE

1

Candice stands in the parking lot behind the nightclub at which she works on the corner of Venice and Hauser, just northwest of Sugar Hill, where the moneyed Negroes live. They started moving into the neighborhood, taking over the mortgages of dried-up oil barons and derailed railroad magnates, during the Great Depression, and the neighborhood's northern border, Washington Boulevard, still stands as a sort of racial equator, with colored folk living primarily to the south. The nightclub is closed and silent, the voices and laughter which earlier enlivened it now only drunken memories, the neon-tube sign out front – which can normally be read from six blocks in either direction, pinning a name on the place, the Sugar Cube – is dark as the night itself, and but for two cars, the lot in which Candice now stands is empty. She leans against one of them, a blonde woman with her lips smeared red, her hair pin-curled, her dress inappropriate for a woman in almost any other profession.

She works as a B-girl, flirting with men, dancing with them, getting them to buy her watered-down drinks at premium prices. A hand on the knee. A kiss on the corner of the mouth. A suggestive look. It can be a difficult job. You must laugh at stupid jokes. You can't allow yourself to cringe at the stink of garlic on breath. Your feet get bruised as the clumsier ones are always tenderizing your meat out on the dance floor.

And the men get grabby. Sometimes they get violent.

She's been accosted on more than one occasion in this very parking lot by drunken men who wanted to take what she was unwilling to give them – or sell them.

Men are animals. You have to be careful with them. You have to tempt them, let them hope they might get to see what's hidden under your skirt without ever letting them believe it's a promise. If you let it get too far you'll find yourself in a dangerous situation.

It's made worse by the fact that some of the girls have a price. There's a dressing room upstairs, and it's a rare night that Candice doesn't see men get dragged up there by their ties like obedient puppies on leashes.

Only once was she unable to fight off an attacker. He left her torn and bleeding in this very parking lot, a mere twenty feet from where she now stands, took the money she'd earned that night, spit on her, called her a cunt and a whore.

For two weeks afterwards she looked like she went several rounds with Rocky Marciano, and though she couldn't afford the time off, she stayed home until the bruises healed. Once she returned to work the mere thought of walking out here in the dark was traumatizing. She couldn't do it alone. She tried to be strong on her first day back, to put on a brave face, but halfway to her car she found herself shaking and crying, unable to force her feet further into the darkness. She stood paralyzed until one of the other girls saw her and walked her to her car.

It took months before she could walk out here by herself.

She's more cautious now, more careful. Men are animals. And she has a boy to raise, a boy whose father is already absent. She doesn't want him to lose his mother as well. She wants him to retain some innocence for as long as possible.

She lights a cigarette, inhales deeply, looks toward the Sugar Cube's back door. Vivian said she'd only be a minute, said she just had to use the ladies' room, but it has to have been a quarter hour now, and Candice isn't dressed for this chill night air.

She looks up at the moon, bright behind a thin film of disintegrating clouds, and feels a small surge of anger. Directed neither at the moon nor at Vivian, but at her husband Neil, who's probably asleep on the couch in their little falling-down house on Bunker Hill. Once again he left her stranded. When he gets off work – he's head mail clerk at a downtown office building – he often hops on a street-car and takes it here to the nightclub, says hey, just wanted to see your pretty face, I'll only stay a few minutes, but minutes turn into hours, and by the time he's pushing out the door, the streetcars have stopped running. So what does he do? Sometimes he gets a cab, but too often he stumbles to the car, drives it home, collapses onto the couch, and falls into a drunken sleep without even realizing he's once again left her without a way home. It happens at least once a week, usually after a busy Saturday night when she's at her most tired, when her feet are killing her, when she's been grabbed one time too many by one chump too many, and wants nothing so much as the comfort of her own bed.

She cares for Neil, despite his flaws, despite the way he treats her son, but sometimes she feels like strangling him till he's dead. He can be so thoughtless, and all tomorrow's apologies mean nothing to her now. They'll mean very little then.

Vivian finally pushes through the back door and sways across the parking lot toward her, saying sorry about that, had to get some money out of Heath.

'Money for what?'

'Leland did some work for him couple weeks ago, asked me to collect it.'

Candice nods, takes another drag from her cigarette, offers it to Vivian, who pinches it between two fingers, sucks the last drag from it, and flicks it out to the asphalt. It hits the ground and a small scattering of orange embers flash on the air, briefly looking like a miniature fireworks show – one for the ants and beetles – before going dark.

'Where's he been lately, anyway?'

'Leland?'

She nods.

'Had a movie last week, five full days of work.'

'Yeah?'

'Twelve hours a day every day.'

'Was it a speaking part?'

'Not this time. But maybe soon. It's about building relationships with producers. You know, it's less to do with talent than knowing the right people.'

'Come on,' Candice says, pulling on a locked door, 'my lady parts are freezing off.'

They get into the car and Vivian starts the engine.

'You need to do something about Neil. The way he leaves you stranded is rotten.'

'He doesn't mean it.'

'If it only happened once I'd believe that.'

Candice shrugs, and as Vivian pulls the car out of the parking lot and into the street she turns to the passenger's-side window and looks through it, out at the city, her breath fogging the glass in front of her.

She likes this part of the night. The bars have closed and the night owls have gone home, everyone from the zoot-suited Mexicans to the Negro-speaking hipsters, but it's too early yet for even the earliest risers to be pushing through their front doors. The city is still and silent and possesses the feeling of possibility, like an unhatched egg. You can almost forget it was long ago parceled out and sold. You can almost forget that crooks live in its mansions while honest people live in tarpaper shacks. You can almost forget that racial violence rages everywhere, from Hollywood Stars games at Wrigley Field to burning crosses in the yards of Negroes who dared to buy homes in white neighborhoods. You can almost forget that gangsters dine with famous actors and grin from newspaper photographs while honest, hardworking men die unknown.

You can almost forget, but not quite.

She knows the chief of police, William H. Parker, has promised to clean the place up, but she knows too that the Bloody Christmas beatings were only three months ago now, and if the man can't control his own cops, how is he supposed to control a city?

The answer's simple. He can't. And in truth she doesn't blame him for that. Los Angeles is a monster, a beast whose primary nutrients are Hollywood glitter and dumb violence. No one could control such an animal.

They drive north till they hit Sunset Boulevard, then head east, past the point where it hooks right and becomes Macy Street. A few minutes after that Vivian turns the car left onto Bunker Hill Avenue, and Candice finds herself surrounded by the comforting familiarity of her neighborhood, crumbling though it is.

The car rolls north on a street punctuated by potholes. Up ahead, on the right, in front of their small house, their small crumbling house with its asphalt-shingle roof, sits their car, a 1948 Chevrolet Fleetmaster. The driver's-side door hangs open. Key's probably still jutting from the ignition as well. It wouldn't be the first time. Lucky the car wasn't stolen by some leather-jacketed hoodlum looking to joyride.

Sometimes she could just—

Her thought is cut off by the sight of something on the asphalt beside the car, something about the size of a man. Not only the size of a man but the shape. A man on his back with his head tilted to the right, toward the parked car.

Whatever it is, the sound of the approaching vehicle doesn't cause it to stir. It simply lies there, still as a mountain.

'Oh my God,' she says.

'Maybe he's just passed out.'

Candice doesn't respond. As the car slows down she pushes open the door and steps out into the chill April air. She walks toward the sedan, moonlight reflecting off the chrome grille. Looks down at the man lying on the asphalt beside it. Looks at his left hand. The fingers are curled and dirt is crusted under the nails, black crescents lining the tip of each one. She looks at his face, looks into his eyes. He doesn't look back. He's incapable of looking back. He's incapable of anything. The left side of his face is covered in blood. There's a black dot like a wormhole in his temple. A five-pointed star carved into his forehead. The gashes deep and red, white bone visible beneath them.

She steps back. She puts her hands over her mouth. Her face feels numb. Her legs feel numb. She can't feel her legs at all, and no wonder, they must have disappeared, they must have simply vanished out from under her, because now she's sitting on the cold asphalt in the middle of the street, and the only way that could have happened is if her legs vanished. A second ago they were holding her up.

Why is Neil outside? Why is Neil lying in the street? That's such a silly, stupid thing for him to be doing.

'Neil,' she says, 'we have to go inside. It's late.'

2

Sandy stands looking through the dirty glass of his bedroom window. He watches his mother push her way out the passenger's-side door of Vivian's car. He watches her walk toward the place where Neil lies. He watches her face contort. Watches the eyes go glossy, and the mouth open and close, open and close, like a goldfish that's just been fed. He watches her put her hands to her mouth and collapse to the asphalt. Under normal circumstances it would make him sad to see his mother in such a state – he loves her and doesn't like to see her hurt – but right now all he can think about is getting caught. And getting locked up.

He tried to make it look like his stepfather was murdered by a serial killer. He read a story about a serial killer not too long ago and tried to make it look like that, like one of those killings, and if he did, if he was successful, maybe he won't get caught. But he isn't sure. He did it in a panic. He didn't think about how to cover up his crime until it was committed, and he might have done a poor job of it. All he knows is he did the best he could. In a panic, his mind spinning, his heart racing, he did the best he could. If he'd planned he'd have done better, but he didn't plan. He didn't really believe he was going to do it. Even while he did it he didn't really believe it was happening. It was as if the part of his brain that could tell fantasy from reality went black in those moments, just turned off completely. I'm tired, good night. If he'd believed it was real he would have planned.

But right after the second shot, the shot that sent his stepfather slumping to the floor in a strange motion that seemed somehow deliberate, as if he'd simply decided to lean forward and rest on his head with his behind in the air, reality came back to Sandy and he panicked. He paced the floor. He prayed to God to let him take it back. He promised he'd never hurt anyone ever again if only God would take it back. But still the body remained, dead as ever, and Sandy realized he would have to do something with it. He would have to make it look like someone else murdered his stepfather. Unless he wanted to get locked up. Unless he wanted his mother to know what he'd done. And he couldn't stand the thought of that. That was the worst.

His mother could never, ever know.

At first he could think of nothing. All he felt was panic and he couldn't get his mind under control enough to form coherent thoughts. Red crayon in an angry fist scribbled across the walls of his mind. Then he got an idea. He walked to the front door and opened it and looked around, afraid that people might have heard the gunshots, afraid they might be outside talking, wondering what had happened. Did it wake you up too, Sandy? But the street was silent. The windows in the other houses and apartments were black. If anyone had heard they hadn't come outside to investigate. And probably no one had heard. These gunshots were not like in the movies.

He might be able to do this. He might be able to get away with it.

He dragged the body outside. It took a lot of work. He had to stop to catch his breath more than once. Neil weighed twice as much as him, maybe more. If it weren't for the terror coursing through his veins he probably wouldn't have been able to do it at all. But finally he managed. He got the body out to the street and next to the car. He opened the door to make it look like it happened as Neil was stepping out of the vehicle. He went back inside and grabbed a straight razor from the bathroom. He leaned over the body and carved long gashes into its head. They came together to form a five-pointed star. Neil didn't even seem to be a person anymore when he did it. Sandy could have been carving into anything. Had he thought about it he wouldn't have been able, the image in his mind would have made him feel ill, but by moving without thinking, by simply acting, he managed without hesitation.

That's what the serial killer had done in the story he read: carved stars into the foreheads of his victims.

He went back inside again and washed the razor and put it away. Then grabbed the keys from the table by the front door and a pair of shoes from the floor. He put the keys into Neil's hand and the shoes on his feet. He tied the shoes, making bunny ears from the laces and looping them through one another.

His third trip inside was his last. He locked the door, then turned to face the room. He flipped over couch cushions to hide the bloodstains, then moved the couch forward a couple feet to cover the stains on the carpet. He undressed, hiding his now-bloodied T-shirt between his mattress and box-spring. He put the gun and the spent shells into a shoe-box under his bed. He lay in bed and stared at the ceiling. Everything he'd done caught up to him. He lay there and felt sick to his stomach, afraid, like he should just run away. But running would be an admission of guilt. His mom would know what he'd done. And the police would know. He had to stay and simply hope she never found out.

He prayed again to God to please let him take it back, please.

He looked out his window, saw Neil's brown shoes jutting past the front end of the car, knew nothing had changed and nothing would, no matter how many times he said please, no matter how sincerely.

God's silence was an answer and the answer was no.

His mother's eyes are glossy like when she's been drinking. Her mouth is open. She looks like a little girl to him right now, a little girl who's just been slapped in the face and doesn't know how to react, confused by the shock of what's happened.

He'd do anything to take it back, but can't, so he simply stands there and watches as Vivian helps his mother to her feet and guides her toward the front door. Then the angle is wrong for him to see anything. They disappear from sight.

The front door unlatches. He hears it.

He walks to bed and crawls into it. He holds his pillow tight to his chest, feeling like a little baby, helpless and alone.

All he can do now is wait to see what happens.

3

Candice walks toward the front door. She feels lost, detached from everything, a rudderless boat adrift on the sea. Vivian reaches out and grabs the doorknob, turns it, pushes open the door. Candice can see it all happening, can feel Vivian guiding her into the house with a gentle hand pressed against her back, can feel her legs moving under her, step after step, but she also feels that she's very far from all this, feels that she's not a part of it at all.

She walks across the living room to the couch. Vivian helps put her into a sitting position. She sinks into the couch and stares across the room to the wall.

The wall is white.

Vivian walks to the telephone. She calls the police. She says hello, there's been a murder. A man's been killed. Yes, killed dead. I think he was shot in the head. She gives the address. She hangs up the telephone.

She looks at Candice and says, 'Do you want me to make some coffee?'

Candice thinks no, no I don't want any coffee, it's late, and how could I drink coffee while Neil lies dead in the street, but instead of saying that, instead of saying anything, she nods her head.

'Okay,' Vivian says. 'I'll put the percolator on.'

'Can you check on Sandy first? Can you make sure he's okay?'

'Oh, God,' Vivian says. 'Yes – of course.'

She disappears into the hallway.

4

Three quick taps on the door, the rattle of the knob. Sandy sits up expecting to see his mother, but when the door swings open it instead reveals Vivian, the right half of her face splashed with light from the living room, the left half covered in shadows. He's glad it's her. He wasn't ready to look into his mother's eyes. He wasn't ready to lie to her.

'Sandy?'

'I'm here,' he says in the darkness. 'Is everything okay?'

He wonders what's next. He heard their voices but couldn't make out their words. He wonders if somehow they already know what he's done, if his pretending at innocence will only make it worse for him. He knows it's a possibility, but the alternative is to admit guilt before anyone has expressed suspicion, and that he won't do, can't do. The consequences are far too great.

'No,' Vivian says, 'everything isn't okay. Why don't . . . why don't you come out to the living room?'

'Did something happen?'

'Come out to the living room.'

'Okay. I have to get dressed.'

'Get dressed, then come right out, okay?'

'Okay.'

She pulls the door closed.

Sandy turns on his lamp and gets to his feet and pulls on his pants and a shirt.

He walks out of his bedroom, down the hall, to the living room.

His mother sits on the couch, her back to the hallway entrance. He can see her blonde hair, her slumped shoulders, the way her head hangs forward, but not her face. Vivian sits at the dining table on the other side of the house, looking at him sadly.

'What happened?'

His mom turns around. Her eyes are very red and swollen, her lipstick smeared, and when she tries to smile, to comfort him despite her own pain, he sees lipstick on her teeth.

'Sandy,' she says.

She reaches an arm out toward him beseechingly. He walks around the couch, walks to her, feeling sick in his stomach. If everything else hadn't yet made it clear, his mother's face lets him know it: the shock in her eyes, the way her mouth is turned down, and the crease between her eyebrows all tell him the same thing: he was wrong and wrong and wrong.

But it's strange. He still feels nothing for his stepfather. He knows he should, but he doesn't. He's sad because his mother's sad, and he's afraid he might get caught, and because of those things he would take back what he did, but if she weren't so sad, and if he knew he would never be found out, he'd kill him again.

He hated the man almost as much as he loves his mother.

She wraps her arms around his neck and pulls him close. She kisses his cheek and his forehead and says his name. She cries.

He sits silently beside her, afraid to speak. Afraid his mother will find out he's responsible and will hate him. She will hate him forever if she finds out, and he's sure she will find out.

In his heart, where he keeps his secret fears, he's certain of it.

She's going to find out, you know she will. She has to. She's your mom. She knows when you've lied about doing your homework; how could you ever have thought you would get away with this? How could you have possibly—

He swallows back his fear.

He tries to block all the worries from his mind, all the bad thoughts. He imagines them being shoved into a chest and the hasp slammed into place and a lock through the staple and the lock latched with a click.

He manages to say, 'What's wrong, Mom?'

'It's Neil,' she says. 'He's . . . he's been murdered.'

'What?'

Mom nods. 'I know.'

He can't stop looking at the lipstick on her teeth.

Then the windows flash with red and Sandy knows the police have arrived. Mom gets to her feet, but Vivian tells her to sit down, then walks to the door herself. Mom does sit down. She collapses back into the couch.

Sandy wants to be sick. He thinks he might be sick all over himself.

He looks at Vivian. She stands in front of the door, staring at it, waiting. He doesn't know why she doesn't just open the door, but she doesn't, not for what seems like a very long time.

Sandy closes his eyes and imagines himself far away from here. He imagines himself as a bindlestiff, clothes on a stick flung over his shoulder. He imagines himself walking alongside rusty railroad tracks, surrounded by trees, the sun shining down on him, birds singing, a dog trotting alongside him, another outcast befriended, and the sky as blue as it's ever been, so blue it hurts your eyes to look at it. He could disappear into that world and never come out. Everything would be perfect in that world. There would be laughter and friendship and no one would ever hurt him ever again.

There's a knock at the front door.

Sandy opens his eyes.

Vivian grabs the doorknob, turns it, and pulls.

SIX

1

Look at this man wearing nothing but a pair of tattered underpants and one argyle sock. Look at him with his pale white belly gone soft. Look at him with his stick legs lined with blue veins and his once-muscular arms now wasted. Look at the gray hair on his head thinning at the temples and the dry riverbed wrinkles in his face. Look at the purple smears like bruises under his eyes.

Look at the pale band of skin on the ring finger on his left hand.

He snores quietly, lying on top of the green wool blanket stretched over his narrow, sagging mattress. If he's dreaming it doesn't show. His face is still and without expression, and, being expressionless, free of the scowl he puts on daily, like a hat, before stepping into the morning sunlight. In sleep he looks innocent. It would be a shame to wake him, to bring reality back to that face, to the brown eyes now lidded, to the weary mind behind them.

A knock at the door.

The man shifts in his sleep but the shutters of his eyes remain fixed.

Another knock. A woman's voice speaking his name.

Carl Bachman opens his eyes and sits up with a curse. He stares at the blank wall. He clears his throat, crawls out of bed, pads to the door. He says what. He's told there's a phone call for him. He says okay and pulls open the door, squinting at his heavy-set landlady, Mrs Hoffman. She looks away from him, clearly embarrassed by his lack of clothing. He scratches himself and yawns. She says you shouldn't be getting calls at this hour. House rules say no phone calls after nine o'clock. You should respect the rules, being a policeman. He says he didn't exactly call himself and won't be held responsible for other people's actions. Besides, he says, this is probably police business. He pushes past her, walks down the hallway in his stained underwear to the telephone stand, picks up the telephone and says ugh. Captain Ellis, Homicide Division, sounding like he was just awakened himself, speaks into his ear, telling him there's been a murder. You and Friedman are next in the rotation so you probably want to catch the scene. He says okay, writes down the address on a pad of paper which rests on the telephone stand, hangs up.

He feels sweaty and sick in his stomach. His legs feel cramped. He rubs his face, walks back to his room, grabs a clean pair of underwear. He looks at the brown paper bag in the top drawer of his dresser, tucked in beside his underclothes, but tells himself no, don't, not right before a job. You have to keep this in check. You can't let yourself lose control. He pushes the drawer closed, tries to massage the cramp out of his left thigh.

Ignore it.

He grabs a towel from the back of a chair where he set it out to dry and walks down the hallway to the second-floor bathroom. His landlady walks behind him telling him no showers after nine o'clock, it wakes the other tenants. He tells her your running mouth is more likely to wake them than running water, so why don't you clap your trap. Then he walks into the bathroom and closes the door in her face. He turns on the shower and waits for the water to get hot. While he waits he pulls off his underpants and kicks them into the corner. He steps into the shower with one sock still on his foot, curses, pulls it off his foot, throws it over the curtain rod. It hangs there, dripping water onto the floor.

He washes himself quickly – armpits, asshole, face, and feet – steps out of the shower, dries off. He wipes the mirror and looks at himself, deciding he doesn't need to shave. He puts on his clean underwear and pads back to his room. He slips into blue slacks, a white shirt, a holster, a red tie, a coat. He runs his fingers through his wet hair and puts a fedora onto his head. He clips his badge onto his belt.

The telephone in the hallway rings again.

He walks out and picks it up himself.

'Captain?'

'Friedman.'

'Shit.'

'Nice to hear your voice, too, Carl. You mind picking me up on the way?'

'It's not on the way.'

'You mind picking me up not on the way?'

'Yeah.'

'Will you do it anyhow?'

'You need to get yourself a more reliable car.'

'This week. Will you pick me up?'

'Yeah.'

He drops the phone.

Locks his room door.

Heads down the stairs to the front of the house.

Two steps from the exit door, his stomach goes sour. He turns around, walks to the first-floor bathroom (which none of the tenants are supposed to use, but he isn't walking back upstairs), unsnaps his belt, hooks his thumbs in, and pulls down his pants and underwear in one motion. He sits on the toilet just in time. He's been constipated for two days and now diarrhea. While he's there he checks his pockets for cigarettes, finds a crumpled packet of Chesterfields, slips one between his lips, lights it. He takes a deep drag. When he's finished with his shit he wipes twice, pulls up his pants, buckles his belt. He checks his stool for blood, but finds none. He always expects blood in his stool, but there never is any. Sometimes he's disappointed, sometimes relieved. Depends on his mood. He flushes, takes another drag from his cigarette, heads once more toward the front door.

This time he makes it through, pulls it shut behind him, trudges across the lawn to a black Ford parked at the curb.

It takes three attempts to get it started, but finally the engine rumbles to life.

He rolls down the window and inhales the chill night air. He takes another drag from his cigarette and steels himself for what's coming.

He likes the puzzle aspect of being murder police, likes fitting together the pieces till he has a picture of what happened, but the blood and loss he hates. The dull shocked expressions on the faces of those left behind. The swollen eyes. The question there's no answer to: why. You try to wall yourself off from that part of it, crack jokes (as long as survivors aren't around), pretend you don't care, but you can't block it all out. It simply can't be done.

Still, you try.

He's become, in the last several months, better at it than many.

He puts the car into gear and gets it rolling.

Despite what he will have to deal with at the scene he's glad to have a case. It might distract him from everything else that's going on in his life right now. Something outside himself and his own bullshit. Even someone else's pain would be better than his own, and he'll do his best to avoid even that. He'll focus instead on how the pieces fit together. If you think of human troubles, you're thinking human thoughts, and those just get in the way. Human emotions get in the way. The trick is to feel nothing. The trick is to keep your soul winter-numb.

He drives in silence through the night, stopping only once between the boarding house and the murder scene. His partner Zach Friedman is already in front of his house when Carl pulls to the curb. He's standing on the porch sipping coffee from a red cup.

He pulls open the car door and gets inside.

'Thanks for picking me up.'

'You're buying breakfast when we get done with this.'

'Deal.'

Fourteen minutes after pulling away from one curb they pull up to another. Carl brings the car to a stop behind a row of police vehicles. Wooden sawhorses stand in the street, cordoning off a large area, and uniformed police officers stand with them, smoking cigarettes and drinking coffee from thermoses. Other cops are already knocking on doors, asking questions. And the crime lab boys are going about their business flashing bulbs and taking swabs.

Carl and Friedman push out of the car and walk toward Captain Ellis, who stands smoking a cigarette and watching the madness.

To no one in particular Carl says, 'What do we got?'

Sam Avery from the crime lab says, 'White male

between thirty-five and forty years old. About five foot ten, one ninety-five. Supine on the street beside a motor vehicle. Gunshot wound to the left temple, another to the crown of the head. Five-pointed star carved into the forehead. Doesn't look like he put up a fight. Gunman must've took him by surprise.'

'Interesting,' Carl says.

The trick is to keep your soul winter-numb.

2

Candice leans against the outside wall, hugging herself, shielding herself against the night. Vivian stands silent beside her. Candice's favorite thing about Vivian is that she knows when not to speak. You wouldn't think it to look at her, you wouldn't think she'd know two plus two, her large eyes seeming lifeless as empty fishbowls more often than not, but she can be surprising in her intelligence, and in how she's intelligent.

Most people don't know when to keep their mouths shut.

Candice watches the chaos. Several police cars, a coroner's van, sawhorses, cops knocking on doors, voices overlapping one another. Do you know what time it is? I don't care if you *are* the police. Has anyone told you what his wife does for a living? That poor little boy. And below the voices she imagines she can hear the steady grinding sound of the world turning on its axis, a sound like a great stone rolling.

And Neil is dead. Her husband of four years is dead. The only man who'd ever stuck around once he learned she had a son. He's dead in the street while the world continues to turn and somewhere someone's laughing. There is no justice.

She finds a man, a man with a decent job, a man who loves her, a man willing to be a father to her son after his biological father decided to take a powder, and he gets murdered in the street.

She's not a regular churchgoer, but she believes in God, she believes He's looking down on the world, and right now she hates Him for what He allowed to happen. She knows it's wrong, she knows there's a reason for everything, but she hates Him anyway. Because right now she doesn't care what the reasons are; she doesn't care about reason at all. Right now all she sees in God is meanness, set-a-cat-on-fire cruelty. One moment Neil was alive and now he's dead and God allowed it to happen.

She closes her eyes, tells herself not to cry. When she opens them again she sees two men walking toward her. They're not uniformed officers but they're both clearly cops. They have that cop walk. They're both wearing suits and fedoras, but they remove their hats as they approach, one revealing wavy black hair, the other thinning gray hair.

The older of the two puts out his hand and says,

'Detective Bachman, ma'am. I'm very sorry for your loss. This is my partner, Detective Friedman.'

Candice shakes his hand. He has a firm grip, but his palm is sweaty.

'I understand your son was home when it happened.'

'He was asleep.'

'I'd like to speak with him, if I may.'

'He doesn't know anything.'

'Just the same, I'd like a few words with him.'

'What for?'

'Ma'am, I understand your loss, I understand you being angry, but I'm trying to find out who killed your husband. I think speaking with your son might get me closer to that end. May I speak with him?'

Candice believes him when he says he understands her loss. It's in his eyes. Though his face is expressionless the eyes are red and rheumy with sadness. He looks directly at her without blinking.

After a long moment she nods.

'He's inside.'

'Thank you, ma'am.'

The two detectives, whose names she's already forgotten, step through the front door and into the house.

She follows them in.

3

Carl believes someone in this house knows what happened. He believes someone in this house is responsible for what happened. He isn't sure why he believes that, but he does. Maybe it's the fact that most murders are done by people who know the victim, or maybe he instinctively understood some piece of evidence he isn't even aware he saw, but his gut tells him the answer is right in front of him, and he's a man who pays attention to his gut. Always has been. He's already told Friedman he should wander away as soon as possible, look around the house, see what he can see. Carl will talk to the boy, watch how the mother reacts to the exchange. Between the two of them they should find at least one loose thread worth pulling on.

As the two men step through the front door Carl sees a wallet on the floor next to a table. It shouldn't be here. If the man was killed in the street, killed on his way home from a bar, killed before his feet passed over the threshold, it shouldn't be here. It should be in his hip pocket, or his inside coat pocket. Carl can imagine the dead man drunkenly walking through the front door, tossing his keys onto the table and his wallet, only his wallet misses and falls to the floor. He had to be alive for that to happen. So how did he end up back outside – and dead?

Carl turns to look at the blonde woman, the decedent's wife. He wonders if she was the one who pulled the trigger.

Goodbye, bad marriage. He wonders if her friend is simply covering for her, giving her an alibi. It's possible.

'You told my captain that your husband left the night-club about an hour and a half before you did.'

She nods.

'People at work can confirm this?'

'Of course.'

'Did he, by chance, get free drinks?'

'Nobody got free drinks, why?'

Carl shrugs noncommittally, turns back to the living room, sees a small boy sitting on a couch, hugging himself defensively. A pale boy with freckles dotting his cheeks. His lips are chapped. His eyes are large and glistening with fear.

Carl walks toward him, says, 'Mind if we talk a minute?'

The boy licks his lips. 'Okay.'

'Maybe at the dinner table?'

The boy nods and pushes himself off the couch. He walks to the dinner table, feet dragging on the carpet, pulls out a chair, sits down. He puts his hands on the table and clasps them, then pulls them apart and puts them in his lap.

He looks sick.

Carl wonders what's happening behind the eyes.

Then Friedman touches his shoulder and nods toward the floor behind the couch. Two dents in the carpet where the couch was sitting prior to its recently being moved. Maybe it has nothing to do with the murder victim outside, or maybe the couch was pushed forward to cover something. Coincidences that look like evidence happen, of course, but not as often as you'd think. He nods.

Walks to the dinner table. Sits across from the boy.

The boy's mother sits down as well.

The other woman stands by the door, looking in, silent.

Friedman wanders off, meandering toward the hallway before silently disappearing into it. No one else seems to have noticed.

Carl looks toward the boy and says, 'This must be hard for you.'

The boy nods.

'Were you and your stepfather close?'

'They weren't real close, but they got along okay.'

'Ma'am,' Carl says, glancing toward the boy's mother, 'I don't mind if you sit here, but I need your son to answer the questions himself.'

For a moment it looks as though the woman will protest. Something flickers behind her eyes and she opens her mouth to speak. But before any words get out she closes her mouth once more and nods. But she's tough. If she hadn't just lost her husband, if she was fully herself, he doesn't think he'd be sitting here at all, much less telling her how the conversation would go – not without a fight.

She's tough like his wife was tough.

But now's not the time to think about such things.

He looks to the boy.

'Son?'

'I don't think he liked me.'

'Why not?'

The boy shrugs.

'A shrug isn't an answer.'

'He was mean.'

'All the time?'

'Most of the time.'

'Then you must have tried to avoid him whenever you could.'

'I guess.'

'I bet your spent a lot of time alone in your room just so you wouldn't get in his way.'

'Yes, sir.'

'How was dinnertime?'

The boy licks his chapped lips. 'It made me feel sick.'

'Because you didn't know what might set him off.'

'Yes, sir.'

'Because if you chewed too loud, he might hit you. Or if your knife scraped the plate wrong. Or if he just didn't like your posture.'

'Yes, sir.' His eyes are moist with tears.

Carl glances at the mother, sees that the boy's emotion has put a crease into the center of her forehead. She hadn't known how bad it was for him, what turmoil it created within him. All she knew was that after her husband walked out she was alone with a mortgage payment and a son, struggling to make ends meet. All she knew was that there was a fellow with a job and an engagement ring who was willing to lighten her burden if she said I do, and she said I do. And all she saw in his behavior was a man trying to be a father to her son, and her son didn't have a father.

People see what they want to see, or what they need to see. Sometimes they're the same thing.

'Was he meanest when he was drunk?'

'Yes, sir.'

'So you must have really paid attention if he'd been hitting the bottle.'

The boy nods.

'But you didn't hear anything when he came home?'

'I was asleep.'

'That's what your mother said. But I had a father like your stepfather when I was growing up, and I think I would have woken up if I heard the car pull up. I would have woken up and listened, made sure he wasn't on a rampage, made sure he wasn't looking for someone to take something out on, made sure I didn't have to hide in the closet or crawl out the window. I was a light sleeper when I was a boy, listened for any hints that trouble might be near. I noticed your bedroom screen was missing. Do you sometimes sneak out the window like I used to do?'

'He was killed outside, detective,' the boy's mother says. 'I don't like where these questions are going.'

'I don't much like it either, ma'am. But your husband's wallet is on the floor by the front door and he would have needed it if he was buying drinks tonight. I'd like to know how it got there if he was killed outside.'

'I don't know anything about that.' The boy's face is pale, full of fear.

'Also, the couch has been moved. There are dents in the carpet.'

'What does that have to do with anything?' the boy's mother says.

'I'd like to know why the couch was moved, that's all.'

'Sandy,' the boy's mother says, 'did you move the couch?'

The boy shakes his head.

'Why'd you move the couch, son?'

'I didn't.'

Carl gets to his feet and walks to the couch. He pushes it back, revealing stained carpet. He leans down and touches one of the dark stains. His fingers come away red.

'Is this why you moved the couch, son?'

'I didn't move it, I swear.'

'Bachman.'

He looks up, looks toward the hallway entrance. Friedman is standing there with a shoebox in his hands. He pulls a zip gun from inside.

'From the boy's room.' He sniffs it. 'It's been fired.'

Carl turns to the boy.

'You weren't being completely honest with us, were you, son?'

'I don't know how that got there.'

Carl can't help but feel for him. Part of it is the fear in his eyes, the sheer terror, but only part of it. Truth is, there were times growing up when he wanted to kill his own father. He thinks he understands what drove the boy to do what he did. There are things that happen in relationships that people can't see from the outside. Little things that accumulate one by one. A tree gets chopped down one swing of the axe at a time, but eventually it falls. And sometimes it falls on the person who did the chopping.

Carl leans toward the boy, catches his eye, and says, with kindness, 'I'm afraid we're past the point where lying will do you any good, son.'

4

Sandy can't believe what just happened. He'd thought he might get away with what he did, but knows now there was never any chance of that. His construct fell apart so quickly, so easily. A few jostles and it collapsed, leaving behind a mere heap of rubble. He looks from the detective to his mother, but can't stand to see what he sees in her eyes, disbelief and horror combined, so he looks back to the detective. There's sympathy there at least. He's understanding, if merciless.

'We're going to have to go over this step by step, son.'

'I don't know anything.'

But that, of course, is a lie. He knows plenty. He knows he's caught. He knows it's over. He knows lying further is pointless. But he can't let it go. He can't put the words into the air that he needs to put there.

The detective is silent a moment. He scratches his cheek. He looks to the corner a moment, then back to Sandy, eyes full of understanding.

'Would this be easier if your mother wasn't in the room?'

For a long moment Sandy doesn't move. But finally, knowing there's no way out of this, he nods.

'Okay,' the detective says.

5

'Do you mind, ma'am?'

'Do I . . .'

Candice looks from her son to the detective. She feels dizzy. This is like a dream. This is the sort of thing that happens to other people. This is the sort of thing you read about in the paper. You shake your head at such horrible goings on, the world's just spinning out of control, isn't it, and you sip your coffee, and it's sad, very sad, and it's so distant from where you are that you can actually afford to feel sadness. Being in the middle of the experience she feels nothing but a kind of shocked disbelief, a strange unbelieving numbness. This simply isn't happening.

She looks again toward Sandy but can't see murder in his face. She should be able to see it on him, some horrible red blotch like a birthmark on his face, but when she looks at him she sees only her boy, her baby, whom she loves more than life, and she thinks of holding him in her arms, of nursing him, of his infant mouth on her nipple, of his infant tongue against it, pulling – not of death, not of murder, not of a black hole in her husband's temple from which the life has oozed – so he couldn't have done it.

He could not possibly have done what they say he did.

'Ma'am?'

'I'm not leaving him alone with you.'

'Ma'am, we just want to talk to him.'

'He couldn't have done what you think he did. He *couldn't* have.'

'I think it would be easier to do this here. I can take him down to the station and do it there, I can do that, but this is better. For him.'

'He didn't do it.'

'Ma'am.'

'He *didn't*.'

'If you don't step outside for a few minutes while we talk to your son, we'll have you escorted out.'

'This is *my* house. You can't kick me out of my own house.'

Vivian, who till now has been standing silently by the door with her arms crossed, walks to Candice, puts a hand on her shoulder, and says her name. Candice looks up and sees her friend's kind eyes glistening with empathy.

'They're just gonna talk to him, hon.'

'They think he murdered Neil. I can't leave him alone with them.'

'We'll be right outside.'

She helps Candice to her feet, and even though Candice doesn't want to leave, even though she's thinking no, I should stay, I should stay here with my son, her body rises, and she finds herself being led outside, led into the dark April morning, and was her biggest problem two hours ago that Neil had taken the car and left her without a way home? Is that really possible?

6

Carl pushes the front door closed behind the women and turns around to face the room. He looks at the boy but the boy doesn't return his gaze. Instead he stares down at the table, looking sick. Carl knows the feeling. His stomach is cramped. The sweat beading on his face feels slick and oily. He can smell his own armpits, the awful stink of ill health. And an itch at the back of his brain that only one thing can scratch.

But he shouldn't think about that. He can't think about that. He needs to think only about what's happening with this case.

He takes the box with the gun in it from his partner and walks back to the table at which the boy is sitting and once more takes a seat himself. He sets the box down on the table between them. He glances into it. As well as the gun there are several comic books, a Slinky, and three spent bullet casings.

There are only two bullet holes in the man on the street. Probably the boy missed with one, his hand shaking, the gun not having a rifled barrel.

'I guess you know it's over,' he says.

The boy is silent. He swallows. Carl sees the thoughts behind his eyes passing like the shadows of clouds over a green earth as he tries, one last time, to think his way out of this, but he must realize there's no way out because, after a while, he only nods.

SEVEN

1

Here we are, New Hampshire Avenue, a narrow strip of asphalt lined with dark-windowed stucco apartment buildings, trees, and parked cars. For the moment silence covers the street like a blanket. Even the neighborhood cats seem to be sleeping. Then the rattle of a doorknob, a man stepping into the early morning. A bespectacled man with black hair and green eyes. He wears white pants, a heavily starched white shirt with short sleeves, and a black bowtie. Perched atop his head, a white captain's hat.

The air is still and cool and the sky dark, though it's already begun its morning fade to the milky blue-gray of daytime.

A block north Wilshire Boulevard stretches out empty across the land.

This man, just shy of six feet tall, taps an Old Gold

cigarette from its crushed packet, lights it, and walks to his Divco milk truck, all white but for the fenders painted light blue, and, on the side of the truck, also in blue, the words,

H.H. WHITE CREAMERY CO.
In Business Since 1912.

In business since the year this man, this milkman, Eugene Dahl, was born. In business for forty years. In business since milk was delivered by horse and carriage.

He steps into the truck and gets it started. He pumps the gas pedal to keep it running while the four-cylinder engine warms up. It takes a few minutes.

While he waits for the engine to start running smoothly he smokes his cigarette and looks out the windshield at his quiet street.

He spits a bit of tobacco off the end of his tongue.

It's hard to believe this is where life has brought him: to a finicky milk truck in front of his one-bedroom apartment just west of downtown Los Angeles. Once he thought he was going to be something.

Once he almost was.

2

After a childhood of squalor in rural Kentucky, living in a shack with a dirt floor about thirty miles outside of Elizabethtown, surviving only on the meat he and his father could shoot – deer, wild turkey – Eugene made his way to New York to become a writer. He rented a room in Red Hook and got a job in construction. His skills were limited, but he could swing a hammer. After work he'd go home, sit at the typewriter with a glass of whiskey on the table in front of him, and bang out stories with titles like 'Planet 17' and 'The Black Ooze Had a Name'. Sometimes they'd sell to *Astounding Stories* or *Weird Tales* and he'd get a check for twenty or forty bucks.

Usually they wouldn't.

Every once in a while he pretended to work on a novel.

Then, in 1938, he got an idea for a comic book.

He'd spent many a Sunday in his youth learning to draw by copying the funnies, and later by writing and drawing comics to hand out to his friends, so, though he was out of practice, he thought he might have enough ability left in him to create on paper what existed as yet only in his mind.

It turned out he was right.

He spent hours writing and drawing after work. He checked out anatomy books from the library to help him, and books on architecture, and books on animal life. He almost always found an image that could work as a reference when his abilities or his imagination failed him, as they often did. If he couldn't find a reference, or if something was simply beyond him, he drew around the problem.

It took him months to finish, months hunched over his small table after long days of swinging a hammer in the sun. He worked with aching muscles. He worked with blood-blisters throbbing on his fingers. He worked with gashes in the backs of his hands. Then one day he looked up and was finished. He had four seven-page stories written and drawn, and, as far as he was concerned, ready to be printed up and put on newsstands.

It was a superhero comic.

His superhero was called Rabid, but Donald 'Don' Coyote was the name of the man behind the mask. He was a bookstore clerk who spent his days and nights lost in tales of adventure. He lived with his mother, had a cat named Meow he fed every morning, had a crush on a girl at work he was afraid to ask out.

The first story began with Don Coyote being bitten by a rabid dog as he walked home from work. Over the next several days he changed. His cat noticed the difference before he did and began hissing at him when he walked by. Then his hearing improved. High-pitched sounds began to bother him. His teeth grew long and sharp. He began to crave raw beef, and eat it with his bare hands. His muscles doubled in size.

Then he went to work and learned that the girl he liked, Sue, had been mugged the night before. He asked where she'd been mugged and what the fellow looked like. That night he went hunting. He found the man who stole Sue's purse and recovered it. Then he beat the mugger to a pulp and left him on the front steps of the police station with a note pinned to his shirt.

After creating his superhero and spending two stories developing him, Eugene introduced the villain who was to become Don Coyote's arch nemesis.

His name was Reginald Winthrop. He was a heartless businessman whose plane had crashed on a remote island. For months he was presumed dead. His brother took over his business, married his wife. But Reginald wasn't dead. After the crash, a witch doctor found him in the wreckage and nursed him back to health. He'd lost an arm in the crash, but the witch doctor replaced it with an airplane propeller.

He returned to the city. But he was no longer Reginald Winthrop. He now called himself the Windmill. When he tried to reclaim his old life, his brother had him declared insane. He was put into an asylum, but could not be contained. He broke out, smashed the wall to smithereens with his propeller arm – and anyone who got in his way. He went after his brother, demanding his wife and business back. His brother broke down crying and admitted he'd lost all the money. His wife refused him. The Windmill burned down their house with them inside it. He started robbing banks, convinced he could rebuild his empire. He just needed a little capital.

At the end of the last story, Don Coyote, while walking home from work, turned a corner and saw the Windmill leaving a bank with a sack of money hanging from his fist.

The Windmill turned on him, propeller spinning. Don stepped back. The Windmill raised his propeller arm and took to the sky like a helicopter, escaping. Don Coyote went into the bank to make sure everyone was all right. His mother was there. She'd been killed, sliced to pieces. Don Coyote swore to himself then and there, and to his dead mother, and to God, that he would stop the Windmill at all costs.

Even if it was the last thing he ever did.

Eugene was immoderately proud of his creation. He flipped through the pages again and again, looking at it. He'd worked harder on this comic book than on anything else he'd ever done. He believed it might be his escape from poverty.

He knew people liked to say that in America anyone could do anything. With enough hard work a man born in the gutter could become a millionaire, or president. But the truth for most people was different. Poverty was a room with no doors. There were windows, you could see outside, but the windows didn't open. If you hoped to escape you had either to break through the glass and into a life of crime or else dream a doorway into existence. If you could do neither of those things you'd be stuck in that room no matter how hard you worked. He believed *Rabid!* might be his doorway, and he planned to walk through it if he could.

The day after he finished the comic, he took the train into the city, determined to find a publisher. The first two weren't interested. Then he walked into the offices of E.M. Comics on 42nd Street. After waiting for twenty minutes he was called into the publisher's office. The publisher's name was Michael Leonard. He was a thin man with prematurely gray hair, a nose like a snowplow, and a loose-skinned neck.

Eugene's stomach was a knot of anxiety.

He handed the pages over.

Leonard flipped through them quickly, like someone browsing a catalogue with nothing of interest in it. Seeing Leonard scan the pages, seeing his bored expression, Eugene prepared himself for rejection. He prepared himself for another no, sorry, it just ain't our thing. He started thinking about where he might go next. He'd made a list of comics publishers before leaving the house. As soon as he was down on the street again, he'd look it over, see what was close by.

But when Leonard flipped the last page he looked up and said, 'Not bad. I'll give you two hundred bucks for the idea, twenty bucks a story, and fifteen dollars a page for the art. I'll tell you now you aren't getting your own book right away. We'll run these four stories in the next few issues of *Bash! Comics*, see if the kids respond to them. If they do we'll think about it. And work on your drawing. You're at the back end of good. Improve a bit and I'll pay twenty bucks a page, but you ain't there yet.'

Eugene stood silent, unable to believe what he'd just heard. He made a dollar twenty-five an hour doing construction – ten greenbacks a day – and this man had just off-handedly offered him hundreds.

'Do we have a deal?'

Eugene simply nodded.

'Good.'

He had his own comic book within six months. He wrote every story. He had notebooks full of ideas and was always adding more while refining the ones he'd already jotted down. Once each month's stories were decided upon, Leonard would assign them to various artists. Eugene would draw one himself and oversee the completion of the rest. It was a productive, creative time.

Then the kids started to get tired of superhero comics.

Circulation dropped fast.

The last issue of *Rabid!* ran in April 1943.

As the superhero comics were sinking, crime comics were rising. Eugene stayed on at E.M. Comics to write and draw for *Gutterguns*, an anthology comic about lowlife criminals. He handled a story a month for a couple years, making enough to get by on, but not much more. Making less than he had in construction.

This was not the escape from poverty he'd imagined it would be.

In 1945, feeling depressed and creatively stifled by working on other people's projects, he told Leonard he wanted to do a comic book of his own again. It would be a crime comic, but one that allowed him to stretch himself a bit. Every story would be set in a fictional place called

Down City, where dark things were always happening. Criminals ran the place. Albino alligators survived in the sewers, living off the bodies of those unfortunate enough to have crossed the wrong mobster – or the corrupt police department. Each story would reference something that happened in another story, would reveal a previously undisclosed connection, until there was a network of fiction so elaborate that Down City seemed real, seemed a three-dimensional place that a person could step into.

The first issue ran in August 1945. The last issue ran in December 1949. It was never the most popular comic E.M. published, but it was a good run all the same, and Eugene managed to accomplish some of what he'd wanted to accomplish when he began. He'd even seen adults reading his work. Those were proud moments, moments when he felt he'd actually done something worth doing.

But by 1949 he'd been in the business eleven years. He was thirty-eight and he was tired of comics. He decided he wasn't going to do them anymore. The quiet pride he sometimes felt wasn't enough.

He had a little money saved. After eleven years of work in comics he had accumulated enough cash to keep himself out of the poorhouse for six months, assuming he was very careful, and if he really committed himself to it he thought six months might give him enough time to write a novel.

He'd come out here from Kentucky to make it as a writer, to make it as a novelist, but had not yet written a single book. Not even a bad one. He'd written a few dozen short stories, published six or seven of them, but he was still on page twenty-nine of the novel he'd begun in 1936. He wasn't even sure where the manuscript might be. He hadn't seen it since he moved apartments in 1947.

His eleven years in comics now felt like they'd been wasted, like they'd distracted him from what he really should have been doing. He'd made no money and the art he produced, if it could be considered art, ended up getting tossed into trashcans by bedroom-cleaning mothers and Sunday-school teachers. He could stay and continue to turn out tomorrow's trash for twenty dollars a page, or he could do what he should have been doing all along.

But he didn't think he could do it in New York. He needed a change of environment, a change of scenery. He decided to go to Los Angeles. He liked the idea of getting as far from New York as he could without first obtaining a passport. He would go to Los Angeles and he would live off his savings and he would write a novel. He would throw out his twenty-nine pages and start a new novel in a new place. He'd sit on a sun-lit porch or on the verge of a hotel pool with a portable typewriter on his knees and write a novel while sipping rum cocktails. And he wouldn't go back to New York till it was finished.

That was his plan.

And a week later he stepped off a train in downtown Los Angeles, with a cardboard suitcase gripped in his fist and a small fold of cash in his pocket. He was in his new place and his future seemed bright.

But things didn't go according to plan.

In two and a half years he has written not a single word unless the paper it's typed upon has been promptly crumpled into a tight ball and thrown into a trashcan.

He still pulls out his typewriter after work sometimes and rolls in a sheet of paper, especially when he's been drinking. But then he simply sits and stares. The blank page is somehow intimidating. He knows what he wants to put on it – it's clear in his mind – but it won't come. Something in him won't let it out.

With comics it was easy. It didn't feel like it mattered. He didn't even sign most of his work. It was creative, sometimes he did something he was proud of, but in the back of his mind he knew it didn't mean anything. He'd never sent a comic book home to Kentucky as he had the short stories he'd published. He'd never even told his father he was working in comics. Comics were disposable. No matter how good they were, they were trash. There was something creatively liberating about that. If what you do doesn't matter, you can do anything. But this matters. This is his dream. And he knows that as soon as he slams his fingers against those typewriter keys, as soon as he commits to certain words in a certain order, he will have tarnished his dream.

He can't bring himself to do that.

It's better to wait.

Someday the right words will come and he'll know they're the right words because he's been waiting on them for so long. When the time arrives he'll sit down and write his novel. He will do what he's always said he'd do.

Until then, he'll be a milkman.

3

He makes a right onto Wilshire, heading east. The street is empty but for him, and its emptiness makes it lonesome. Like a dry riverbed, it feels almost sad. This isn't how it was supposed to be. It was built for so much more. But he likes that feeling. He likes it because he knows it's temporary.

This isn't failure; it's potential.

He rolls down the empty street, makes a few turns onto other empty streets, and finally pulls into an alleyway, driving along the backs of anonymous warehouses. Trash bins line the alleyway. Tractor trailers parked at docks. Homeless men with newspaper blankets. Then he arrives, rolls past a steep ramp, slams the truck into reverse, and backs up the incline, ignoring the engine's high-pitched whine. He brings the truck to a stop, kills the engine, and steps out of it with a clipboard in hand.

The warehouse guys are sitting at a rickety table playing cards.

Once trailers are unloaded and product is inventoried and stocked, the warehouse crew merely wait around for milkmen like him to arrive so the day's orders can be pulled and loaded. Then, after all the trucks are on their way, they sweep, check inventory once more, and shut the place down. By eight o'clock they're headed home to sleep, or to a bar to toss back a few.

'Eugene,' says the warehouse foreman, Darryl 'Fingers' Castor, looking up from a fan of cards. 'How's the novel coming along?'

'Slow and steady. What about last night's gig?'

'It was sweet, man. You should've been there.'

Fingers drives down to 57th Street every Saturday night to play trumpet, the only speck of white in a six-piece Negro bebop band. Eugene's gone out to see them several times now. He was nervous, and got a few stares, the first time he showed up at the club where they play, but things loosened up once everyone realized he and Fingers were friends, and he ended up having a hell of a good time. Now when he goes, rare as that is, the regulars know him by name. He even took a date once.

'Next time.'

'All right, I'm holding you to it. What's your load like today?'

When Fingers isn't blowing his horn he's usually got something else going on. He knows everybody and has his fingers in everything, which is how he got the nick. People come to him with goods they need to shift – one day it'll be a truckload of Canadian cigarettes, the next a duffel bag full of heroin – and he gets a percentage if he can find a buyer. Doesn't matter what it is, he always finds one.

He's asked Eugene to help him out once or twice, just

need you to drive a truck to the corner of Slauson and Crenshaw, park it, and walk away, but Eugene doesn't have the temperament for criminal activity. Simply knowing he was driving stolen goods or illegal substances would make him sweat. One sideways glance from a cop and he'd crumble. The money'd be nice – the only people who don't seem to know the value of money are those who've always had it – but Eugene's simply too square for that kind of work, and knows it. He won't even sell reefers off his truck, as some of the other milkmen do.

He glances down at his clipboard, looks over the orders.

'Pretty full. You know Sundays. Everybody loading up for the week.' He hands Fingers a carbon copy of today's haul, written in his neat block lettering.

'Dave, Gary,' Fingers says, 'help Eugene out.'

'I'll get the ice,' Gary says, and heads off.

Divco manufactured a few hundred refrigerated trucks in 1940, but the Japanese ended production with Operation Z. After Pearl Harbor was bombed, Divco's resources were instead diverted to the war effort, and despite the war being over for seven years now, the company has yet to pick up where it left off, so they use ice to keep everything cold while en route. And occasionally Eugene will chop off a small block for folks who don't yet have refrigerators of their own. There are still a few people along his route who make do with their old ice boxes, setting their eggs and milk on chicken-wire shelves so the cold can permeate.

'What's first on the list?' Dave asks.

'Two hundred and forty-three quarts of milk.'

Dave nods, then grabs the pallet truck and pulls it behind him, like an uncooperative dog, toward the walk-ins. As he approaches them, a stainless-steel door swings open and Gary emerges from a freezer with two large blocks of ice in a wheelbarrow. In just under fifteen minutes Eugene's truck is loaded.

He thanks Dave and Gary, tells Fingers he'll see him day after tomorrow, and gets into his truck. He starts the engine and rolls down the ramp, through the alley, and out to the street. When he hits his route he'll swivel the seat aside and drive standing up so he can hop on and off the truck more quickly, but for now he'll take the cushion.

He heads east toward Boyle Heights where he delivers, rolling past stacks of newspapers sitting on street corners, waiting for newsboys to arrive. In front of him the early morning light is creating a halo around the jagged urban horizon, the day finally beginning. It will be, he's certain, a day like any other day. And he's right.

Today will be a day to forget.

He'll finish his route and grab lunch at a diner. He'll sip coffee, smoke a cigarette, and read from a paperback novel while his food digests. Lunch will be followed by several drinks at the bar on the first floor of the Galt Hotel. If he meets a woman, he'll take her to dinner at the Brown Derby just a few doors down, then home to his place for one last drink. If he doesn't, he'll simply stumble home, eat dinner from a can, and pull out his typewriter. He'll stare at the blank page for a long time. He'll probably even get a couple sentences down. But when he reads over them he'll see how clumsy they are, how clumsy and false, and he'll wish he hadn't expended the energy it took to bang them into existence. He'll tear the sheet of paper from his typewriter and throw it away.

A day like any other day. A day to forget.

We fall into patterns, boring and comfortable and predictable.

What he cannot predict is that by this time next week his life will be in turmoil.

While he slept two men were murdered, one with a gun and one with a knife, and each of those murders, like stones dropped into still water, sent ripples outward, and eventually those ripples will reach him, rock the small boat that is his life, and send him overboard.

He won't know it till this time next week, but this life he lives is already over.

EIGHT

1

Carl pulls his car to the curb in front of a diner on Broadway. He hasn't had a meal since dinner, day before yesterday, and needs to eat. He isn't hungry, nobody would be after dealing with what he just dealt with, but that hardly matters. His body needs sustenance, so he'll put food into his mouth, chew, and swallow.

As soon as the boy confessed to the murder, Captain Ellis made a call to the Juvenile Division, and their detectives came in, took the boy in for processing, and took over the case. Except for Carl's report and testimony come the trial, his part in it is finished. Yet somehow he was the one left explaining to the boy's mother what was happening. The look on her face was heartbreaking.

But that's over. No point thinking about it.

The trick is to keep your soul winter-numb.

'What do you want?'

'Cheeseburger, I guess.'

Friedman nods, then steps out of the vehicle and walks across the pavement before disappearing through the diner's smudged glass doors.

Carl looks through the windshield to the street ahead. He frowns at nothing. Against his own will he thinks of his wife. He misses her.

2

They found the tumor in her left breast two years ago. Her doctor recommended a relatively new treatment – nitrogen mustard via hypodermic injection. American soldiers exposed to mustard gas during the war had experienced, as well as blisters on the skin and in the lungs, a noticeably lowered white-blood-cell count. Military doctors thought sulfur mustards might have a similar effect on cancer cells and began a series of secret experiments in which they treated patients with them. After the war ended the experiments were declassified. The best results had come from treating certain lymphomas with nitrogen mustard, but there'd been a noticeable effect on other cancers as well. Carl was hesitant, didn't like the idea of injecting his wife with a chemical weapon, but Naomi's cancer was serious and she wanted every possible chance of survival, I'm not ready to die, Carl, so she did it. And started feeling better immediately. The nitrogen mustard appeared to be killing the tumor.

But after a brief period of feeling well, she began to feel worse than she had before treatment. The nitrogen mustard was killing her white blood cells far more quickly than it was killing the cancer cells. After a month they stopped the injections and Naomi had a mastectomy, followed by radium treatment.

She was depressed for a long time. He held her while she cried about the loss of her breast. He told her she was beautiful to him no matter what. And it was true. When he looked into her eyes all he saw was the woman he loved, not the disease that had maimed her. And slowly she came out of her depression, and things began to feel normal again.

But nine months later the cancer returned. It had gone through the chest wall and infested her lungs.

He stayed by her side, he took care of her, he washed the dishes and did the ironing when it got so she couldn't keep up with the housework. But something else happened as well. He felt himself growing colder toward her in a way he hadn't before the cancer returned, felt himself preparing for her death.

He hated what was happening but didn't know how to stop it. Some part of him, some self-protecting instinct, simply went about walling off his heart, and his love, despite his wishes.

He remembered when they were dating, how being near

her had caused his heart rate to increase. He remembered marrying her, how slipping that ring on her finger had been like walking through a strange door ten thousand miles from anywhere you've been before – a strange door standing alone in the middle of the Arctic, say – and finding yourself, once on the other side, miraculously, at home. He remembered the way her laugh could make him fall in love with her all over again. He remembered all this, but each day these things were more distant than the day before. He became more and more removed from the emotions attached to these memories until they could play in his mind and he would feel nothing. It was like the memories were not his own. They were simply stories he'd heard.

That was bad, but worse was looking at her and being unable to feel anything. He would stare into her eyes, search them, trying to reach the love he'd once felt, but could not. She hadn't changed, everything he loved about her was still there, as was his love, but that wall was built, separating him from this woman he was probably going to lose, and soon.

In early December, four months ago now, he did.

They said good night, I love you, and shut off the lights. She swallowed her pain pill in the dark, and they lay together without speaking. He must have known it was coming, for he listened to the sound of her labored breathing for hours before drifting into sleep himself. By the time the sun came up on the next morning she was gone. He didn't cry. It simply wouldn't come.

The emotion was in there somewhere, he knew it was, but it was walled in.

He moved out of the house the next day, packed a few things and left. He still pays the mortgage, but the house sits empty and locked. He can't bear to go back. He's afraid something there – a photograph, a piece of clothing, a scent – might break the wall around his heart, and now that she's gone, gone and unrecoverable, he doesn't want it broken. He doesn't want to feel the loss.

He doesn't want to feel anything.

When Carl told the boy's mother they were going to have to arrest her son, her face contorted with agony and she called him a bastard and a motherfucker and a son of a bitch, and beat on his chest and shoulders with her fists. He let her. He simply stood there placid. He let her and he said he was sorry and he said he understood what she was going through and gave her the number at the boarding house and said she should call if she needed someone to talk to, and she said she'd never call him, never call one of the sons of bitches who took her boy away from her, you heartless motherfucker.

He doesn't want to feel anything.

3

He takes off his fedora and wipes his sweaty forehead. The sweat feels greasy. His stomach is sour. He doesn't know how he's going to make it through the day. He might have to visit his connection in the hop squad, pick up a one-dose bindle, something to get him through. It's become almost impossible to make it clean.

Friedman pushes his way out of the diner and walks to the car. He pulls open the door and slides into his seat.

Carl puts the Ford into gear, pulls it out into the street.

4

Carl walks across the squad room to his desk. He feels much better than he did fifteen minutes ago; he feels nothing at all. He managed to get hold of his connection in the hop squad, pulled him out of bed cursing and met with him beneath the palm trees in the park just south of City Hall. Then he headed back inside and found an empty room, a janitor's closet, locked himself in, and sat alone with a lighter, a piece of tin foil, and a pen casing. After a couple hits he nodded off, tears streaming down his face. When he came back to reality he picked himself up and dragged himself to a restroom, washed his face of sweat, and dried off with a few paper towels.

He's a new man.

He sits at his desk. It's quiet at this hour, the room almost lifeless. His normal shift is eight to four and he's used to the sounds of talking, shuffling papers, ringing telephones, but he's glad those things are absent. The silence of the room echoes against the silence within him, and rings out further and further, making him feel part of a vast emptiness that stretches to the outer reaches of the atmosphere and beyond.

It's perfect.

He thinks of the report he has to type up, looks at his notepad, then at the comic book sitting beside it. The corners are bent and torn. A rip across the front cover has been repaired with tape, yet a rectangle has been clipped from the back, the space undoubtedly once occupied by an irresistible coupon for a Real Sheriff's Badge or Martian Ray Gun. At the top of the page, between the price in one corner and the publisher's colophon in the other, these words:

Everybody falls in . . .
DOWN CITY

The cover shows a man lying in a gutter with a swastika carved into his forehead. A uniformed policeman stands over him with his gun drawn. Behind this scene, a row of warehouses, simple brick buildings with metal roll-up doors. Skyscrapers jut behind the warehouses crooked and malevolent as fangs. The silhouette of a man can be clearly seen flying from one of the skyscrapers' windows. Shattered glass hangs around him.

Carl wonders whether he jumped or was pushed. He supposes it doesn't matter.

Everybody falls in Down City.

He flips the comic open, turns to a story called 'Little Hitler', the story the boy said inspired him to carve that star into his stepfather's forehead, and reads it.

It concerns a man who angrily wanders Down City each night hunting Jewish women. He waits till they're isolated, then comes up behind them and stabs them. After they're dead he carves six-pointed stars into their foreheads. He doesn't want anybody to misunderstand his motives. He might take their money and their jewelry, but they're dead because they're Jews.

One night while he's lurking in the shadows, about to attack, a policeman comes upon him. He runs, but instead of getting away he trips over a curb and falls on his own knife, which, rather improbably, carves a crude swastika into his forehead. Then a truck hauling jars of gefilte fish runs over him as he lies in the street. The policeman stands over him in the last panel, looking down at the mangled corpse, and speaks the final line of the story: 'What goes around comes around, I guess.'

Carl closes the comic.

The boy carved the wrong kind of star into his stepfather's forehead. It wouldn't have mattered even if he'd done it correctly – he tried to frame a comic-book character for the murder, and a dead comic-book character at that – but still, he carved a five-pointed star into his stepfather's forehead rather than a six-pointed star. Somehow that makes it sadder, more pathetic.

But panic will paralyze your mind. Emotion takes over. You know you have to do something and you do whatever you think of, no matter how strange or stupid, just to keep moving. Doing something is important, not sitting still is important, far more important than any action you end up taking. It seems that way in the midst of panic, anyway. It's only later, as you look back on the trail of destruction you left behind you, like a tornado that cut its way through a city, that you realize stopping, doing nothing, would have been wiser. You've only made things worse.

Plus the kid's thirteen. Carl has seen grown men do poorer jobs of covering up their own crimes, men in their thirties and forties and fifties.

He looks to the typewriter. He might as well do it. He pulls the machine toward him, grabs three forms and slips two sheets of carbon paper between them, rolls the paper sandwich into his typewriter. After another moment, and an under-the-breath curse, he gets to work, banging hard on the keys to ensure the marks make it through all five sheets of paper.

NINE

1

Seymour Markley, in blue-and-white-striped pajamas, pads barefoot across his hardwood floor, down the wide book-lined hallway, through the tastefully decorated living room, to the thick, hand-carved maple front door. He grabs the glass doorknob and pulls, wondering who could be knocking at this hour on a Sunday morning.

At first he doesn't recognize her. There's a part of his brain that knows he should – the short brunette hair; the vacant blue eyes; the full, soft-looking lips – but the context is wrong, and at first he has no idea who she is. He blinks at her through his wire-framed spectacles, lips parted but soundless. He's about to say something, yes, can I help you, I think perhaps you're at the wrong house, when recognition comes. It comes all at once, like a fist to the gut.

He glances over his shoulder to make sure Margaret is still in bed, to make sure she isn't standing in the hallway watching this, then looks back to the woman standing on the other side of the threshold. He believes her name is Vivian. That's what she calls herself at work, anyway. She works as a B-girl, and sometimes more, at a place called the Sugar Cube. Out on the street behind her, in a green Chevrolet coupe, sits another woman. He recognizes her as well, but has never heard her name spoken aloud. Or if he has he's forgotten. The woman in the car appears to have been crying very recently. She looks at them, at Seymour and Vivian, through the passenger's-side window. She has blonde hair. Her face is pale. She looks like a ghost.

Or maybe Seymour's simply been unnerved by seeing these women out of context. He feels slightly dizzy.

'What are you doing here? How did you find my house?'

'I'm sorry to bother you at home,' Vivian says, touching his arm briefly, 'but we need help.'

'You can't be here,' he says, glancing over his shoulder a second time, 'you simply cannot *be* here.'

'But I am here, and I'm not leaving until you agree to help.'

'With what?'

'Candice's boy is in some trouble.'

'Who's Candice?'

'The woman in the car. She works with me.'

'What kind of trouble?'

'Legal trouble. Why else would I bother you on a Sunday morning?'

'What did he do?'

Vivian pauses, looks hesitant.

'What did he do? You didn't come here to *not* tell me.'

'He killed a man.'

'What?'

'I know. But you're gonna help us.'

'Or what,' Seymour says, feeling anger start to swell within him, 'you'll tell my wife? Do you really think she'll believe you? You're just a whore. I can claim it's nothing but an attempt at blackmail. Why don't you get the hell out of here?'

'Nobody has to believe me, Seymour,' Vivian says. 'I have pictures.'

'You have . . .' He blinks at her. His eyes feel dry, itchy.

She mimes the taking of a photograph, says, 'Click.'

Seymour cannot think. There's a hitch in his mind. All the gears have locked up. Then, after a moment, after that strange mental hang-up has resolved itself, his brain starts working again and thought returns to him.

'Okay,' he says. 'But we can't talk here. I'll meet you and your friend—'

'Candice.'

'I'll meet you and Candice at nine o'clock. There's a diner called Fred's not far from here. We'll talk there.'

'Nine o'clock?'

Seymour nods.

'You better show up.'

'I will,' Seymour says, and pushes the door closed.

He turns around and puts his back to it. He looks down the length of the hallway, toward the room where his wife still lies in bed. He knew better than to do what he did. He always knows better, every time. But something in him, some base part of him, thrives on that knowledge, and rather than stopping him it pushes him forward. Into places where a man can buy anything so long as he has enough money folded into his wallet. He lets the women lead him upstairs, or to the back room. He watches them undress. He lets them come to him, not at all assertive himself, lets himself pretend he didn't know what would happen, what it would lead to. That's part of the game. Most of the time he has to be so much in control that he likes giving it up on these occasions. But it also makes him feel disgusting to do what he does. After it's over he feels sick. He fears syphilis. He fears gonorrhea. He comes home and scrubs his body in scalding water and tells himself he will never do that again. It's filthy and he's filthy for doing it. He avoids his wife for a week, sometimes two, to make sure he hasn't contracted anything that he might give her, though it's less out of concern for her wellbeing than out of fear that he'll have to explain to her why she must get penicillin shots. But despite the way it makes him feel, despite the guilt, a couple months later he's in his car again, driving, telling himself he's not going where he knows damn well he is.

Sometimes he manages to restrain the urge for as long as six months, but never more. He hates himself for it. Immediately afterwards he hates himself, but the mind is a strange thing, and when the venereal diseases do not arrive, when it's clear that God hasn't punished him for his transgressions, the guilt and shame fade away.

But it looks like God's punished him after all, doesn't it? He's certain he never told Vivian his last name, nor would he ever have told her his job. So how did she find him? How does she know who he is, what he does?

Don't be a fool, Seymour. Your name and photograph are in the newspaper on a regular basis. You were elected to office. You're a public figure who failed to keep his private vices private.

God didn't do this; you've brought it upon yourself.

He walks down the hallway and pushes into his bedroom. Margaret, in bed, opens her eyes and smiles at him sleepily.

'Who was it?'

'Barry. Looks like I'll have to go into work for a few hours.'

'But it's Sunday.'

'I know. You'll have to go to church without me.'

2

Candice sits in a diner with a mug of coffee cupped in her palms. Outside she hears cars rolling by, horns honking. Back on Bunker Hill her next-door neighbors keep chickens in their backyard for eggs, and usually by this time of morning she's spent the last hour or two listening to their rooster greet the sunrise. Neil hated it, swore he would poison the goddamn thing, but she's always liked the rural images it put in her mind: farmhouses and green tractors parked in fields. It reminds her of her youth.

Right now she misses that sound. She misses the comfort of it.

She looks down at the black liquid in her cup. She can't believe her son did what she knows he did. The coffee is thick as crude oil. She thought she understood the relationship Sandy had with his stepfather but she had no idea. Steam rises from the surface of the liquid. What kind of mother misses that much hatred, that much pain? If she'd known, if Sandy had told her, she would have changed things. She would have made Neil move out. She bought the house with her ex-husband, Lyle, but she hasn't seen him in seven years, and though his name is still on the papers at the bank, she's made the last eighty-five payments herself. It's her house. It never belonged to Neil. If she'd known how bad it was for Sandy she would have done it, she would have made Neil pack his bags and leave.

She tells herself that, but it isn't true, is it? Sandy did tell you. Maybe he didn't tell you in so many words, but he's only a boy, and in a dozen other ways he let you know what was happening, and you ignored it. You told yourself it would work out. You were selfish, you wanted Neil around, you needed someone to lie beside you in the dark, so you ignored what you knew was happening. You pretended what was happening wasn't.

She picks up her coffee and takes a sip.

She glances over to Vivian sitting in the booth beside her, looking out a dirty window to the street. Families in their Sunday best heading to church, or maybe to breakfast before service begins.

Without turning away from the window she says, 'He'll be here.'

'Do you think he'll be able to do anything?'

'He's the district attorney. He can do something.'

'Do you think he will?'

'If he wants to keep his wife. If he wants to keep his career.'

'How could I have let this happen?'

Vivian looks toward Candice. She remains silent for a long time. Then she says, 'You didn't let anything happen. It happened, that's all.'

'Neil's gone. My son's gone. They were everything, everything I had.'

'Sandy isn't gone.'

'How could he do something like this? My sweet little boy.'

Vivian shakes her head. Her eyes tell Candice the only answer she has. I don't know.

Candice doesn't know either.

'Drink your coffee.'

She does.

After a long time Vivian says, 'I think there's a place inside everybody where it's always nighttime. A place we keep locked up. But if the latch breaks and lets the night out . . . maybe shadows fall on everything.'

'What time is it?' Candice says.

'He's late.'

3

Seymour parks his car on the street and steps out into the bright morning, all blue sky and white sun and not a cloud in sight. He slams his door shut, glancing once at his reflection in the driver's-side window and dusting a bit of lint off his sleeve before stepping up onto the sidewalk and, two arm-swings later, into the diner. He's wearing a somber blue suit and a hand-painted tie from George's Haberdashery out on Ventura. He wants these women to understand that he's a man of importance and will not be pushed around. Which is also why he's walking through the door ten minutes late. He's a man who sets his own schedule.

His list of campaign contributors during his last run for DA was a veritable *Who's Who in Los Angeles*. He's taken on gangsters and state senators. He's considering a run for Mayor against Fletcher Bowron. He'll not be pushed around by a couple whores. He intends to make that clear; he intends to make that *very* clear.

He will not be pushed around.

The diner smells of burnt cooking grease and breakfast foods – eggs, sausage, fried potatoes. You can feel the airborne grease particles on your skin as soon as you step into the place. A thin layer of it coats everything in here, including the windows, making the world outside look smudged.

He scans the room and sees the women sitting at a booth, a cup of coffee on the table in front of the one he doesn't know. A fat-calved waitress with her hair in a ponytail walks over and refills her cup.

Seymour walks to the table and slides into the booth across from the two women.

'Can I get you something, hon?'

'Two poached eggs, a side of fruit, and a glass of orange juice.'

Seymour isn't hungry but he wants to give the impression that he's not been affected by this morning's threats, that he isn't worried about a thing in the world. He's far too important to be worried about such piddling affairs as these, inconvenient to his day though they may be.

'All right.' She sets down the coffee pot and scribbles

down the order on her pad. 'Either of you ladies gonna get any food?'

Vivian shakes her head. 'No, thanks.'

The other woman only stares down at her coffee.

'Ma'am?'

She looks up. 'What? Oh. No, thank you.'

'All right,' the waitress says, picking up the coffee pot.

Once she's gone Seymour looks to Vivian and says, 'I'm here only to eat. Your threats will get you nowhere.'

Vivian licks her lips, pauses, then finally says, 'Okay. We'll leave you to your food. You can see the pictures in tomorrow's paper.'

'You're bluffing.'

Vivian raises an eyebrow. 'Oh?'

'If you actually have pictures, which I doubt, you won't make them public. If you do, your husband will find out you do more than merely flirt for money. Are you really willing to ruin your marriage simply to ruin mine? I don't think so.'

She looks down at the wedding band on her left hand. He noticed it this morning. She might take it off for work, but it was there when she knocked on his door. She spins it around with her thumb until the stone is centered on the back of her finger. She smiles.

'I won't be ruining my marriage,' she says, looking up at him with amusement twinkling in her eyes. 'Who do you think took the pictures?'

And with those words the courage he spent the last

three hours building up, building up like a dam against the flood of worry, is gone. Visions of newspaper headlines fill his mind. The end of his career. His wife walking out the door. His wife whom he loves. His wife to whom he is good but for these occasional betrayals. Betrayals that hurt her not at all so long as she doesn't know about them.

He stares at the women sitting across from him. He remains silent.

The waitress brings out his breakfast.

He glances down at the food, pushes the plate away.

After a while he says, 'Do you have the pictures here?'

'I have one of them.'

She removes a small rectangle from her purse and slides it across the table. An instant photograph from a Polaroid Land Camera. His face is visible in the shot, as is the length of his body, his pants unbuttoned, his erect penis jutting from the fabric. And Vivian as she kneels before him. He remembers what her breath felt like against his skin in that moment, warm and moist and very, very close. He remembers how quickly his heart was beating. The numbness in his fingertips.

His cheeks feel hot and his head throbs with pain. He closes his eyes. He thinks of the Polaroid Land Camera they have at home. He gave it to Margaret last year for her birthday. They took it with them on vacation to the Grand Canyon last summer. They had a stranger take their picture. A minute later they stripped off the negative and there they were. That picture even now is on the mirror above the dresser. There are a dozen others littered through-out the house.

He will never again be able to look at any them without thinking of this. All of those captured moments ruined.

He opens his eyes.

'Okay,' he says. 'What do you want me to do?'

PAPER MOTHS

TEN

1

Eugene Dahl pulls his milk truck to a stop in front of the Galt Hotel on Wilshire and kills the engine with the turn of a key. He steps from the truck and walks into the hotel's bar, which opens onto the street. All daylight is cut off as the door swings shut behind him. A few dim bulbs overhead and a couple neon tubes on the walls provide what little illumination remains. Every direction you turn the dim room feels like looking through a window screen.

Outside it was a Thursday evening. Outside it was the tenth of April. But none of that matters in here. In here it is forever midnight at the end of the world.

He looks around the room for Trish but doesn't see her, and when he doesn't see her he feels relief at her absence. He took her to dinner a few times last summer, took her on a few motorcycle rides along the Pacific Coast Highway, took her to a Negro bar for dancing and drinks, but after a few dates she became possessive and angry when he so much as glanced at another woman. Yet when he wasn't around she was spreading her legs for anybody willing to buy her a few martinis. First they had fights, then they stopped talking. But neither of them was willing to give up this spot. When you find a good bar, you tend to be loyal. Instead, and without discussing it, they developed shifts. Sometimes there's overlap, but not today.

He walks across the room to a barstool and sits down on cushioned red leather.

The barkeep, Jerry, a balding fellow with a gut that hangs over his belt, white shirt stretched over it like a tarp, dries his hands on a liquor- and mixer-stained towel, grabs a tumbler, and pours a double shot of bourbon into it. He pushes the drink across the counter to Eugene, who lifts it, puts it to his nose, and inhales its fine harsh scent.

He takes a mouthful, closes his eyes, and lets it sit on his tongue. He likes the tingling sensation it brings. He swallows. It goes down warm, feeling acidic, like heartburn in reverse.

He grew up during prohibition, so most of what he drank back home was bathtub moonshine. Occasionally, though, someone's dad would get a prescription and bring home a bottle of Old Grand-Dad, which everyone would nip from for the next day or two. The bottle claimed the whiskey was and while Eugene still isn't sure what medicinal purposes the whiskey might serve – sometimes it was prescribed for gout, sometimes for the very headaches it caused – he believed then and believes still that Old Grand-Dad is unexcelled for drinking purposes. There's nothing finer than a good bourbon. He thinks he'll have another three of these at least before he even considers letting his stool cool off.

He finishes work midday, eats lunch, and still has hours to kill. He loves the way they stretch out before him. He doesn't understand boredom. Sitting on a barstool, sipping a drink, thinking about the book you will soon start writing – soon, but not today – is more than enough to fill the hours.

One need not actually *do* anything.

Thinking is enough. Dreaming is enough. Dreaming is the best. As soon as you *do*, the dream is dead, usurped by reality. It's best to hold onto that bittersweet hope and the knowledge that there's still time, even if it is slowly bleeding down the drain of the world. For now there's time. There's the future.

He again sips his drink.

'Thanks,' he says. 'How are the twins?'

'Short and stupid.'

'I'm not sure those were the wisest names for your children, Jerry.'

'You ain't met em.'

'How old are they now?'

'Ten months. I don't know why they can't be born twelve years old. What good are kids when they're too god-damn small to take out the garbage?'

Eugene shrugs, thinks of his own childhood.

He grew up in poverty, but hardly knew it. He could spend entire days alone, playing, building fantasy worlds around himself as he went on great adventures, hunting nonexistent beasts and discovering imaginary treasures. There was an innocent magic to it that even now makes his chest ache with nostalgia when he thinks about it, though he knows there was ugliness there he's since forgotten, or pushed from his mind. He could remember, but chooses not to. He's simply glad he still has some small magic within him. He's protective of it, never wants to lose it. Maybe this is why he doesn't spend it, why he only dreams. He's afraid if he uses it, the magic will be gone. He's afraid he will use it up completely. Then what will he have left?

The door behind him lets out a high-pitched squeak as someone pushes through. He looks over his shoulder to see a slender woman with wavy red hair slither into the dim bar. She's pale, with fine features, and manages somehow to be both beautiful and ugly simultaneously. There's some-thing oddly, disquietingly, reptilian about her. She sways silently toward the counter, in a brief dress, and sits down, leaving an empty stool between herself and Eugene.

She reaches into a clutch, finds an etched gold cigarette-case, unlatches it with the push of a button, and flips it open. She removes a filtered Kent cigarette with slender fingers, puts it between her lipsticked lips. She glances toward Eugene, her eyes pale blue.

'Have a light?'

Eugene flips open his lighter, a pre-war Zippo, gets a flame going with some effort – he needs to replace the flint – and holds it to the end of her cigarette. She inhales deeply, removes the cigarette from her mouth, the end of the filter now smeared red, and exhales a thin stream of smoke through sensually puckered lips. A smile touches them.

'Thanks.'

'You bet.'

'How'd you like to buy me a drink?'

'That depends.'

'Oh, yeah? On what does it depend?'

'What are you drinking?'

'Is this a test?'

'I guess you could call it that.'

'A man who's particular, I like it. But I'm afraid I'm about to disappoint you. Old Grand-Dad, neat.'

'Old Grand-Dad.' He smiles.

'Did I pass after all?'

'Pass? What say we skip to the end and get married?'

'Ouch, that is the end. Let's just start with the drink.'

'Bourbon for the lady, Jerry. And I'll have another myself.'

Jerry nods.

The woman holds out her hand. 'Evelyn.'

He takes her hand lightly in his own. 'Eugene.'

'You don't look like a Eugene.'

'No?'

She shakes her head.

'What do I look like?'

'A Kurt. That chin belongs on somebody with a hard-edged consonant in his name. I'd even settle for Frank. Eugene, though, I'm not sure it works for you.'

'I've managed to live with it so far.'

'Then I suppose I can too.'

'That's awful generous of you, I appreciate it.'

'I thought you would.'

'You from out of town?'

'Why do you think that?'

'Your accent.'

'I have an accent?'

He nods.

'I'm in from New York.'

'I'd hate to call you a liar.'

A blush touches her cheeks.

'I grew up in New Jersey.'

'What brings you to town?'

'Business.'

'Business?'

Evelyn nods.

'What kind of business?'

'You a private dick?'

'Just making conversation.'

'I work for my dad.'

'Well, what kind of business is your dad in?'

Evelyn downs her whiskey.

'Stop asking questions and buy me another drink,' she says. 'Quick, before you ruin your chances.'

'Another drink for the lady, Jerry.'

2

Evelyn takes a drag from her cigarette and watches Jerry pour her drink from an orange-labeled bottle. She says thanks and takes a sip. It's harsh and unpleasant, but at least it's the real thing. She respects a man who takes his liquor straight. Means he's serious about it. She's serious about it too. She just wishes Eugene had better taste.

But the important thing is that Fingers, one of Daddy's west-coast peddlers, came through on the information. He didn't seem too happy about it, but he came through.

And on short notice.

As recently as yesterday morning Evelyn didn't even know she was taking this trip to the West Coast. She was called into Daddy's office in lower Manhattan and, as usual, asked to wait in his outer office, so she walked—

3

Evelyn walked to Daddy's bar and poured herself two fingers of scotch from a crystal decanter. She held the tumbler up to the light, swirled the liquid in the glass, looked at its honey color. She brought it to her nose and smelled peat and leather.

She downed it in a single draught and set the empty glass on the counter. She walked to the window, looked down at the street below, watched people walk by. They looked small from up here, like they were barely people at all. Amazing how a little distance could change your perspective. Seeing the world from this height she thought she could understand how good wholesome boys – like her brother, George, before the Japs shot him down over Tokyo – could fly over cities and drop explosives on them without feeling remorse, without feeling anything.

But of course, unlike those good wholesome boys who dropped bombs on cities, she did not have the luxury of distance.

She turned away from the window, walked to a couch, sat down. She crossed her legs at the knees and settled in, waiting for her turn to speak to Daddy.

She was obviously called here for a job. She wondered what it was.

4

It was six years ago, when she turned twenty-one, that she demanded her first meeting with Daddy, and two days later she was summoned from their Shrewsbury house to his office in lower Manhattan. She'd never before seen him in that context. He had forever been Daddy and that was how she perceived him. Daddy took her to Coney Island and bought her Foster Grant sunglasses, cotton candy, and hotdogs from Nathan's Famous. Daddy watched her ride the Ferris wheel and waved at her. Daddy brought home presents from his trips to Chicago and Las Vegas.

But in his office he was no longer Daddy.

He was the Man.

She realized it as soon as she pushed through the door. The weather was different here. It was colder.

'What is it you want, Ev?'

'I want a job.'

He nodded but for a long time said nothing. His bulbous face like over-yeasted bread dough was still and expressionless, his eyes vacant. Finally he blinked once and said, 'A job.'

She nodded.

He simply stared, and after some time she realized he wanted her to make her case. She cleared her throat and sat up nervously. She looked down at her skirt and flattened it against her legs with the palms of her hands, pushing it down to make certain her knees were covered.

'Well, see,' she said, 'you don't have a son and I thought—'

'I have a son.'

'George is dead, Daddy.'

He nodded once, minutely. 'I have a dead son.'

'Someday you'll want to retire. Even if George was alive he couldn't take over the business. He was too innocent, like Mom. I'm like you.'

'And you think you can take over my business?'

She nodded. 'Yes, sir.'

A smile shone behind Daddy's eyes but did not reach his wide, moist mouth.

'You have no idea what happens here.'

'I have some idea,' she said. 'I hear talk. But I know I don't know enough. That's why I want a job. To learn.'

'If I give you a job there's three conditions.'

'Okay.'

'First, I might ask you to do some unpleasant things. You do what I say as an employee and don't question it. When it comes to work, I'm not your daddy. You get no special treatment. You're told to do a job, you do it and that's it. You got that?'

She nodded. 'Of course, Daddy. Sir. Of course.'

'Good. Second, you talk about business to no one on the outside. Not even your mother. Especially not your mother. You might do some things weigh on you. You

came across a news item out of Los Angeles. Her brow furrowed as she read and a frown touched the corners of her mouth. But before she could finish the article, Daddy's office door swung open, and she looked up. Louis Lynch stepped out. He wore a black pinstriped suit that accentuated his thinness and stood with his back very straight. To Evelyn he always looked like he should be standing near a casket.

'The Man will see you now.'

Evelyn got to her feet.

'Will I be taking a trip to the West Coast?'

Lou cocked an eyebrow at her.

'Something in the paper.'

'We have to be at Idlewild Airport in two hours.'

'We're flying?'

'Time is of the essence,' Daddy said from the office. 'Come in.'

She walked past Lou into Daddy's office.

'Close the door behind you.'

She did.

7

'You have an accent yourself,' she says.

'I do.'

'Where's it from?'

'Kentucky.'

'I like it,' she says, 'you sound kind of like a cowboy.'

They talk for another hour and half, and throughout it all Eugene can see she's trouble. It's in the sensual way she touches herself when speaking – her own earlobe, her neck, her thigh – and in the way she purses her lips, and in the way she looks at you with eyes behind which there are no nos. But mostly it's in her beautiful-ugly reptilian features. He wouldn't be surprised by a forked tongue. And she's not the kind that'll shake her rattle before striking either. One minute she'll be coiled up beside you, the next her teeth will be gum-deep in your throat.

Yet Eugene finds that attractive. There's something in him drawn to trouble, always has been. He likes fire in the eyes and a knowing smile. He wants to grab onto something wild and hold on as long as possible.

He finishes his seventh or eighth drink, more than he'd planned on having tonight, and sets his tumbler on the bar. He smiles at Evelyn.

'How'd you like a dinner companion tomorrow night?'

'Why, do you know someone less annoying than yourself?'

'Ouch.'

She laughs and says, 'That sounded meaner than I thought it would. I'd love dinner.'

'There's a place on 8th Street I think you'll like,' he says. 'Where are you staying?'

'At the Fairmont across the street.'

'And you didn't go to the Palm Frond?'

'Too cheery for me. Like sex, drinking should be done in the dark. It adds mystery to the whole experience.'

'God,' he says, 'are you sure you don't just wanna get hitched?'

'Do I look like a horse to you?'

'All right,' he says. 'I'll settle for dinner. Pick you up around seven?'

'Are you leaving already?'

He taps his empty glass. 'One more drink and I'll be crawling home.'

'Hey, Jerry,' Evelyn says, 'pour one more for Gene. He's promised a show.'

Jerry glances toward them, but Eugene waves him away.

He gets to his feet, bowing slightly. 'It was lovely meeting you.'

He takes her hand in his and kisses the back of it. It's cool and dry and soft and he can smell perfume on the inside of her wrists, something light and flowery and unlike the woman herself.

'I look forward to tomorrow night, Evelyn.'

'Room three twenty-three,' she says.

'Room three twenty-three.'

He turns and heads for the door, pushes through it, staggers into the night. He blinks at his milk truck parked by the curb and feels a moment of internal conflict. He knows he's had a few too many, probably shouldn't drive, but he knows too that he doesn't feel like walking despite the fact it's only a few blocks.

He lights an Old Gold, inhales deeply, exhales through his nostrils. He spits tobacco from the end of his tongue. He pulls his keys from his pockets and looks at them in his open palm.

'Fuck it.'

Five minutes later he's parking the milk truck in front of his building. He steps from his vehicle and tosses what remains of his cigarette into the street. A car passes by. He waves at it for no good reason and when the man behind the wheel doesn't return his wave he wishes him an early death, or at least a sprained ankle. He walks into his building, up the stairs that lead to his front door, and as he walks up the steps he sees that something has been nailed there. A white envelope. The nail pierces its center, making it look to Eugene – perhaps because he's drunk – a bit like an insect specimen.

'And here,' he says to nobody, 'is the rare paper moth of Peru.'

He walks the rest of the way up the stairs and stands facing his door. He looks at the envelope nailed to it. There's nothing written on the outside; it is just an envelope. It could contain anything.

After a moment he grabs the nail between the pad of his thumb and the side of his index finger and wiggles it back and forth and, once he has it loose enough to pull it from the door, does so. He turns the envelope over in his hand, but doesn't open it. Instead he unlocks his front door and steps into his small apartment.

The kitchen is just inside the front door, tiled in blue. Cabinets hang over the counters. To the right of the kitchen is the living room, with only a counter between them. Next to the counter, a small table with two chairs sitting in front of it. On top of the table, a black case containing a portable typewriter. Beside the typewriter, a stack of blank paper beginning to yellow with age.

Eugene shuts the door behind him, looks at the typewriter, and thinks maybe he should try to get some writing done. He walks to the table and sits down, setting the envelope aside unopened. He pulls the typewriter toward him, unlatches the case. He looks at the typewriter, a green Remington with white keys. He bought it for five dollars when he moved to New York. The keys look like grinning teeth to him. He doesn't like the grin at all. It's full of contempt.

You're really gonna do this again, eh?

'Shut up.'

If you wanna pretend you're a writer, go ahead. No skin off my nose.

'I said shut up.'

He rolls a piece of paper into the machine.

He stares at it, blank.

The machine stares back, but says nothing more.

He's just drunk enough to write the first sentence of his novel. He will dream this doorway into existence and he will walk through it. He's done it before. He puts his fingers on the keys. They're cold to the touch. He types.

CHAPTER ONE

I wasn't supposed to be in the car when it
went off the cliff.

He stops. He stares at the sentence for a long time. He blinks. He tears the paper from the machine, crumples it up, tosses it onto the table.

I knew you couldn't do it.

He closes the typewriter case to shut the thing up. It only speaks when he doesn't want it to, when he wishes it wouldn't.

He pushes it away. He gets to his feet. He looks to the envelope on his table.

It can wait till tomorrow.

He walks to the back of his apartment and falls into bed, still clothed. He imagines he can hear the typewriter's muffled voice mocking him from within its case. Eventually, though, he hears nothing at all.

Soon after the typewriter goes silent he's snoring low rhythmic snores.

On the table, the envelope waits.

ELEVEN

1

A dark hardwood desk sits near the back of Seymour Markley's large office, and Seymour himself sits behind it in a brown leather chair, his back straight, his hands clasped before him. He faces three chairs, one of them occupied.

He pulls a white rag from his pocket and gives it a quick snap to remove all lint, then takes off his glasses and cleans them methodically. He thinks about this situation, this bleeding of his personal life into his professional; he doesn't like it one bit. He sets the glasses back on his nose, folds the rag into quarters, and slips it out of sight. He looks across his desk to Barry Carlyle, his chief investigator.

Barry is cue-ball bald, with a black mustache on his lip about the width of his nose, which is itself blade-thin, granny glasses resting on it precariously. His narrow shoulders give way to a large belly and backside before he dwindles down once more to skinny legs. He's shaped a bit like an egg, and like an egg looks as though he may topple at any moment when standing upright. His legs are currently crossed, calf on knee, a pale bit of one ankle visible between his garter-clipped argyle sock and the hem of his gray slacks. He wears a poorly knotted red bowtie.

It's nearly six o'clock in the evening on the seventh of April, the day after his meeting with those two whores in that San Fernando Valley diner, the sun's hovering over the sea, threatening to sink into it hot and sizzle out, and Barry has just arrived. Seymour's been nervously awaiting this meeting all day. He made phone calls, talked to Chief Parker about a few cases, spoke with his chief deputy about a troublesome witness, and more, but he did it all with the absent confidence and knowledge of a professional who can do his day-to-day work without full attention. Eighty-five per cent of his mind was on this bit of blackmail which has threatened his career and marriage. He awaits what Barry has to say with the same palm-sweaty dread with which he awaits a verdict in a case he's unsure of.

'Well?'

'I've looked over the boy's file, talked with the detectives covering the case, and done some other digging besides,' Barry says in his nasal but toneless voice. 'I think there's a smart way to handle this, a way that might, with a little luck, even help to advance your career. Let me give you the facts and we'll go from there, but they seem to me to suggest a fairly straightforward approach.'

'Fair enough.'

'Okay.' Barry opens a folder in his lap and studies it a moment. 'Okay. Here are the facts. One,' he says, counting off with a finger, 'the boy killed his stepfather and was inspired by a comic-book story to carve a star into the man's forehead. Two, psychologists such as Frederic Wertham have done research into comics and believe they damage young minds and turn normal boys to violence. Three, the comic book that inspired the boy was published by E.M. Comics, which utilizes the Manning Printing Company of Newark, New Jersey, to do all of its comic books and magazines. And four, said printing company is owned by none other than James Douglas Manning.

'Now, I did some asking around, lined a few palms with silver, and while I don't have any solid evidence of it at this point it looks like Manning controls and funds the publishing company as well, uses both it and his printing company to clean dirty money. To twice-filter it, so to speak.' He pauses, glances down at his file, flips through the pages, looks up again. 'Okay. Those are the facts.'

Seymour nods but says nothing. He licks his lips, shuffling and reshuffling the information in his mind to see what kind of hand he might deal himself. He taps his fingers on his desk. The clock ticks. After half a minute of silence he leans back in his chair and puts his hand over his open mouth, covering an unbelieving smile. Then, in a hushed tone, as if he might frighten the fact of it away if he speaks too loudly, he says, 'This could make my career.'

Barry nods.

'I mean, Kefauver's all but guaranteed the Democratic nomination come July, and all he did was bring a bunch of gangsters down to various courthouses to plead the fifth on television. J. Edgar Hoover's been trying to get to Manning since the days when his business was confined to breaking kneecaps in New Jersey, and I actually have a chance to nail the son of a bitch. Forget taking on Fletcher Bowron. If this goes right I could have the governorship.'

'Oh,' Barry says. 'I forgot the most crucial part of all this.'

'What's that?'

'The Sheriff's Department arrested James Manning's accountant last night. Picked him up in front of one of those gambling joints out there on Sunset Boulevard west of LAPD jurisdiction.'

'What'd they get him on?'

'Murder.'

'You're kidding me.'

'I wouldn't do a thing like that.'

Seymour shakes his head, barely able to believe it. Up until only a minute ago he'd thought his career might be finished.

'I'll talk to the accountant tomorrow morning. I want you to head over to the juvenile-detention facility and talk to the boy, see how malleable his recollection of the evening might be. Take the mother along if you think it will help.'

'Right,' Barry says, and gets to his feet. 'I'll take care of it.'

2

Next day Teddy Stuart is sitting at a metal table in a white room. His hands are cuffed. They rest like dead spiders on the table, only inches from a glass ashtray with three smashed cigarette butts in it. He doesn't know why he's here. There's no reason for him to be in an interrogation room. The next step should be the arraignment, at which he'll plead guilty. He's already confessed to killing the card dealer. He'll take what punishment they prescribe without argument.

Last night he dreamed about it: the murder. He believes he'll be dreaming about it, red splashed across the walls of his mind, till the day he dies.

The door opens and a neat little bespectacled man in a blue suit walks in. He looks like the kind of man who'd use tongs to hold his own dick when taking a leak. Hanging from his right hand is a black briefcase.

The door closes behind him and as it latches he twitches slightly. Then he walks to the table and sits across from Teddy. He sets his briefcase on the table, nudging it so its edges are parallel to the table's edges.

'You're Theodore Stuart.'

'I am.'

'My name is Seymour Markley. I'm the district attorney.'

Teddy doesn't respond. He looks down at his dead-spider hands, brings them to life, pressing his fingertips together, pushing them until the skin beneath the nails is white. He doesn't want to talk to this man. He knows prison will be difficult, knows he might not make it through, but he knows also that he could. Meanwhile this man, this district attorney, is here to suggest that Teddy commit suicide. Teddy knows it without needing to be told. There's no other reason for either of them to be here.

Teddy regrets what he did, but he wants to live.

It's true there's some small part of his mind, some biblical corner, where his being stoned to death is the only true justice, and that corner of his mind is sometimes given voice at night, when the moon is the only light in the sky and the shadows on the ceiling move like the living, but it's morning now, and beneath the sun that part of his mind is silent as the dead.

After a while the man says, 'Do you not want to know why I'm sitting across from you?'

'I know why you're sitting across from me.'

'You do?'

'Because we don't know each other well enough for you to sit in my lap.'

'You're facing a long prison sentence, Mr Stuart. Do you want to know why I'm here or not?'

'Like I said, I already know why you're here.'

'Enlighten me.'

Teddy shakes his head. 'I've confessed to what I've done. I've signed my confession. I want nothing to do with anything else.'

'I just want to talk.'

'That's exactly what I *don't* want to do.'

'Do you go by Theodore or Teddy?'

'My friends call me Teddy.'

'What would you like me call you?'

'Mr Stuart.'

'No, that won't do. I think we can be friends. In the end I think you'll want us to be friends, Teddy.'

Teddy knows a threat when he hears one and knows he's hearing one now. It's in the tone of the district attorney's voice. He doesn't need it spelled out. He's confessed to murder in this man's county; he owns Teddy. At least he believes he does.

'What do you want to talk about?'

'James Manning.'

Teddy blinks, but for a moment doesn't respond. Then: 'Who?'

'You don't know who James Manning is?'

'I'm afraid I can't help you.'

'You must be the only person who lives on the East Coast who wouldn't recognize the name. He runs criminal activity in half of New Jersey and in the last ten years has spread his influence to lower Manhattan, particularly Greenwich Village, where he controls the heroin trade. He has associates in Chicago and Las Vegas and Los Angeles.

He's been connected with two dozen murders. He's most decidedly not smalltime.'

'He's done all that, huh? Someone should arrest him.'

The district attorney leans in toward Teddy. 'I know you know who Manning is.'

'I think I've heard of him.'

'You've more than heard of him. You work for him.'

'You've been misinformed. I'm a small-business owner.'

'A small-business owner whose client list consists of a single name.'

Teddy says nothing.

The district attorney frowns a moment, then says, 'I'm trying to help you, Teddy.'

'You're trying to help yourself.'

'Is that so bad if it also helps you?'

'Prison doesn't frighten me as much as the grave.'

'You're afraid of Manning?'

'I don't step in front of trains either. That doesn't mean I'm scared of em.'

'I can protect you.'

Teddy laughs. 'You gonna pray for me?'

'I can keep you in protective custody for a start.'

Teddy shakes his head. 'I can't help you.'

'Can't or won't?'

'It amounts to the same, doesn't it?'

The district attorney taps his fingers on the metal table and cocks his head to the left, looking at him as though he were an interesting species of insect.

'What do you want, Teddy?'

'Nothing.'

'I can offer you immunity.'

'Only God can offer me that.'

'This card dealer you killed, why did you do it?'

'Doesn't matter.'

'The deputy who brought you in said you were a wreck. Said you wept. And I've heard you haven't been eating much. You don't *look* like a man with small appetites.'

Teddy shrugs again but says nothing.

'You've worked for Manning a long time. You must now the details of a dozen murders or more. You must know the names of a dozen widows. I don't want them. All I want is information on his businesses, how they're financially connected.'

'I can't help you.'

'I want you to think about something. If you give me this information, it's possible you can prevent more death. It's possible, if you do this, that you'll be saving more lives than you've taken. You mentioned God earlier. I think God might take notice of the balance of your life, might see you've done more good than harm. And if you give me this information, you *will* have done more good than harm. The card dealer you killed will still be dead, of course, and that's a terrible thing, a tragedy, but it's nothing compared to how many lives you can save.'

The district attorney gets to his feet.

'Think about it,' he says.

He puts a card onto the metal table and pushes it toward Teddy.

Teddy picks it up and looks at it. Then he looks to the district attorney. He thinks of the card dealer, Francis, lying dead on the asphalt. The red gashes. The white bone beneath. The blank eyes. Blood pouring from him, then the blood stopping as the heart quit beating.

'If you change your mind about talking to me, call.'

The district attorney picks up his briefcase, turns to the door, and walks away. Teddy watches the door close behind him, then looks once more at the card.

3

On Wednesday, the ninth of April, before the sun has even risen, Seymour Markley sits on the couch in his pajamas, waiting. He'd have taken a shower and dressed, but didn't want to wake Margaret from her sleep, so he padded out here and here he remains, seated, watching the windows go from black to gray, watching green yards and beige houses and blue sky emerge slowly from the darkness as if surfacing from the depths of some murky sea. He thinks of the phone call he got from Theodore Stuart a mere hour after meeting with him. He thinks of yesterday's last-minute press conference. He thinks of the future.

A soft thump on the front porch.

Seymour gets to his feet and walks to the door. He pulls

it open to see this morning's paper lying on the welcome mat. He leans down and picks it up. He inhales the cool morning air, glances out to the street, watches the paperboy ride his bicycle deeper into the block and throw a roll of newsprint toward the Smiths' front door.

And . . . thump.

He steps back into the house, closing the door gently behind him.

Back at the couch he sits down and opens the paper. His photo dominates the front page below the fold. His hair combed neatly. His mouth open in silent speech. Fist gripping a copy of a comic book.

As he reads the accompanying text, a smile touches his lips.

TWELVE

1

On Monday morning, the seventh of April, while Seymour Markley is asking his chief investigator Barry Carlyle to look into a rather important matter and get back to him before the end of the day, and three days before Eugene Dahl will come home to find an envelope nailed to his front door, Sandy Duncan is sitting on a white-painted school bus, looking out the window at the world as it passes by; he sees a blur of color as the road moves under him, as it sweeps beneath the bus like a great gray ribbon, bringing the juvenile-detention facility closer to him, and closer still.

He spent the night in a holding cell with several other boys, most of whom were older than him, as most of the boys on this bus are older than him. It was frightening. He couldn't sleep at all. He lay awake, listening to thirty or forty other boys breathing, snoring, yelling out in their sleep. He thinks he heard someone masturbating. He thinks he heard someone else weeping almost silently. He knows early this morning he heard someone's muffled cries as he was punched repeatedly, and when sunlight arrived he saw a boy of fourteen or fifteen sitting alone in the corner with a face both purple and bloody.

They were given food, gray undifferentiated slop they called oatmeal, served in dented metal bowls like dog-food dishes.

Then, after breakfast, a white-painted school bus arrived. He heard its engine's rumble through the large holding cell's single window.

A guard called out names and the boys were lined up alphabetically and marched to the bus. Sandy was, of course, among them. A Negro boy of fifteen or sixteen walked behind him and once they were on the bus sat beside him. They looked at one another and nodded but didn't speak. The boy had a cane in his hand. Sandy looked from the cane to his feet and saw polio braces jutting from his pants, hooking under the heels of his shoes. He thought of the polio scare two years ago at the public swimming pool. Part of him had wished he would get polio. He could die and everyone who'd been so mean to him would regret everything they'd done. They'd go to his funeral and weep and apologize. It would be incredible.

The bus continued to fill with people.

In less than ten minutes the seats were full. The doors closed with a hydraulic hiss. A guard called out names again, ensuring everyone was on his bus, then counted heads to make sure no one answered for someone who wasn't actually present.

After that the bus rolled out into traffic.

3

They've been on the road for forty-five minutes or more now, heading east, moving further inland. The densely packed streets of downtown Los Angeles have given way to quiet suburbs, which have in turn given way to occasional industrial buildings emitting noxious fumes and foul smells.

And finally they arrive.

They pass the front of the institution. It could almost be a normal high school or university campus, except it's surrounded by an eight-foot fence topped with barbed wire, and there are guards, and no one's leaving at the end of the day – not him or any of the other boys in here with him, anyway.

The bus makes a left turn into a dirt driveway. Dust wafts into the air behind them. When the bus reaches a metal gate the driver honks his horn. A moment later the gate is pulled open by a guard in a khaki uniform. He stands aside while the bus rumbles past him, sending dust flying into his face.

Once the bus has passed him he closes the gate.

Sandy can see the buildings before him, all brick and mortar, thick walls and small black windows reflecting no life or light. The closer they get the less it seems it could be a normal campus, the more it seems some great inorganic beast reaching for him, reaching out to him, wanting to take him into its guts and never let him go.

He misses his mother. He feels the sting of tears in his eyes. He sniffles.

'Don't cry,' the Negro boy says to him, the first words he's spoken.

Sandy blinks several times to clear his vision and looks at him. The boy looks back with kindness and understanding.

'You can't let nobody see you cry around here,' he says. 'If you need to cry, lock yourself in a toilet stall and try not to make no noise. I'm serious.'

Sandy nods and wipes his eyes with his knuckles.

A moment later the bus comes to a jerky stop in front of the building.

The brakes hiss.

Sandy swallows. He's arrived.

4

The bus doors sigh open. The guard standing at the front, by the driver, tells them to get off the bus in an orderly fashion, one row at a time. The boys in the front seats stand and start out, followed by those in the seats behind them, and so on. It looks as though many of the boys have been through this before. Sandy's glad of that. He can just watch them and do what they do and not stand out. If he does that he might be able to make it through this.

Finally his turn to stand arrives, and he does so. Then he walks down the length of the bus, down the narrow aisle between the seats, and steps out into the light of the white morning sun.

There are four lines of boys standing in formation and more boys stepping into place. At the head of the formation a guard watches with his hands clasped behind his back, shouting orders when necessary to get everyone squared away. After everyone is unloaded and in formation, the bus rumbles off.

A cloud of dust floats through the air.

'My name is Mr Fisk, but you can call me sir,' the guard at the front of the formation says. 'Welcome to the East Los Angeles Juvenile-Detention Facility and Reform School. I'm your chief monitor here while you await arraignment and trial. I expect good behavior at all times. There will be no cursing. We will march to all destinations. When I say left, you step with your left foot. When I say right, you step with your right. When I say right face, you turn right. When I say left face, you turn left. When I say attention, you stand straight with your arms at your sides and your heels together. When I say at ease, you may have your feet eighteen inches apart and your hands clasped behind your back, as I'm standing now. You swing your arms at your sides when we march. Your hands will not be in your pockets. Your fingers will be curled, your thumbs pressed against your fists. There will be no fucking around. Is all of that clear?'

'Yes, sir.'

'Good.'

After that they're marched past a fenced-in recreation yard littered with basketball courts, handball courts, and benches. Marched to a red-brick building with

'A' COMPANY

painted in white letters on its side. The windows are cover-ed in wire grates. The dull gray metal doors look like they'd be difficult to swing. Two elderly women stand just to the right of them. They're both thick in the middle and look as though they must stink of stale cigarettes and mothballs. They have large canvas laundry sacks at their feet.

'Group . . . *halt!*'

Mr Fisk turns and faces the boys. 'You are now a part of Alpha Company and will remain so until you've gone through trial and, if convicted, been assigned to one of the resident companies. But for now you don't need to worry about that. What you need to worry about is this. One of them ladies over there by the door is about to call each of your names. When your name is called, you are to collect two pairs of pants and five shirts and head into the barracks. Just inside, the desk monitor will tell you your room number. The hall monitor will then ensure you get into your room. You are not to leave. Once in your room, you are to change clothes. There will be socks and under-wear waiting for you in a chest under your bunk. Your bunk will have your name on it, so unless you're so stupid you can't read your own goddamn name there shouldn't be any confusion. Your chest is the one that isn't yet padlocked. You will find the padlock inside. You're to use it. You're responsible for your facility-issued belongings. Once you change clothes you will wait. The hall monitor will then collect your civilian clothes, with the exception of your shoes, which you will continue to wear.

'Enjoy your stay.'

Soon enough his name is called. He walks to the two women standing by the door. One of them hands him two pairs of khaki slacks. The other hands him three white T-shirts and two heavily starched khaki shirts with the facility's initials stenciled on the back in block letters. He walks into the building.

A young man sitting behind a desk says, 'Name?'

'Sandy.'

'Full name.'

'Sanford Duncan.'

He scans a sheet of paper. 'Room one-sixteen.'

He walks toward the hallway, where another young man sits, his arms crossed in front of him, a cigarette tucked behind his ear.

'Room?'

'One-sixteen.'

'Third door on your left.'

Sandy walks down the hallway to the third door, pushes it open, steps into his room. There are four bunks, two on the left wall, two on the right. Two chests sit on the floor beneath each bunk bed. The walls are white. There's a small metal desk at the back of the room, and a chair. Above the desk, a single window covered on the outside by a wire grate. A cool breeze blows into the room through the open window. It feels good on his skin, which is hot and covered in nervous sweat. His stomach feels sour as well, like he might have diarrhea, and there's no toilet in this room. He wonders where a toilet might be. He doesn't want to ask. He's afraid to ask.

He reads the name tags on the bunks. The top bunk on the left wall has his name on it, so he tosses his new clothes onto the thin mattress. The other three bunks are covered in thin white sheets and green wool blankets, but his mattress is bare. It's off-white but lined with blue pinstripes. It's stained yellow in places with sweat or urine, dark orange salt-crusted lines marking the edges of each island splotch.

He reaches under the bed and pulls out one of the trunks. It's padlocked, so he replaces it and pulls out the other. This one's unlocked. He unlatches the lid and opens it. Inside are five pairs of white socks and five pairs of white underpants, as well as a sheet, a pillow, and a neatly folded green blanket. The underpants look like they're about two sizes too big, but he supposes that's just the way it is. Next to the clothes, a bible, and on top of that a padlock with the key still in it. A long chain is threaded through the key so that it can be worn around the neck.

Sandy undresses, checking his underwear to make sure there are no skid marks in them. He knows he has to hand them over and doesn't want to be embarrassed. He once had to spend the night at a schoolmate's house because their mothers were friends and forgot his underwear there. The boy brought them to class the following Monday and showed everyone that they were stained. Little baby made a shit-shit. If there were skid marks he might find a place to hide them instead of handing them over, but they're clean, so he folds his clothes neatly and puts on a facility-issued outfit. He tosses the blankets and pillow onto his mattress, and closes his trunk. He locks it and slides it under the bed. Hangs the key around his neck.

Makes his bed.

Then he turns in a circle, lost. Everything around him is alien and he's alone in this alien place. There are rules and procedures, but he doesn't yet know what most of them are. Nobody's thought to tell him. He's no longer a person. He's only an object to be moved from one place to another, preferably without incident.

He walks to the desk and opens the drawers and, but for the nub of a pencil and some pencil shavings and a smell that reminds him of school, a sort of waxy crayon smell, finds them empty. He looks out the window.

The sky's very blue and cloudless. The grass is green but for a few dead patches. He can see the fence that surrounds this place in the distance. He wants more than anything to be on the other side of it. To be anywhere but here, to be any when but now.

He sits at the desk and wonders what's next.

But nothing much is next.

The hall monitor comes and takes his clothes. He gathers the courage to say he has to use the bathroom and is permitted to. There's a large bathroom with four toilet stalls, six urinals, and a shower area at the end of the hall. After using the toilet, he heads back to his room. He stays there till later in the afternoon when his roommates return from their classes. School is from eight till three. Everybody awaiting arraignment or trial goes to the same classes regardless of age or grade, but his roommates are all within a year or two of him. He learns their names but immediately forgets them. They sit on their beds and draw in their notebooks, or talk, or read books they checked out from the library. He does nothing until dinnertime, which is six o'clock, at which point they are marched to the cafeteria. They eat chicken and boiled potatoes and peas. They're marched back to their rooms. At nine o'clock the overhead lights go out. But there are still bright lights outside, illuminating the yard, and of course there's the light of the moon, which is almost full.

Sandy stares at the ceiling.

And, after a while, closes his eyes.

THIRTEEN

1

Next morning, nine o'clock, Candice sits on a chair in the corner of the living room, her back straight, her hands resting flat on her thighs. She wears a gray wool skirt and a white blouse with ruffles running down the front, conservative when compared to her work attire, and her blonde hair is pulled back and twisted into a tight bun, making her look severe. She wears no makeup. Someone used to seeing her at the Sugar Cube with lips smeared red, eyes shaded blue, and blush on her cheeks wouldn't recognize her. Compared to that woman this one is thin-lipped and terribly sad.

She stares at the couch, at the bloodstains on the floor in front of it. It's a strange thing, a thing she doesn't understand at all, but despite the fact she misses Neil very much, there's a part of her that is angry with him. Angry with him for dying, yes, and angry with him, too, for being the reason her innocent boy is no longer innocent. The reason he's no longer here. Neil's the one who filled him with so much violence he could no longer contain it. Neil's the one who taught him what violence was through demonstration. The lessons we remember are the ones that hurt us. She knows Neil thought he was doing right. She knows he wanted Sandy to be strong and good and was trying to make him that way. But he was wrong, and now he's dead.

And Sandy's locked away.

There's no logical reason for it to be so, but she believes she can feel the distance between her and her son, a great sucking hollow. Some antediluvian instinct, some primordial soul-nerve, feels her son's absence, and there is within her a great urge to get him back, whatever the cost, to get him back to fill that empty space.

She thinks she's going to take the couch out to the curb later today or tomorrow morning. She can't stand to sit on it. She knows that's where Neil was killed and can't stand even to be near it.

Then there's the pity and hatred in her neighbors' eyes. They pity her for her loss, of course, poor thing, but there's something in people that makes them also hate someone who's been the victim of a tragedy. Part of them believes she must have had it coming. She must have had it coming because nothing like that could ever happen to them.

They're safe. They're secure. They need worry neither about God's indifference nor the unlocked door.

The bell rings and Candice jumps, her heart pounding wildly in her chest.

'I'll be right there,' she says once she is again calm.

She gets to her feet, pulls open the door, and is greeted by an egg-shaped bald man in a blue suit and a red bowtie. He says hello and she says hello.

She walks with him to his car and gets into it.

2

She speaks very little on the way to the detention facility. She sits in this tidy Buick and looks ahead at the road and wonders if this man from the district attorney's office will really help her son. She supposes she'll find out soon enough.

The road hums beneath the car tires. The radio plays jazz music softly.

3

After forty-five minutes on the road, the car turns left into a dirt driveway. It rolls up the driveway, stopping at a metal gate. A guard asks the man behind the wheel what his business is. He shows identification and says he's here from the district attorney's office to see Sanford Duncan. This is the boy's mother. The guard opens the gate, waves them through, shuts the gate behind them.

They park and are greeted by a gray-haired man in a wrinkled suit. He leads them into a small room with a table and four chairs at its center. There's a glass ashtray in the middle of the table. It's lined with a film of gray ash. Any cigarette butts it once contained have been removed. Simply the sight of it makes Candice want to smoke – that and her nervousness – but despite the urge she doesn't reach for her cigarettes. Something about Mr Carlyle reminds her of a strict schoolteacher. She feels the need to be on her best behavior lest she take the metal edge of a ruler against the back of a wrist. Shoulders straight, young lady.

Mr Carlyle sits at the table and opens his briefcase, looking through it briefly. He leans back, absently reaches to his nose, pinches a hair between the pad of his finger and his thumbnail, yanks it from his nostril. He flicks it to the floor, folds his hands in his lap, waits. Blank-eyed, the picture of patience.

Candice paces the floor – back and forth, wall to wall – wondering why on earth this room is as small as it is. And the more she paces, the smaller it feels. It seems like it takes fewer steps to pace the width of the room each time she does it. She knows that's impossible, but it feels that way just the same.

Then the door opens. Sandy stands on the other side.

At first his face is blank, then he sees her and it contorts with sad hope and love and after a moment of hesitation he runs to her and hugs her, wraps his arms around her neck and puts his face into her hair. She hugs him back. He says he's sorry, so sorry.

'I'm sorry, Momma.'

He hasn't called her Momma in years but he calls her that now. She says she knows he's sorry, she knows that, she should have seen what was happening, it's as much her fault as his. She should have seen what was happening and stopped it.

'I'm sorry too, Sandy.'

She believes what she says.

'Our time is limited,' Mr Carlyle says, his voice even. 'Perhaps we should get to the matter at hand.'

Candice stands and wipes her eyes. 'Of course.'

Mr Carlyle leans toward Sandy and introduces himself.

Sandy shakes his hand when it's put forward.

'Why don't you and your mother have a seat?'

'Yes, sir.'

Sandy sits down across from Mr Carlyle. Candice takes a chair to the side. She looks at her boy, at her son, whom she was breastfeeding only twelve years ago, and tries to see a murderer, but cannot. And yet, she realizes now, a small part of her hates him as a small part of her hates Neil. The part of her that knows what he's done despite the fact she cannot see it on him or in him. It's a horrible feeling, to love someone completely and to simultaneously hate them. She's never experienced it before and now she feels it both with Sandy and the man Sandy killed. It makes her feel there's a diseased cavity within her heart, black and decaying. She imagines she can feel the disease eating the good parts away from the inside out, leaving a black hollow, like the trunk of a rotting tree.

'I'm from the district attorney's office,' Mr Carlyle says.

Sandy says nothing. He wipes at his nose with the back of his wrist.

'I'm here today,' Mr Carlyle says, 'because I think we can avoid your case ever going to trial. You see, my boss, Mr Seymour Markley, believes that you are, in all likelihood, every bit as much a victim as the poor man who was killed, just as much a victim as your stepfather.'

Mr Carlyle removes something from his briefcase and sets it on the table: a comic book. Candice recognizes it. It's clear from his expression that Sandy does as well. He's pale and a bit sick-looking.

'We believe,' Mr Carlyle says, 'that this comic book is the reason your stepfather's dead. We believe its violence and filth contaminated your mind. We looked into your school records. You've not been in many fights. You don't act out in class more than any intelligent boy would. You haven't missed an excessive amount of school. You get good grades. Yet you killed your stepfather. You took a straight razor to your stepfather's forehead, same as a character in this comic book does. I look at these facts, and I see where the anomaly is. Now,' Mr Carlyle licks his lips, 'now, when did you start reading comic books, Sandy?'

FOURTEEN

1

And here we are again: Thursday, the tenth of April: the day Eugene Dahl meets Evelyn Manning; the day he drives home and discovers a white envelope nailed to his apartment's front door. We are, in fact, smack-dab between those two events, standing outside the bar on the first floor of the Galt Hotel.

Step inside.

2

Evelyn sits on her stool, smiling at Eugene. He's just asked her out to dinner, as she'd hoped he would, as she needed him to, and she of course has agreed. She watches him get to his feet. He grabs the edge of the counter to maintain his balance. He bends at the waist in a drunken imitation of a bow.

'It was lovely meeting you,' he says, taking her hand in his and kissing the back of it. His lips are soft. They feel good against her skin and send a pleasant shiver through her body. 'I look forward to tomorrow night, Evelyn.'

'Room three twenty-three,' she says.

'Room three twenty-three.'

Then he turns and walks away. She watches him leave, watches him disappear into the night. She's surprised she likes him, she didn't expect that she would, but even liking him, liking him and knowing what she has to do to him, she feels only a slight twinge of guilt, and if you asked her she would deny feeling even that. It can't be guilt. This is business, where guilt has no place. It's nothing more than one too many glasses of that low-grade whiskey he likes.

Speaking of which . . . she finishes her last swallow, sets down the tumbler, wipes moisture off her fingertips and onto a napkin, and gets to her feet.

She waves goodnight to Jerry, the bartender, and heads outside, the door swinging shut behind her. Eugene's milk truck, which was parked on the street when she arrived, is now absent. The spring air is cool and brings gooseflesh to her arms. She's glad she doesn't have far to travel. She stands on the sidewalk and waits for traffic to clear. Once it has she walks across the street, heels clacking against gray asphalt.

She walks into the lobby of the Fairmont Hotel to find great white columns holding the ceiling up, red floral carpeting spread across the floor, leather couches littering the carpet, and dark hardwood wainscoting lining the outer walls.

She weaves her way through this feeling slightly dizzy, cuts past the sounds of people talking and the telephone ringing at the front desk, and takes the elevator up to the third floor. She walks down the wide corridor – past several pairs of shoes set out for the night, waiting to be collected and polished – to room 321.

She raises her fist, hesitates, and, after a brief pause, knocks.

A moment later Louis Lynch opens the door. He wears only slacks and an undershirt, his pale arms thin to the point of emaciation. His joints, elbows and shoulders, are thick knots holding together mere twigs. A revolver hangs from his right fist, comfortably, like it grew there. His long narrow face is pockmarked, cheekbones jutting, cheeks hollow, the eyes buried beneath heavy lids and set deep. His hair is slicked straight back with pomade, adding to an already skeletal appearance.

'Would you like to come in?'

'No,' Evelyn says. 'I'm a little tight. I want to hit the mattress and sleep it off.'

He nods. 'But it's done?'

'Tomorrow night,' she says.

'Good. Have him home by midnight.'

She nods. 'Yeah. I'm going to bed.'

'You got everything you need?'

'I have the knife. Is there anything else?'

After a moment's pause: 'I guess not.'

'Okay.'

She turns away from his door and toward her own.

3

Lou stands in the doorway, looking out into the corridor. He watches Evelyn key open her room. She looks at him and smiles a tight-lipped smile he knows she reserves only for people she dislikes. The feeling is mutual. He smiles back. She disappears into her room and the door latches behind her. He closes his own door and walks back to the bed and lies upon it, setting the revolver on the night table next to the Gold Medal paperback novel he was trying to read when she knocked.

Nobody tells you when you get into this kind of life that you spend most of your time looking for ways to fill the hours. Jobs require some planning, of course, but mostly, in Lou's experience, they require patience. It doesn't matter what the job is, it will require many hours of not doing a goddamn thing. You wait for the time to strike or else you wait for others to move so you can see if they step into the trap you've set or else you do the job and must lie low until the heat dies down. You learn to fill the time. You have a few paperbacks handy, a deck of cards, a bottle of something that'll blur your vision.

You try to stave off boredom.

He feels impatient sometimes when he knows what he has to do but must wait. This is the case now. But everything must be laid out properly for this to work. It's chess with living players, with people, and with people there are no rules. There's simply no telling what they'll do, how they'll react to a given situation. In chess you know it's safe to put a piece directly in front of a pawn, for pawns can't get at you straight, but people aren't predictable in that way. They don't live by such rules. But you do the best you can, and that requires forethought. And patience.

But he wasn't born patient. Forty-two years ago he forced his way into the world months early, with underdeveloped lungs and fingers with no nails, and he hasn't developed patience since. His seeming patience is not patience at all. Only through force of will can he find it in himself to wait. He must will himself to sit still. Every muscle tight, ready to twitch. The waiting period in this case, though, is almost finished.

Lou is glad.

4

Seymour Markley in bed beside Margaret. She lies prone, her head resting on his shoulder, her arm stretched across his chest, fingers combed into the hair at the back of his neck. He stares at the ceiling. Since his plans went public he's fielded many worried phone calls, most of them from people in the movie industry, people who contributed to his last campaign, people worried that what he's doing will have repercussions they don't like. They already must work within the confines of the Hayes Code. They already must worry about McCarthy's unsubstantiated redbaiting. This could be one step too far. Fletcher Bowron himself called and expressed concern. He's tried to alleviate all worries, telling everyone who'd listen that he's only going after entertainments for children, that movies for adults can and should have adult themes, that he's not at all interested in changing that, but he isn't certain he's convinced everyone. He will, but it's going to take time. Probably he'll have to speak with the press again, put it on public record.

Tomorrow he's meeting with the whore and her husband to collect the photographs. First thing he intends to do is burn them. He'll not even wait till he gets home. He doesn't want them within a mile of his wife. He'll find an alley and set them on fire and watch them bubble and blacken and curl and melt.

He turns to the right and kisses his wife's forehead. He loves her very much.

He closes his eyes.

5

Carl Bachman sits in his car and looks through the window to the house across the street. He hasn't stepped foot in it since the day after his wife died. The yard is dead, the house dark; it should feel abandoned. But it doesn't. His wife's presence fills it even now; a warmth that shouldn't be here, but is.

He lights a Chesterfield and smokes it down to the knuckles of his yellowed fingers. He flicks the butt out to the street, starts his car, and pulls away from the curb. His headlights splash on the gray asphalt before him as he cuts his car through the dark night. He drives to the boarding house where he's been living, and as he thinks about what he plans to do when he gets up to his room, he feels saliva building up at the back of his mouth, as if in preparation for being sick.

By the time he parks and steps from the car his face is beaded with sweat. There's an unbearable itch at the back of his brain that demands scratching.

He walks into the boarding house. Mrs Hoffman is washing dishes in the kitchen. She says hello as he walks past the door, you're coming home late, and he says mind your own business and heads up the stairs and down the hallway to the bathroom. The door's closed. He knocks. No answer. He opens it and finds the room empty. He steps into the room and closes the door behind him and locks it.

He walks to the toilet and pulls down his pants and sits. If he doesn't take a shit now, it'll be another day before he's able to, and it's been two days already. He's trying to remain as healthy as possible, trying to function normally.

He spits between his knees.

He looks at the wall across from the toilet and sees a framed Norman Rockwell picture. It shows a little girl holding a doll out to a doctor. The doctor holds his stethoscope to the doll and pretends to listen to its heartbeat. He's never noticed it before. He idly wonders how long it's been there, but doesn't really care.

He grunts, trying to get something out. He looks down at the tile floor between his knees and curses. After a while he gives up. He wipes anyway and pulls up his pants.

He walks to his room and closes the door behind him and locks it.

He pulls open his dresser's top drawer and there he finds a crumpled paper bag. He grabs it and holds it tight, as if someone might try to take it from him, and walks to his bed. He opens it and pulls out a blackened piece of foil, a pen casing, a pocket knife, and a small paper bindle.

The first time Carl smoked this stuff, in the weeks following his wife's death, he can't remember exactly how soon after, it's all a fog to him now, he overdosed himself, smoked far too much, and vomited. Next thing he knew he was lying on the floor beside his own sick feeling nothing at all but quiet calm. There was no feeling of elevation. There was just conscious nothingness. Which, to him, was better than bliss. He understood what Heaven must feel like, and he knew his wife was there, and he was glad, because he was there too. They were together even though they were apart. They were together in feeling. The feeling was not-feeling, and it was perfect.

Everything was perfect.

With shaking hands he unfolds the paper bindle and knifes a bit of the brown powder from the bindle into the foil, which he has creased into a canoe shape. He puts the pen casing into his mouth like a straw, holds the foil under his chin, and with a lighter slowly cooks the brown powder. It forms a bead and runs along the length of the foil, leaving a trail of black behind it. He inhales the vapors through the straw, chasing the bead across the foil, the taste like rotten tomatoes and vinegar, and it burns the back of his throat harsh and strong, and he closes his eyes, and tears stream down his cheeks. He feels slightly sick, but he doesn't care. He smokes another hit, and sets the foil and lighter down on the table beside his bed. He falls back on his mattress and looks up at the ceiling. At first there's nothing but anticipation and mild nausea. Then the anticipation fades. For some time he thinks he's simply stopped waiting for the drug to take hold, stopped caring, then he realizes it has.

6

Sandy lies asleep in bed, a small boy in a big world.

7

Teddy Stuart stands at a window and looks to the night street six floors down. He's alone in a small hotel room. Below him the hotel's sign hangs from the corner of the gray stone building, giving it a name:

THE SHENEFIELD HOTEL

He wonders, not for the first time, if he's made the right decision.

He's afraid he hasn't.

Two days ago, on the eighth, the Los Angeles County Sheriff's Department turned him over to the LAPD and the LAPD brought him here, to this downtown hotel where they keep a block of rooms. A series of uniformed police officers have been standing outside his door since, working in shifts. They don't speak to him except to tell him it's time for a shift change, or to tell him room service has arrived.

Teddy doesn't think they'll be able to do anything to stop the Man if he decides he wants to silence him, but worrying about such things does no good.

He pulls the curtains closed and walks toward the bed. He pulls off his coat and tosses it onto a chair in the corner. He slips out of his suspenders, unclips his cufflinks and sets them on a table, unbuttons his shirt and tosses it on top of his coat, sits on the bed and kicks off his shoes.

He wonders if part of him doesn't *want* the Man to come after him, if part of him, that small biblical corner of his mind, doesn't view that as the necessary next step in the righting of the world. His sins absolved in blood. He thinks maybe part of him does want that. A very small part of him. Some pure ancient part uncorrupted by everything else that surrounds it, by everything else that he is.

But he can't worry about that either. He can only do what he's agreed to do.

Whatever else happens happens.

8

Outside, the stars shine. The moon, nearly full, moves across the sky. The drunks leave bars and head toward home, some of them losing control of their vehicles, running them into streetlamps, into the sides of buildings, into other people; some of them making it home and passing out; some of them furiously beating their wives or their children with clenched fists or open hands. The streets empty of people but for the homeless, covered in newspapers and rags. The city goes quiet. The world turns on its axis, grinding away the hours like a great stone. The dark night turns gray as morning approaches. A light touches the horizon. Tomorrow becomes today.

FIFTEEN

Eugene, showered and dressed but not yet fully awake, stumbles from his bathroom and walks down his narrow hallway. He has the day off, but finds it impossible to sleep past four o'clock even when he has nowhere to be, even when he's a bit hung over, as he is today. His time as a milk-man has ruined him for sleeping in.

As he walks toward the kitchen his shower-fogged glasses clear in the cool morning air. Coffee should be done percolating and he needs a cup. He grabs a mug from the cupboard and pours thin brown liquid into it. He checks the fridge, but is out of fresh milk. An empty bottle sits in the door beside a jar of mustard. His mind's working just well enough that he finds the empty milk bottle amusing. He shuts the fridge and starts looking through his cupboards for an alternative. After shoving several cans of peas and green beans and Spam aside he finds a can of condensed milk. He can't find his can opener, so he punches a couple holes into the lid with a screwdriver and pours the thick syrup into his coffee.

Then, with mug in hand, he walks to the dining table and sits. He intends to drink his coffee in silence and stare blank-eyed at the wall thinking nothing at all, but instead his eyes fall upon the envelope he found nailed to his front door last night.

He'd forgotten about it until now. Drunken memories seem to remain drunk long after you yourself have sobered up. Pulling the note from the door, walking inside, trying to write: it's all a blur.

He picks up the envelope and looks at it. It's blank, white. He holds it up to the sunlight but can't see what's inside. He tears open the top and finds within the envelope a newspaper clipping. At first he's staring at an advertisement. Think of it! A new cylinder-type vacuum cleaner! Only $13.95 complete with attachments! He flips over the thin sheet of paper and reads this headline:

D.A. SEYMOUR MARKLEY SAYS COMICS CAUSE MURDER!

Beside the article is a picture of a rather prim-looking man in his late forties or early fifties. He wears wire-framed glasses. His thin-lipped mouth is open in angry speech. He's holding up a copy of *Down City*, which Eugene recognizes immediately. It's one of the dozen or so issues for which he drew the cover. Below the headline, the story:

LOS ANGELES – District Attorney Seymour Markley announced yesterday that he would be launching a grand-jury investigation into whether it might be possible to charge those involved with the creation and production of a comic book with criminally negligent homicide. The grand-jury investigation comes on the heels of a Bunker Hill killing in which a thirteen-year-old boy allegedly used a so-called 'zip gun' to shoot his stepfather before, in imitation of a crime comic book called *Down City*, carving a star into the dead man's forehead with a straight razor.

Markley said that the boy's testimony to LAPD detectives indicated to him that he was not fully culpable for his actions. 'Anybody familiar with the work of psychologist Frederic Wertham,' Markley said, 'can tell you that comic books are a terrible influence on the youth of today. There's a reason church groups across America are calling for this trash to be burned, to be incinerated. These small boys are susceptible to the morally corrosive influence of entertainments filled with sex and violence, and the inevitable result is tragic deaths like the one we saw a few days ago, a death which has not only ended the life of a man, but which could destroy the life of a small boy before it is even fairly begun. When the boy testifies before the grand jury, I believe the influence, the guilt, of this gruesome comic book and its creators will be clear. And I hope this investigation causes other comics publishers to think twice about what they're printing – what they're filling the minds of impressionable youths with.'

According to Markley, his office has evidence that

E.M. Comics, a subsidiary of E.M. Publications, which also publishes adult magazines such as *Nude Sunbathing and Hygiene*, is run behind-the-scenes by James Douglas Manning – also known as New Jersey Jim and the Man – and used as a means of laundering ill-gotten money through overpayment for printing services.

A source within the D.A.'s office has also said, on condition of anonymity, that Mr Manning's accountant, Theodore Stuart, has agreed to testify against his employer during the grand-jury investigation, though he did not know the extent of the information Mr Stuart might be willing to divulge.

If the investigation goes the way the D.A.'s office intends, and the grand jury returns a 'true bill,' James Manning and others involved in the production of *Down City* could be the first individuals in American history charged with homicide for the creation of an entertainment.

For a long time Eugene only sits and stares unthinking at the gray newsprint, coffee on the table beside him forgotten. He sets down the news item and gets to his feet. He walks to his porch and lights a cigarette. He takes a drag and exhales in a sigh. He looks out at the dark, empty street. The air is cool. He tries to consider what this might mean for him.

Worst case: he's convicted of a crime he had nothing to do with and he spends years in San Quentin. Best case: nobody ever finds out he was involved in any way. He never signed his work with more than an offhand E., and usually he didn't sign it at all. There are people who could easily point to him, of course, but not one of them, so far as he knows, lives in Los Angeles. Yet someone nailed this news item to his front door. Somebody knows who he is and where he is. And the implication is clear. A threat is implied.

He can't imagine that a grand jury would agree that he should be charged with homicide, even criminally negligent homicide, for the creation of a comic book . . . except for one thing: it would be a way to nail James Manning, who has been a known criminal for thirty years. Authorities have never managed to put him in jail, despite what everyone knows he is, and this could be a way to do it. A jury could be convinced. And if Eugene ends up a casualty of a witch-hunt, so what, that's nobody's problem but his own. He has no friends in high places. He has few friends in low places.

And nobody will defend comics.

Everybody agrees they're wretched. Everybody agrees they're trash. Everybody agrees they corrupt children. Books have been banned, and bookstore owners arrested for carrying them. Aren't criminal charges such as these the next step? If books can be too dangerous to read, they can certainly be dangerous enough to rot the minds of impressionable children.

He takes a drag from his cigarette. He needs to remain calm.

Whoever left the article nailed to his front door was

making an obvious threat. I know who you are. I know where you are. I know what you did. I will tell. But the only reason to say all that rather than simply to do it is if there's an unless. I will tell unless.

Unless what?

Eugene doesn't know. And the only way to find out is to wait.

SIXTEEN

1

Seymour Markley sits alone in a booth. He looks out the grease-spotted window to the street but doesn't see them. He looks around the diner for the second time, scanning the faces of the other patrons, but none of them are familiar. They didn't inadvertently cross paths. They aren't waiting for him at some other table. They simply haven't yet arrived.

He takes a sip of orange juice, straightens his tie. Though he doesn't plan to eat, couldn't eat if he tried, he wipes the water-spotted flatware off with a napkin and sets each piece down parallel to the others, fork, knife, spoon.

He can't stand that these people have turned this around on him. Despite the fact that he might be able to advance his career because of it, it bothers him. He's an important man. He's an important man and he's being made to wait by unimportant people: by scum: by a whore and her cuckold husband. It's almost too much to take.

The door swings open and he looks toward it.

A fellow in a cowboy hat walks into the diner wearing dark pants, a checkered shirt with pearl buttons, and a bolo tie. On the pinky finger of his right hand he wears a blue topaz ring. His mustache is thick and long, hiding his mouth, and the ends are waxed to ice-pick points. Seymour feels like he knows him from somewhere, but can't imagine where, unless he's put him in prison before.

But he doesn't think that's it.

Behind the cowboy walks Vivian in heels and a brief dress.

The cowboy scans the room. Then, tipping two fingers toward Seymour, he says in an oddly cheery voice, 'That him, darlin?'

'That's him.'

The cowboy walks over and drops his hand like an axe in front of Seymour's face. Seymour blinks at it.

'Leland Jones. Wasn't sure I recognized you with your clothes on.' He smiles.

Seymour lets the hand hang for a long time, then says, 'You can put that away. I'm not going to shake.'

'Well, shit, that's all right, sugar. I wasn't dying to wring out your sweaty dishrag paw anyways.'

He slides into the booth. Vivian sits down beside him.

'Hi, Seymour.'

'We're not friends, whore. Do you two have the pictures?'

Leland Jones leans in, smile gone. 'You best watch the way you talk to my wife.'

'Is your wife not a whore?'

'My wife is a beautiful woman, and you'll respect her. What she does for work don't have nothin to do with who she is.'

Seymour knows suddenly where he's seen this man before. He remembers him from *Fort Apache*, and is almost certain he's seen him in other Western movies as well. He didn't have any lines that Seymour can recall, he was just human background, but yes, that's why he seemed familiar.

'Do you have them?'

'What's that?'

'The pictures.'

Leland Jones reaches into his back pocket and removes an envelope that's been folded in half. He tosses it onto the table. It lands between the salt shaker and a bottle of hot sauce. Seymour blinks. Then reaches out and picks up the envelope, pulls it open, looks inside. Three Polaroid pictures. He flips through them twice, frowns.

Looks up at Vivian and says, 'The first picture you showed me isn't here.'

Vivian looks confused. 'It's . . . what?'

'Yeah,' Leland Jones says, looking at him with blue

eyes, his relaxed way of speaking stretching the word like verbal taffy, 'I wanted to talk to you about that.'

'Leland, what are you doing?'

'Yes, Leland,' Seymour says, 'what are you doing? We had an agreement.'

'You and the ladies had an agreement. But these pitchers don't really belong to the ladies. They belong to me.'

'We talked about this, Leland.'

'All right, darlin, I get you're mad, but let Leland take care of business.'

'I held up my end of this agreement,' Seymour says.

'I appreciate that. Candice is a hell of a woman and she don't deserve to have no pain in her life. That's why I'm willing to give you that last pitcher for a mere hundred dollars. A bargain when you think about it.'

Vivian stares at her husband, clearly furious, her face white but for hot pink blotches on her cheeks, but she says nothing.

'How do I know,' Seymour says, 'that once I pay for this last photo, another one won't turn up? And another after that?'

'I don't mean to insult you, Mr Markley, but I don't think Vivian had your pants down more'n five minutes before you was putting em back on. There just wasn't no time to take a lotta pitchers.'

'That's not good enough.'

'Then you'll have to trust me.'

'Trust a man who makes an agreement and then

changes his mind when the other party has fulfilled his end of said agreement? I don't think so.'

'"Fulfilled his end of said agreement."' Leland laughs. 'You *are* a lawyer, aren't you? But last I heard Candice's boy was still locked up.'

'These things take time. The point is this: that last photograph has been paid for and I'm not willing to pay for it twice.'

'I don't see that you got a choice. I ain't givin it back till you do.'

Seymour simply stares at him.

'Tell you what, think it over. I'll call your office at five o'clock and we'll have us a little chat. Till then, I'll bid you adieu.'

Seymour watches them stand up from the booth and walk toward the exit.

He doesn't move for a long time.

2

Leland sits on the couch at home, staring at the television's blank gray screen. Ever since they left their meeting with Seymour Markley Vivian's been telling him what a goddamned idiot he is. You know the rule, Leland. You don't put your fucking hand in the same till twice. Well, it isn't *his* rule. He'll grab as much as he can, and if that means two fistfuls instead of one, all the better.

He looks at his watch.

It's time to call Markley. He knows what the man's decision will be – he knew before he stepped through the diner's front door and out into the sunlight – but he wanted to let him think it over. He wanted the man to realize on his own that he really doesn't have a choice in the matter. He wanted to let it sink in.

Better to simply pay and be done with it. Better to put the situation behind him.

He knows what Markley's decision will be, but he might as well hear it.

He gets to his feet and walks to the kitchen. He pulls the phone from the wall and puts it to his ear. He dials Markley's office.

3

Seymour knocks on the blue door in front of him. A moment later a Negro woman pulls it open. She's about thirty-five, and pretty, with broad cheekbones and a heart-shaped face. Her skin is very dark and smooth. Her hair's been ironed straight and pulled into a tight ponytail. She's wearing night clothes.

'Yes?'

'I'm not sure I have the right address.'

'Well, who you looking for?'

'Barry Carlyle.'

'Oh, you're Seymour. Barry said you might be stopping by tonight. Come on in.'

She steps aside and he walks into the apartment. The walls are covered in striped green wallpaper. The couch is green corduroy. An oak coffee table sits in front of it, glowing with candles. A large oak record player sits against the wall. Bebop music plays, a trumpet screeching wildly while brushes slide against a snare drum.

'Thank you,' Seymour says as the woman closes the door behind him.

Barry, drying his hands off with a dish towel, walks into the room from the kitchen. 'Seymour, I see you found the place. This is Maxine, in case you haven't gotten to the introductions yet. She helps out around the place. I apologize for the delay but I was peeling shrimps. Maxine gets squeamish about that part of the process. Pulling the heads off, you know. All that orange head fat. Anyway, have a seat.'

Seymour's never seen Barry like this – no coat, no tie, shirtsleeves rolled up, top button undone, suspenders hanging loose around his hips. He almost seems a completely different person.

'Have a . . . yes, of course.' He sits down on the corduroy couch.

'Would you get Seymour a – what would you like to drink?'

'Water's fine.'

'Would you get Seymour a glass of water, hon?'

'Sure,' Maxine says.

Barry sits on the couch beside Seymour and tosses the dish towel onto the table.

'She helps out around the house?'

'That's right.'

Seymour clears his throat. 'That's all?'

'If I'm not mistaken, Seymour, you're here to ask a favor.'

'Of course. You're right.'

'What is it you need?'

'I have an appointment tomorrow with Leland Jones. I'm to give him money, he's to give me the last, uh, compromising photograph he has. I'd like – and I know this is a big favor – I'd like you to search his place while he's out with me, make sure he doesn't have any other photographs. I want this to be the end of it.'

'Seymour, this goes well beyond—'

'I know that, Barry. I wouldn't ask if I didn't think it was important. And, of course, if my career moves forward I'll bring you along with me.'

'Can't it be someone who—'

'I need it to be someone I trust. You're someone I trust, Barry.'

Barry sighs, scrapes a bit of shrimp out from under his fingernail, wipes it on the dishrag. He stares thoughtfully at nothing. Finally: 'Okay.'

'Thank you.'

'Just give me the address, Seymour.'

'Of course.'

Maxine returns with a glass of water.

SEVENTEEN

1

Candice has the evening off and wishes she didn't, but the funeral's tomorrow and she couldn't imagine trying to sit through it on four hours' sleep, so here she is, sitting in the corner of the room, looking at the place where her couch used to be, wishing she was somewhere else. The couch is now curbside and will be until someone who doesn't know its history makes off with it. She hopes it happens soon. She'd like to look out the window and see the damned thing has vanished.

Tomorrow she'll go to Sears & Roebuck to look for a new one, because right now it's the mental equivalent of a missing tooth. Her eye keeps going to the spot where it should be, looking, looking, looking, while her mind plays over the reason it's gone.

She doesn't want to be here.

She gets to her feet and walks to the telephone on the wall. On the counter below it, a telephone book. Stacked on top of the telephone book, business cards and scraps of paper. She picks up the paper with Detective Bachman's phone number on it. She knows she shouldn't call. She hit him and screamed at him and told him she would never forgive him for taking her son away. She called him a bastard and a motherfucker. But he told her he understood what she was going through, understood her loss, and there was something in his eyes that made her believe him. And she can think of no one else who might know what she's thinking and feeling.

Vivian's her friend, has done more than anyone to help her, but she's probably at work, and wouldn't understand anyway. And even if she did understand, there's something about talking to a stranger that appeals to her, that feels safer. A stranger can't judge you, and if he does judge you it doesn't matter. You can simply walk away.

She picks up the telephone and makes the call.

A woman picks up.

'Hoffman Boarding.'

'Is Detective Bachman in?'

'Hold on.'

The telephone is set down. This is followed by a knocking sound, the woman saying call for you, Bachman, are you there? Open the door. And then silence.

After a while the woman's voice in her ear: 'He isn't in.'

'Can I leave a message?'

'Okay.'

'Can you tell him Candice Richardson called?'

'Candice Richardson?'

'Sandy's mother.'

'Does he have your phone number?'

'Trinity nine five one fifty.'

'Would you like to say what it's regarding?'

'No,' she says, 'thank you.'

She sets the phone down.

She wonders if he'll call back. Part of her hopes he doesn't.

2

Evelyn steps into her dress and pulls it up over her shoulders. The fabric is smooth and delicate and feels good brushing across her skin. She zips up the back of the dress, feeling inexplicably nervous. She tells herself it's not going to be a real date; it's work. Speaking of which: she walks to her suitcase and in one of the side pockets finds a black-handled switchblade knife. She presses a button. The spring-loaded blade flips out, and she examines it a moment, looking at her distorted reflection in its steel. Then she folds the blade into the handle and slips the knife into her purse.

Lou has a second knife, identical to this one, which he'll use elsewhere when the time is right.

She walks to the bathroom, picks up a lipstick from the bathroom counter, smears it on her lips. She rubs her lips against one another, liking the slightly grainy feel of the lubrication the lipstick supplies. She blows herself a kiss.

She's ready.

Eugene isn't due for half an hour, and when he arrives she'll still make him wait ten minutes, simply sit up here flipping through a magazine, but she wants to look good, needs to look good.

Needs him to fall for her.

3

Carl steps from his car, slams the door shut, and walks toward the boarding house. He's covered in oily sweat and disgusted by his own stink, a sour smell like curdled milk. He spent his last two hours at work doing nothing but watching the clock, refusing to let himself leave early. If he left early that would mean he was no longer in control. Things have been slipping lately. He found a way to use at work every day this week – once while locked in a toilet stall, hoping against hope that no one would walk in and smell that distinctive smell and know. Every day this week he's used at work. Every day but today. He realized he was losing control. He needed to prove to himself that he could regain control of the situation, of himself. And he did. He made it. He made it through the work day without using.

True, the last two hours it was all he thought about, getting into his room at the boarding house and unfolding his bindle, but thoughts are not actions. Only actions are actions.

And he acted like a man in control.

He *was* a man in control. Barely in control, perhaps, but in control.

He pushes through the front door and hurries up the stairs, tripping on his way, hurting his wrist and cursing under his breath, but not stopping, scrambling on all fours up the last few steps, and then into his room. He locks the door behind him. He walks to the dresser sitting against the back wall and pulls open the top drawer. He removes the brown paper bag, walks to the bed with it, sits down. Then his eye catches something on the floor, a white piece of paper. Mrs Hoffman must have slipped it under the door. He wonders for a moment if he's late on rent, but rent is due on Mondays and he knows he already paid this week. He should pick it up and see what it says. If he's in control of himself he'll pick it up and see what it says. A normal person would do that, and he's a normal person. Things have been slipping lately, but they're under control. He's under control. He wills his fingers to let go the bag and sets it on the bed. He picks up the slip of paper and looks at it. Someone named Candice Richardson called for him.

Who the fuck is Candice Richardson?

He closes his eyes and tries to think. First he thinks of nothing, just the itch at the back of his brain, then her face appears in his mind, and then other images float forward, as if emerging through a fog. A 1948 Chevrolet with a man lying beside it. A zip gun made from a car antenna. A comic book. The mother of the boy who killed his stepfather. He should call her. He told her to call him if she needed anything and she did, despite the fact she told him she never would, despite the fact she told him she would never forgive him for taking her boy away from her. She called because she saw it on him, or smelled it on him: death. He's someone who understands.

He should call her back.

But not now. After. He made it through the day. He deserves this.

He picks up the paper bag and one by one removes the items from within it, setting them out on the bed in a neat row, in a tidy line, almost enjoying the discomfort of his need now that it's about to be satisfied, enjoying the ritual.

He'll call her back after.

4

The elevator doors open. Evelyn emerges from within, like some creature hatched from an egg, and sways toward Eugene, svelte and fluid and serpentine. A smile touches her lips as she walks toward him, and her eyes are alive with humor and sensuality. He called up to her room over ten minutes ago, but it was certainly worth the wait. He gets to his feet and takes a step forward to greet her. Seeing her is almost enough to make him forget the envelope he opened this morning and what he found within it. Almost. But even though the worry floats around the back of his mind he knows he can do nothing about it. He must simply wait, see what happens.

He leans in and kisses her cheek. He can smell clean sweat on her, the kind of sweat you want to lick off, and soap, and that soft flowery perfume that's so unlike the woman herself.

'You look beautiful,' he says into her ear.

'I know,' she says.

5

The knock at the door comes sooner than expected. He only called her back fifteen minutes ago, and she wasn't sure when they got off the phone that he'd actually show up. He seemed distant and strange during their conversation, halting in his speech, but despite this she is inexplicably looking forward to seeing this man who helped to arrest her son. She walks to the door and pulls it open. Detective Bachman stands on the other side in a wrinkled gray suit and scuffed shoes, his weathered face hanging there dead till he sees her and puts a smile on it. He removes his fedora and holds it in front of his chest as if she were the national anthem.

'Mrs Richardson.'

'Candice.'

'Candice, then. Are you ready?'

His eyes seem glossy and far away, and much of the emotion that was evident on his face the night she met him appears to have vanished, is completely absent. She wasn't herself that night. Perhaps she misjudged him. Perhaps her memory of him was distorted by what she was going through. She hesitates, wondering if this was a bad idea, wondering if she should just stay home.

She glances back over her shoulder and cannot stand the sight of her empty house. It feels oppressive, the emptiness, and she wants to get away from it. At least temporarily.

'Yeah,' she says. 'I'm ready.'

'Good,' he says, and steps aside.

6

The restaurant is dimly lit. A chandelier hangs from the ceiling, lighting the center of the room, but Evelyn and Eugene are sitting at a small two-top in a back corner, in darkness but for the flickering light of a guttering candle. It makes it difficult for her to read his expression.

He takes a swallow of his beer.

'Is that really so bad?' she says.

He remains silent for a long time. Finally he shakes his

head and says, 'I just don't know how anyone can *not* like Humphrey Bogart.'

'I didn't say I don't like him.'

'That's what it sounded like to me.'

'I like him fine when he plays scoundrels. He was perfect in *The Treasure of the Sierra Madre*. But his teeth are disgusting. Every time he kisses a woman onscreen all I can think about is what his breath must smell like. I see him with Lauren Bacall and I simply don't believe it.'

'But they're *married*.'

She shrugs. 'They say love is blind. Maybe it doesn't have a good sense of smell, either.'

Eugene laughs.

She smiles and sips her wine.

7

Carl and Candice sit across from one another at the Brown Derby on Wilshire Boulevard. He watches her eat a bowl of chili and sips his coffee, good and bitter and hot. The place is busy and filled with the sounds of people talking, of forks and knives scraping against plates, of chairs being scooted in and out. He likes the sounds; they blend together, creating a cloud of noise that's almost as peaceful as silence.

'It was my wife,' he says, 'the end of last year. Cancer.'

'I'm so sorry.'

'I moved out of our place the next day and haven't been back since.'

'Really?'

He nods. 'Park on the street sometimes, look at the house, but I can't bring myself to go inside. Too many memories there.'

Candice nods her understanding. 'Things used to happen there, and now they don't, and the place feels emptier because of it. Emptier and lonelier.'

'And the worst thing is that the more full of memories it is,' Carl says, 'the more hollow it all seems now.'

'It's like that old riddle,' Candice says, taking a bite of her chili. 'What gets bigger the more you take away from it?'

'A hole,' Carl says.

8

Eugene and Evelyn walk along 8th Street beneath a bruised evening sky. Behind them, what remains of the sunset – a thin line of pink being crushed by dark night from above. In front of them, the skyscrapers of downtown Los Angeles. Automobiles roll by, headlights throwing out beams of light. Then one of the yellow streetcars heading east.

'How far is your apartment?'

'About five blocks.'

'Let's walk there, have a nightcap.'

'Maybe your hotel room would be better.'

He doesn't want Evelyn to see his apartment. He's taken women there before after picking them up in bars. Drunk, they're delighted by his milk truck. Next morning as he drives them home, however, they often seem vaguely embarrassed by the whole experience. Waking up in a small apartment furnished in yard-sale finds. Being driven home in a delivery vehicle. The fact they can't quite remember his name. Often they ask him to drop them off at the end of the block and walk the rest of the way home.

He likes Evelyn, likes her a lot, and doesn't want any embarrassed silences come morning. And maybe he feels she's out of his league and his apartment will reveal that fact to her. He isn't sure, exactly.

But Evelyn shakes her head at his suggestion.

'No?'

'I can't let anybody see me take a strange man into my room. That wouldn't look good. Besides, I want to see where you live.'

'I'm not sure I have anything to drink at home.'

'We'll stop somewhere on the way, pick up a bottle.'

Eugene gives up, shrugs. 'Okay.'

Evelyn smiles at him and puts her arm in his arm and leans her head on his shoulder as they walk. It feels strange and unnatural and new and fine.

'Now I think of it, I probably do have a half bottle of whiskey in the cupboard.'

'Perfect.'

After a few more minutes of silent strolling along the cracked sidewalk they make their way up the stairs toward Eugene's front door, their feet thudding against the bare wood steps. The walls are lined with smudges, the banister black from grimy hands dragging up and down it over the years.

Once at the top of the stairs he glances to Evelyn and smiles.

'Here we are,' he says.

'Here we are.'

He unlocks the front door and pushes it open. 'Ladies first.'

'What if there's a burglar?'

'That's why I'm sending you in first. To protect me.'

'Coward.'

She heads into the place, smiling, and Eugene follows. He closes the door behind him and turns on a lamp, illuminating the small living room.

'Have a seat,' he says. 'I'll get the drinks. Neat?'

'Neat.'

He pours them each two fingers of bourbon, carries the glasses out to the living room, sits down. He hands Evelyn her drink.

'Thank you,' she says. She holds up the glass. 'To a lovely evening.'

'To a lovely evening,' Eugene says, tapping his glass against hers before taking a swallow. She sips hers as well, her soft mouth smashing against the glass, her tongue teasing the lip of it. Then she pulls the glass away, and must feel him watching her, because she glances toward him, and suddenly they're staring into each other's eyes.

Eugene's heart pounds in his chest. He leans in toward her, close enough that he can feel her breath on his skin, and hesitates. He feels like an adolescent boy, like he's never done this before, his dozens of one-night stands forgotten. He feels unsure of himself and awkward and they stay that way for a long time, their faces mere inches apart, looking back at one another uncertainly.

'Do it,' she says.

He does.

9

Carl and Candice sit in his car in front of her house. They're silent. Carl feels strange. He feels close to Candice and very far from her. He scratches his cheek and looks through the windshield at the dark, empty street. The asphalt is gray, houses lined up on either side of it, facing one another like formations of soldiers about to do battle. Most of the windows are closed for the evening, the curtains drawn, secret things taking place behind them. Awful things, as secret things so often are.

'Thank you,' Candice says finally.

He looks over at her. She looks back, smiles.

'For what?'

'Understanding.'

'I wish I didn't.'

'I know. But it helped.'

'I can't imagine I said anything useful.'

'Understanding was enough.'

She leans in and kisses him on the corner of his mouth. Then the car door's opened and shut and she's walking up the path to her house. The windows are black.

He watches her walk to the front door, unlock it. He watches the door open and shut like the blink of an eye. One minute she's there, the next she's not. In between those two states she glances back at him and smiles.

He touches the corner of his mouth where she kissed him. He blinks.

Her living-room window lights up. He can see her moving behind the glass.

He starts the car.

10

Eugene finds himself in a small room, with no idea how he got there. He walks to a window and looks out. Sees gray sky, lightning flashing in the distance. Thunder follows, shaking the glass. He puts his fingers to the glass and feels cold from outside. Below him, a dense layer of clouds he can't see past; they block his view of the ground below, but the mere fact of the clouds lets him know he's very high up in a very tall building. His reflection tells him he's wearing a gray suit. He isn't sure he owns a gray suit. He turns around to face the room. On the wall opposite, an oak desk with a telephone and a typewriter on it. He walks to the telephone, picks it up, puts it to his ear. Hears first a shallow silence, then a pounding sound coming from far away.

Thud, thud, thud.

The entire room shakes.

Eugene sits up in bed. There's someone beside him, but he doesn't know who. Then he remembers. He can feel her skin smooth and warm against his skin.

Thud, thud, thud.

Suddenly he knows what the pounding is. He crawls out of bed, walks to his closet, grabs a .38 Smith & Wesson revolver from the top shelf. It's been months since he last touched it, perhaps years, and he's surprised by its weight, but also comforted by it. He checks the cylinder that it's loaded.

Then, with it gripped in his fist, thumb on the hammer spur, he walks to the front door and yanks it open. No one there, but he hears feet pounding down the stairs. He follows, taking the steps two at a time, the wood cool against the soles of his bare feet. Then out into the chill night where he sees a figure heading toward a car with the engine running, smoke wafting up from its tailpipe. The figure pulls open the driver's-side door, jumps inside, slams the door shut. The taillights glow red. The car pulls away.

Eugene stands in the wet grass, feet cold, body covered in gooseflesh.

He turns around, heads back up the stairs. His door stands open.

There's an envelope nailed to it, yet another paper moth. He tears the envelope from the door, leaving the nail in place, and walks into the apartment. He closes the door behind him. He sets the gun down on the dining table beside his typewriter.

He stares at the envelope.

'What is it?'

He jumps, startled, and looks up.

Evelyn stands in the hallway with a sheet wrapped loosely around her otherwise nude body, revealing a hint of breast he would under normal circumstances find very sexy, but right now he's too disoriented, too distracted, to find anything sexy. Moments ago he was pulled from dream sleep and now holds in his hands an answer he isn't sure he wants. This morning he read that newspaper clipping and knew it implied a threat, I will tell unless, and knows he now holds the rest of that sentence in his hands. Unless what? Just look inside.

'What is it?' Evelyn says again.

'I don't know.'

He tears the envelope open.

STUPID HEART

EIGHTEEN

1

Eugene, wearing only a pair of wrinkled slacks, walks Evelyn to the front door. She looks at him with her large eyes, purse clutched in her hands. Once more she is wearing the dress she wore last night, though it seems strange in the early morning, out of place, and it's wrinkled from having spent the night on the floor. Most of her makeup has been rubbed away and her pin-curled hair is a frizzy mess. Her chin is pink and raw from kissing him, from rubbing against his sandpaper-rough five o'clock shadow.

She looks beautiful.

He touches her arm as he pulls open the door.

'Sorry about this,' he says.

She smiles. 'It's probably better this way. I can sneak into my room without anybody seeing at this hour.'

'I'm glad you're not upset.'

'Will you call me?'

'When I get this resolved.'

'What are you gonna do?'

'I don't know yet.'

'Okay,' she says. 'Call me.'

'Are you sure you don't want a cab?'

'It's only a few blocks.'

She turns and walks down the stairs. He watches her go. When she's out of the building he closes the apartment door and sets the deadbolt. He puts his forehead against the wood and stays there a moment before turning to face the room. He walks to the dining table and picks up the note, unfolds it and looks at the gray lettering on the white page. It was typed on a typewriter in need of ribbon replacement. The 't' is cocked to the right, making it look a bit like a malformed 'x'. The 'h' sits higher than the other letters. The note says:

$1000

1:30 p.m.

535 South Grand Ave.

645

He should have known what the unless was. Unless you give me money. It almost always comes down to money, doesn't it? Money or love. But there was never any chance this would be about love. What he can't figure out is, why the paper moths? Why the coyness? Why not simply brace him? Is it someone he knows? He thinks it must be. It must be someone he knows. He worked with a lot of people when he was doing comics, writers and artists, and it could be any one of them. That could be the reason for the paper moths. The man behind this maybe doesn't want to reveal his identity. Maybe if he did reveal his identity the threat would vanish on the air, like a lover's promise.

And he still finds it difficult to believe the district attorney will actually come after him for negligent homicide. He might try to pin something like that on James Manning, but Manning runs the whole publishing enterprise. Eugene's a nobody. He isn't worth going after. Except for this – he wrote and drew the story in question. If his name came out he could very well end up a codefendant, couldn't he? Of course he could.

Of course he could.

These are strange times. Living in the shadow of the atomic bomb. Politicians pointing in every direction and shouting communist. Baseball desegregating despite Baton Rouge and other southern cities banning Negro players from their fields; fights over race down at Wrigley Field when the Los Angeles Angels play the Hollywood Stars. Church groups all over the country burning comic books and blaming them for juvenile delinquency. Psychologists claiming they incite violence. Jonas Salk's polio vaccine still only a hope while kids continue to die. Flying saucers being spotted in the sky across the country while the military denies any responsibility. The world is as frightening as it's ever been and only getting worse.

And when people are scared, anything might happen.

So Eugene has no answers to his dozens of questions and having no answers he knows not what to do. There are too many unknowns.

You don't stand on a ledge and leap into darkness. You shine a light into the shadows to see what's below you.

Could he simply ignore the note? Crumple it up and throw it into the trash and pretend he never received it?

And then what? Wait for something to happen? Wait for the police to come pounding on his door with their guns drawn?

Or maybe he'll throw the note away and simply go on with his life. Maybe a month from now he'll stop expecting something terrible to happen; he'll stop waiting for gray clouds to blow in. Thoughts of the threat will fade into the background, like a radio heard from three blocks away, and he'll eventually be deaf to them. Five years from now he'll have forgotten about it altogether.

He doesn't know what to do.

He looks at the clock. He has to leave for work in twenty minutes.

He tosses the note onto the table.

He tells himself he needs to get dressed and out the door, but for a long time he can't do anything but stand there and look at that piece of paper.

Then he finds he can move. He turns and heads down the hallway.

2

Evelyn walks down the third-floor corridor. It's lined with freshly polished shoes, a pair outside nearly every room. She feels a great urge to scuff them all, to walk by and drag her heel across their shining leather tops. That would kink a few mornings. The thought puts a sour smile on her face, but she doesn't do it. Instead she walks to Lou's room and knocks.

Cursing, the creak of a bed, a grunt that means what or who is it.

She tells Lou, open the door.

She's glad she woke him. She hopes he just got to sleep after nailing that envelope to Eugene's front door. Hopes he was having a good dream and she pulled him out of it. She feels awful about what she's doing to Eugene. She's done worse to other men, but she liked none of them the way she likes him. She knew she shouldn't get attached to the man – he was a mark, nothing more, and from the beginning he was going down – but maybe you can't help who you get attached to. It doesn't matter. It won't stop her from doing her job. Just makes it unpleasant, that's all.

Lou pulls open the door. She pushes into the room past him.

'It smells like asshole in here, Lou.'

'Why are you here?'

'To get this over with,' Evelyn says. Then she unzips her

purse. With a white napkin she removes a revolver and sets it on a table. Then she removes a folded-up sheet of paper with writing on.

'His fingerprints should be all over both of them.'

'What's the paper?'

'You know how to read.'

'And the knife?'

She shakes her head. 'I fell asleep last night and this morning had to do what I could. I got you the gun.'

'Will he notice it missing?'

'He has work, then his appointment. I doubt he'll have time to notice it missing. I'm going to bed.'

She turns and walks back out to the corridor. She walks to her room and keys it open and steps inside. She's surprised by how much she hates herself for what she's doing. She tells herself to be hard. She tells herself to get her head right. This is business. If there's no room for God in this business, there's no room for love.

Love? There's sex and there's marriage; she doesn't even know what love is.

She unzips her dress and lets it fall to her feet and kicks it away. She crawls into bed. She can still smell the man she spent the night with on her skin, she can taste him in her mouth. She covers herself in blankets and closes her eyes, hoping she might be able to catch a few more hours' sleep. But she can sense the morning's swift approach. Soon it will be daylight and her mind knows it.

This is the reason there's no chance of sleep. This is the reason her mind will not go silent. There's no other possible explanation.

This is business.

3

Eugene's experience of his day is like a dream remembered. There are faces and colors and places, but they don't combine to create an experience. He goes to the warehouse and picks up the day's work; he drives his route and delivers his milk; he collects payment when payment is due; when he sees someone he knows he says hello, yeah, it does look like a storm might be brewing, hope I get done with the job before it starts pouring – but none of his conscious mind is present, and when the day's over and he's parking his truck in front of a hotel at 535 South Grand Avenue, he remembers very little of it.

He lights a cigarette and inhales deeply and pulls it from his mouth. He holds it between his fingers and looks at the orange glow of the cherry. He glances over at the Shenefield Hotel, a fourteen-storey block building made filthy by smog. Inside it, someone awaits his arrival. He wonders if he's making a mistake coming here without the money. There's a chance he is, a chance he's making a serious mistake coming here at all, but there was no alternative. He doesn't have the money. He doesn't know a way of getting it. He tells himself, too, that even if he could get the money he wouldn't. He tells himself there's no way he'd bring a thousand dollars down here without knowing what he was walking into, without knowing who was doing this to him. He tells himself that, but he doesn't believe it. If he had the money he'd pay. The district attorney might not care about such a nobody as him. The grand-jury investigation could end with the district attorney being told there's no case. The grand jury could decide there is a case, but the trial result in a not-guilty verdict. Any number of things might happen. But mights and coulds don't make for restful nights. Even certain doom is somehow better than not knowing. You can wrap yourself in the dark blanket of doom and get some comfort from it. It's warmer, anyway, than the frigid air of uncertainty.

He steps from the milk truck, tossing his hat onto the seat. He runs his fingers through his oily hair, takes a final drag from his cigarette, flicks it away. Walks under an American flag snapping in the breeze and, doorman pulling the door open for him, thank you, into the hotel lobby.

After taking a few steps inside he stops and stands and does nothing else. He exhales in a sigh and tells himself God hates a coward. Maybe it's even true.

He walks to the elevator and hits the call button.

A minute later he's stepping off the elevator and onto the sixth floor.

The corridor is wide and carpeted with red carpet. The walls are white. A man is walking toward him. He was stepping out of one of the rooms as Eugene was stepping off the elevator. Eugene didn't see which room. He wonders if it's his man come to greet him. He's a thin man with a pale, skeletal face, his black hair slicked back with pomade. Eugene continues to walk as if everything were normal, but he watches as the man approaches him. Watches him with great caution. The man wears a black pinstriped suit. He also wears black leather gloves, despite it being spring in Los Angeles.

They pass one another. The man nods, makes brief eye contact, and is gone. It wasn't his man. Of course it wasn't. His man's in room 645.

Eugene wishes he'd thought to bring his gun. Instead it lies useless on his dining table back home. It'd be a good thing to have. Or maybe it would be yanked out of his hand and he'd be shot with it.

He stops at the hotel room. The door's unlatched, the doorframe cracked, the wood split. He glances back toward the man who walked by him, the thin man with the gloved hands. He stepped out of a room – was it this room? Eugene doesn't know.

And the corridor is now empty.

He steps forward and something squishes beneath his foot. He looks down. A puddle of liquid on the carpet, darkening it. He reaches down to touch the puddle. His fingers

come away wet with red liquid, with blood, and the blood's
still warm, near body temperature.

He closes his eyes, exhales, opens his eyes.

Then opens the door.

NINETEEN

1

Vivian pulls a black dress from her closet and holds it up at arm's length to give it a once-over. She picks a few pieces of lint from it. It's a nice dress and aside from being perhaps too brief quite funereal in its simplicity. She believes it'll do. She will, after all, only be sitting in a pew beside Candice while a man of the cloth speaks of death and the departed and how the soul may move on but our memories remain, God bless us all, amen. She wonders how Candice is feeling. She seems to be holding up fairly well, as well as could be expected under these circumstances, but people put up facades. It's hard to tell what's going on inside another person's mind.

Sometimes it is. But she's fairly certain Leland knew exactly what she was thinking when he walked out the front door fifteen minutes ago, when he left to meet with

Seymour Markley. He stood in the entry sulking, saying don't be like that, darlin, like he thought he could just do whatever he wanted, ignoring her protests, and she had to be okay with it. She isn't okay with it. She might be a whore, as Markley said, and she might be a blackmailer, but she's not a liar. She wasn't until Leland made her one.

And aside from any ethical qualms she has with what Leland is doing – and despite who and what she is, she does have those: how she makes her money might not be legal, but it's honest – there's another reason she's upset with him. She lives by a rule that Leland's breaking. You do not put your hand twice into the same till. Not unless you want your fingers cut off when the drawer slams shut. Leland knows this, they've been through this before, but once more he's being stupid about it.

It infuriates her.

It doesn't even matter if it works out. It has before. That isn't the point. Every time it works out, it only encourages Leland to try something like this again, and next time it won't work out. Or the time after that. You have to do things the right way. You have to be honest. You're dealing with important people who aren't used to being made vulnerable. You're embarrassing them. You're making demands. You have to be straight with them if you expect to come out of that unscathed.

It's simple self-preservation.

She walks to the bathroom and hangs the dress from

the door. She turns on the water in the tub, plugs the drain, watches the tub slowly fill up.

After a few minutes she slips out of her nightgown and steps into the water. She has about thirty minutes to soak before she needs to get ready for the funeral.

2

Barry parks a block from the house. He's never before done what he's about to do, but knows better than to park directly in front of the place he intends to burgle. Every neighborhood has at least one bored retiree more than happy to scribble down a license-plate number and call the police about this bald fellow seems to be snooping around and I don't recognize him, and Barry would rather not get caught. It would almost certainly be the end of his career. He steps from his car and locks the door. He walks along the sidewalk toward the house. The sky is overcast today, gunmetal gray, and the air, while still warm, is beginning to cool. He expects rain is on the way, blowing in from somewhere, but it's not here just yet. As he walks he listens to the hollow echo of his shoes against the pavement. It reminds him of his days in the army. The synchronized thudding of combat boots on hard-packed soil, the smell of well-oiled rifles, the sound of flags snapping in the wind.

The men didn't respect him. Commissioned officers are

often disliked by soldiers under their command, but this went beyond that. The men didn't respect or like him personally. They wouldn't willingly drink with him when the uniforms came off. He thinks now there was some reason for that. He was young and stupid and arrogant, an unpleasant combination. His father expected him to be a career military man as he had been, but instead he left after two years. He'd always loved the piano, had been getting lessons since he was ten, and thought he might have a career as a pianist, but in truth he wasn't good enough. He could sit in a barroom and impress with clunky renditions of Chopin, but he simply didn't have the skill to command a stage. Somehow life was missing from the music he clinked out. His fingers lacked grace. Fortunately, the Los Angeles district attorney's office looked favorably upon his university education and his military record or he might be banging the ivories yet in some western bar with filthy spittoons on the floor. Or maybe not so fortunately. Right at this moment that life doesn't sound so bad to him. Almost sounds romantic.

He'd at least be doing something he loved.

He arrives at the house, walks to the front door, knocks. Seymour told him the place would be empty, told him the occupants would be meeting with him fifteen miles away, but one must be cautious in moments like these.

No one answers his knock.

He turns away thinking he'll walk around the house and find a window to crawl through, and wishing he hadn't worn a suit for this job, but turns back only a moment later. He might as well try the knob. He has no hope for it, but should make sure before resorting to anything else.

He turns the knob and the door unlatches. He pushes and the door opens. He glances once over his shoulder and sees no one and nothing but empty street. He steps into the house and closes the door behind him.

He looks around the living room, a small room with white-painted pine floors. A couch sits in the middle of the room on a brown rug with tattered strings hanging from its edges. A small Philco television sits against the wall opposite the couch, an empty bottle of beer on top of it, resting directly in front of a coat-hanger antenna.

He walks deeper into the house, wondering where the compromising photographs might be hidden, still having no idea someone else is here with him.

3

Vivian stretches out her right leg, resting her foot on the protruding bathtub faucet, the dull gray metal hot against the arch of her foot. She soaps her leg up, covering it in a film of lavender-scented bubbles, and gets to work with one of Leland's Gillette safety razors. She starts with her toes, scraping the small brown hairs from the knuckles, and then works her way up her leg, dragging the blade toward her knee, then over her knee and up her thigh. Occasionally she stops to rinse the blade in the tub, shaking it around in the water. Short nubs of hair, not much bigger than grains of sand, float on a scrim of soap which lines the water's surface.

Her father forbade her to shave her legs while she lived under his roof, nor would he allow her to wear makeup. The only book he allowed in the house was a bible. This book contains everything worth knowing; you start lookin for answers outside the bible, what you're really lookin for is trouble.

She went out and looked for trouble, anyway, and if she couldn't do the things she wanted while living under his roof, she wouldn't live there. She ran away at sixteen and never regretted it, not even during the hardest of times.

She pauses with the blade halfway up her leg, tilts her head to listen. She could have sworn she heard something, a knock at the front door maybe. All she hears now though is the water running.

She sets the razor down on the edge of the tub and turns the water off. Now all she hears is the drip . . . drip . . . drip of the faucet. If someone was at the door they must have left, for there isn't a second knock. Not that she would answer the door if there were. She's in the middle of a bath and isn't about to run soaking wet to the front door just so she can tell a salesman she isn't interested in his full set of stainless-steel cookware or his amazing bottle of stove cleaner, you'll never have to scrub again.

She's reaching forward to turn the water back on when she hears the floor creak.

Her first instinct is to call out to Leland, you home already? But she knows it isn't him. He should just be arriving at his appointment. She sits perfectly still and listens. The floor creaks again. She gets to her feet, the splashing water sounding very loud in her ears, though she attempts silence. Water drips from her body. She steps from the tub, moving slowly. She dries herself with a towel.

Someone's going through the dresser in the bedroom now. She can hear wood sliding against wood as drawers are opened and closed. She feels very naked. She walks to her nightgown and slips back into it. It clings to her still-damp body. The bathroom door is cracked. She walks to it and looks through the crack in the doorway. A man in a suit, a bald man in a suit, not your typical burglar, is digging through her dresser, pulling the clothes out and setting them aside before replacing them neatly. Her first thought is that he's a pervert looking for panties to sniff while he plays with his thing, but that isn't right. It isn't panties he's after. He's searching for something else and isn't finding it.

She turns back to the bathroom looking for a weapon of some kind. At first she sees nothing of use. A toothbrush. A tube of Pepsodent toothpaste. A yellow latex douche/enema bag flung over the shower rod.

The shower rod.

She pulls it from the wall and walks once more toward the bathroom door. She pulls open the door and stands silently in the doorway a moment, watching the man now pulling open the bottom drawer of her dresser.

She opens her mouth but nothing comes out. She's afraid to speak. Part of her thinks it might be best if she said nothing at all. She could step back into the bathroom and close the door, lock it, wait for him to leave. That might be the best thing to do. It might be the safest thing to do.

But she won't simply allow this man to dig through her belongings. She can't.

She grips the rod in her fists tightly, her knuckles going white. She swallows. Her hands feel cramped from the tension in them.

Finally she finds it within herself to speak.

'Find what you're looking for?'

4

Barry turns around to see a doe-eyed brunette woman standing in an open doorway. She wears a wet nightgown which clings to her skin, the shape of her breasts and her hips clearly visible beneath its thin fabric. She holds a metal rod in her hands like a baseball bat.

He blinks at her, unbelieving. The house was supposed

to be empty. Seymour promised him it'd be empty. He knocked and there was no answer. So why is someone standing across the room from him with a weapon gripped in her fists?

'What?'

'Did you find what you were looking for?'

She takes a step forward. Barry takes a step back.

'I think there's been a misunderstanding.'

'Misunderstanding? Did you *accidentally* break into my house?'

Barry cannot think of a response. He's not a stupid man, but he feels stupid right now. His mind has failed him. He wants to run, but she's standing between him and his way out of here. And he still hasn't found any pictures. It could be that there aren't any. It could be that Seymour now has them all. But he'd feel better about coming to that conclusion if he had time to finish searching.

The woman takes another step toward him.

He has to get out of the house. If he gets out of the house and gets to his car he'll be fine. He can forget about it. The pictures are Seymour's problem, not his own, and he can walk away without a worry. He stole nothing. No one will investigate. She probably won't even call the police. If he gets away he'll be fine.

Goddamn it, the house was supposed to be empty.

'You better say something.'

'The . . . the door was unlocked.'

'The *door* was unlocked?'

She raises the pole in her hands.

He swallows, glances from her to the doorway. There's a moment during which neither of them moves. Then he runs for it.

As he rushes past her she swings, bringing the pole down fast at a diagonal.

It connects with the side of his head, sending a great ringing through the hollows of his skull, and sending him to the floor. He blinks, disoriented, and rolls over. He looks up to see the woman stepping toward him, brow furrowed, arms swinging again. The pole comes chopping down toward his face like an axe. Once, against the forehead. Twice, he reaches out and manages to catch it. There's a terrible stinging in the palm of his hand, sharp and somehow acidic, like a slap. He ignores it and pulls the pole from her hand, yanking her forward with it till she loses her grip. He gets to his feet.

Fear flickers in the woman's eyes and it's her turn to take a step back.

It does something to him, the fear visible on her face. As does her subtle retreat. It erases all thought of leaving. He could now simply turn and walk away, and everything would be fine. There may or may not be more pictures, but the house was supposed to be empty. It's no longer his responsibility.

Except the woman backing away pulls him toward her, as if there were some invisible cable connecting them to one another. She moves back so he moves forward. It's as simple as that.

'Where are they?'

'Where . . . where are what?'

'The pictures.'

TWENTY

1

Lou steps off an elevator and walks down a corridor that stinks of the cigarettes smoked behind the doors lining the walls on either side of him. He can see a cop standing in front of the door he wants to walk through. The cop is about twenty-three years old and wears a heavily starched uniform. His red hair is cut short and freckles dot his cheeks. His hands are clasped behind his back and he stares straight ahead at the wall, mouth a soggy teeter-totter drooping over his chin. Lou's guessing this young cop used to be a marine. It's in his posture. His older brother saw combat, has stories about storming the beach at Normandy, battling on vast fields of blood, bayoneting teenage warriors and feeling no remorse, for it was us or them, and we had God on our side. He's unhappy that he was too young to join before the end of World War II and was unlucky enough to be discharged before the Korean War began. Probably he left to join the police force after two years at Camp Gordon, Georgia, or some other place equally as boring, hoping for action in the city if not on the battlefield. He wants to taste blood. That's what Lou sees as he walks toward this young cop. That's what he sees, but he hopes he's wrong, because if he's right it might mean trouble.

He approaches the cop, walking casually, hands in pockets. The hand in his right hip pocket grips the cool handle of a switchblade knife. If things had gone to plan, there'd be an identical knife in the milkman's apartment. Evelyn bungled it, but he still wants to use the knife here; a gunshot will give Teddy Stuart too much warning. The cop looks toward him without moving his head. His eyes shift left, that's all. Lou smiles at him and gives him a small nod. The cop does not return Lou's smile.

Instead he says, 'I think you're on the wrong floor, sir.'

'No, it's all right, I'm just going—'

And then Lou's upon him. He moves quickly, pulling both hands from his pockets simultaneously. With the left he reaches out and grabs an ear and pulls down, bending the cop forward. With the right, before the man can recover, before the hat which has fallen from the cop's head has even hit the floor, he flicks open the switchblade and plants it in the back of the cop's neck, slamming it straight down, aiming for the spinal cord. The cop crumples to the ground, unsheathing the blade now dripping with blood, nothing remaining of him but a pile of blue laundry, no sound escaping him but the single grunt he made when Lou grabbed him by the ear.

His blue hat lies on the floor a few feet away.

A strange chuckle escapes Lou's throat. He'd thought the cop might be trouble but he wasn't any trouble at all. If the police were going to use such an incompetent to protect Teddy Stuart they should have just left him unattended. It would have saved a life, and while Lou doesn't get emotional about murder, not at this point, he sees no reason to commit the act unless it's necessary. It is, after all, a messy and dangerous affair. Especially when the victim's a cop.

He wipes the blade off on the cop's uniform and puts it away. Later he'll throw it into the ocean and have an ice cream at Santa Monica pier. But for now he must get on with business. He reaches into his coat pocket and grabs a pair of leather gloves. He slips his hands into them, removes the milkman's revolver from his waistband, thumbs back the hammer.

He pulls back with his right foot and kicks. The doorjamb cracks but doesn't give completely; he kicks again, it splinters, and the door swings open. He grabs the cop by the back of his collar and drags him into the room, which appears to be empty. No sign of Teddy Stuart. He dumps the cop just inside the door. Then he grabs the hat from the hallway floor and throws it on top of the corpse. It flips off the body and onto the carpet, where it lies upside down. He closes the door. It won't latch, but at least it'll provide a temporary barrier if Teddy Stuart makes a run.

'Now,' he says, taking a step deeper into the room, 'if I were a rat, where would I hide? Under the bed, maybe.'

He leans down and looks. There's nothing there but floor.

'Maybe the armoire,' he says. 'Rats like the dark, don't they?'

2

Teddy sits in bed wearing nothing but pants and an undershirt. He has a couple days of beard-growth on his face. He's been stuck in this hotel room for four days and each day he feels less inclined to groom than he did the day before.

First couple days he got up early, showered, shaved, put on a suit – and spent the rest of his daylight hours sitting alone in this goddamn prison of a room. Last two days he hasn't really bothered. There's no point in hygiene. Hygiene is for other people and right now there are no other people.

He looks through the newspaper absently, reading headlines, sometimes the first paragraph of a story, but mostly he flips through pages simply to be doing something. His thumbs are black from the newsprint rubbing off on them. Nothing interests him. Each day he's here he fades a little more out of existence. Soon he'll go transparent and shortly after that will cease to exist altogether. Air will fill the space he once displaced.

He needs to go for a walk. He needs to grab a hamburger at a hamburger stand and eat it while making small talk with the man perched next to him. He needs to smile at pretty girls and feel the sunshine on his face. Only four days and he's tired of being protected. He isn't sure how much more he can take.

This thought, then a sound just outside his door. A grunt. Then another sound. The heavy thud of a man collapsing to the floor. His first thought is that the cop guarding his door fainted, but he knows that isn't right. One doesn't grunt before fainting; one grunts while being knocked unconscious.

The Man has come for him. The Man has sent someone to kill him. He knew this might happen, knew it probably would happen, and now that it is happening the biblical corner of his mind which before was preaching so loudly has gone silent. That feeling of fading from existence is also gone. He feels fully in himself, fully alive, and his only concern now is for survival.

He lifts his heavy frame from the bed, cringing as the springs creak, wishing he hadn't let himself get so fucking fat. He pads to the bathroom, eye on the door, every moment expecting it to open, to see a killer revealed. His first thought is that he can hide behind the shower curtain, but as soon as his feet are on cold tile he sees there is no shower curtain. The shower's enclosed in glass. He knew that. He's been here for days.

Why didn't he—

Someone in the corridor kicks at the door and the doorjamb cracks without giving completely. A few jagged splinters of wood fall to the carpet.

He pushes the bathroom door shut, knowing he's only delaying the inevitable, knowing it but not having the courage to face head-on what's coming.

Another kick at the room door and this time it swings open.

Death has just walked in, but he'll not greet it. Every second he can cling to life is a second he wants, filled with terror though it might be. It's a second that belongs to him rather than God.

3

Lou pulls open the armoire. Empty wood hangers line the length of the warped dowel, interspersed like crows on a telephone line. On the left side of the dowel, a coat, a few shirts, a few pairs of pants. Two black shoes sit on the floor, empty of feet.

He pushes the door shut and turns around.

A smile touches his lips.

'You're in the bathroom, aren't you, Teddy?'

He walks toward the door, stepping slowly, moving

fluidly. He knows that Teddy Stuart's behind that door. There's nowhere else for him to be unless he's not here, and he is here. The cop was guarding the door because of what was on the other side of it.

Though he remains calm and his actions deliberate Lou knows he needs to get this done quickly. He called the police before taking the elevator up, called them from the lobby and said he needed to report a murder, told them that Teddy Stuart had been killed, and now he must make that killing happen and get out of here before the police arrive.

He reaches the door and toes it open.

It swings wide, revealing the man whose life he's to end. He stands barefoot on the bathroom floor in a pair of wrinkled slacks and a Dago T-shirt. He holds in his hands the heavy lid of the toilet tank. He holds it over his head, ready to swing it down – except Lou is not within swinging distance. His eyes are red, face unshaven and tired-looking. Lou can almost find it in himself to feel sorry for the son of a bitch.

Almost.

He raises the gun.

'You had to know the Man would send someone,' Lou says. 'He liked you. He trusted you. And you betrayed him.'

4

Teddy looks through the doorway and down the barrel of a gun. Behind the gun, the skeletal face of a killer. He thinks of his ex-wife. They lived together unhappily for a decade, but she was the only person he ever loved. He wonders why he couldn't find happiness. He's going to die now and he never knew happiness. A few good and true moments, yes, but it wasn't enough.

He's not going to die now. He can't die. He doesn't deserve to die.

He wants more, and he needs it.

He throws the toilet tank's heavy lid at the man standing across from him. It flips end over end once. The killer puts up his arm to block the object. It hits the arm and he grunts, ugh, and falls backwards to the floor, and the porcelain lid lands beside him.

Teddy looks from the killer on the floor to the hotel room's door. It's only ten steps away and it isn't latched. Loose splinters of wood hang from the doorframe. He can make it. If he can get to the door and through it he might actually live.

He can make it.

He takes a single step.

5

Lou pulls the trigger. The revolver explodes in his hand. A small dot appears on Teddy Stuart's forehead, dead-center, like a birdhouse door, tweet, and his brains and small flecks of bone splatter the white wall behind him. The scent of cordite and the coppery odor of blood fill the room. He shoots again, hitting the already dead man in the shoulder as he falls to the floor. One clean shot in the head would look too much like a professional hit. Two shots, though, one in the shoulder and one in the head, well, maybe the shooter got lucky.

He tosses the revolver to the floor.

He pulls a sheet of paper from his back pocket, one of the milkman's H.H. White Creamery Company stock-request forms. It includes the milkman's name, truck number, and how much product he needed for his route three days ago.

Lou drops it.

It falls to the carpet, looking like planted evidence.

He picks it up, crumples it up a bit, walks to the armoire. He drops it to the floor. With his toe he pushes it till it's half hidden beneath the large piece of furniture, more than half hidden, just a corner of paper poking out of the shadows. That's better. Looks less obvious and therefore more real.

His job is now finished. He glances at his watch. He

needs to get out of here. The police will be arriving soon. The milkman will be arriving soon.

He steps from the hotel room and into the corridor, turns left and walks toward the elevator. As he does he sees a man stepping off said elevator. The man's about five-ten, an inch shorter than Lou himself. He's wearing well-ironed white slacks, a white shirt, a black bowtie, and a pair of tortoiseshell glasses.

Eugene Dahl, right on time.

Lou strolls toward him casually, not a care in the world. They nod at one another the way strangers sometimes do when passing, giving simple courteous acknowledgments, and then Lou steps onto the elevator. Before the doors close he watches Eugene Dahl continue his walk down the corridor, toward the murder scene.

TWENTY-ONE

1

Seymour watches Leland Jones push in through the finger-printed glass door. He stands in the doorway and scans the room, squinting and turning his head slowly like a light-house lamp. Then catches sight of Seymour and smiles. He holds up a hand like an Indian in a Western picture. Big Mustache say How. Seymour nods a cool greeting without, he's certain, so much as a hint of smile. There's no humor in him, nor kindness toward this blackmailing hillbilly peckerwood (as the southern Negroes Seymour's put in prison would rightly call him). He looks past Leland, expecting Vivian to walk through the door behind him. But he appears to be alone.

He walks to the table and slides into the booth saying, 'You need to relax, sugar. You look more nervous that a pussycat in a roomful of rockin chairs.'

'Don't worry about me,' Seymour says. 'Where's Vivian?'

'You miss her purty face, eh?'

'I just want this finished.'

'Fair enough. You got the money?'

'I have it. Where is she?'

'She's at home. What's it to you?'

'At home?'

'Yup.'

A hot lead ball drops into Seymour's gut with a heavy plunk, like a fishing weight, splashing bile up into his throat and the back of his mouth. He tries to swallow but cannot. He removes a white cloth from his coat's inside pocket. He snaps it to remove any lint and cleans his glasses. He rubs at the sore spots on his nose where his glasses usually rest. He puts his glasses back on. He folds the cloth into quarters and slides it back into his pocket. He swallows. He wonders if Vivian called the police when Barry broke into the place. He wonders if Barry might talk to get himself out of trouble. He wonders what kind of investigation that might lead to.

The precarious nature of his situation makes him feel sick. He hopes none of what he's feeling is visible on his face, but believes it must be. His face feels numb and for a moment he can't seem to move it.

'Well,' he says once he again has some control of himself, once he thinks he can speak with a voice that isn't shaking, 'let's get this over with, then.'

'Let's,' Leland says.

Seymour puts five twenty-dollar bills on the table.

Leland smiles and scoops the money up and counts it before shoving it into the breast pocket of his pearl-button cowboy shirt.

'Thanks, sugar,' he says. 'Vivian said you might be a problem, but I think you handled the situation real good. You didn't act scared. Business had to be done and you done it. I appreciate that.' He slides out of the booth and gets to his feet. 'Oh. Here's your pitcher. It really is the last one, you know. I don't believe in prolongin unpleasant business.' He reaches into the back pocket of his pants, pulls out a Polaroid, tosses it onto the table top. He touches the brim of his Stetson cowboy hat, makes a clicking noise with the corner of his mouth, the way a man will sometimes do to call a horse, and turns away.

Seymour picks up the photo, gets to his feet, walks across the checkered vinyl floor to a payphone in the corner.

He slips a dime into the coin-slot and dials a phone number.

After three rings a woman picks up. 'Carlyle residence.'

'Hello,' he says, 'this is Seymour Markley. May I speak with Barry, please?'

'Barry isn't in.'

'He's not back yet?'

'No.'

'Okay,' Seymour says, 'thank you.'

'You're—'

He drops the phone into its cradle.

2

Keeping one eye on the woman standing wet in a night-gown, holding the weapon in his left hand, ready to swing if necessary, Barry reaches to the top shelf of the closet with his free hand and pulls down a hat box. He knocks the lid away and looks inside. No hat, but dozens of Polaroid pictures. They're rubber banded into small stacks of two, three, or four. Most of the pictures are labeled, names written across them in black marker. Barry recognizes several of the names, and the faces within them as well. Men in the movie industry, men in politics. The same room appears in every photograph, a dingy room with peeling wallpaper lining the walls, with a couch and a sink and a rolling clothes rack with a few dresses hanging from it. The photographs were all taken from the same strange angle, the photographer undoubtedly hiding from his primary subject.

'My God.'

'You never had sex before?'

'How long have you been doing this?'

'What do you care?'

'I'm taking the pictures.'

'I figured.'

'You're not going to try to stop me?'

'No.'

'Okay then. I apologize for threatening you. It seemed necessary. In fact, it still does. Don't move till I'm out the front door. Please.'

Barry backs out of the bedroom, walking slowly, keeping an eye on the woman standing across the room from him. He backs his way across the living room, the wood floors creaking beneath his feet. It'll be okay if he can just get out of here. These people can hardly call the police about the missing photographs. As soon as he's out the door everything will be fine. He can stop sweating.

He's at the front door, ready to throw down the pole and leave, ready to grab the doorknob and make his exit, when he hears the sound of a vehicle pulling into the driveway. The engine rumbles and the brakes squeal, and then the engine stops rumbling. A door squeaks open, a door slams shut. Boot heels thud against the concrete walkway, coming ever nearer.

And the woman's now standing in the bedroom doorway, looking at him, despite the fact he told her not to move.

'Who is that?'

'It's Leland.'

'Okay,' Barry says, backing away from the door. 'Okay.' He leans down slowly and sets the box on the floor. He raises the pipe over his head. He looks again to the woman. 'Don't you make a sound.'

The doorknob turns. The door swings open.

A man in a Stetson cowboy hat is on the other side, smiling beneath a thick mustache and saying, 'I told you everything would be fine. It went smooth as—'

Barry swings the pole down with all his might, hitting the man on the side of the head, hitting him so hard the shock of the blow makes his palms ache. The pole bends at the contact point, forming an elbow. The large man collapses to the floor, knees first, then forward, but he's not knocked unconscious. He immediately starts picking himself up, glancing back toward the door with a confused look on his face, like he somehow tripped over his own feet and simply can't figure how it could have happened.

Barry swings again, against the back of his head, the soft part, and when the man hits the floor this time he doesn't try to pick himself back up.

Barry looks to the woman. She hasn't moved.

'I'm sorry.'

'I told him this would happen.'

There's resignation in her tone. Barry's glad to hear it. It means this is over.

He picks up the box of pictures.

'Even so, I apologize,' he says, and heads out, stepping over the unconscious gentleman blocking the doorway.

3

Seymour's sitting on the green corduroy couch in Barry's living room, rocking nervously and gripping a cup of water in both hands. Maxine, who helps out around the house, is sitting in an easy chair, her legs crossed, looking at him. Neither of them speaks. The door swings open. Seymour gets to his feet. Barry walks through, his bald head beaded with sweat, a pink knob on his forehead, a box under his arm. He closes the door behind him, looks at Seymour, and says, 'You assured me the place would be empty.'

'I know. I'm sorry. Is everything okay?'

'The place wasn't empty.'

'What happened?'

'I don't want to talk about it,' he says. Then: 'Look at this.' He tosses a hat box onto his coffee table. It lands with a clap.

'What is it?'

'Take a look. I need a drink.'

Maxine says, 'Are you okay, Bear?'

'I need a drink,' Barry says again, and heads into the kitchen.

The refrigerator opens and closes. There's a pop, a small hiss, silence. Barry returns with a small bottle of Blatz gripped in his fist.

Seymour sits down and pulls the box toward him. He looks down into it and sees dozens of photographs, and at first thinks these are all pictures of him with whores, and feels shame and disgust and terror. How long have they been following him? How long have they been photographing him? Has he really had this many transgressions? Then the faces in the pictures reveal themselves to him and he realizes they're not of him. He picks up several rubber-banded batches, reading the names on them, flipping through the pictures. Some of the pictures are of nobodies. Most of those are unlabeled. But many more of the pictures are of important people in Los Angeles. An ex-mayor, a police captain, two different state senators, a clean-cut actor with a spotless reputation.

'My God.'

Barry takes a swallow of his beer. 'That's what I said.'

TWENTY-TWO

1

Eugene steps into the hotel room, feeling a strange vibration within him, a sort of dissonant internal buzz. He can hear it as well as feel it, this discord within, echoing in his skull. He looks to his right. A cop on the floor, dead. He lies on his side, head tilted down, arms limp in front of him, one hand turned up, the other turned down, a pool of black blood beneath him. His uniform shirt is bunched up under his armpits, untucked, revealing a bleached undershirt and beneath that bare white stomach. His eyes are open. They're blue. The bare stomach is somehow the worst part. You never see a man naked in that way, with his clothes pulled away and rumpled, unless he's been assaulted, and it's usually drunk fellows who've been rolled by hoodlums. It reveals a vulnerability that, somehow, is both terrifying and embarrassing. You see your own vulnerability in it and must look away.

Two instincts war within him. The first and most basic is the instinct to flee. Blood, death: they make him slightly dizzy. The shock makes him feel as though he's stuck within a nightmare. His heart is pounding in his chest despite his stillness; it's telling him to get ready to move, and fast. But something else pulls him further into the room, a deeper survival instinct perhaps, hiding behind simple curiosity. What's going on here and what does it have to do with him? It must have something to do with him, he was brought here, and if he leaves now he won't get any answers.

A man can warm himself even beneath the blanket of certain doom.

He walks further into the room, looks to his left, and sees a gun on the carpet. A revolver. Then beyond it, and beyond an open door, another corpse lying on the white-tiled bathroom floor. Blood and brains are splattered on the back wall, running down it, sliding down it, thick and gelatinous as cold chicken fat. More blood running along the grout lines on the floor as if the areas between the tiles were a maze and the blood possessed some sort of primitive intelligence.

No one in the room is living but for Eugene.

Everything about this is wrong. There's nothing to discover here but death. But running is not the thing to do. He needs to call the police. He needs to call the police and tell them what happened, every last detail, even if it means the district attorney becomes aware of him. This is obviously bigger than anything he can handle on his own.

He turns around, looking for a telephone.

But a piece of paper on the floor catches his eye. A crumpled piece of paper mostly hidden beneath an armoire. He walks to it, not sure what he's doing, why he's walking to it – you need to call the police, Eugene; stop fucking around and call them already – and leans down to pick it up. He flattens it out and looks at it, an H.H. White Creamery Company stock-request form. His name is written on it, in his handwriting. He turns back around to look at the gun on the floor, a .38 Smith & Wesson revolver with a six-and-a-half-inch barrel. He's not a gun person, doesn't give a tin shit about guns, but he recognizes it all the same. Recognizes it because he has one just like it. He set it on his dining table next to his typewriter case early this morning before the sun had even touched the horizon. He set it down and tore open an envelope. Within the envelope was a typed note, the typed note that told him to be here, to be here now. Is it possible Evelyn took it, picked it up from where he left it and stowed it away in her purse? He knows that it is. From the moment he got the note his mind was on only that and what it meant. She could have grabbed a freight dolly and wheeled out his refrigerator without his noticing.

He thinks of meeting Evelyn. He thinks of her evasive responses when he asked why she was in town, what kind of business her father was in.

He doesn't want to believe what he's beginning to believe. He likes Evelyn, or once did. Her liked her a lot. He thought they shared something. He knows they shared something. You can't fake moments like the moments they had, moments where electricity seemed to spark between them. He hopes such moments can't be faked, anyway, and knows he never experienced anything like that before. Part of him believed such experiences were mythological, simply the stuff of bad poetry. But since he met her his idle fantasies of the future have had her in them. And yet he knows he's been framed and believes he knows by whom.

He needs to collect the evidence against him and get out of here.

He needs to do it now.

Outside: sirens wail.

He walks to the window and looks out, looks down to the street to see two LAPD radio cars screeching to a stop in front of the hotel, doors swinging open, uniformed officers stepping from their vehicles.

He shoves the paper into his pocket. Then grabs the gun and stuffs it down the front of his pants, untucking his shirt to hide it, hoping no one notices the shape of the gun under its fabric. If he stays calm, calm and collected, he might be able to walk out of here. Walk out of here and get rid of this evidence. Then he can find out why this was done to him. He knows Evelyn was part of it, he's sure of it, and the more he thinks about it the more certain he becomes, but he's also sure she didn't do this on her own.

There were others involved. He needs to find out who, who and why, and he needs to find out how to fix it.

But now isn't the time to be thinking about such things.

Now is the time to be getting the fuck out of here.

He steps into the corridor, his foot sinking into the bloody puddle. He looks left. The cops will be coming up in the elevator. He needs to find the stairs. He turns right and walks, hoping he isn't actively working to pin himself in. He feels sweaty and nervous and though he's innocent he's certain guilt is written across his face.

Innocent or not, he feels guilty.

At the end of the corridor he finds a white door. He thumbs a paddle and pulls, revealing a stairwell. He steps into it and starts down, gravity making it easy. And the worry pressing upon him.

The stairwell has a damp, dusty smell to it, like the smell of impending rain.

He trudges down, wondering what he's going to find when he reaches the bottom and pushes through the last door, but he doesn't have to wonder long, because soon enough he's pushing through it.

He's at the end of a corridor very much like the one on the sixth floor. At the other end, the hotel lobby. It looks calm. The uniformed police are probably upstairs now, about to discover the bodies he just left behind. He might be able to get out of here with no trouble, get out of here and get to his milk truck and drive away. He can worry about what happens after that once he gets there, because if he doesn't get there, there won't be any after that to worry about.

He walks down the corridor, hoping there are no cops at the front.

Nervousness and fear begin to take him over. He was not made for this sort of thing. There are born soldiers, and their home is the battlefield. There are born spies, and their home is Moscow. He's a born dreamer, and his home is nowhere in this world. He doesn't know how to tolerate this sort of stress, and though he tries very hard to maintain a placid expression he can feel small muscle twitches on his face and throughout his body. He imagines he must look like a man being electrocuted while simultaneously trying to walk.

He steps into the lobby, barely maintaining control, and looks left to the front door. He can see sunshine. A bellhop standing just inside the door, hand on a rolling cart. A doorman outside. But no cops.

He heads toward sunlight telling himself to just act normal despite the fact he feels jerky and stupid and unnatural. Just stay calm and wear a blank expression. Blank faces are forgettable as unmarked paper.

He's halfway there. Then he cuts the distance in half again.

He thinks of something he heard once, about a philosopher who supposedly proved it was actually impossible to reach a destination because to do so you must cut the distance there in half, and in half again, and in half again, infinitely, and since there's no limit to how small the distances can be cut, you arrive nowhere. You end up forever cutting distances in half. He's always before thought it a bit of ridiculousness, but now he wonders if there isn't some truth to it. He certainly feels now that he will never reach the door. He must have been walking for several minutes now, for hours, days. It must have been days. The sun must have set and risen again many times by now. His mouth is incredibly dry. How long has it been since he's had a glass of water? It was only fifty feet from the start, how is he not out yet? How is he not escaped?

How is the door still ten feet away?

Now it's five.

He's nearly upon it when the doorman opens the door and a man in a gray suit and a fedora walks in. He's in his fifties and sweaty but walks with purpose, his glassy eyes on something in the distance, the elevator perhaps. He bumps Eugene's shoulder, sending Eugene spinning around.

The man stops and catches Eugene by the arm. The gun falls from Eugene's waistband. He watches it flip end over end on its way down and swipes for it with a sweaty hand but misses.

The man says, 'Sorry about that, buddy, I—'

The gun hits the floor with a thud and a rattle.

Eugene looks down at it, can't I catch a single fucking break, and then looks up at the face of the man in the fedora.

His grip tightens on Eugene's arm.

'What's with the weapon, son?'

Eugene pulls away from the man in the fedora, pulls hard, gets his arm out of the grip, though it feels bruised and sore, and rushes the front door. He bangs through it, tripping over the doorman. He falls forward, peeling skin off the palms of his hands as he catches himself on asphalt. Doesn't even feel it. Doesn't feel anything. Simply struggles to his feet, glancing over his shoulder to see the man in the fedora pull a revolver of his own from a holster. Sees a police badge clipped to the man's belt. Then he's looking forward again, stumbling along, looking for escape, a way to get away.

That's all he wants in this moment: away.

2

Carl Bachman, in wrinkled gray suit, lies in bed and stares at the ceiling. The ceiling doesn't stare back. He thinks of his wife and smiles and doesn't long for her but simply enjoys the mental images. She was so beautiful. Her face was effervescent. When she scrubbed herself free of makeup at night and her skin was pink and clean she was at her most beautiful. She was the most beautiful creature he'd ever known.

The mattress beneath him is very comfortable.

The telephone in the hallway rings. It's probably for Langer.

Harold Langer is a college student who stays in the next room. He's studying mathematics. Carl's talked to him some but they don't have many overlapping interests so their conversations are short and halting things. Still, seems like a good kid. But he's been seeing a high school girl, a little paper shaker who calls him at least five times a day, and the ringing phone sometimes gets on Carl's nerves. Now, however, isn't one of those times. He likes the sound. Like singing. He listens to it ring and ring.

Until Mrs Hoffman picks it up, choking off the sound. He can hear her voice but cannot make out what she's saying. Then she stops saying anything. A moment later, a knocking sound. It's very loud in his ears. She must really be pounding on Langer's door. The pounding goes on and on, nothing like song. He wants to yell, answer the door, Langer, but he also wants not to yell it, and he guesses he wants that more because he says nothing. The ceiling is stained yellow from cigarette smoke.

The banging continues.

Then: 'Mr Bachman, are you in there?'

The name sounds familiar.

After a while he sits up. 'Yeah.'

'Telephone.'

'Oh. Okay.'

He gets to his feet and looks around the room. He picks up various items – foil, bindle, pen casing – and shoves them into a brown paper bag. He shoves the brown paper bag into his dresser's top drawer and slides the drawer closed. He walks to the door, unlocks it, and pulls it open. Mrs Hoffman stands on the other side, hands on hips. Looks at him with disapproval.

'What took you so long to answer?'

'I was taking a nap.'

'It's the middle of the day.'

'That's when naps happen. If it's nighttime you're just sleeping.'

He walks past her to the telephone stand.

'Hello?'

Captain Ellis tells him there's been a report of a murder. A man under LAPD protection might have been killed. No answer in the room, no word from the protecting officer at the scene. Two radio units are already on the way and hotel staff have been told to stay clear. By the way, do you know where Friedman is? We can't get hold of him.

Carl says it's Saturday, he's probably at synagogue, keep trying till you get him. Then he requests the address. Ellis gives him a number on South Grand Avenue and he scribbles it down, hangs up the telephone, tears the paper off the notepad. He walks to the bathroom and splashes water onto his face and looks at himself in the mirror. Some sad-eyed old man with a face like melted wax looks back. He touches the bag under his right eye. It's tender and hurts when he touches it, stings with pain. He wonders if he accidentally did something to it to make it hurt.

He turns away from the glass, steps into his room and grabs his fedora from the bed, trudges downstairs, walks to his car.

He drives beneath an overcast sky, wondering if there isn't going to be rain today.

Less than fifteen minutes later he's stepping from his vehicle, walking past two radio cars toward the Shenefield Hotel, a gray block building on the corner of 5th and Grand, in the heart of the city.

A doorman sees him coming and pulls open the glass door. He gives the guy a nod and makes his way into the lobby. A couch, two chairs, a table with today's paper on it and an ashtray. At the back of the room, a desk with a bell on it, and a desk clerk flipping through a magazine.

As he walks he bumps into someone, a young man in a white shirt and a black bowtie with tortoiseshell glasses on his face, and sends the poor fellow spinning. He reaches out and grabs the guy by the arm to help steady him.

'Sorry about that, buddy, I—'

But the sound of something heavy thudding to the floor cuts him off. He looks down at the carpet and there sees a revolver, a black revolver with a long barrel and a wooden grip. He looks from the revolver to the man standing beside him, the man whose arm is gripped in his fist.

Fear is written across the man's pale face and guilt flickers in his eyes.

'What's with the weapon, son?'

The man yanks away from Carl and runs for the door,

pushes through it. He trips over the doorman, hits the ground hard, scrambles back to his feet without slowing down, looks over his shoulder as he runs.

Carl pulls his service revolver, feeling detached from this moment but having some sense that he needs to act, and runs after the guy. He gives chase, shouting stop, goddamn it, and only caring because then he could stop running himself. But the man in the bowtie doesn't stop. He makes a sharp right turn, pivoting off his left foot, and cuts down an alleyway instead, vanishing behind the brick corner of a building.

About halfway to the alleyway Carl gives up running. He holds his hand to his side and walks quickly, as quickly as he can, breathing hard, feeling dizzy, hating himself. By the time he arrives at the alleyway it's empty. Of course it is. Murderer isn't simply going wait for him, oh, I see you're out of breath, I'll give you to the count of thirty before I continue.

Trash bins line the alley, giving off the stink of old garbage. At the other end of the alley, an empty street. Then a car rolls by.

'Fuck,' he says, and leans for a moment on the brick wall to his left.

Once he has his breath again he walks back toward the hotel. He's no longer a young man in uniform and is apparently incapable of doing the things he once did. It doesn't matter. This was not a hoodlum, thug, or gunsel. This was a guy with a job, an address, and square friends who don't know better than to talk to cops. That was clear by looking at him. Carl will find him, he'll track him down to his front door and knock.

That's what he tells himself, anyway.

He hopes he isn't lying.

3

Eugene's shoes pound the sidewalk. He feels scared and upset and absolutely drained. He doesn't know what to do. He had to abandon his milk truck at the scene, and a single phone call to the H.H. White Creamery Company will tell the police that truck number twenty-seven is his. A police detective saw him in his milkman's uniform with the murder weapon, which even now lies in the hotel lobby, unless it's already been collected as evidence. And he ran rather than cooperating with the police. Not that he had a choice. They wouldn't have believed his story. The obvious answer is often the correct answer, it usually is, and it looked like he killed those men upstairs, so he must have. No amount of protest on his part would have changed their minds. And every action he took only worked to smear more red across his hands. What he did seemed right in the moment but he finds it hard to imagine doing anything that would have incriminated him further. But there was no right thing to do in that situation. There was one wrong choice or another wrong choice. That there's always a right thing to do is a lie you tell to children.

But now what?

The grand-jury investigation is an irrelevancy. For him it is. He's now wanted for murder, real murder, actual physical murder, his thumb on the hammer spur, his finger on the trigger, and one of the victims was a cop. If the police don't have his name yet they soon will. His only hope is that it takes them a couple hours to put it all together and get to his place. He wants to gather some clothes as well as a hundred dollars in cash he has folded into a sock.

He hops onto a streetcar at 6th Street and rides it west to Vermont.

In ten minutes he's back on foot, and back on foot he lights a cigarette and makes his way to New Hampshire. He keeps his eyes on the street, looking for radio cars, wanting to make sure he sees any cops before they have a chance to see him.

He needs to get out of these clothes; they're too conspicuous.

He walks up the stairs to his apartment, unlocks the front door. The place is empty but he doesn't know how long he has so he must hurry.

His revolver, which he's certain he left lying on the dining table, is absent, as he knew it would be. Evelyn. Goddamn it. He knew she was responsible, at least in part, but even so there was a part of him that hoped he'd walk in here and find the revolver where he left it. That would at least have cast some doubt on her involvement.

Stop bellyaching, Eugene. There's no time for it.

He walks to the bedroom and pulls a cardboard suitcase out from under his bed, the same suitcase he used when moving here from the East Coast. He also finds a locket lying on the floor, a small gold locket with an intricate design etched into it.

With the suitcase in one hand and the locket in the other he gets to his feet. He tosses the suitcase onto the bed, examines the locket. A thin gold chain is strung through it, the chain's clasp broken. He thumbs a button on the side of the locket and it opens. Inside, a picture of a teenage girl sitting beside her father. She's in a dress, he's in a suit and tie. He recognizes her despite the fact the picture is probably more than ten years old. He also recognizes the man, though he's never seen him in person. He's seen his scowling image on the front page of several newspapers over the years. A person of interest. Suspected of bribing public officials. Suspected of murder. Connections to the underworld in several major American cities. Then, months later, a different story on page three. No charges filed. Acquitted. Bad information. Lost evidence. Sloppy police work.

James Manning.

The Man.

Eugene would be willing to bet green money on Evelyn's last name. When she told him she worked for her father she was telling the truth. She simply neglected to mention who her father was. Who he is. And *what* he is.

He tosses the locket into the suitcase, then piles clothes on top of it, pants and shirts and underwear. He opens his sock drawer, pulls out several pairs, throws them into the suitcase. At the back of the drawer he finds a lone sock folded over itself. He unfolds it and removes ten ten-dollar bills, all the money he has in the world. He sets the money on top of his dresser. He closes the cardboard suitcase, tries to latch it and finds the latch broken. He wraps a belt around it to keep it closed. He changes into a different set of clothes, a pair of khaki pants and a checkered shirt and a cardigan; fresh socks and a pair of casual two-tone shoes. He grabs the money from the dresser and shoves it into his pocket. He lifts the suitcase.

He has a motorcycle parked in the garage, a Harley–Davidson with a two-cylinder panhead engine. He hasn't touched it in almost a year. Rode it often last summer, then garaged it and forgot about it. The milk truck is always right out front.

He hopes he can get the bike to start. He's about to find out.

Without knowing where he might go, without knowing what he might do, having no idea what might be in store for him at all, he heads out the front door.

TWENTY-THREE

1

Seymour Markley sits at his desk in his home office, the door shut and locked. He doesn't want Margaret to walk in on him, as she sometimes does, offering a snack or something to drink. He doesn't want her to see what he's looking at, dozens of potential blackmail photographs. He's amazed by how many there are. But it makes sense. None of the men in these pictures would dare speak up about being blackmailed. If they did they'd have to reveal *why* they were blackmailed, and if they were willing to do that they couldn't have been blackmailed in the first place. The numbers added up because no one would reveal himself as a whoremonger.

Seymour faces the same shameful problem. He'd like to use these pictures to some political advantage, but doesn't want anyone to know he too was photographed.

Of course that evidence is bubbled black film in a trash bin now, and while some of these men might suspect something, he learned many years ago that suspicion isn't evidence. It isn't even close.

So how does he best use these pictures to his advantage? He doesn't want to blackmail anyone. He wants these men on his side. He wants these men in his corner come a political fight.

Perhaps the best move is to simply hand the pictures over to their subjects and suggest they remember the favor. But some of them might not even know the pictures exist. In fact, it's certain. The pictures Vivian and her cuckold husband had of him were from over a year ago. They held onto them until they were useful. They were patient. Some of these men with whom he has old rivalries might even assume he hired someone to get the pictures himself, and that would only serve to make them mistrust him further. It could convince them that he should be buried, and there are those among them who *could* bury him.

So he'll be careful. He'll only give the pictures to those already on his side. He'll put them in envelopes and hand them over and say, thought you might want these back. If the fellow responsible for them has been bothering you, that's finished now. If not, I saved you some serious trouble. The rest of the pictures, he'll hold on to.

In most cases he'll ask for nothing in return, not until he needs help.

But there are a few people he needs favors from

immediately. He believes he'll start with Woodrow Selby at Monocle Pictures. He'll hand the photographs to Selby and mention that he's seen this background actor Leland Jones in several of his Western pictures. He'll say he doesn't like to recognize background actors, it pulls him right out of the action. He'll ask Selby if he doesn't find it distracting as well.

The telephone on his desk rings. He jumps, feeling guilty, grabs a handful of photographs and throws them into the box, then realizes how absurd that is and lets the others remain where they lie, spread out across his desk.

He picks up the telephone.

'Hello.'

'Seymour. It's Bill.'

There are only a few reasons Bill Parker would be calling Seymour on a Saturday evening, none of them good. He and the chief of police have a fine professional relationship, but that's the only relationship they have. They've not spoken a dozen words to one another outside the context of work.

Seymour clears his throat. 'I'm almost afraid to ask.'

'It's your witness.'

'Theodore Stuart?'

'That's right.'

'What about him?'

'He's dead.'

Seymour finds it difficult at first to process the sentence, a mere two words though it is. He remains silent for a long time. He stares down at the photographs on his desk. He blinks.

Finally he says, 'I thought he was under police protection.'

'His police protection is dead too.'

'James Manning?'

'Too early to say. We have homicide detectives on the scene and boys from the crime lab are on their way. We'll see what we get.'

'I want to talk with the detectives on the case.'

'When?'

'Tonight.'

2

Seymour drives through darkness, his stomach empty and sour. Margaret tried to get him to eat some dinner, but he had no appetite. She wrapped his plate in tinfoil and put it in the fridge. It'll be here when you get home. She kissed the corner of his mouth, looked into his eyes. You work too hard.

Be back in a while.

He turned, headed out the front door.

Theodore Stuart's dead, murdered, and it almost has to have been James Manning behind it. People don't murder people under police protection without good reason, there's too much risk, and Seymour can think of only one man with a strong enough motive to take said risk.

The fact that he could get to Stuart means, too, that Bill Parker's department has been compromised. That's the problem with money. It can make even good cops spill. You get in a little over your head on house payments, or the vigorish on your gambling debt gets out of control, and along comes some grinning mustache with a fat wad of cash, and he doesn't want anything from you but a few words, what's the harm, really?

He pulls his car into the parking structure and brings it to a stop.

3

He looks at the three men sitting across the desk from him, Captain Ellis crisply suited while to his left a couple homicide detectives – Bachman, clothes nearly as wrinkled as his face; and Friedman, the youngest man in the room by at least a decade – slouch red-eyed after a long day on the job.

Seymour exhales in a sigh.

'So,' he says, 'what do we have on Manning?'

The silence stretches out.

Finally Detective Bachman sits up and clears his throat. He scratches his left eyebrow and looks uncomfortable.

'Nothing,' he says.

'Nothing?'

'Well, uh . . .'

'As of this moment,' Captain Ellis says, 'it doesn't look like James Manning was responsible for the murder.'

'You're kidding me.'

'I'm afraid not.'

'What do you have?'

'Our primary suspect is a milkman named Eugene Dahl,' Bachman says. 'He was at the crime scene with the murder weapon on his person. He escaped capture, but we've just searched his apartment and found shoes with blood on them and a box of shells. Guys from the crime lab are matching footprints at the scene to the shoes we found in his apartment. The evidence is solid.'

Bachman shifts in his chair, looking physically pained. Indigestion perhaps, or kidney stones.

'A milkman?'

'He used to write comic books,' Friedman says.

'Is it possible he was hired by Manning?'

'It's possible, but we don't have any evidence to suggest it.'

'Look into it.'

Captain Ellis says, 'We have every intention of finding a connection if there is one. We're looking into everything.'

'I don't think he was working for Manning,' Bachman says. 'If he did this, and it looks like he did, he did it on his own.'

'What makes you say that?'

'He's not a professional. He's a failed writer working as

a milkman. Been a milkman since he moved out to Los Angeles in forty-nine. No connection to organized crime, not even a tenuous one so far as we can tell, though we'll continue to look into it. But the bottom line is, he's simply not the kind of guy who'd get called in for a job like this.'

'What's his motive?'

'He was afraid Stuart would spill his name during his grand-jury testimony. And we think he had reason to be.'

'How's that?'

'We found what might be a blackmail note in his apartment.'

'Who was blackmailing whom?'

'Looks like Theodore Stuart was trying to get money out of the milkman.'

'That doesn't make sense.'

'It does if Stuart was scared,' Friedman says. 'Good way to collect some cash so that once this grand-jury thing was finished he could disappear.'

'So he tries to blackmail the milkman and the milkman kills him.'

'That's the way it looks,' Bachman says.

Seymour shakes his head. He doesn't like it. It makes as much sense as any scenario he's been able to imagine, more sense than several, but it doesn't feel right. Or he's telling himself it doesn't feel right simply because he needs there to be a connection to James Manning. If his key witness is dead, then the investigation might be dead with him, might be dead before they've even presented the indictment to the grand jury, and he was taking an enormous political risk on this one. He'll have to think it over.

'How did this milkman find out where Stuart was being held?'

'It was on the blackmail note.'

'None of the officers watching Stuart saw what he was up to, saw that he was busy blackmailing this milkman?'

'They were outside his room,' Captain Ellis says. 'They were there more to make sure no one got to him than to monitor what he was doing while hidden away. And in truth, it's possible one or more officers worked with him for the promise of money.'

Seymour nods unhappily, then leans back in his chair to think.

Captain Ellis must see the worry on his face because he says, 'We're gonna get this milkman. We want him in an interrogation room by Monday. Once we've got him nailed down, we'll get the answers we need.'

'You think you can have him in custody by then?'

'He's square,' Bachman says. 'He'll probably turn himself in.'

Seymour nods. He likes the sound of that.

'Okay,' he says, and gets to his feet.

TWENTY-FOUR

1

Next morning, the thirteenth of April, Carl finds himself in a chair in the corner of his room at the boarding house in nothing but tattered gray underpants. His soft white belly bulges out over the elastic waistband as he slouches before a small table on which rest the accouterments of what is quickly becoming the point around which his life orbits: a glass of water, a small paper bindle, a shining spoon he took from the kitchen downstairs, a syringe, a pocket knife, cigarettes, a lighter. His forehead is covered in sweat, his legs are cramping. His stomach and liver hurt. His eyes itch.

He stares at the syringe. He told himself he'd never do this. He told himself he'd never shoot up. But he can no longer afford not to. Smoking wastes too much. It burns away, unused and useless.

Candice said her husband's funeral was yesterday. She

told him on Friday, tomorrow's the funeral, and it occurs to him now that her saying that might have been her shy way of asking him to attend, might have been her way of asking him to sit beside her during a difficult moment. He should call her and see if she's okay.

She needs a friend.

But his legs are cramping badly. He won't be able to focus on the conversation if he calls her now. He'll do this, then call her. That's the correct order of things.

He picks up the syringe and brings it to the glass of water and pulls back the plunger, drawing in a few cubic centimeters of liquid. He sets it on the table. He knifes powder from the bindle into the spoon, then carefully squirts the water from the syringe onto it. His stomach is cramped, a painful knot. He's sick. He picks up his lighter and makes a flame. His hand shakes involuntarily. He moves the flame back and forth beneath the convex surface of the spoon's underside until the brown powder has dissolved. The flame blackens the spoon. He sets down the lighter. With the tip of the syringe he mixes the liquid, then draws it into the glass tube by pulling back the plunger. He sets it down on the table.

He reaches down to his pants to remove his belt, but finds he has no belt, because he's not wearing pants. The pants he last wore lie in a pile on the floor and within the belt loops is a narrow strip of leather. He needs that strip of leather. He gets to his feet, grabs the belt, walks back to the chair. He puts the belt around his arm, pulling it taut, grips it in his aching teeth. He wonders if his gums are bleeding. He makes a fist and picks up the syringe.

He told himself he'd never do this, told himself he'd only smoke it, like they do in China. He wasn't going to use the needle, had seen too many burned-out hipsters and jazz musicians to fall into that trap, and had been told that if he smoked it like opium he wouldn't develop a dependency.

He believes he was lied to.

He shakes his head. He isn't addicted. He isn't. He's just being smart. It's wasteful to smoke it. This means nothing. It doesn't mean nothing, it means he's smart. It means he doesn't want to waste the stuff. It isn't free, you know.

He brings the needle to his arm, holds it mere centimeters above the flesh. A few drops splash onto the pale skin on the inside of his elbow. He pierces the skin, feels a sting of pain. He finds a vein on the first attempt. He believes so, anyway. He draws back the plunger, bringing blood into the needle, watching a cloud of it dissipate into the heroin. He thumbs down the plunger, opens his hand, lets go the belt from his teeth.

An indescribable feeling swims through his entire body, liquid emotion washing over him like a great wave, and his head drops down – just for a moment, or five minutes, or an hour; it doesn't matter – and the world goes gray.

Then he's back, back but better, back but perfect.

He looks down at the syringe hanging from his arm,

stares at it for a long time. Finally, after some indeterminate period, he pulls it away, sets it on the table.

Blood leaks from the hole in his arm. It's very red; it's beautiful. No one ever thinks about what a beautiful color blood is.

He should call Candice. He will. Of course he will. But first he's just going to sit here. It's nice to just sit somewhere. It feels good to just sit somewhere.

So that's what he's going to do.

2

He stands in the hallway for a long time, unmoving, and stares down at the telephone. It sits on a stand. A notepad lies beside it, ghost-writing visible from whatever was scrawled across the top sheet before it was torn away. Rain pounds down outside. He doesn't remember it starting, but it's going full-force now.

He came out here for a reason but can't remember what that reason might have been. Then he sees the rectangle of paper in his right hand, pinched between the pad of his thumb and the side of his index finger. He looks at it. A telephone number. He picks up the telephone and dials.

After some time, an answer: 'Hello?'

'Candice.'

'Who is this?'

'Carl.'

'You sound funny.'

'I think it's allergies,' he says. 'But listen: I was calling to see how you were doing. I remembered you saying that . . . well, I guess yesterday was hard on you.'

'Oh. The funeral.'

'You holding up?'

'I want my son back.'

'What kind of deal did you make with Markley?'

'It's not settled, the lawyers have to work it out, but it looks like after Sandy testifies he can come home on weekends at least. He'll probably have to stay in reform school a while, though.'

'That might be good for him.'

'He doesn't handle that type of discipline well.'

'The walls that keep him in also keep trouble out. Somebody who was supposed to testify before the grand jury got murdered yesterday.'

'What?'

There's panic in that word, that *what*, and the fear in her voice makes him wish he hadn't said anything. He thought it would be comforting, your son's being protected by those walls, so don't you worry, but as soon as it was out of his mouth, he knew he'd said something he shouldn't have. By then, however, it was too late: you can't unsay a thing.

'It doesn't mean your boy's in any danger.'

'What does it mean?'

'It means—' He scratches his cheek. 'I don't know. He's

in a secure location. He's safe. That's what I was trying to say.'

'He's coming into the city tomorrow to go over his testimony with Mr Markley.'

'The Sheriff's Department will be driving him, his name hasn't been released to the public, nobody knows where he's being held. He'll be fine. I shouldn't have said anything. I'm sorry I scared you.'

'I would have read it in the paper anyway. Do you know who killed him?'

'Who killed who?'

'The man who was killed.'

'Oh. We think we got a pretty good idea. We have police out looking for him.'

'Good.'

'Do you want to get dinner tonight?'

A long silence on the other end of the line, a palpable hesitation, and then finally: 'Okay.'

'Yeah?'

'But you should know I can't get into a relationship right now. I just lost Neil. I won't pretend he was the love of my life, but I cared for him, and I feel something like hatred when I think of my son, even though I love him more than I ever loved anyone. I hate him for what he did. I can't get involved with someone else. It would be too complicated. Everything is confused right now. *I'm* confused right now.'

'It's just company.'

'So you understand?'

'I have to work today, but I'll pick you up at eight.'

'Okay.'

'Okay. See you then.'

He drops the phone into its cradle.

TWENTY-FIVE

1

Eugene steps out the front door of his motel room and into the wet, gray morning. The rain that was threatening to come down all day yesterday is finally splashing against the asphalt and concrete which line the floor of the city. Something about the smell of rain always makes him feel nostalgic for an earlier, more innocent time in his life. Never more so than now, with everything broken. Even the small life he's been living for the last three years – small, yes, but pleasant enough – even that is gone, vanished like something draped beneath a magician's cape.

Goodbye, white rabbit.

Last night after checking into this crummy motel he lay in bed, stared at the ceiling, wondered if his life might be recovered. When he finally fell asleep he dreamed again that he was high up in an office building. He dreamed that he was stuck in that building alone. He called out but no one answered. He tried to find an elevator but there was no elevator. Where it should have been was only an empty shaft. When he looked down into it, vertigo sweeping over him, he could not see the bottom. It went down and down into darkness. He took the stairs. He walked for a very long time but never reached the bottom. In the dream he walked for months, for years, but it was never over. He just went down forever. Until he woke up, anyway.

He should have brought his typewriter. He's owned it since he moved to New York eighteen years ago. Every story he published he banged out on that machine, and now it's gone. Somehow, even with everything that's happened in the last few days, it feels like a great loss. Some big part of him sunk to the bottom of a murky sea.

He flips up his collar. He lights a cigarette. He walks along the sidewalk, down Whitley Avenue to Hollywood Boulevard, looking for a newsstand. Two blocks on, the rain-soaked paper holding his cigarette together breaks apart. He spits it into the gutter and it's immediately swept away on a filthy river.

He finds a newsstand on Cahuenga, red bricks resting on top of the stacks of newspapers to keep the wind from carrying the profits away, an awning overhead doing a reasonable job of protecting them from the rain. He grabs a local paper, pays, heads back to the motel with the news tucked under his arm. He's almost afraid to look at it. He is afraid to look at it. Afraid he'll see his picture on the front page. Wanted on suspicion of murder. That might make it difficult for him to get around the city without being recognized, and he thinks he's going to have to get around the city if—

First just read the goddamn paper and see how bad it is, Eugene.

He walks to his motel room, number 13, marked by a stone by the door with the number painted on it. He keys his way into the place and steps into a pile of squalor he immediately wants to scrape from the bottom of his shoe. A sagging bed in the middle of the room with a small night table on either side of it. In the corner, an easy chair with torn upholstery. A card table with gashes cut across its gray surface. Two wooden chairs on either side of the table, and a lamp with a torn paper shade sitting on top of it. Everything seems old and dirty and used, even the lamp's dim light.

He walks to the bed and sits down. He arms water from his face, wipes it from his eyes with the heels of his hands. He unfolds the paper and looks at the front page:

KEY WITNESS IN COMIC CRUSADE MURDERED!

LOS ANGELES – Theodore Stuart, a New Jersey accountant with alleged ties to organized crime on the East Coast, was found dead in his room at the Shenefield Hotel early yesterday evening after police received a tip from an anonymous caller that he had been murdered. Mr Stuart was under police protection at the time of his murder, pending his testimony before a grand jury. The officer charged with protecting him, whose name has not yet been released, was also killed.

District Attorney Seymour Markley believed that Mr Stuart's testimony would prove there were ties between James Manning, long suspected of being a major figure in organized crime, and a comic book called *Down City*, which is believed to have inspired a recent Bunker Hill murder. The purpose of the grand-jury investigation was to determine whether there might be enough evidence to charge James Manning and others involved in the creation of the comic book with negligent homicide. It would be the first such case in American history.

We reached Markley at his home yesterday evening, and he said that despite this set-back, the investigation would continue.

'But our focus right now should be on the tragic loss of two lives. A man with courage and a willingness to testify against dangerous criminals was murdered, and along with him, one of our city's finest officers.'

Despite Theodore Stuart's ties to organized crime, and the nature of his stay at the Shenefield Hotel, police do not currently believe James Manning was responsible for his murder. Markley said that the LAPD's lead investigator on the case, Detective Carl Bachman, had reason to believe a local man, who may have been involved in the creation of the comic book himself, was responsible. 'We believe he was worried about being implicated during Mr Stuart's grand-jury testimony.' He said, however, that police are currently unwilling to release the suspect's name. For the time being, they are 'gathering evidence and chasing down every possible lead'.

The rain outside is now pouring down. He can hear it drumming on the roof like ten thousand nervous fingers. He walks to the window and pulls back the curtains. Sheets of rain fall from the sky. Within twenty minutes the streets will be flooded. Tomorrow great chunks of asphalt will have been washed away, leaving enormous potholes.

He turns away from the window, looks around the room.

Decides to venture once more into the rain.

2

Eugene walks to his motorcycle, kick-starts the engine. It rumbles grumpily. He straddles the large leather seat, throttles some gas into the engine, revving it up. A moment later he pulls out into the street, tires sliding against the rain-wet asphalt, rear end fishtailing momentarily before regaining traction and control.

He didn't bring a jacket. In his rush to get out of the apartment he neglected to consider that he might need one. He merely stuffed his suitcase with what his hands grabbed. He wears only a thin cotton sweater to protect him from the elements, and it merely serves to soak up the rain.

By the time he gets where he's going he's wet to the bone. A quick but violent shiver works its way through his body. He steps from the bike and toes down the kickstand. He takes his glasses from his face and shakes them off, then sets them once more on the bridge of his nose. He looks through them to a smudged and water-spotted world beyond. A rectangular block of apartments stands across the street. The building is pink stucco guarded by a pair of palm trees like wind-tattered umbrellas which bend toward the southwest. He's only been here once before.

He hopes Fingers is home. His shift is midnight to eight, but if he's warming a barstool somewhere Eugene could be waiting for hours.

He walks to the front door and gives it a knock.

For a long time there's no answer, then there is. The door creaks open and his friend looks out at him bleary-eyed, the skin beneath his eyes swollen and pink.

'Eugene,' he says. 'What happened to you today, man?'

'I need your help. Can I come in?'

Fingers stares at him a moment, silent, then nods and steps aside.

Eugene steps into the tiled entrance. His clothes are soaked through, couldn't get any wetter if he were dunked in a tub of water. He's very cold. The apartment is warm. He can feel the gas heater and smell the pleasant scent of heated ducts and the dust and spiders within them. Eugene's glasses fog up in the warmth. He wipes them off on his undershirt.

Fingers shuts the door.

'Don't move.'

Then he's gone, disappeared into the hallway.

The living room has brown carpet and brown furniture and the walls are tacky and yellow with wallpaper paste, though the wallpaper itself has been steamed away. A few pictures hang on the walls, mostly of musicians playing their instruments.

When Fingers returns he has a towel in his hand. He tosses it to Eugene, who catches it and wipes himself down with it.

'Thanks.'

'What's going on, man? You okay? You haven't missed more than a handful of days in almost three years, and never without calling. Boss is mad, says the police were asking about you yesterday.'

Eugene rubs his hair dry with the towel and combs his fingers through it. He looks toward his friend. His friend looks back. Finally he says, 'I need a gun.'

'What?'

'A gun. I'm sorry to ask, but I need one.'

Fingers sighs and scrapes at the corners of his mouth with index finger and thumbnail, rolls up what he finds there between his fingers, flicks it away.

'I got some guns,' he says, 'but they're bought and paid for and not by the kind of people I want to be fucking with. What kind of trouble you in, Gene?'

'The serious kind.'

'You really need a gun?'

Eugene nods.

'Okay.'

He once more disappears into the hallway. When he returns this time he's carrying a green canvas duffel bag. He sets it on the floor in front of Eugene.

'Take your pick.'

'Are these guys gonna go ape on you?'

'They'll box my ears a little, but I'll live.'

'You don't have anything else? I don't wanna put you out.'

'I got a Baby Browning used to belong to a girlfriend of mine. But you can't walk into a situation with a lady's gun as your primary.'

'It's fine. I don't want you in a spot.'

'You sure?'

'Yeah.'

Fingers gets him the small gun from a kitchen drawer and a box of rounds as well.

'Thank you.'

Fingers nods. 'You frail? I got some money stashed away.'

'I have a little money.'

'Is there anything else I can do?'

'I don't think so. I'm on my own on this one.'

'Okay,' Fingers says. 'Good luck.'

TWENTY-SIX

1

Sandy sits at the desk in his room. He looks out at the rain. There are great puddles in the recreation yard, reflecting clouds and looking like small pools of sky, though the rain continually breaks apart the images, and the storm is slanting down diagonally, and the light seems somehow ill.

He doesn't like it here.

The other boys with whom he shares this room are playing a card game, he can hear them behind him talking and laughing, but he wasn't invited to participate. He's still not made any friends. He thought he might make friends with his roommates at first, they talked to him and tried to include him in things, but within the first couple days they decided they didn't like him. They flicked his ears. They wiped boogers on his shirt just to see how he'd react. Now he avoids them. There's something about the way he speaks, or his posture, or something, that people simply don't want to be around. During recess, which they call recreation period here, he plays alone. If there's a free basketball court he shoots baskets, despite the fact that he's not very good. If there isn't a free court, and usually there isn't, he bounces the ball against a brick wall and catches it, until someone takes it away from him, as someone inevitably does. He doesn't know why people pick on him. He hasn't done anything to anybody. He wouldn't care that they don't like him if they would just leave him alone. If everybody would leave him alone he'd be fine.

So far it hasn't been that bad, but even so he feels something vicious inside him, something he's afraid of, some terrible black liquid filling him up again. He poured some of that violence out when he shot his stepfather but a week later he's once more near to overflowing.

He gets to his feet and walks to the door and steps through it. He looks to his right. The hall monitor sits in his chair. He seems bored.

'Permission to use the bathroom.'

'Go ahead.'

He turns left and walks to the end of the hallway.

Once in the bathroom he stands in front of a urinal and unbuttons his fly and pulls out his penis. He's glad no one else is here. When other boys are in here they make fun of the way he stands. Why you stand with your legs apart? You squirting from a little pussy and don't want it to dribble down your leg? Why don't you sit down to pee like all the other girls? Have you started your period yet?

He has to wait a long time. He didn't really have to go. He just wanted to leave his room. He was tired of sitting at the desk, tired of staring out the window, tired of listening to his roommates play behind him. He wanted to be alone, even if only for a couple minutes. Finally he begins to urinate. It's just a trickle.

He stares down at his penis and wonders if it will always be so small. He's seen some of the other boys in the shower. It makes him embarrassed. He hates to be naked in front of them. Some of them are beginning to look like men, but his body looks the same as it did last year, and the year before that.

Skinny and hairless and pale.

Behind him, out in the hallway, the sound of a door creaking open and swinging shut. Two voices: request, response. Footsteps echo in the hallway, growing louder.

He finishes with a final spurt, shivers, shakes off, tucks his penis away. He should have gone into a toilet stall. He could have been alone for a little while. Now someone else is coming and will see him and he'll have to leave. He can't just stand around doing nothing while someone else is in here peeing. That would be weird. People already don't like him, already think he's strange.

He doesn't want anyone to think he's a pansy.

He walks to the sink and turns on the water. He washes his hands. In the mirror he sees another boy walk into the bathroom, and recognizes him. A couple days ago he came up to Sandy and took the basketball he was playing with and threw it across the recreation yard. Sandy wanted to punch him in his stupid face, but the boy's much bigger than he is, and already has a mustache.

His name is Raymond.

They make eye contact in the mirror.

'What are you looking at, germ?'

Sandy drops his gaze to his hands, rinsing the soap away. 'Nothing.'

He turns off the water. He grabs a few paper towels and dries his hands and throws the towels into the bin. He turns around.

Raymond stands inside the bathroom door, leaning against the tile wall, arms crossed. He stares at Sandy.

Sandy tries not to look back, tries to pretend he doesn't notice him at all, and walks toward the bathroom door. I don't see you, please don't see me, please don't see me, please don't see me.

Raymond puts out his arm, blocking Sandy's path.

'What's wrong with you?'

'What?'

'You retarded or something? You a retard?'

Sandy blinks, feeling something terrible inside. 'No.'

'I think you are.'

'Just leave me alone.'

'Just leave me alone.'

'Please.'

'Please.'

Sandy tries to push past Raymond's arm, to get out of the bathroom, but Raymond pushes back hard. He sends Sandy backwards. His legs can't keep up with the force of the shove, and after a couple scrambling steps he loses his footing and falls onto the tile floor. He bites his tongue as his backside hits, bites the left side of his tongue between molars, and tastes blood.

Tears of pain sting his eyes.

'Such a retard you can't even walk.'

'I didn't do anything to you.'

'I didn't do anything to you. Drop dead, germ.'

He kicks Sandy in the thigh, sending an immense pain through his leg. Sandy rolls onto his side and clutches himself. From the corner of his eye he sees Raymond pulling back to kick again. He scrambles out of the way quickly. Raymond's leg continues past the spot he expected Sandy to be, and Sandy, with tears still stinging his eyes and with fury in his heart, moves in and takes the other leg out from under him, rushing forward and knocking it away. Raymond falls sideways, tries to catch himself on the wall, and instead hits his head on it before continuing to the floor.

Sandy leans over him and punches him in the nose. It sends a sharp pain up his arm from his hand, from the backs of his fingers. It hurts terribly, but the pain feels good too. He punches again. Raymond holds out his hands to block the blows, but Sandy shoves them aside with the swipe of an arm and swings again. He can see blood on Raymond's face now, and he's glad of it. He doesn't feel guilt or remorse or anything like empathy. He feels mad glee. His fist is simply screaming with pain, and he's glad of that too. The pain in his hands is pain inflicted as well.

'I told you to leave me alone,' he says, and swings again, and again, and again, until the hall monitor comes rushing in and pulls him off the other boy, and even then he continues swinging at the empty air in front of him.

2

He sits in a chair just outside an office, Raymond beside him with wads of blood-slicked tissue shoved into nostrils and a bruise swelling around his left eye.

His hands are clasped in his lap, the right one throbbing with pain. He likes the sensation. It reminds him that he's done something. He pulls his hands apart and looks at his knuckles, his middle finger swollen and blue, so swollen he can barely bend it. He likes that too.

It felt good to do what he did to Raymond. It felt good to give something back.

He's done being picked on. Done being a receptacle for other people's violence.

He thinks of how he felt the night he killed his stepfather, the night he put two bullets into his stepfather's head, how he wanted to take it back. He no longer wants to take it back. He's glad his stepfather's dead. He still wishes he could have kept what he did from his mother. It still hurts him to see that anger, and that small hatred, in her eyes. But he's glad his stepfather's dead. Even on that night he only wanted to take it back because he was afraid of getting caught. Even then he didn't regret the loss of life.

He hated the man. He hated him and is glad he's dead. From now on he'll only pour violence out.

When he goes into the principal's office he'll say he's sorry. He'll say it won't happen again. He'll say those things, but he'll be lying.

There was a time when he was confused, but things in the last week have helped him to understand the world in a way he didn't before. He feels like he's been given a glimpse at the machinery of the world, all the gears and pulleys and levers and belts.

There was a time when he saw everything as a threat, as potential pain, and tried to avoid it at all cost. He would ditch school so he wouldn't have to face a teacher who hated him, or a classmate who had been picking on him. He hid from his stepfather, cowering in fear.

Even when he came here he was thinking only about how to avoid being noticed, how to avoid being picked on. He was thinking only of how to become and remain invisible. But that doesn't work, he sees that now.

If you try to disappear the world sees a hole where you should be and pours its rage into you, pours its violence into you, in order to fill that hole.

He glances to his left, to where Raymond is sitting. The boy is staring down at his lap. His eyes are red from crying.

Sandy's glad.

A door opens and a heavy-set man in a wrinkled suit stands on the other side of it. He has thin, finger-combed white hair, a cowlick at the back of his head. His eyes are turned down at the corners. His nose is red and bulbous. His fly is open, his wrinkled blue shirt hanging from it, and there are ink stains on his slacks.

'Mr Duncan,' the man says.

Sandy gets to his feet and walks toward the office, preparing to lie. For here's a fact: you can say you're sorry and feel nothing at all.

TWENTY-SEVEN

1

Carl drives through the rain while his windshield wipers cut water off the glass, squeaking with each swipe of their thin rubber blades, clearing his view of the empty street before him. He thinks about Eugene Dahl, the milkman, and the evidence against him. He was at the scene with the murder weapon in his possession. They searched his apartment and found bloody shoes that matched shoeprints tracked all over the room in which Stuart and that cop were killed. They also found a box of bullets and a blackmail note. Cases don't get much tighter than that.

During their brief encounter he didn't strike Carl as the kind of man who'd be able to cold-bloodedly sever a man's spinal cord with a knife, but in this situation that's less important than where the evidence points. People, everyday people, can be surprising in their brutality.

Carl would like it better if they knew who tipped off the police, and he'd like to get his hands on the typewriter used to bang out the blackmail note, but those are insignificant pieces in this otherwise finished puzzle, corner pieces that won't change the overall image even if he finds them. Maybe the milkman told someone his plans while drunk and that someone called the police before the murders even happened. Maybe the accountant had an accomplice who typed up the blackmail note and delivered it. Those things don't matter. There's simply no way the milkman didn't do the murders. Not a chance. The pieces fit together too well for them to go any other way.

He parks the car in front of Friedman's house and gives the horn two quick taps. He lights a cigarette and takes a deep drag. He rubs at his eyes with the heels of his hands. They're dry and they sting.

Friedman steps into the car and slams the door closed behind him.

'Ready?'

'Ready.'

Carl puts the car into gear.

2

They step from the vehicle. Carl flicks his cigarette butt into the gutter. He squints up at the gray clouds overhead, bulbous and seemingly solid as mountains. Rain splashes against his face. It feels good on his hot skin. He takes off his fedora and combs his fingers through his oily but brittle gray hair. He turns to the door and finds his partner already pushing his way through to the interior. He follows.

As soon as the door closes behind them the outside world ceases to matter. The bar feels like its own dimly lit pocket universe. The world outside could be crumbling in a great earthquake, streets opening up, fires blazing – but here that would mean nothing. Grab a stool and get yourself a drink, friend.

Several patrons sit at tables nursing their cocktails, several more sit at the bar. Mostly they're old men of retirement age or older in moth-eaten cardigan sweaters and clip-on ties, men with rheumy red eyes and sagging faces like overloaded trash bags, filled with regrets. There are also a couple younger men in rags present, men spending their unemployment insurance on drink. And a woman in her late thirties, a redhead with a flushed face that would be beautiful if not for the damage years of hard drinking and heavy smoking have done to it, sitting at a table with a man in a blue mechanic's jumpsuit and a greased duck-butt hairstyle.

They all make a point of not looking at the two newcomers.

Carl puts his hands in his pockets, pushing open his jacket so the barkeep is sure to see the badge clipped to his belt, and walks to the bar. Friedman walks beside him.

The barkeep, a heavy-set fellow with a white shirt stretched over his substantial belly, nods at them while drying off a glass and setting it on a metal drainer.

'You guys drinking?'

Friedman shakes his head. 'I don't drink.'

'And I'm on the clock.'

'Then what can I do for you?'

'You can tell us about Eugene Dahl.'

'Never heard of him.'

'He's a regular here.'

'News to me.'

Friedman pulls a sketch from his pocket and unfolds it. 'You know him.'

'I might've seen him a time or two.'

'According to his neighbors he's a regular.'

'Could be.'

'Was he here yesterday?'

'I don't remember.'

'What about today? Have you seen him today?'

'No.'

'When's the last time you remember seeing him?'

'Days all blend together. Why you looking for him, anyway?'

'What do you care?' Carl says. 'You don't even know the guy.'

'Curiosity.'

'Look how that turned out for the cat.'

'What cat?'

'He killed someone,' Friedman says.

'I don't believe it.'

'That's the thing about reality,' Carl says. 'It's there even if you shut your eyes.'

'Who'd he kill?'

Carl lights a cigarette.

'Maybe you answer our questions.'

'When's the last time you saw Dahl?'

The barkeep exhales through his nostrils, looks away. After a while he speaks: 'Few days ago. Thursday I think.'

'Notice anything unusual about him?'

'Like horns growing out his head or something?'

'Did he seem wound up?' Carl says.

'Wound up?'

'Nervous.'

'No, he seemed himself. Met a dolly. Been meaning to ask him how it went.'

'This girl anyone you knew?'

The barkeep shakes his head. 'She was from out of town.'

'How far out of town?'

'East Coast. Did Gene really murder someone?'

'We aren't here cause of his tickling habit,' Carl says.

'Does he meet a lot of women?'

'Women like him,' the barkeep says, 'then they hate him.'

'That's how it goes.'

'Do you have any idea where he might be?'

'No.'

'Friends? Relatives?'

'Gene drank alone. Like I said, he sometimes left with a girl on his arm, but he always arrived by himself.'

'And he never talked about anything?'

'Never about anything personal.'

'What did you talk about?'

'Impersonal stuff.'

'And he never mentioned any friends?'

'No.'

Carl pulls out a card and slides it across the bar.

'If you see him, call.'

The barkeep looks at the card but doesn't reach for it. Simply lets it lie there.

'If he's on the run I don't think he'll be stopping in for a drink.'

'Nobody asked for your thoughts.'

'If you see him, pick up the phone.'

Carl butts out his smoke on the bar and turns toward the door.

3

They step from the bar and make their way through the rain to the car. Carl lights another smoke, already beginning to feel the itch. He thinks about the syringe in his pocket, but knows it's too early to use it, knows he needs to wait. Except that an itch needs to be scratched before it'll stop. The more you try to ignore it, the less you can focus on anything else, and he needs to be able to focus on work. He thinks about heading to the toilet, but tells himself no. It's only been a few hours and the day stretches before him long and gray; if he uses now he'll have nothing for later. He only brought enough for one shot.

A knocking sound pulls him from his thoughts. He looks up to see the redheaded woman from the bar standing just outside the car.

Friedman rolls down his window. 'Get in back.'

She steps into the backseat and pulls the door closed behind her.

'Either of you got a cigarette?'

Carl taps a cigarette out of his packet, lights it using the cherry from his own, and hands it back to her.

'Thanks.'

'Is that all?'

'It's a cigarette. You want me to give you head?'

'That's not what I meant.'

'Do you have something to tell us about Eugene?'

'I might. You got five dollars?'

'What's your name?'

'Trish. You got five dollars or not?'

'I might. Trish what?'

The redhead takes a drag from her cigarette. She looks out the window.

'Forget it,' she says.

Friedman pulls a leather wallet from his inside coat pocket, removes a five-dollar bill. He holds it out to her but when she reaches for it pulls it back.

'Now you know I have the five dollars,' he says. 'Let me know you have something worth it.'

'I used to date him.'

'Did you? Candlelight, all that?'

'Fine, I used to fuck him.'

'And?'

'And he took me to this nigger bar down on 57th Street where his friend was playing in a bebop band.'

'And?'

'And give me five dollars or I go back to drink my drink.'

Friedman hands her the five-dollar bill.

TWENTY-EIGHT

1

Evelyn, wearing only her silk nightgown and a cotton robe, her hair mussed, her eyes red from lack of sleep, knocks on the door in front of her. After what feels like a long time Lou pulls it open from the inside. He wears black slacks and an undershirt, his pale feet bare, and small for a man of his height. Greasy strands of pomaded hair hang over his Neanderthal brow.

'Have you seen this?'

She thrusts today's paper forward, holding it out for him to examine.

'I've seen lots like it.'

'They didn't catch him.'

'What?'

'Eugene. The police didn't arrest him.'

Lou takes the paper from her and silently reads the

news story. When he's done reading it, he hands the paper back to her and shrugs.

'So what? They know who he is and they have evidence against him. That's all that matters.'

'What do you mean, that's all that matters? He's still out in the city and knows he's been framed for murder.'

'They'll catch him today or tomorrow. He's a goddamn milkman, Evelyn, in way over his head. It don't matter if he knows he's been framed, he's been framed. The evidence points to him and he ran, as a guilty person would. When they catch him he can say whatever he wants. Denial won't mean nothin.'

'And if they don't bring him in in the next day or two?'

Lou shrugs again. 'I don't care. I got nothing against the guy. Point was to make it look like he was responsible for Teddy Stuart's murder. That's been done. What happens to him now, whether the police catch him or he gets away, that's got nothing to do with me, and it's got nothing to do with you.'

'He knows I framed him.'

'He knows he was framed. He might not know you're behind it. But say he does, you really think he'll come after you?'

'I think he might.'

'He's wanted for murder. He's on the run. He's not coming after anybody.'

'What if he does?'

'What if he . . . I don't know, Evelyn. What do you want to do?'

'Get a room in a different hotel.'

'If everything goes well we'll be out of here day after tomorrow anyway.'

'You're not the one at risk here.'

'You're not either, and if I thought you were you'd know it, because if you're at risk, I'm at risk. Your dad would kill me dead if I let anything happen to you.'

Evelyn is silent. What Lou says has the ring of truth to it.

And yet part of her also knows that Lou wouldn't mind at all if she took two to the back of the head. Until she started working in the business it looked like Lou might take over once Daddy retired. Now it looks like Lou will be working for her, and a man like Lou doesn't want to take orders from a woman. She doubts Lou would want to take orders from anybody. He planned on inheriting the business. He spent years working for Daddy, getting close to him, becoming his most trusted friend, and in she wanders, all of twenty-one, and puts everything he's worked for into question. Evelyn thinks he'd be just fine if her blood went still. He might look sad at the funeral, hug Daddy and tell him it's a great loss for everyone, but in the privacy of his home he'd celebrate her death with a shot of something strong and a thank you, Jesus.

She's sure of it.

And yet: what he says has the ring of truth to it.

If he let anything happen to her Daddy would kill him.

And he's probably right. Her initial fear at hearing Eugene avoided apprehension was the fear of a woman used to dealing with criminals. He isn't thinking about her, he's thinking about how to avoid arrest. Hell, he's probably at the border by now, about to cross into Tijuana. And that's a good thing, isn't it? She felt crummy about what she had to do to him, about helping to frame him. He deserves to get away.

'You're right,' she says.

'The police probably have him in custody already.'

'Maybe.'

But she hopes not. She likes the idea of him living in Mexico, wearing colorful tropical shirts and white canvas shoes, drinking beer by the ocean.

'Are we done? I have to talk to someone about a job.'

'Okay,' Evelyn says.

'Okay.' Lou closes the door.

She turns toward her room, and blinks at what she sees.

Eugene stands in the corridor, soaking wet, his hair hanging down around his face in clumps. In his right hand he holds a Baby Browning, a lady's gun, but lady's gun or not it shoots bullets, not flower petals, and it's aimed at her face.

'Evelyn.'

'Eugene.'

'We need to talk.'

2

Lou unlocks his room safe and pulls from within it a small bundle wrapped in brown paper. It's the shape of a brick though thinner and considerably less weighty. He tucks it into his inside coat pocket, grabs an umbrella, and steps from his hotel room.

Once in the corridor he gives Evelyn's door three quick taps with his knuckles.

'I'm stepping out,' he says, a smile on his lips, 'you might want to make sure your door is chained. Don't want the milkman to get you.'

Then he heads down the corridor, toward the elevator.

He takes the elevator down to the lobby and walks toward the front door. The doorman pulls it open and steps aside. He walks out into the rain, holding his umbrella overhead. As he makes his way across the lawn to the street a gust of wind catches the umbrella and nearly tears it from his hands, but he manages to keep his grip on it, and forces his way through the bad weather.

As he approaches Wilshire he sees a large truck, a barn-red Mack wrecker, parked on the street waiting for him. The right front fender is dented up, and there are great gouges running along the length of the door, and the right half of the split windshield is spider-webbed with cracks, but at least his man is on time. If he'd had to stand in the rain he might have gotten irritable.

He pulls open the passenger's-side door and steps up into the truck, shaking off the umbrella and pulling it in behind him. The truck's seat and floorboard are littered with food wrappers, greasy pieces of cloth, coffee mugs, washers, nuts, and bolts. The upholstery is gouged and torn. The stink is incredible, an old human stink whose fumes hit the back of your sinuses like horseradish.

The stink is coming off the man behind the wheel, a fat man in a greasy T-shirt and a pair of Levis. He has a dirt-tanned round face in need of soap and a razor. It glistens oily in the gray light. His hands rest on his thighs, grime under the fingernails, fingers wrapped in filthy band-aids. The right thumbnail is black, and a hole has been drilled into its center to release the pressure. There's a bead of blood there like a jewel.

The rain on the metal roof is cacophonous.

'Got a cigarette?'

'I didn't bring them out with me,' Lou says.

'Shit.'

The man reaches to the ashtray and picks through the butts till he finds one of decent length. He lights it with a match, inhales deeply, then casually blows a series of smoke rings.

He cracks the window.

'You got the money?'

'I've got it. Are we clear on the job?'

'It ain't exactly complicated.'

'Even so.'

'We're clear.'

'Good. Then you know that part of what you're being paid for is silence. No matter how tough the police get, you keep your mouth shut.'

'How would the police know it was anything but—'

'Irrelevant. The point is, your silence has been purchased and paid for, yeah?'

'Yeah.'

'Good.'

Lou removes the package from his pocket and hands it to the man.

'Tomorrow morning at eight o'clock.'

'Consider it done.'

'I'll consider it done when it's done,' Lou says.

With that, he pushes his way back out into the rain.

After the stink of the truck, it's a relief.

3

Eugene walks out of the rain and into the lobby of the Fairmont Hotel. He looks around. No one looks back. Last time he was here he was anticipating a date, an evening out with the beautiful-ugly woman he'd met the night before. Now he's back to meet the same woman but has no idea what to expect. He has no plan at all except to point his gun and get answers. Will she provide them? He doesn't know. He doesn't think he could shoot her if she refused to talk. If she calls his bluff it's over. He thinks it is. But then you don't have to shoot someone to prove you mean business. He could hit her. Could he hit her? After what she did to him he thinks maybe he could. Punch her square in the nose and watch her bleed. Part of him is repulsed by the idea, one does not hit a lady, but another part knows that civilized behavior doesn't apply to situations such as these. Besides, she's no lady, and you don't sip tea with a serpent.

The pistol feels cold against his stomach.

He walks across the lobby to the elevator and takes the elevator up to the third floor. He isn't sure how he's going to get into her room.

He stands in the corridor feeling strange, disoriented, lost in a dream, as he felt when he was a child with high fever. He could simply walk to the door and knock, see what happens. And if she doesn't answer? He doesn't know. But he doesn't know what else to do either.

He walks to her room, pulls the pistol from his waistband.

He raises his left hand to knock.

But before he can he hears the sound of the chain being pulled away from the door, then the sound of the deadbolt being snapped out of place. He takes several quick steps away from the door, backing around a corner.

Paranoid thoughts run through his mind. He's suddenly convinced the lobby was being watched. When he entered the hotel a call was made. Now a gunman will emerge from Evelyn's room and end his life.

The door swings open.

Evelyn pushes through. She walks to the hotel room next to her own and knocks, a newspaper gripped in her left hand. The knock is answered.

'Have you seen this?'

4

'Evelyn.'

'Eugene.'

'We need to talk.'

'Okay.'

'Let's head into your room.'

'I'm not going in there with you.'

'Then you'll die out here.'

'I could scream.'

'Then you'll die screaming. I'm already wanted for murder, Evelyn. I have no problem becoming what the police already think I am.'

She licks her lips. After a long time she nods.

'Okay.'

TWENTY-NINE

1

Carl stands in the rain. He looks at the door in front of him and waits for the slow bastard on the other side to pull the thing open so he can put a roof between himself and the pissing gray clouds overhead. Friedman stands beside him. Neither man says a word. After a while Carl raises his hand and knocks again. The crease at the top of his fedora catches rain while he stands and waits. The water pools there till the crease can no longer hold it, then it pours down the front of his head in a stream, splashing on the brim of his fedora and down to his scuffed shoes.

Finally someone pulls open the door. That someone is Darryl Castor, known to most people as Fingers. His eyes are red and he looks tired. He blinks to clear his vision and glances from their faces to their badges and back again.

'Detectives.'

'Mind if we come in?'

He steps aside.

Carl enters the small first-floor apartment. Friedman follows.

The curtains are drawn, giving the place a claustrophobic feel, making it seem smaller even than it is, darkness crowding the corners.

Darryl Castor scratches his head and sniffles. 'Excuse the place. I work nights and I was trying to catch a little shut-eye.'

'We'll just be a minute,' Carl says. 'We're here about Eugene Dahl.'

'Thought you might be.'

'Why's that?'

'He hasn't come into work last couple days, boss said the police called and asked after him, and next thing I know two detectives are banging on my door. I ain't a genius, but I can do a little arithmetic.'

'That's all?'

'What do you mean?'

'Has he been in touch with you?'

'Why would he be in touch with me?'

'You're friends,' Carl says.

'We work together.'

'You never associate except on the job?' Friedman says.

'We might.'

'You either do or you don't.'

'Then I guess we don't.'

'I hear different,' Carl says.

'What did you hear?'

'I hear you're a horn player.'

'Trumpet.'

'And I hear you play bebop music in a Negro bar.'

'Okay.'

'And I hear Eugene Dahl's gone down to see you play. Rumor has it he even took a dolly once or twice.'

'So what?'

'So that makes him your friend,' Friedman says.

'Lots of people come to see me play.'

'Lots of white people?'

'I don't see how that has anything to do with anything, man.'

'Fellow drives down to 57th Street to see me blow my horn in a Negro bar, I'd call him a friend.'

'Fine, he's my friend. So what?'

'So you admit to lying?'

'About what?'

'You said you didn't see him outside of work.'

'I don't see him outside of work. Every once in a while.'

'Was one of those times in the last two days?'

A slight pause, then: 'No.'

'I think you're lying,' Carl says.

'I think you're ugly.'

An open hand whips out and slaps his mouth.

'Enough bullshit,' Friedman says.

Darryl Castor touches the corner of his mouth, fingertips coming away red. He absently rubs the blood between his fingers.

'Look,' he says finally, 'I can't help you.'

'We know your reputation. Even if you don't have anything to tell us now, you know people. You can get information.'

'I got no reason to stick my neck out for a couple cops never did nothin for me. Especially not to help you get to Eugene.'

'He's a murderer.'

'Murderer. Man sends back steak if it's bloody. He's a good guy, but square all the way down.'

'People are surprising.'

'Not in my experience. And like I said, I'm not in a position to help you.'

Carl scratches his cheek, thinking. He didn't want to have to do what he's about to do, but it looks like the only way to get the information they need.

'You know,' he says, 'I've heard your name more than once in the last couple years. You're smart enough not get mixed up in murder, so I never paid much attention, but when I heard it again today I called a friend of mine in the hop squad. He's been watching you, even dug into your history some.'

'I've never been arrested for anything, man.'

'Not your arrest record I was interested in.'

'Then what?'

'Your mother.'

'What?'

Carl pulls a notepad from his inside pocket, ignoring the syringe tucked in beside it, and flips past several pages of unrelated case notes. Finally he reaches the correct page and scans his own handwriting, telling himself to only think about what's happening right now in this dimly lit room.

'Darryl Castor,' he says, 'born Darryl Jefferson in Metairie, Louisiana, forty-two years ago to a widowed Negro cook named Loretta Jefferson, and sent to an out-of-state boarding school by Herman Castor, the Louisiana businessman your mother worked for. You attended boarding school until you were sixteen, at which point you ran away, disappearing for several years before turning up in California, where you began passing as white. Does your boss know you're really an eight ball? What about the people you work as an intermediary for? They have a lot of colored folks in their organizations? When I talk with them all I hear is nigger this and spade that, so I have my doubts. And what about the people at the Negro club where you blow your horn? You think they'd look kindly on a man who denies what he is so he can enjoy the benefits of society they're not entitled to, meanwhile slumming with them when the urge strikes? Seems to me you could find yourself in some seriously ugly situations if it got out that you've been lying about what you are for the last twenty years.'

Darryl Castor stands silent for a long time, expressionless. Then, after the silence has stretched to nearly a minute, he speaks. 'Herman Castor raped my mother and faced no consequences for it. Some folks who knew about it even blamed her. She tempted him, right? She must've. But I remember when I was six or seven this colored boy whistled at a white lady in town, and two days later he was found strung up in a tree, beetles feeding on his corpse. Just a boy, thirteen years old. Maybe she smiled at him, or swayed her hips in that way ladies sometimes do when they know they're being admired. Don't matter, though, because it's always the nigger's fault. They just can't control their animal urges, right? A white man rapes my mother, it's her fault. A Negro boy whistles at a white lady, gets lynched for it. That's the way of the world we live in. I'm not ashamed of what I am. I never lied to nobody. I just let people think what they want to think. I might as well benefit from what my mother had to endure. And I guess I'm as much that man's son as I am my mother's. I only look like this because of it.'

Carl closes his eyes, opens them.

'That's a tragic story,' he says, 'but it doesn't have anything to do with what's happening right now. You have a decision to make. You can continue to be stubborn, in which case we start fucking with your life, letting people know you've been passing, and what happens as a result of that happens. Or you can be sure of things and help us get to Eugene Dahl, a murderer despite what you may believe, in which case nobody finds out anything. I'm a Johnson myself, a live-and-let-live type guy, and I'd rather not have to meddle in your business. But like I say, the choice is yours.'

Darryl Castor looks down at the floor for a long time. Finally he says, 'I'm gonna pour myself a drink. You guys want anything?'

Carl shakes his head and taps a Chesterfield from his packet.

Friedman simply says no.

'Okay.'

Darryl Castor turns and walks into the kitchen, and when he emerges once more a few minutes later, it's with a glass of something strong on ice. He walks past them and sits on the couch. He stares off at nothing. He takes a swallow from his glass.

'What's it gonna be?'

2

Fingers stares at his reflection in the gray surface of his television screen, forearms resting on his knees, glass of dark rum gripped in both hands. He looks at his light skin, his wavy hair. He thinks of his mother, whom he hasn't seen since he was twelve, thirty years ago now. He wonders if she's still alive. He can't imagine she is. He feels small and impotent, and hates that he's been made to feel that way. He doesn't want to betray his friend a second time.

He betrayed him once already.

Louis Lynch called, said he'd been talking to people all day with no luck, asked did he know Eugene Dahl, and he answered without thinking. When Louis Lynch asks a question he's asking for the Man, and when the Man wants an answer you provide it. It's simple as that.

He gave him a gun, offered him money, tried to correct his mistake. But Eugene's on the run because of what he did, wanted for murder, and he's being asked once more to betray him, only this time it's coming from the cops. He doesn't want to do it, but he doesn't want his life to come crashing down around him either. It makes him sick. He's not ashamed of where he came from, nor of what he is. He was born of adversity and that makes him strong. Part of him thinks he should tell these cops to go fuck themselves, and every part of him wants to. They'll spread the word and he'll be who he is. He's already who he is. The only difference will be, everybody'll know it.

That might be fine.

Except he'll lose friends. He might lose his job. People he's worked with for years will stop talking to him. He's built a life, a good life, and he doesn't want it reduced to rubble. He doesn't want to have to start over, and at a disadvantage.

'Eugene came by earlier today,' he says. He stares at his own reflection in the television when he says it, can't bring himself to look at these men as he betrays his friend. 'About an hour ago.'

'Why'd he come by?' the older cop asks.

'He wanted a gun.'

'What for?'

'He didn't say and I didn't inquire.'

'Have any theories?'

He shakes his head.

'Did you give him one?'

'One what?'

'A gun.'

'I did.'

'Do you know where he's staying?'

'No.'

'I think you do.'

'I don't.'

'Okay,' the older cop says. 'I want you to do what you can to find out, and if he gets in touch with you again you let us know.' He pulls out a card, walks to the coffee table, sets it down.

'Thanks for your time.'

Fingers doesn't respond. He continues to stare at his reflection in the television screen as the two police detectives let themselves out of the apartment, as the door latches shut behind them.

He hopes to God Eugene stays as far away from him as possible.

3

Carl sits in his car with both hands gripping the steering wheel. His palms are sweaty. The seat rumbles beneath him as the car idles. His head is turned to the right. He watches through the rain-spotted passenger's-side window as his partner walks into his house to greet his wife and his two children, and disappears behind the door.

Sometimes Carl feels as though he's spent his entire life watching people walk away.

He thinks of using the syringe now, but it's only a thought. A junkie might not care about being cautious, but he isn't a junkie.

He has a job he cares about, responsibilities.

He can't shoot up in broad daylight while parked in front of his partner's house.

He puts the car into gear. He looks into the mirror and sees a rain-spattered rear window, exhaust pipe emitting a steady cloud of white smoke which the rain then hammers out of existence. Behind the exhaust fumes the street is clear of vehicles. Rivers of water rush along the gutters. He pulls his foot from the clutch while gassing the engine and rolls his vehicle into the street. He'll wait till he gets home. It's only a fifteen-minute drive. He's waited all day, he can wait another fifteen minutes. Of course he can. He isn't a monkey. He's in control of his own actions.

He isn't a goddamn monkey.

He feels sick and sweaty and cramped. His stomach is boiling. His sphincter is twitching, and he thinks he might have to be careful he doesn't involuntarily shit. He feels weak and heavy, as though his limbs have been drained of blood and the blood replaced by lead. His eyes are dry and it's difficult to focus.

The windshield wipers squeal across the glass. The sound is maddening. Someone needs to invent a windshield wiper that doesn't make such an irritating fucking sound. He wants to park and step outside and rip the wipers off the car. He wants the throw them into the street and run over them.

He wonders if Darryl Castor will help them get to Eugene Dahl. He thinks there's a good chance he will, but feels rotten about the way they broke him. He tells himself he shouldn't feel bad, he was just doing his job, but that doesn't make the feeling go away.

The trick is to keep your soul winter-numb.

He pulls into an empty parking lot. He kills the engine. He peers through the rain-spattered windshield at the building he's parked in front of. All the lights are off, doors locked. But for his car, the parking lot is empty.

He pulls the syringe box from his pocket and puts it into his lap. He slides out of his jacket, shrugging it off his shoulders and tossing it aside. He rolls up his shirtsleeve, revealing the black dot on his arm where last he used the needle, and a pink dot like a pimple where he used before that. Beneath the skin, they've become hard little knots. He whips his belt from his pants and puts it over his shoulder so it's handy. Looks down at the box in his lap. Reads the lid:

BD YALE
Becton, Dickinson and Company
Rutherford, N.J.
One 10cc Syringe

He opens it and within finds a syringe, a needle, and a paper bindle. He removes his lighter, his spoon, and his foldaway knife from the right-hip pocket of his slacks. He sets the objects, but for the syringe, on his left leg, a nice row of his favorite things. He removes the syringe from its box, as well as the Yale reusable needle, and puts them together.

His mouth, which was dry, is now watering. He swallows.

He's supposed to meet Candice for dinner tonight. He made a date. He should go back to the boarding house and get showered and changed.

He looks at his watch. He has two hours. Two hours is plenty of time. He'll do this first and then finish his drive home and get cleaned up. This first, then that. She'll understand if he's a few minutes late. He'll tell her it was work. That's how it goes sometimes, nature of the job.

He flips open the knife and with the tip of it scoops a small bit of brown powder from his paper bindle into the spoon, then he realizes he has no clean water.

He closes his eyes, tells himself it's okay. Tells himself it's for the best.

This isn't something he should do in his car anyway, not when there's still daylight outside. He lost control for a moment, but this isn't something he should be doing. Of course it isn't. He's only minutes from home.

He picks up the spoon telling himself he'll just pour the powder back into the stash and fold his bindle up, telling himself he'll pack everything else up and drive home.

Instead he brings the spoon to his mouth and spits into it, gently. He lets a bead of liquid form on his lips and eases it into the spoon. It doesn't seem like enough to cook the heroin in so he does it a second time, and then a third.

He already has everything out, after all. It would be silly to pack it all up at this point.

He loops the belt and puts his arm through it.

He picks up his lighter.

THIRTY

1

Eugene watches Evelyn walk to her hotel room and key open the door, following closely as she slips through so that she can't shut the door in his face. Once they're both in her room, he slides the deadbolt into place.

'Sit down.'

She sits on the bed. He looks at her and she looks back. He hates to admit it, but seeing her again, even after what she did, stirs something within him. They've spent only hours together, but those hours were somehow both comfortable and exciting, and the way she's looking at him, not with fear but with sadness, makes him believe that despite what she did afterward, she felt the same as he did.

But that's over now. That's a faucet he needs to shut off.

'I'm sorry for what I did.'

'I don't care.'

'Just the same, I'm sorry.'

'I thought . . . I thought we had—'

'We did. We do.'

'You framed me for murder.'

'It was my job.'

'I know.'

'That doesn't mean I don't care for you, Gene.'

'Shut your fucking mouth, I'm not here to work this out with you. You can go to hell, and the sooner the better. I'm here to find out how to clear my name. I'm here to find out how to get out of this mess you got me into.'

'You can't. It's too late for that.'

'I'm innocent.'

'You're wanted for murder. I can't make that go away. I'm sorry for my part in it, but it's done. The best I can do is help you get to Mexico, and get you some money, enough to live on for a long time down there.'

'I don't want your money. I want my fucking life back.'

'But can't you see that that's over?'

'Don't you try to tell me what's over. You don't get to make that decision. You don't get to make any—'

A knock at the door, three quick taps. Eugene's first thought is that he was too loud, that the man in the next room heard him in here, heard him and is now just outside the door, waiting to make sure everything is okay.

Then he speaks: 'I'm stepping out. You might want to make sure your door is chained. Don't want the milkman to get you.'

Then silence stretches out for a full minute.

'Don't move,' Eugene says.

Keeping an eye on Evelyn he walks to the door and unlatches the deadbolt. He pulls open the door. He glances left, then right. The corridor is empty. He closes the door and locks it once more, the deadbolt clacking into place.

He turns his attention back to Evelyn.

'Where were we?'

2

Evelyn sits on the bed, looking across the hotel room to the man who only a couple nights ago was inside her. The flesh on her chin is still a bit raw from his beard stubble scratching her as they kissed, and she's still a bit sore. She should have trusted her first instinct. She could see from the beginning, from the night she met him in the bar, that he was not a man to run from trouble but rather to grab onto it and try to bring it to its knees. Not that there was time for her to do anything; she only found out he slipped away from the police thirty minutes ago, and even now, while he's here in the room with her, while he's threatening her with a gun, part of her is glad he did. If he'd not had this sort of thing in him she wouldn't have been attracted to him in the first place.

'I'm sorry, Gene,' she says, 'but there just isn't—'

Then something occurs to her, something both terrible

and great. She thinks there might be a way to do what he wants. It'll take planning and forethought, and he'll have to trust her when trusting her is likely the last thing he wants to do, but it might be possible to clear his name. If it's something she really wants to do.

After a moment's consideration she knows that it is. She even lets herself believe that once Eugene's name is cleared they might be able to pick up their relationship where it left off. They might be able to have something together.

'What?' Eugene says.

'I think there might be a way.'

Hope flickers in his eyes, but the shadow of suspicion quickly clouds over it.

'Do you?'

'I do,' she says, 'but you're gonna have to trust me.'

'After what you did?'

Evelyn knows convincing him will be difficult, but she has to try. She closes her eyes a moment to think. She opens them again and looks at Eugene. Looks at him and allows herself to feel what she feels. She prepares herself to speak, and when she does the words that leave her mouth are honest ones.

'I like you, Gene. We have something. I did what I did because it's what I came here to do. It was my job. But when I came here I hadn't met you. I've felt crummy ever since I last walked out of your apartment, and that isn't like me. You have to understand, I'm not a soft woman. I've done worse to men than I did to you and lost no sleep. I know that doesn't speak well of me, but there it is. Whatever Daddy has in him that makes him who he is, I have it in me too. But it was different with you. I've felt rotten. I haven't slept. When I read that you'd escaped the police, part of me was glad, despite the fact that I knew you might come after me. That's the truth. Now I'm telling you another truth. I think I know a way to get you your life back. All I'm asking you to do is listen to what I have to say, listen to my proposal. If it sounds like something you're willing to do, if it sounds like something you're capable of, I want to help you. I want to help you because I still think we might have something between us, and I've never felt like this about anyone before.'

As difficult as it was to allow herself to be vulnerable, it felt good too. It feels good. She looks at Eugene, searching his face for something other than suspicion, for something other than complete mistrust.

Finally, she thinks she sees it.

'Okay,' he says after a while. 'What do you have in mind?'

3

Eugene steps out into the rain. The sky overhead is dark with clouds, only diffused gray light seeping through the cover. He walks toward the street wondering if Evelyn's plan could possibly work. He believes it could. He believes that, like a hammer, it's so simple it almost has to work. But there's no reason to believe she has any intention of following through on it, no reason to believe she'd be willing to bring heat down on her father to save him, some guy she met less than a week ago. No reason to believe it beyond her saying so. And there's plenty of reason to doubt what she says. He wants to believe her, more than anything he wants to believe her, but he'd be a goddamned fool if he let himself take her at her word.

She betrayed him, planned to betray him before they even met, walked into that bar on the evening he first saw her with a sensuous smile on her lips and fluttering eyelids, with the knowledge that she was going to do things that all but guaranteed he'd end up sitting in a chair wired for death.

Yet standing in her hotel room only minutes ago pointing a gun at her, looking at her as she looked back, he wanted to believe every word she said, and some innocent part of his heart did believe, and wanted to embrace her, and feel close to her again.

But his mind is not so stupid as his heart.

After three attempts he manages to kick-start the motorcycle, then straddles the leather seat and gives it some gas.

No, his mind is not nearly as stupid as his heart. Maybe Evelyn's being straight with him, anything's possible, but he can neither believe it nor act as if that's the case. Until he knows better, he'll have to operate under the assumption that every word she spoke to him was a lie. He'll use her if he can, and it seems to him he may be able to, but he'll not trust her.

Only a fool would do that, and in this situation he refuses to play the fool. It happened once. It won't happen again.

THE ROYAL

THIRTY-ONE

1

Eugene wakes in darkness. He wakes from a dream. In the dream he was trapped in an office building, a skyscraper. Because the elevator was broken, he walked down the stairwell, trying the reach the bottom. He walked for days and days but the stairs never ended. There was nothing to eat. He lost weight. At first he believed he was alone, believed the building was empty but for him. But soon enough he began to hear voices. They were distant, always a floor below. Sometimes there was laughter, and the laughter wasn't the laughter of the sane. He checked the corridors, the offices, but they were always empty. So he'd continue down the stairs. Then one time an office wasn't empty. He walked into the room and found four men in tattered clothes, covered in filth and blood, with long beards and long hair, sitting in a semi-circle. In the middle of the semi-circle was another person, a young boy. He was lying on his back. He was dead. His eyes were open. They had a white film over them, like the eyes of a rotten fish. The mouth was open, swollen tongue protruding. Eugene felt like he should recognize the boy, and in some shadowed corner of his mind he did, but his conscious mind couldn't pull it from the darkness. Some mental barrier prevented it. One of the four men reached out with a knife and cut a piece of meat from the boy's arm. He put it into his mouth and chewed. Then grinned at Eugene through filthy teeth. He cut off another piece. He held it out to Eugene. Blood dripped from the meat, ran down the man's grimy hand.

'No,' Eugene said, 'thank you.'

'You might as well. It'll spoil soon, anyway.' Then the man laughed the mad laughter Eugene had heard so many times before. Spittle flew from his mouth, clung to his tangled beard.

Eugene turned and ran, ran down the corridor to the stairwell, pulled open the door, stepped through, and the door slammed shut behind him.

When the door slammed he woke.

And now he lies here in bed, staring at the ceiling, his heart thudding wildly in his chest. He wonders what time it is. He feels lost. He feels like he felt the first time he slept away from home as a child – a week at his grandfather's – and woke up in unfamiliar surroundings, recognizing nothing.

He reaches to the night table and grabs his watch. He

blinks at it in the darkness, holding it close to his face, as he isn't wearing his glasses. His hope is that it's nearly four o'clock. He knows it won't be later, he's up by four every morning, but he hopes four o'clock is near. After a few moments his eyes adjust and he can see the time. It's just past midnight, two minutes past, and he knows his sleep is over despite the fact he tossed and turned till at least eleven.

After he talked with Evelyn yesterday there was nothing for him to do. He was filled with adrenalin from the confrontation, but there'd been nothing in it to expend the energy. They had a conversation, came to a tenuous agreement, and he left. He came back here. He listened to the radio. He listened to the radio and he thought. He thought about Evelyn's plan. It was simplicity itself. It was a hammer. Frame for murder the man who committed the murder. It shouldn't be difficult.

But they need to get into his room and find out what evidence is still in his possession, perhaps plant further evidence, and that means getting a key. Evelyn has promised to do so. He'll call her hotel room at eight to see if she got it, but eight is almost eight hours away, and already he feels as though he's waited too long. He remembers thinking recently that he didn't understand boredom. He still isn't sure he does, people who get bored must think themselves very poor company, but he understands something that lives right next door to it. The emptiness of waiting for something to happen. The nagging at the back of the mind from which nothing can distract you. Could be something as simple as a letter in the mailbox or as catastrophic as the bomb, the point is the wait. The empty hours in which distraction is an impossibility. The time between each tick of the clock carries in its short span an entire day – a day filled with the sound of the sea, like your ear to a shell – and nothing in it but nothing.

He looks at his watch again. It's still two minutes past twelve. He throws the watch across the room. It hits the wall and falls to the floor. He will lie here and go back to sleep and he will not think of the time. He won't think of time at all. He won't get up and find the watch. He won't obsessively check it. He'll lie here and close his eyes, like this, darkness on top of darkness, the cover of eyelids over the cover of night, and he'll picture sheep jumping over a brick wall, a red brick wall, two feet high – one, two, three, four, five, six, seven, eight, nine, ten, eleven, twelve . . . twelve-oh-two. Maybe it's twelve-oh-three by now. It almost has to be. He should find out.

He gets to his feet and walks through the darkness to the place he heard the watch land. He sits on his haunches and feels for it blind, his fingertips moving across the coarse surface of the carpet, occasionally brushing over a strange and suspect crumb. Eventually he finds it. He gets to his feet. He looks at the watch.

Twelve-oh-two.

It doesn't seem possible. A single fucking minute hasn't passed? He's almost able to convince himself it's broken, but the second hand is moving, tick, tick, tick, around the face of the watch.

He stares at it. And stares at it.

Twelve . . . oh . . . three.

2

The next eight hours are a shiftless nightmare. He tries to sleep on his back. He tries to sleep on his stomach. He sits on the edge of the bed and stares at the wall. He sits on the opposite edge of the bed and stares out the window, waiting for the blanket of night to be pulled away. But it doesn't happen. The black remains black. He counts down from a thousand. He wishes he had a bottle of booze. If he drank a pint of something hard he might manage to get a little more sleep in. He does as many push-ups as he can, seventeen, and as many sit-ups as he can, thirty-two, and tries again to sleep. He fails again. There's grime on his back from lying on the filthy carpet to do sit-ups. He gets to his feet and brushes crumbs from his back. He lies down again. He puts the pillow over his head. It smells like sweat and pomade. He rolls to the other side of the bed, where the mattress is cool. This helps not at all. He feels sweaty and sick.

This night will clearly never end. It will never fucking end.

3

At seven thirty Eugene steps into the shower. He washes himself. He dries off with a coarse white towel that smells of bleach. He gets dressed in a pair of dry khaki pants and a white T-shirt and a short-sleeve button-up shirt and a cardigan sweater. He combs his hair. He brought only the shoes on his feet when he left his apartment, so he slips into them despite their being wet. They make a squishing sound and water leaks through the seams and runs down over the lip of the sole to the beige carpet.

With his shoes on and his laces tied he gets to his feet.

He's tired and disoriented when he steps into the daylight at seven forty-five. His eyes sting and feel grainy, as if he'd spent hours at the beach on a windy day. But he's glad daylight's arrived and he smiles as he squints at the blue, blue sky.

He heads to a diner on Hollywood Boulevard, finds a payphone in the back, and drops a dime into it. It falls into the empty change receptacle, sending out a hollow clink as it hits, then settles. He dials the Fairmont Hotel. A woman at the switchboard picks up and, after a brief exchange, patches him through to Evelyn's room.

'Hello?'

'Did you get it?'

'Eugene?'

'Did you?'

'I had to bribe one of the hotel girls.'

'What if she talks?'

'She won't.'

'How can you know that?'

'The one thing hotel workers know how to do better than anything else is keep their mouths shut, Gene. Silence is a commodity they can sell, and they do.'

'Okay, what's next?'

'Next we find out what we have to work with. I'll meet you at noon to give you the key. By then I should have some idea how I'm gonna get Lou out of his room. Where are you staying?'

'We'll meet somewhere else.'

'You don't trust me?'

'Not yet.'

'Fair enough. Where do you want to meet?'

'Schwab's.'

'I'll see you at noon.'

The line goes dead.

Eugene pulls the telephone away from his ear. He looks down at it. It was nice to hear her voice, and he wants to trust her, but he doesn't.

He hangs up the telephone, drops it into its cradle.

He doesn't trust her, but she got the key, so their plan moves forward.

His plan moves forward, anyway. Too bad he doesn't yet know what his plan is. Too bad he doesn't have the slightest clue. Well, he has another four-hour wait on his hands. He can think about it then. He can think about it over breakfast and a few cups of coffee. He's starving. Thinks he'll have some eggs over easy, a fat steak, and some well-done hash browns.

He walks to a booth and sits down.

Maybe with a full stomach he'll be able to think.

THIRTY-TWO

1

Sandy watches the deputy at the counter scrawl his signature across a form in order to take custody of him. Then the two of them, he and the deputy, walk side by side down a white corridor, through a metal door, and into the crisp morning air. Though the rain has stopped, it stopped last night while Sandy slept, small pools of glistening water still dot the ground, marking its low points, leveling the earth. The puddles reflect blue sky and wispy white clouds and bursts of glistening sunlight like jewels.

The deputy, who will be driving him to his meeting with the district attorney, has a reddish-blond mustache, graying sideburns, and light-blue smiling eyes. He folds a stick of Wrigley's chewing gum onto his tongue.

'Trying to quit smoking. Wife hates the smell. Car's over there.'

He nods toward the vehicle. It's splattered with mud, which is drying in the morning light, forming a dull crust on the fenders.

Sandy and the deputy walk toward the car.

Today is the day he finds out just what lies he's to tell when he testifies before the grand jury. He doesn't even know what a grand jury is. Probably something like a grandmother: a jury of really old people. Maybe they're wiser than a normal jury. It doesn't matter; he doesn't want to do it. Just thinking about talking in front of a group of adults makes his stomach ache. He isn't sure he can lie the way he's supposed to lie. In the past when he's lied it was to get out of immediate trouble. It was thoughtless lying. Like a tapped knee kicking out, a reflex lie shot out of his mouth before he could think to be honest. This will be a story given to him by someone else, a story he's supposed to speak as if it were truth remembered. He's afraid he'll forget what he's supposed to say, or say it wrong.

He can't do that. This is a lie to get him out of trouble too, more trouble than he's ever been in before, and he doesn't even have to concoct a story, only remember one. He can do that. He'll be nervous and sick to his stomach the whole time, but he can do it. They probably won't even think there's anything strange about him being nervous. Anybody would be. Even someone telling the truth.

He can do it. He can do it because he has to.

He reaches for the back-door handle.

'You can sit in front with me if you want.'

'Okay.'

He slides into the front passenger's seat and pulls the door closed behind him.

The deputy slips in behind the wheel, his weight rocking the car.

'I got a boy about your age,' he says. 'Good kid. Great shortstop. You any good at baseball?'

'No, sir.'

'Bet you would be with a little practice.'

Sandy doesn't know what to say to that, so he says nothing. He simply looks at the deputy for a moment, wondering what it might have been like to have a father like him, a father with smiling eyes and easy conversation, then, realizing he's been staring too long, he looks away embarrassed. He looks out through the water-spotted windshield to the dirt driveway curving out to the street. He's glad to be leaving this place. He knows it's only temporary, but he's glad all the same.

The deputy starts the car. The engine rumbles to life. The deputy puts the car into gear, and they roll down the driveway.

Sandy looks back over his shoulder and watches the buildings shrink. He wishes they would get so small they'd disappear.

Then he wouldn't have to come back.

2

Fred sits in his Mack truck. The truck is parked on the side of the road, half on the shoulder and half on the gray asphalt. He sits with a porcelain mug of coffee resting on his fat stomach. The collar of his T-shirt has mostly torn away from the rest of the shirt, sitting apart like a cotton necklace. He sips his coffee and fishes through his ashtray for a butt worth smoking. He should have bought a packet of cigarettes this morning. Usually when he fills up his tank with gas he paces the area and finds several good lengths of cigarette on the asphalt – he especially likes the ones with lipstick on the end; it feels sexy to smoke them, like he's kissing the women whose lips last touched them – but after yesterday's rain there's nothing but smears of paper and loose tobacco.

Goddamn rain ruins everything.

He finds a butt with at least half a dozen hits left on it and sticks it between his lips. He wipes the gray film of cigarette ash off his fingers and onto his Levis. He strikes a match and lights his cigarette and takes a good deep drag. The cigarette is old and inhaling its smoke tastes like licking an ashtray. He doesn't care. He takes another drag and follows that with a swig of coffee.

The sheriff's car rolled by him, heading toward the juvenile-detention facility, about fifteen, twenty minutes ago. It should be heading back soon, and this time with the boy in it.

He starts the truck. It rumbles to life, the big engine turning over slowly.

The driveway's about a mile further up the road, which should be enough distance for him to get this hunk of rust up to speed. With the weight it's got behind it, it'll do just what's needed. And it'll look like an accident too. So long as it goes the way he wants it to, and so long as there ain't no witnesses around to contradict him.

He takes another drag from his cigarette and follows that with another swig of coffee. He wishes a man could live on cigarettes and coffee. If he could live on just that he'd never eat nothing else ever again. Except maybe the occasional donut. A man without a sweet tooth is a man who might as well hang himself in his coat closet, because he don't know what life is for.

The Sheriff's Department ain't gonna be happy about one of their own getting killed in an accident, but so long as it is an accident there won't be much they can do. It'll just be one of those tragedies that no one could have predicted. They'll put a flag on his coffin and shoot some rifles at the clouds and call it a day.

He watches the sheriff's car pull out of the driveway, just a toy at this distance, and turn toward him. He puts his truck into gear, eases off the clutch. The truck jerks and rolls out into the street, rumbling like the great metal beast it is. As he picks up speed, he slurps down the rest of his coffee and tosses the mug aside. It bounces off the seat and clunks to the floorboard, clattering against the litter lying there – another mug, a Mason jar lined with black mold, a few nuts and washers, loose paperwork, a red brick. He takes a final drag from his cigarette, sucking the smoke deep into his lungs, and tosses it out the window. He waves the smoke from his eyes, wipes his greasy forehead with the back of a wrist, grips the wheel in both hands.

It's time to earn his money.

The deputy's car is only three quarters of a mile away and the distance is closing.

He shifts into second, then third. He checks his rearview mirror. No one behind him, the road is clear. This is good, better than good. It's necessary.

As the deputy's car approaches Fred yanks his steering wheel left, into the oncoming lane. The car's horn honks. Fred can barely hear it over the rumble of his truck's engine, like a goat's dumb bleat.

He shifts into fourth gear.

Now the two vehicles are less than a quarter mile apart. Fred's speedometer claims the truck is going just under fifty. Add in the speed of the deputy's vehicle and that should be plenty.

Another bleat from the deputy's car.

Then it swerves into the lane his truck should be occupying. This is just what Fred was hoping for. Deputy was trying to pass another car, see, swerved into his lane, and he couldn't help but run straight into him. He was coming right at me, officer, what the hell could I do? Run myself off the road? Get myself kilt?

Just as the vehicles are about ready to fly past each other, Fred jerks his steering wheel to the right. Hard.

3

Sandy sits in the passenger's seat and looks down at his right hand as the deputy pulls the car from the driveway and into the street. His middle finger is still swollen and purple. The swelling makes it difficult to bend. He pushes the bruised finger against the armrest. It hurts, but he likes the hurt. It reminds him of what he did to that boy.

'What the hell is this guy doing?'

Sandy looks up at the deputy. The deputy is squinting at the windshield, confusion on his face. Sandy looks out the windshield and sees a large barn-red truck approaching them. It's in their lane, and seems to him that it's leaning toward them as it rushes forward.

The deputy honks his horn.

The truck continues toward them, straight and steady, as if it were on tracks, and rather than slowing down appears to be gaining speed.

Sandy watches it with his mouth open. He doesn't feel afraid. He feels instead a strange exhilaration. He unconsciously grinds his bruised finger against the armrest. They're going to crash. He's sure of it. He's sure, too, that the man in the truck means for it to happen. He must.

The deputy honks the horn again, then, when the truck

continues undeterred, changes lanes, yanking the wheel to the left.

'Fine, you stupid son of a bitch,' he says, 'we'll trade lanes.'

Sandy watches the truck. It continues on its path. He was wrong. They aren't going to crash. The two vehicles are going to pass without incident. It's almost too late for anything else to happen. But something else does happen. The truck makes a hard turn toward them, leading with its rusty grille, and Sandy can see the face of the driver behind dirty glass, a fat face with a scraggly beard and yellow teeth revealed in a grimace or grin and black porcine eyes.

For a moment the world freezes.

Somewhere a feather floats gently to the earth.

Then an explosion of noise, like being inside a thunderclap. Sandy's body is thrown forward, then to the side. The deputy makes a frightened animal noise. Something smashes against Sandy's face. His shoulder twists with pain. The world spins, then flips upside down, all the trees now rooted in the green sky.

Sandy falls to the roof of the car.

The car wobbles. There's a crinkling sound and the weight of it shrinks the distance between the roof and the seats. Windows explode from the pressure.

He looks toward the deputy.

The deputy is standing on his shoulders, his neck bent at a strange angle, his feet caught under the crushed steering wheel. He groans and flecks of teeth crumble from his mouth and run down his cheek toward his eyes on a tide of mucus and blood.

Sandy lies on the roof of the car, dazed. He's too much in shock to know how badly he's hurt, or whether he's hurt at all.

So he simply lies there.

4

Fred leans down to the floorboard on the passenger's side of his truck and grabs a red brick. He doesn't know how it got there, but he's glad he has it now. He has to make sure the folks in the deputy's car are dead, and it seems to him the damage he does with a brick will look an awful lot like something that might have happened in a car accident, so with it gripped in his meaty fist he steps from the truck and walks toward the deputy's car, which is upside down on the side of the road.

The wheels still spin. A dripping sound comes from somewhere. A groan.

'Is everybody all right in there?'

Another groan.

Fred walks around the car. He leans down and looks in through the shattered side window. A sheriff's deputy hangs upside-down, legs pinned in under the dashboard, drool and blood running from his mouth and into his eyes, into his hair. Pieces of windshield jut from his face.

His mouth looks like a saw blade, teeth jagged.

'You all right there, fella? You look an awful mess.'

The deputy manages, despite the angle of his neck, to turn toward Fred. He groans pleadingly, desperation clearly audible despite the lack of any actual words.

'Don't you worry,' Fred says. 'I'll make it stop.'

He brings the brick down hard into the deputy's face. There's a strange two-stage wet sound, like something heavy breaking through a thin sheet of ice, then splashing into the liquid below. The deputy tries to scream, chokes on his own blood, and sprays a mouthful of it. He puts his arm out to block Fred, or to push him away, or to punch him, Fred can't tell which, but the arm is broken, seems to have developed an extra elbow, and its movement is strange and somehow inhuman.

'Don't do that,' Fred says. 'It only makes it sad.'

He brings the brick down again, and again. And again.

Finally, the deputy stops moving.

5

Sandy knows he's next, knows it without a doubt, and knowing it he knows too there's but one thing for him to do: run. The problem is this. He feels lightheaded and sick and isn't sure he could walk, forget running. But he thinks he's going to have to try, because what's the alternative? Lie here and wait to have his brains bashed in? Let's just call the whole thing off. No, he won't do that. He's gonna have to run. He's gonna have to try. And he's gonna have to move now, right now, because the man outside the car is getting to his feet, is walking around the vehicle toward him, his feet grinding against shattered glass, and he has a bloody brick gripped in his fist, a brick he's already used to kill the deputy.

Then Sandy sees the deputy's revolver.

It lies on the roof of the car surrounded by blood and shattered glass and broken bits of plastic. It's black. It has a wooden grip. He isn't sure he knows how to shoot it, he's never fired a real gun before, but it seems to him it offers a better chance than running. It seems to him it offers a much better chance.

He wraps his hand around the grip.

'What d'you got in mind for that thing?'

Sandy turns toward his window.

The killer sits on his haunches, looking at him, the brick he killed the deputy with gripped in his fat hand. A long string of blood hangs from it, thick as snot.

'Were you gonna shoot me with that thing?'

Sandy doesn't respond. He swallows. His throat is dry.

'How old are you?'

Sandy knows he needs to respond. Every second he can keep this man talking is a second he remains alive. But the words don't want to leave his mouth. He feels trapped in an unresponsive body.

Finally, though, he makes himself speak: 'Thirteen.'

'Thirteen years old. What did you do that someone wants you dead?'

'I,' he swallows again, licks his chapped lips, 'I don't know.'

'That's a shame.'

The killer moves in toward him, and he swings the gun around and aims it at the man's face. He thumbs back the hammer, having to push down with both thumbs to make it click the way he's seen in movies. It's more difficult than you'd think. The cylinder rotates a notch. The metal trigger is cool beneath his finger.

'You got some fight in you, kid. I respect that. But I got no time to fuck around.'

He reaches for the gun.

Sandy pulls the trigger.

The gun kicks hard, almost causing him to punch himself in the face with it. Flame shoots from the cylinder as well as the barrel, burning Sandy's left hand, burning his index finger. He'd expected it to be like the .22 rounds, but this was different, deafeningly loud and intense. He blinks, shocked.

The smile falls from the killer's face. A moment later the rest of him falls too, tilts to the left and drops, hitting the moist earth like a burlap sack filled with potatoes.

Sandy crawls out of the car and gets to his feet. He looks down at the killer. The killer turns his head to look back at him, one eye opened, the other nothing but a black hole. He reaches for Sandy's leg, grabs his khaki pants, says please. Sandy pulls his leg from the killer's grip and kicks the hand away.

He licks his lips, aims for a second shot.

6

Fred isn't sure why he can't open his left eye, but knows he can't. The world over there has vanished. But with his good eye he can see a small boy standing over him. The gun in his right hand looks enormous, like a cannon. The boy looks down at him. There should be panic in his eyes, after everything that's happened there should be panic in his eyes, but there isn't. There isn't even pity there. There's nothing in his eyes at all. It's like someone turned off the switch. He reaches for the boy's pants and says please. He wants to make the boy understand what's happening to him. The boy pulls his leg away, kicks Fred's hand. He points the gun at Fred's face. Fred cannot believe this is how it happens. He simply cannot believe this is how it happens.

7

Once it's finished Sandy tucks the gun into his pants. He turns and looks at the detention facility in the distance. He doesn't ever want to go back there. He won't go back there. The deputy's dead. This man who was trying to kill him, for reasons he doesn't even understand, is also dead. Nothing is keeping him here. There's no reason to stay, but there are reasons not to. If he stays he's in danger. Someone knew he was here and tried to kill him. They might try to kill him again. But if he's going to get out of here he needs to get out of here now. Another car is bound to come along soon.

He glances once more at the wreck on the side of the road, at the killer lying beside it, then turns and starts walking. He walks faster and faster until the walk becomes a run. Away from the detention facility. Away from all of this. He knows the city is miles from here. He knows he'll have to hitch a ride to get there. But he knows too that first he needs to get some distance between himself and this wreckage. He needs to get some distance and he needs to get out of these clothes.

It feels good to run.

It feels good to draw great breaths of air.

It feels good to get away from the detention facility.

He doesn't know what he's going to do once he gets back to the city. He wants to go home. He wants to tell his mother he loves her and sleep beside her. But those are baby thoughts, and he can't afford to be a baby anymore. He knows he can't go home, no matter how much he wants to.

He's on his own now.

THIRTY-THREE

1

Carl stands naked over the bed for a moment and looks down at the sleeping woman who lies upon it. She's on her side, one of her arms tucked beneath her pillow, the other stretched across the bed as if feeling for the man who should be lying there. Her blonde hair is splayed across her pillow. Her eyes are closed, her lips slightly parted. The blankets were kicked to the foot of the bed during the night, but she's covered in a thin sheet to the waist. Her upper half is bare. Her small breasts hang slightly, the left resting in her armpit, the right hanging toward the middle of her chest, which is marked by a small patch of freckles. Only hours ago his mouth was on those breasts, on that stomach, buried in the woman's sex now hidden beneath that sheet. It's difficult to understand how it happened. But it did, and part of him is glad it did. Maybe most of him is glad. It felt strange and wonderful to be close to a woman again. Several times while they made love he thought of his dead wife, and in the end he wasn't able to orgasm, but that didn't seem to be the point, neither for him nor for her. Being close to another human being was the point. He slept the night through lying beside her. He slept with his back to her and she had her arms wrapped around him and he could feel her breasts pressed against his back and her heart beating there as well like a small bird fluttering.

It made him feel, for a time, almost human.

But now he feels as though it was a betrayal. His wife is dead, but her spirit still occupies their house, and he has yet to face it. He has yet to say goodbye.

But it was the cramps and the sweating which pulled him from her bed, and the urge like a rash in his mind needing salve.

He picks up his pants from the floor and steps into them without bothering to fasten the button. He grabs his coat from a chair in the corner and walks out of the bedroom, down the hallway. He looks out to the living room where Candice's new couch sits, a blue couch with red stripes. He walks to the bathroom and closes the door.

He doesn't want to do this here. He wants to be normal. He wants to cook eggs and bacon and sit across the table from Candice while they eat breakfast and talk about nothing, flipping through the paper, chuckling about something amusing in one of the comics. But what he wants doesn't matter. His legs are cramped. He's covered in sweat. He feels sick to his stomach.

He drops his pants and sits on the toilet. His guts come rushing out. He either can't force out anything or else he has diarrhea, there's no in-between. And there's that itch at the back of his brain. That itch that demands attention. That itch that will not allow him to focus on anything else until it's scratched.

Goddamn it, he misses his wife.

Goddamn it, he wishes he could have a relationship with someone new without fucking it up and without it feeling like betrayal.

Maybe someday. He hopes so. But not today.

He wipes, checks for blood, flushes, and sits back down. He grabs the syringe box from the inside pocket of his coat. He looks at the inside of his arm, at the puncture wounds dotting it. He's glad it was dark last night when he and Candice undressed one another. He'll have to put on a shirt before she wakes up.

He opens the syringe box.

2

Candice sits up in bed. She's glad the space beside her is empty, though she hopes Carl hasn't yet left for work. She simply wants a few minutes to wake up. She wants to brush her teeth and wash the makeup from her face. Usually she washes it off before bed. Last night that didn't happen. She's certain that with her makeup smudged as it is she looks a bit like an out-of-focus picture, and she doesn't want him to see her like that just yet. They haven't known each other long enough for that level of comfort.

It's been a long time since she's shared a morning with someone new, and she hadn't planned on such a thing happening today. Despite the fact she told him on the phone there could be nothing between them, she knew she had feelings for him; she told him there could be nothing between them because she *did* have feelings for him, and she didn't think she was ready to step into something new, and she didn't want to sabotage whatever this was – if it was anything at all – by hurrying into an affair so soon after she lost her husband. She feels raw. Despite the fact that she's holding herself together, she feels perpetually close to a breakdown. But she doesn't regret that it happened. It felt right in the moment and good, and she needed something that felt good after all the bad she's suffered. Even if this morning turns out to be awkward she won't regret last night. Even last night had its awkward moments, but despite them, or because of them, it felt wonderfully human. Last night she felt like herself for the first time since Neil was murdered. It made her wonder where she'd been.

This morning she must again deal with this mess her life has become. She must drive down to the district attorney's office to sit with Sandy while he's coached on his testimony. She must discuss the terms of Sandy's deal with Markley and her lawyer, with whom she's only spoken once before. If everything's in order, then paperwork can be signed, making the arrangement official.

But last night let her know that this isn't all she can have. There's something beyond this, even if she isn't yet there. Last night was a glimpse of it. She hopes, though her hope is a cautious one, that Carl might take her hand and help lead her there. Maybe she can help him too.

She gets to her feet, finds a pink nightgown hanging over her door, and slides it over her head. The material is night-chilled and as it slips over her body it brings out gooseflesh on her arms.

She walks to the living room.

'Carl?'

No response.

She wanders through the living room and the dining room to the kitchen, but the kitchen too is empty. A brief but intense sadness overwhelms her, like a wave crashing on the shore and then quickly retreating. He left without saying goodbye. Maybe he left a note for her somewhere. Or maybe he simply stepped out to get some fresh morning air. There's almost nothing finer than a spring morning after it's rained.

She walks to the living-room window and looks out. She doesn't see him, but she does see his car, which means he hasn't left after all. Simply seeing his car parked out there on the street causes a smile to touch her lips.

She turns from the window and makes her way to the bathroom. She has to use the toilet. She hopes it doesn't burn when she pees. The first time she urinates after sex is sometimes less than pleasant. She might have a urinary-tract infection. It'd been so long that she'd forgotten she often gets them after first making love with a new partner. She supposes she'll know soon enough.

The bathroom door is closed. She gives it a tap with her knuckles, says Carl's name, and when he doesn't respond pushes the door open.

As the door swings wide she sees flesh, sees Carl sitting on the toilet, smells the stink of shit, and starts to pull the door closed with sorry on her lips. But before the door can latch she stops. There was something strange about what she saw. Carl didn't look up at her with surprise in his eyes, didn't look up at her at all. He just sat there, slumped. There's something very wrong about that.

Slowly she pushes the door open again.

'Carl?'

Still he doesn't move. His legs are sprawled out in front of him, feet jutting from wrinkled slacks, pale and gnarled. The toenails are yellow. His head is tilted down, chin resting on his chest. His eyes are closed. Drool hangs from his open mouth. Spittle clings to the patch of hair between his pectorals. It runs down his pear-shaped stomach.

A needle hangs from his left arm, a glass syringe.

She looks from that to his face and understands.

She thinks of her first husband, Lyle, always drunk; controlled by the bottle. Often he'd barely manage to stumble home before passing out on the lawn in his own sick. He couldn't hold a job. He was married more to his addiction than to her, and of course he finally chose it over her. You need to quit or leave, Lyle, that's your choice.

Then goodbye.

No. She will not be anybody's mistress. She will not be second in anybody's life. She's been through too much. She's worth too much.

She walks into the bathroom, stands over Carl. She says his name, and when he doesn't respond she says it again.

He picks up his head and looks at her. He smiles.

'Candice,' he says. 'G'mornin.'

'You need to get out.'

'What happened?'

'You need to get dressed and you need to leave.'

'What?'

'Now,' she says.

'What did I do?'

'What did you—'

She stops. She leans down and pulls the syringe from his arm and holds it up in front of his face.

'This is what you did. I'm not having that in my life. I'm not. I won't.' She throws the syringe down and it shatters on the tile floor. She feels the sting of tears in her eyes, and blinks repeatedly, wanting to hold them off, wanting to get control of her emotions. She exhales.

'You need to go,' she says again.

This time she says it calmly.

3

Carl looks down at the shattered syringe on the bathroom floor. He can see through the shards to the black and white tiles on which they lie. He looks up at Candice. She glares down at him angry, her brow furrowed, her mouth a narrow line. She shouldn't be so angry. She should smile instead. He should tell her that.

'You . . . you should—'

'Get out of my house.'

She wants him to leave. He supposes it's best if he does. They can talk about this later. He'll call her later and they can talk about it then. He'll make her understand that it's not how it looks. He isn't an addict. He would never let himself become an addict. He needs to explain that to her. He'll do it later, though. Right now she's too angry to listen to him. Right now she's too angry to listen to reason.

'Okay,' he says, and gets to his feet.

The syringe box, his bindle, his lighter, and his spoon all fall to the floor.

'Oh.'

He leans down and picks up his belongings. He puts them into his pockets. He looks at Candice again. She stands with her arms crossed in front of her chest. When he tries to make eye contact she looks away.

'Okay,' he says again.

He walks to the bathroom door. He can hear glass cracking beneath his feet. He supposes he can feel it too, though it doesn't feel like much. It doesn't really feel like he can feel it, but he guesses he must.

'You're cutting your feet.'

He looks behind him, sees a trail of blood.

'Sorry,' he says. 'I'll clean it up. I'll go get something to clean it up.'

'Just go,' Candice says.

'Okay. We'll talk later.'

'I don't want to talk later. I don't want to see you again.'

He doesn't respond to that. There is no response. He turns and walks to the bedroom. He sits on the edge of the bed and brushes glass from his feet, picking shards from his flesh when he needs to and setting them on the night table. Then he puts on his socks and his shoes, his shirt and his tie. At first he cannot find his coat. After a few minutes he remembers he took it to the bathroom. He doesn't want to go back there. Candice is angry. He'll leave it.

He walks to the living room. His fedora hangs by the door, the lone fruit on the hat tree. He plucks it from where it hangs.

'Shit in it and pull it down over your ears,' he says to himself before setting it on his head. He looks over his shoulder. Candice stands in the hallway entrance, arms still folded over her chest.

Blood fills his shoes.

He takes a step toward her, thinking maybe he can hug her goodbye. If he hugs her, if she can feel how much he cares for her, she'll forgive him. She'll soften in his arms and forgive him and everything will be fine.

But before he can take a second step she's shaking her head.

He turns around without responding and unlatches the deadbolt. He grabs the doorknob. It's cool to the touch.

He pulls.

4

Candice watches him walk out the door. As soon as he's gone she slides to the floor and puts her face in her hands. That was hard to do. He showed her kindness, he made her feel understood, he made her feel there might be something good on the other side of all this shit she's been wading through, but she will not be second to an addiction. She's been that woman before and she'll not be her again. She simply won't.

After a few minutes she forces herself to stop feeling sorry for herself. She wipes at her nose with the back of her wrist. She gets to her feet. She walks to the bathroom and looks at the mess on the floor. She needs to clean it up, then she needs to get showered and dressed.

She still has to meet with the district attorney and her lawyer.

At least she gets to see Sandy today. That will be the single bright spot on what she thinks is bound to be an otherwise black square on her calendar.

5

Carl sits in his car and stares through the windshield at nothing, blank as a blackboard during summer vacation. After five minute he blinks and thoughts once more begin passing through his mind. He starts his car. He looks down at his feet. Blood is leaking from his shoes. He probably shouldn't have stepped on that glass. He didn't mean to. He didn't think about it.

Candice shouldn't have thrown it on the floor.

He puts the car into gear and pulls out into the street.

He considers heading straight to work. He doesn't want to be late. But he knows he can't do that. He knows he has to be careful. If he isn't careful other people will find out something's wrong. He needs to clean up, bandage his feet. He thinks he can fix things with Candice. He just needs to make her understand that he isn't a junkie.

He isn't.

But nobody else can find out what he's doing.

He drives toward the boarding house. He's going to be late for work, but that's better than showing up looking like he does right now.

THIRTY-FOUR

1

Leland Jones stands in the bathroom, looking at himself in the mirror. He wears no shirt, only a pair of dark pants. He isn't muscular, but his torso is tree-trunk solid and tanned from mowing the lawn shirtless every Saturday. His hair is wet and finger-combed back. His nose is swollen and purple. His eyes are black.

2

Two days ago, on Saturday, he was bashed twice on the head with a shower rod. He fell face-first to the wood floor and broke his nose. He was knocked out. When he came to, the house was empty. He woke and called out to Vivian but received no response. He got to his feet. Blood ran from a gash on the back of his head. It ran down his neck, staining the collar of his shirt. More blood ran from his face. He felt wobbly and unbalanced. He walked to the couch and sat down. He stared at the ceiling and held his nose so blood wouldn't run from it. Instead it ran down the back of his throat. He had no idea what had happened. He walked through the door saying that everything went smooth as a baby's backside and next thing he knew he was on the floor. He called to Vivian again while sitting on the couch, his voice sounding strange with his nostrils pinched shut, but knew she wasn't home. She'd had a funeral to attend.

He couldn't believe she'd leave him lying on the floor bleeding. It didn't make any sense. It wasn't like her. It didn't make any sense at all.

Then it did make sense.

She was mad at him. She'd told him you don't put your hand in the same till twice if you don't want to lose your fingers when the drawer slams shut. She'd told him that, but he'd ignored her, and now he was sitting on the couch with a broken nose and a gash in the back of his head.

The son-of-a-bitch district attorney had sent someone to do this to him as punishment for the blackmail. That's what had happened. That's what he thought had happened. But two hours later, when Vivian returned, he learned he was wrong. The district attorney hadn't sent someone here to beat him up. The district attorney had sent someone here to get any pictures Leland might not have handed over, and that someone had left with all the pictures, his retirement.

His first thought was to go after Markley, but Vivian talked him out of it. They'd pushed him and he pushed back – it was the way of the world, downright Newtonian even – and Leland shouldn't have expected any different. If he pushed again, Markley would push back again, and that wouldn't be good for anyone. Anyway, they could take more pictures. She still had a pussy, after all, and he still had a camera.

He agreed to let it go. He was angry and he wanted to do something but in the part of his mind where emotions didn't rule he knew she was right.

And he knows it still.

3

He blinks at his reflection and wonders briefly if he might be able to use Vivian's makeup to cover the bruises on his face. He has a meeting with a producer at Monocle Pictures about a speaking part in a Western movie. His character would have a duel with the film's hero and get shot down. The guy's given him background work before. Leland had pictures that ensured at least twelve weeks of work every year, that's the agreement they came to, but a speaking role is a different matter.

He walks to the bedroom and looks at Vivian in bed with her eyes closed.

'You asleep?'

She opens her eyes to slits. 'Not anymore.'

'Can I ask you something?'

'What?'

'Think I should try to use some of your makeup to cover up these bruises?'

'What for?'

'I got a meeting with a producer.'

'What kind of part?'

'I have a duel with the hero and get shot down.'

'No, keep the bruises. They make you look like a ruffian, which is probably what they want. Now shut up and let me sleep.'

'You don't think—'

'Shut up and let me sleep. I worked last night, in case you forgot.'

He puts on a pearl-button shirt and a bolo tie. He slips into socks and black alligator-skin boots. He perches a Stetson on his head, grimacing as it slides over a bruise. When all that's done he walks back to the bathroom and looks at his reflection once more. He decides Vivian's right. The bruises make him took tough. He scowls at himself, squinting and looking mean, then the scowl breaks into a toothy grin.

He grabs his keys and walks toward the front door.

4

Leland parks his powder-blue Ford pickup truck on the south side of Sunset Boulevard, glances into the side-view mirror, sees the street's clear, and swings open the door. He steps out into the morning air, boots thudding on asphalt, inhales the lingering scent of yesterday's rain, and slams the truck's door shut. He heads inside, feeling good.

He slaps his hand on the counter and smiles at the pretty little secretary sitting behind it. She was painting her fingernails fire-engine red as he approached but now she looks up and smiles back at him coolly, no trace of the smile in her eyes. She screws the top back onto her bottle of nail polish.

'Good morning, sir.'

'It's Leland Jones, darlin, and good mornin to you.'

'How can I help you?'

'You can pick up that phone and let Woodrow Selby know that Leland Jones has arrived and is ready to speak with him about a part. I'm an actor.' He gives her his most winning smile.

'You and everyone else in this town.'

She picks up the phone, says a few words, and hangs up again.

'You can have a seat,' she says. 'Mr Selby will call down when he's ready.'

'Is it gonna be long?'

'Do I look like Nostradamus to you?'

'Don't know, I never met him.'

'He'll call when he's ready.'

Leland's first instinct is to snap at the woman, but he knows that'll get him nowhere. They'll have an argument, he'll get angry, and his day will be ruined. He doesn't want that. He wants today to be a good one. He needs it to be.

'Yes, ma'am,' he says, touching the edge of his hat.

He walks to a couch against the wall opposite and falls into it. He leans back, settling in. Tilts his hat down over his eyes. Pictures himself in a dusty one-saloon town, standing in the middle of a dirt road, facing some do-gooding sheriff in a white hat. They stand twenty paces apart, elbows bent, hands at the ready mere inches from the butts of their weapons, fingers twitching. Leland's got a smoldering cigarillo in his teeth. He gnaws on it, squinting at the man standing across from him as the man squints at him. Leland's got the advantage. The sun's behind him. A wind kicks up. Something rattles to the left, a pie tin rolling along the boardwalk. White-hat's eyes shift that direction. Leland takes the chance, draws. Not fast enough. His barrel hasn't even cleared his holster when he feels something like a sledgehammer thudding against his chest. He stumbles back two steps, looking down at his blue shirt blossoming red. It's all over now. It's—

The telephone rings.

Leland pushes his hat up, away from his eyes, and looks

across the room to the secretary. She picks up the telephone, says yes sir, okay, and hangs up.

'He'll see you now.'

Leland gets to his feet.

5

He steps into daylight. He's been ruined. That son-of-a-bitch district attorney has ruined him. Forget speaking roles in movies. He'll be lucky if they let him shovel the horseshit from the dusty streets after a day of shooting. It's over, he's over. The district attorney didn't stop when he had someone bash Leland in the skull, and he didn't stop when he got the pictures. He only stopped when he made sure Leland was ruined. The son of a bitch is giving the photographs back to the men pictured in them. Leland has had these men scared for years, made them feel like nails with a hammer about to fall, and now they will see there is no hammer, no danger, and they'll resent the threat.

These are powerful people. He's done.

He should have known this was coming. What did he think would happen once the district attorney got his hands on those photographs? He can't believe he let himself get talked out of going after that son of a bitch.

He stomps to his truck and flings the door open and slides inside. He pounds his steering wheel, cursing, every foul word he can think of flying from his mouth and spittle as well. If he'd done what he wanted to do this wouldn't have happened. If he'd done what he wanted to do on Saturday the district attorney wouldn't have had time to do this. He'd have kicked the shit out of him and taken the pictures back.

Now he's going to kill him: kill him dead.

He digs through his pocket till he finds his keys.

A moment later the engine rumbles to life.

6

The truck comes to a screeching halt in front of City Hall. He hopes like hell the district attorney's in his office. He doesn't care who sees him, he doesn't care what the man can do to him. He's already ruined. If the district attorney had stopped when he got the pictures, stopped there, this wouldn't be happening. But he didn't do that. He had to rub Leland's face in his own defeat. He'll not be anybody's bad dog. He'll not be treated like he shit the rug. He gets out of his truck, walks around it, steps up onto the sidewalk.

'Leland?'

He stops, looks to his left.

Candice stands on the sidewalk. Her blonde hair is pulled back into a bun. Her face is free of makeup or nearly so. A thin man in a dark suit stands beside her.

'Candice.'

'What are you doing here?'

'I was just— Shit. Nothin. What about you, darlin?'

'Meeting with Sandy and the district attorney.'

'How's Sandy doin?'

'He was okay last time I saw him.'

'What about you? I didn't make it to the funeral like I planned.'

'That's all right.'

'But how you doin?'

She looks away, blinking, then swallows.

'I better head in, Leland. Tell Vivian I said hi.'

'Will do. You take care of yourself.'

'I will.'

Leland watches Candice and her lawyer walk up the path toward the building, watches her walk up the steps and disappear inside. He heads back to his truck and steps into it. He stares through the windshield to the street. He needs to get himself a drink.

THIRTY-FIVE

1

Seymour Markley pulls a white cloth from his pocket, snaps it, and cleans his glasses, wiping the lenses in a circular motion one after the other. Without them, the men sitting across from him are mere flesh-colored smudges without eyes or noses or mouths, like someone smeared out their oil-paint faces with the swipe of a thumb. Once the glasses are clean he puts them back on and blinks at Barry and the man sitting beside him, Peter Burton, the deputy district attorney charged with providing the grand jury with legal advice on this investigation once the indictment is presented. They have once more been made human, features having grown from their faces as he placed the glasses upon his nose. He folds the cloth into quarters and puts it back into his pocket.

He has but one question on his mind. What are they

going to do about this investigation now that Theodore Stuart is dead? The police haven't yet apprehended the man who killed him, despite their confidence two nights ago, so he can't question him about a possible connection to James Manning, and even if he could it doesn't look like there is one. And he needs one.

He'd planned on presenting the indictment to the grand jury tomorrow morning, once he'd finished lining everything up. He wanted to hand them most of a case. But just as it was coming together, fate knocked it apart. He's postponed till Friday. He needs at least fourteen members of the twenty-three member grand jury to return an affirmative vote if they're going to indict, and this is unprecedented legal ground.

When he had Stuart in custody he was sure he'd get the votes, and with a true bill from the grand jury he wouldn't be standing alone behind a shaky case. Their vote for indictment would protect him, to some degree, from allegations of recklessness. He'd still have to work hard to convince his supporters in the movie industry that this case wouldn't end up hurting them – he's gotten more pushback than he expected there, but then the threat those whores made against him clouded his thinking – but at least he wouldn't be standing alone. Now he's not so sure the jury will come back with the votes, and if he doesn't get the votes, it's over. And his career is irreparably damaged.

Seymour looks at the two men sitting across from him.

Barry, with his elbows on the arms of his chair and his fingertips pressed together, looks like a man preparing for prayer.

Peter Burton, all nerves, with a head of curly blond hair in need of a trim, sits peeling the paper off a cigarette while bits of tobacco fall into his lap.

'Okay,' Seymour says. 'The way I see it, the investigation must to do three things if there's to be a case. One, it must result in evidence that James Manning is the money behind E.M. Comics. We had testimony to that effect until Theodore Stuart was killed, now we don't, but I'm confident we can get there. You can't run a business without leaving a paper trail somewhere. We just need to uncover it. Two, it will need to result in evidence that *Down City* compelled the boy to commit a murder he would not otherwise have committed. We'll have the testimony of the boy himself for that, as well as the testimony of Frederic Wertham, an expert in the field. With the way people feel about comics these days, this is the least of our worries. Mothers are already throwing them into trash bins and church groups are burning them. Half of the grand jury will be convinced before any evidence is presented to them. Three, it must result in evidence that James Manning was criminally negligent in allowing the comic to go to press. We need evidence that he knew of the dangers and let the comic end up on newsstands anyway. That's the tough part, and that's what might stall the case before it's even begun. We're out on a limb here, and to be perfectly frank, it has me worried. Any thoughts?'

Seymour's telephone rings.

He looks down at it. It rings a second time. He told his girl not to put any calls through, so why is his telephone ringing? It had better be important. He holds up a finger to the two men sitting across from him, picks up the receiver midway through the third ring.

2

Barry watches his boss pick up the telephone, put it to his ear.

'Yes?'

He looks down at his hands, at his fingertips touching, pushes them hard against each other so the skin goes white beneath the fingernails. He thinks of the discussions he's been having with Maxine.

'Put him through.'

He's been talking with her about quitting. They discussed it over dinner last night and the night before. Maxine always asks the same thing. What will we do about money? It's a good question, an important one, and his answer now is the same as it was then. I don't know. But he knows this. He's been compromised by his work here. He wanted this job because of his respect for the idea that he lived in a nation governed by laws, and that breaking them meant you faced consequences, and that those consequences were meted out to the guilty without regard to who they were or what their social status might be. The problem is, it's bullshit. It's a lie. And he's been actively participating in that lie.

'What bad news?'

He doesn't know what he's going to do, but he doesn't think he can continue doing this. He knows he can't. Maybe he'll bang on the ivories in a piano bar somewhere. At least he'll be able to look himself in the mirror.

'Are you certain?'

He looks up to see his boss's face drain of color.

Into the phone Seymour says, 'How could this happen?'

He puts his hand over his opened mouth.

'You need to find him.'

He hangs up the phone and looks across the desk.

'There was an accident.'

'What kind of accident?'

'Automobile.'

'What happened?'

'A sheriff's deputy crashed into a Mack truck. He was transporting our witness.'

'Is anyone hurt?'

'The deputy's dead from injuries and another man's been shot.'

'In a car accident?'

'It's confused right now.'

'What about the boy?'

'Fled the scene. And it looks like he took the deputy's service revolver with him.'

3

Seymour closes his eyes and rubs his temples with the first two fingers on each hand. His head is throbbing. He can't believe what a nightmare this has become. It might be time to end it. Without Theodore Stuart or the boy to testify they have very little to work with. They have the Bunker Hill murder and a weak connection to a comic book with a weak connection to James Manning. They have the skeleton of something, maybe, but the meat has been torn away from the bones and hauled off by hyenas.

And the threat against him has been eliminated.

He won't be able to simply drop it. He made the grand-jury investigation a public matter, and the public will demand answers. His career will suffer, probably permanently, but if he cuts his losses now it won't be over. He needs to think this through.

The telephone rings again.

He looks at it hatefully, considers picking it up and

dropping it right back down into its cradle. He wants it silenced.

Instead he grabs it, puts it to his ear.

'What now?'

'Candice Richardson and her lawyer have arrived.'

THIRTY-SIX

Sandy hops out the back of a truck, swinging out over the side and dropping to the sidewalk, both feet slapping the ground. He wears a pair of khaki slacks and a T-shirt. The khaki shirt with the detention facility's initials stenciled onto the back is now lying in a ditch several miles away. The revolver is tucked into his pants, pressed against his stomach. He lifts a hand to the driver and says thanks mister though he doesn't know if the driver can hear him. The driver lifts a hand in return, then pulls his truck back out onto Olympic Boulevard. Sandy watches it shrink and disappear. Once it's gone he turns in a slow circle, taking in his surroundings. He's never felt more alone. The streets have never been wider, nor the sky emptier. He's back in the city and has no idea what to do. He can't go home but has nowhere else to be. He feels planted where he stands, rooted, and his brain won't help him, frozen in indecision.

His stomach growls. He's hungry and should get

something to eat. He likes that idea. It gives him a way to move forward. He begins walking. At first he drags his feet, but he doesn't like the sound of that or the feel, so he begins taking big steps instead, begins stomping. That's better. His feet like hammers falling. Cars roll by to his left. He wishes he had a cigarette. He would feel like a man if he had a cigarette. He's smoked a couple before, on the back of Bunker Hill, sitting on a truck tire that had been tossed there, and it made him feel sick, but it also make him feel ten feet tall. He should feel like a man right now, not lonely or scared. He never has to go to school again. He never has to say yes sir or no sir or please. He never has to tell other people's lies.

Not if he doesn't want to.

He has a gun tucked into his pants. That means he can do whatever he wants. It doesn't matter that he's thirteen years old. It doesn't matter that he's small. Being meaner than everybody else makes you bigger than you really are, and having a gun makes you bigger still. He only wishes he'd learned that lesson sooner. He spent so much time being scared. Even now he feels afraid and hates it. He wishes he could banish the feeling from his heart. That's why he killed his stepfather. Because he didn't want to be afraid anymore, didn't want to feel sick to his stomach every time he walked through his own front door. He tells himself there's no place for fear. He's not a lightning rod and he's not a cup. He's a vicious dog. He's a wild horse. He's anything he wants to be.

Up ahead on the right he sees a small shop. He decides he's going to get his lunch there. He's hungry and he's going to get lunch and it doesn't matter that he has no money. He doesn't need money. He'll take what he wants. That's what men do. They take what they want and they don't say please.

He steps into the store and walks up and down the aisles looking at the loaded shelves, at the jars of pickles and mayonnaise, at the tubes of toothpaste. He stops in front of the canned meats. Rows of corned-beef hash, Spam, tinned herring snacks in sour cream, oysters, sardines. He glances toward the man behind the counter. He's looking directly at Sandy, watching him. When they make eye contact he nods. Sandy quickly turns back to the canned meats. He shouldn't have looked. He doesn't know why he did. Now the man behind the counter will know he's up to something. But he has no choice. He's very hungry.

He picks up a tin of sardines, reads the label as if considering the purchase. Boneless, skinless sardines in cottonseed oil. Lightly smoked. He nods to himself and steps away from the canned meats. Continues down the aisle toward the back of the store. He wants to find a place where the man behind the counter can't see him. Then maybe he'll be able to slip the sardines into his pocket. Then maybe he'll—

'I know what you're up to.'

He turns around and looks at the man behind the

counter. His face feels suddenly hot. The skin tingles. The man looks back, a heavy-set Greek guy with a bushy beard and a sweat-glistening forehead. He stands casually, one hand resting on the counter near a glass ashtray, a brown cigarette between his lips sending up a thin stream of smoke toward the ceiling. He has sleepy eyes. He blinks at Sandy. A small breeze blows in through the glass front door, disturbing the stream of smoke, breaking it apart, and causing a small plastic American flag jutting from a cigarette rack to wave briefly before once more going still.

'What?'

He takes a drag from his cigarette, taps ash into the tray, blinks again.

'I know what you're up to.' His tone is flat, unconcerned.

'I'm not.'

'You got any money? You gonna pay for those sardines?'

Sandy has a decision to make. After a moment's thought he nods and walks toward the counter. He licks his lips.

Then grabs a packet of cigarettes from the rack on the counter, knocking the rack over in the process, cigarettes spilling across the counter and falling to the floor, and runs for the exit. The man behind the counter yells after him, get back here you little shit, but he doesn't stop and he doesn't look over his shoulder. He runs through the door, out into daylight. He runs down the sidewalk. His feet pound against the pavement. Thud, thud, thud like falling hammers.

Once he reaches the corner he stops running. He looks back. The man stands in the shop's doorway, looking in his direction, but he doesn't give chase. Sandy turns away and turns the corner, heading up a small street, looking for a place to eat his lunch.

He should've pulled out his gun. He should have waved it around. That would have let that fat Greek bastard know he meant business. Then he could have taken his time, took as many cans of sardines as he wanted and as many packets of cigarettes too. He could have emptied the register and had a nice lunch at a restaurant, like it was Easter or something. That's what he should have done, but he didn't think to. Still thinking like a little boy, he only wanted to get away. He needs to stop that, needs to stop thinking scared. Next time he goes into a store it's with his gun drawn.

He's a vicious dog. He's a wild horse. He's anything he wants to be.

As he continues north apartment buildings give way to houses with neat square lawns. Eventually he arrives at one with a

FOR SALE

sign planted in the grass and walks up the oil-spotted driveway to look inside. He hops up three steps to the front porch, puts his face to the glass, sees an empty living room. The beige carpet has been recently vacuumed. The walls are white. A few nails jut from them where pictures once hung. He checks the door and finds it locked, and there's no key under the mat. He walks around the building looking for a window to crawl through. He finds one cracked open a few inches at the back of the house and pries the screen out of the way, leaning it against the outside wall. Then pushes the window the rest of the way open and climbs inside.

He walks around the house, exploring the empty rooms, inhaling the scent of fresh paint. He checks the kitchen cupboards and drawers, hoping for a discovery of some kind, but they're empty with the exception of a box of matches in a drawer near the stove.

He carries the box with him to the living room and sits down on the floor, leaning against the wall. He pulls the gun from his pants and sets it down beside him. Then he pulls the key from the side of the sardine tin, puts it into the metal eye at the top, and begins peeling the lid off, pulling away a twisted metal ribbon.

He'll have to eat the sardines with his fingers. He doesn't care. There's no one around to yell at him for eating with his hands, no one around to smack him upside the head and call him a piggy little shit, so there isn't any reason to care.

Once the lid is free of the tin he sets it on the floor beside the gun and plucks a sardine from within. He puts it into his mouth and chews. It tastes good. He licks the oil off his fingers, then eats another sardine, and another, and another.

When the tin is empty he sets it on the floor and wipes his fingers clean on the carpet, front and back. He stares at the white wall in front of him. He likes this, sitting here alone, not worrying about anything, not answering to anybody.

He thinks of his mother.

He knows he can't go home. He knows that, he isn't a baby. But he thinks maybe he should let her know he's all right. She must be worried.

But not right now. He wants to be nowhere else but here right now, alone in this empty room, alone and safe. He was almost killed this morning, had to shoot someone to get away. The police are probably looking for him. He doesn't want to go back out into that world. It's a mean world filled with traps you can't see till you step in them.

He unwraps the cellophane from his packet of cigarettes, peels away the foil, and plucks one from within. He lights a match and inhales.

The world shouldn't scare him like that. He tells himself he shouldn't let the world scare him. The world might be full of meanness, but he can handle it. He's meaner.

He's a vicious dog. He's a wild horse.

He doesn't need a mother. He doesn't need anybody.

He's a vicious dog. He's a rampaging bull.

He begins to cry.

THIRTY-SEVEN

1

Eugene leans hard into a turn, swinging onto Sunset Boulevard, and speeds his way west toward Schwab's Pharmacy. He squints ahead at the palm trees lining either side of the street, narrow trunks bending into the air topped with sagging fronds both brown and green. Behind them, a sky the color of faded denim in which a few wispy clouds blow past slow as they disintegrate.

He still doesn't know what to do. He only knows what not to. He simply can't go along with Evelyn's plan. He'd never walk away alive. The police need someone to pin those murders on and he is that someone. He can blather all he wants and they'll simply think he's trying to talk his way out of the rap. It's what a guilty man would do. But if he manages to pin the murder on Louis Lynch, he's no longer of use to James Manning. Instead he's a threat, he knows too much, and there's only one way to ensure that guys who know too much don't say too much: fill their mouths with dirt.

If he knew he could trust Evelyn he would tell her his concerns. Maybe together they'd be able to work something out. But he doesn't know he can trust her. Just the opposite. He's almost certain he can't. He wants to, his heart wants him to, but hearts are stupid. And love is a liar.

For now he must keep his thoughts to himself. He must start planning what he's going to do. In the back of his mind, in the darkness beyond the light of conscious thought, just beyond the edge at which that lamp's glow fades, something is pulling itself from the mud, an idea, but he doesn't yet know what it looks like. He can merely sense that it's there, picking itself up, taking shape.

He pulls to a stop at the curb behind the Schwab's delivery motorcycle. He steps off the bike, toes down the kickstand, and walks across the wide sidewalk to the front door. He pushes through.

Just inside the doorway he lights a cigarette, picks a bit of tobacco from the end of his tongue, and scans the anonymous faces lining the counter. He and Evelyn see one another at the same moment. She raises her hand in a wave, a touch of a smile on her gash-red lips. He nods, takes a drag from his cigarette, and makes his way toward her, reminding himself that she betrayed him, that she can't be trusted, that she's a serpent and has proven it by striking once already. But as he approaches her his palms begin to sweat. His mouth goes dry.

2

Evelyn watches Eugene walk toward her, a smile touching her lips as he approaches, but despite the smile this is serious business. Doing this will put Daddy at risk. She came out to the West Coast to take care of some trouble, but instead she's here creating it. And the most horrible thing is, she doesn't care. She *should* care, it's her job to care, but she doesn't. She can't. For the first time in her life something other than her mind is guiding her, and she's going to let it.

And despite the fact she's creating trouble for Daddy, she's fairly certain he'll be fine. He can walk through a fire and come out the other side unharmed.

He certainly won't go to prison.

They'll arrest Lou and question him about why he killed Teddy Stuart. They may even bloody him up some. But Lou won't talk. He's a professional.

Not that he'd have a chance to open his mouth if he wanted to. He'd be dead before he could put his hand on the bible. He'd be dead before he got anywhere near a courtroom. It'd be another suspicious death in a string of them, but Daddy's had suspicious deaths dragging behind him like anchors for thirty years. There's no reason to think this would be the one whose weight would finally stop him.

And this will get Lou out of her way. For six years they've been in conflict with one another. This will put an end to it. A definitive one.

For the first time in her life something other than her mind is guiding her, and so far as she can tell, it's wiser than she is.

Eugene sits down on the stool beside her.

'Evelyn.'

'Gene,' she says, 'I'm glad you came.'

He doesn't respond. He simply takes a drag from his cigarette and nods without taking his eyes off the napkin dispenser sitting on the counter in front of him. His eyes are bloodshot, his shoulders slumped.

'You look tired.'

'Trouble sleeping.'

'Me too. I kept thinking about you.'

A barmaid walks over and asks them what they'll have. Evelyn orders a turkey sandwich on rye. Eugene asks for coffee.

After the barmaid leaves Eugene says, 'Do you have the key?'

'And the knife.'

She reaches into her purse, removes them, and hands them to Eugene. When their fingers touch he finally looks at her, finally makes eye contact, and he holds it for longer than is comfortable. He seems to be looking directly into her.

Then he breaks away, glancing down at the objects she's handing him.

'Thanks.'

'Be sure to wipe your prints from the knife. And wear gloves when you go into Lou's room. There can't be any evidence that you were there.'

He nods.

'What time will you have him out?'

'We're having drinks at eight o'clock. Told him we needed to discuss business.'

'This knife,' he says, 'you were supposed to use it to frame me?'

'I was supposed to plant it in your apartment.'

'But you didn't.'

'I didn't.'

'Why?'

'I'm not sure.'

'You still did plenty.'

'I'm sorry for that, Gene.'

'I know.'

The barmaid returns with Evelyn's sandwich and Eugene's coffee, the coffee spilling over the edge of the white cup and into the saucer when she sets it down.

Evelyn pulls the top slice of bread from her sandwich and sprinkles salt and pepper onto the mayonnaise smeared across it before setting it back down. Then she wipes her hands of rye seeds and stares at her plate, not the least bit hungry.

Eugene sips his coffee black, grimaces, and gets to his feet.

'I'm gonna go.'

Evelyn reaches out and puts her hand over his hand.

'Gene.'

He looks at her.

'Do you think there's any chance for us after this?'

He doesn't answer for a long time. Then: 'I don't know.'

3

He walks back out into the daylight, squints at the blue sky, takes a final drag from his cigarette. He holds it pinched between finger and thumb a moment, looking at it thoughtfully, then flicks it out into the street. He tried not to show it, but seeing her did something to him. It always does. But he knows he must be careful.

He walks to his motorcycle and kicks it to life.

He straddles the bike, knocks the kickstand out of the way with his heel, pulls out into the street. The afternoon air feels good rushing against his face.

He needs to buy a pair of gloves.

THIRTY-EIGHT

1

Carl walks through the hallway. He looks down at his scuffed black shoes as they kick one in front of the other. His feet are beginning to hurt as the drug wears off, but at least he managed to stop the bleeding. He wishes he felt better. The junk doesn't do for him what it used to do. It used to make him feel blissful nothingness. Now it simply takes away the sickness, and that horrible itch at the back of his brain. That's something, of course. But he can't bring back that bliss, that feeling that he's a silent echo bouncing against the emptiness of the universe, bouncing out further and further into nothing, free of trouble and thought and doubt and worry.

He needs to make Candice understand that he's not addicted. If he can do that maybe he won't feel sad anymore.

The trick is to feel nothing. To keep your soul winter-numb.

He pushes his way through a door labeled

HOMICIDE DIVISION

and into the squad room. He starts toward his desk, but only manages three or four steps before he sees Friedman get to his feet and start toward him. He's about to say good morning, how you doing, but doesn't get the first word out before Friedman grabs him by the arm and starts pulling on him. He says what are you doing, have you lost your god-damn mind, but Friedman doesn't answer, only pulls him into the bathroom.

'Do you think you're fooling anyone?'

'What are you talking about?'

'How long have you been using?'

'What? I don't—'

'You think people don't talk? You want to know what most secrets are? They're things everybody knows but whispers about in hushed tones. If more than one person has a piece of information, it's not a secret anymore. How long have you been using?'

Carl says nothing. He stares at his partner and wonders about his future. Will he be suspended? Lose his job? Go to jail? He doesn't even know if he wants answers to those questions. He supposes he doesn't. He supposes he'd like to echo against the emptiness and pretend none of this is happening. He doesn't want answers, but his mind forms the questions anyway.

'I was hoping you'd pull yourself out of this, but all I can see is you sinking deeper into it. You're not far from drowning in it.'

'I'm fine, Zach. It's fine.'

'You're not fine. You're not even close.'

'Why are you doing this?'

'Because you're my friend and I can't watch you kill yourself when—' He looks away, blinks several times, looks back. 'Because you're my friend.'

'Fine, then. We're no longer friends. Go fuck yourself.'

'Carl.'

'No, if you're doing this because I'm your friend, then I won't be your friend. We'll be enemies instead. Come on.'

Carl puts his fists up in front of his face, swaying slightly, glaring at Friedman. He wants Friedman to hit him. He doesn't know why, but he does.

'Come on.'

'I'm not gonna fight you.'

'Then I'll fight you.'

He throws a punch, fist swinging only through air as Friedman pulls back, and next thing he knows he's lying on his back looking up at Friedman and past him to the glowing lights in the ceiling. They're very bright.

Friedman holds a hand out, offering to help him up. Carl slaps it away.

'Fuck you.'

Friedman nods.

'Okay. But you need to pull yourself together. I know things have been rough for you since Naomi died, I know you're having a hard time, and I understand it. I'd fall apart if I lost Deborah. But you're killing yourself. You're killing yourself, and I refuse to stand by and watch it happen. Think about that.'

Friedman pushes out of the bathroom, leaving him alone on the cold tile floor.

He doesn't move for a long time. Then after a while he does. He pushes himself up to a sitting position, finds a packet of cigarettes in his pocket, lights one. He reaches to the counter and pulls himself up.

He pushes out of the bathroom, then out of the building.

He's going to lose his job anyway, and maybe he should. He doesn't care one way or the other. Why should he? It's pointless work. Everybody dies. Take all the murderers off the streets and the very next day someone will die choking on a cold roast-beef sandwich. You can't arrest a heart attack and you can't arrest cancer.

You can't prevent death. You just pretend you can so the living can remain oblivious to it right up until a pain shoots through their left arm or they find the tumor.

The dead, meanwhile, don't care; it's a one-way door they've gone through.

He walks to his car and gets inside. He starts the engine, puts it into gear.

He doesn't know where he's going. Somewhere.

2

Candice parks her car in the driveway and kills the engine. She looks through the water-spotted windshield to the paint-peeling garage door. She feels slightly dazed. She can't believe her son did what the Sheriff's Department thinks he did. It's impossible.

They think he caused an accident by trying to steal a deputy's service revolver while the man was driving. They think another man tried stop his escape after the accident and Sandy shot him because of it. They think he's a badly warped record that plays different from the rest of us. Of course he is. He killed his stepfather, so he must also have done what the Sheriff's Department thinks he did.

But something else must have happened.

She wants to believe something else must have happened.

And she would, but for this. She's been worried about her son since last year when she saw what he did to that bird. It was a small bird, a sparrow maybe. It flew into one of the windows, but didn't die. She heard it hit the glass and walked over to see what had happened. Sandy was hunched over it in the dirt, poking it with a stick, watching it twitch and writhe and flap its broken wing in its attempt to escape. He poked at it and refused to let it get away. His eyes were distant. There was a small smile on his lips. She didn't say anything. She told herself he was a boy being a boy, a boy discovering what death was. But it bothered her.

Now that her husband is dead it bothers her more.

But she doesn't want to believe her beautiful boy is a monster. She knows he killed his stepfather, that's indisputable, but that doesn't make him a monster. It doesn't make him anything but a boy who reached his limit.

She should have seen it. She did see it.

But she's seen too that there's sweetness in him. Can monsters have sweetness in them as well as evil? Can they wrap their arms around their mothers' necks and say I love you for no reason at all? Can they make their mothers breakfast in bed simply because they want to be nice?

She doesn't know.

Whatever happened out on that country road, two men are dead and her son's gone missing.

She steps from her car, walks to her front door, and pushes her way into the living room. It feels dark and lonesome. She wishes she could talk to Carl. He understands the overwhelming sense of loss you sometimes feel when you walk into an empty room. She wants to call him and talk to him, but she won't do that, she refuses to do that, refuses to be mistress to a man married to his addiction. She's done it before and won't do it again.

She walks to her new couch and sits down. She stares at the wall and wishes she could go out and look for Sandy, but she'd have no idea where to begin. He could be any-where – anywhere but here. He's not in the kitchen where he took his first steps, or in the bedroom where he spent so many hours sprawled across his bed reading comic books, or at the dining table where he sometimes did math home-work, or out back where he often played alone.

Maybe he'll come back to her.

If he did, would she turn him over to the police? Know-ing what he is, would she do that? She doesn't think she would; she doesn't think she could.

Someone knocks on the front door.

Her first thought, of course, is that it's Sandy. She hopes it is. She hopes it isn't.

She gets to her feet.

3

Carl stands waiting at the door. He watched her walk inside, so he knows she's on the other side of it. She was gone when he first arrived, but turned her car into the driveway only four cigarettes later.

She pulls open the door with a somehow hopeful expression on her face – her eyes wide and expectant, her mouth on the verge of a smile. He removes the fedora from his head and says her name. The hope drops from her face.

'What are you doing here?'

'Hoping to talk to you a minute.'

'I meant what I said. We're done.'

'I can stop.'

'Then stop.'

'You don't understand. I just need to—'

'I can't deal with this right now. I can't deal with *you*.'

'But if you just let me—'

'My son is gone and I don't know where he is. I'm scared and I'm alone and I can't deal with your bullshit right now.'

'Your son is gone? What happened?'

She looks at him for a long time, seems as though she may soften, then shakes her head.

'No.'

She closes the door in his face.

4

Candice watches through the peephole as Carl turns and walks away, head hanging down, shoulders slumped. He drags his feet. Then he's gone, and she's glad that he is. She can't deal with her own troubles and his as well. She simply can't.

But as well as being glad she's sorry.

5

Carl sits behind the wheel of his car, which is parked across the street from his house. He has the window rolled down and a breeze blows against his face. Since he began using he has experienced fewer and fewer moments during which he feels neither wasted nor sick, but he's experiencing one of those moments now. He feels almost like the man he was before Naomi died. It makes him feel strong. It makes him feel he doesn't need the junk. He should stop taking it. Friedman was right. Candice was right. He should stop taking it, and he can. He knows he can.

He should also tell his wife goodbye. If he told his wife goodbye his continuing to live without her wouldn't feel like a betrayal. He should tell her I loved you more than I ever loved anything or anyone and I don't know how to live without you in my life, and I'm afraid of sitting at our dinner table and looking across it to an empty chair, but you're gone and I have to say goodbye. I have to say goodbye because even though I'm afraid of facing my life without you I'm more afraid that you will haunt me forever. So let me go, let me go, let me go.

He pushes out of the car and walks across the street and stands on the sidewalk in front of his house and looks at it. His haunted house. The most terrible thing about it is that the ghost within it is kind.

Don't soothe me while I say goodbye. It only makes it

harder. Don't tell me it's okay when it isn't okay and can't be.

He walks up the path to the front door, his front door, over whose threshold he carried Naomi on the day they moved in. They'd been married two years already, but this was their first home, their only home. Before they bought it they lived in a furnished apartment on De Longpre. He looks at the brass handle. He looks at the keyhole. They had no furniture their first two days, so they made love on the floor and slept in sleeping bags. Then Sears & Roebuck delivered their furniture, and they slept together in bed, the same bed which even now sits inside holding Naomi's scent within its fabric.

He closes his eyes.

Go in and tell her goodbye. It's what you have to do, so do it.

I will. Right now. I'm going to reach forward right now and unlock the door, then I'll push into the living room and—

He turns away from the door and walks back to his car.

THIRTY-NINE

1

Leland Jones stumbles from the bar, the evening air cool and crisp. He was in darkness, inhaling stale air for hours, so stepping outside feels a bit like stepping from a dream with the dream still clinging to him. As a boy he felt this way when he left a movie theater following a double feature. He'd been so caught up in the film experience that it still seemed more real than reality, even as he walked through reality. The films were more vibrant and alive than the small Texas town he lived in.

But now he's caught in a different kind of dream.

When he first arrived at the bar he simply sat hunched over his beer, drinking slowly, thinking the situation through and wondering what he might do about it. But the more he drank the angrier he got. He began telling the barkeep what was on his mind.

The district attorney is a miserable son of a bitch, ruined my life. Thinks he can just kick me like a bad dog and he won't get bit. He's got a surprise coming. Leland Jones has teeth. I'm gonna make that no-good son of a bitch pay for what he done to me. He ruined my life and I'm gonna make him pay for it. You see if I don't.

He feels disoriented and unsteady. And he feels angry.

He squints at the darkening sky. Night is coming. The moon visible as well as the egg-yolk sun, which is spilling across the horizon. Thin haloed clouds scud by overhead. The brighter stars have begun revealing themselves, making the sky look like a nonsensical connect-the-dots picture.

That cocksucker.

He walks to his truck and slides in behind the wheel. He starts the engine. It rumbles to life.

He's gonna make that son of a bitch pay, and unlike this morning, ain't nothin gonna stop him. He won't be able to live with himself if he lets the district attorney get away with what he's done. He won't feel like a man.

He puts the truck into gear and pulls out into the street.

2

To get home Seymour Markley should pull out of the parking structure and turn left on Main, heading north. He turns right instead. He knows better than to do this. He knows what it will lead to. He should stop immediately. He should turn his car around. If he doesn't turn his car around he'll end up doing something he regrets. He's certain of it. Nearly certain of it. Nearly certain, yes, but it doesn't have to be that way. He might merely stop in somewhere for a drink or two. He could absorb a little atmosphere and, having done that, head home to his wife, whom he loves very much. But he won't go straight home. Today has been stressful, today has been nothing but the world collapsing down around him while he tries desperately to hold it up, and he needs to forget it. He needs to go somewhere where nothing is required of him. It doesn't mean anything untoward will happen. It doesn't mean anything at all. Besides, he already called home and told Margaret he was working late. If he goes straight home she'll think he was lying when he called. So he has to follow through. He'll have a few drinks and leave. If he wanted a whore he could go to any number of places in Hollywood. Or he could rent a hotel room, make a phone call, and have one delivered. That isn't what he's after. What he's after is a few drinks in a relaxed environment, and that's all. He works hard. He deserves that much. No one would say different.

He cannot believe he's doing this. After how close he came to losing his career and his wife he cannot believe he's doing this.

Maybe he isn't. Maybe he's merely driving somewhere to get a few drinks. Maybe he just wants to sit in a room where no one will make any demands on him. Every time the phone rings it's a problem or a question. Every time there's a knock on his office door it's the same. He goes home and his wife wants to know if she can buy some new curtains she saw in a catalogue and she talked to Ophelia down the street, how about they invite the Loorys over for dinner and cocktails on Friday, they're such delightful people. A man deserves reprieve.

No one would say different.

He parks on Washington Boulevard in front of a crumbling stucco building with

The Pink Flamingo

hand-lettered across the facade above the door and a painting of the same just to the right of it. He steps from his vehicle, feeling excited about the evening's possibilities while simultaneously denying they exist. He'll simply drink his drinks and watch the crowd and enjoy the music. He can do that.

He pushes into the Pink Flamingo and stands for a moment by the door.

The place is dimly lit. A few lighted signs hang on the walls advertising Schlitz and Ballantine and Budweiser. A jukebox in the corner plays Billie Holiday's rendition of 'Mon Homme', her silken voice explaining how she dreams of a cottage by a stream with her man. Two couples are dancing to the song, but it's early yet, and except for them and five ladies lining the bar like birds on a telephone wire the place is empty.

He walks to the counter and orders vodka with a twist. He sips it and glances toward the five ladies at the bar. He smiles at them and they smile back, one even waving like a beauty queen on a float, then he turns away and carries his drink to a table in the corner, only a few feet from the jukebox. He likes the music loud, he likes it to overwhelm him. It makes thinking impossible, which is just what he requires of these evenings: the cessation of all thought.

This is the third time he's been here, and he knows there's a room in the back where the ladies will take you if you respond correctly to their signals. If you don't, they'll simply ask you to buy them drinks and flirt and touch your thigh suggestively. But really, the choice is yours.

He sits down and sips his vodka. The couples on the floor continue to dance. They smile as they dance, looking natural, looking like they're having a swell time; you'd never know from looking at them that their arrangement is a financial one.

Buy me another drink, sugar?

That isn't anything he's going to do tonight.

He's here for a few cocktails and nothing more.

The Billie Holiday song ends and the jukebox changes records. The needle drops once more and after a moment of crackling there's a blast of horns. The horns give way to Lorenzo Fuller singing 'Too Darn Hot'.

One of the five ladies at the bar, a blonde woman with

her lips painted burgundy, a blonde woman in a black dress that hides none of her curves, peels herself from the stool on which she's been perched and sways her way toward Seymour.

'I remember you.'

'Do you?'

'Mm-hm.'

She sits in a chair across from him, her leg brushing against his leg.

'Do you mind if I sit down?'

'It's a free country.'

'That's what I hear,' she says, 'but it seems these days everything has a price tag on it. How'd you like to buy me a drink?'

'I don't know,' Seymour says, feeling a familiar fluttering in his stomach and an anticipatory heat between his legs. He licks his lips. 'I wasn't really planning on meeting anyone tonight.'

'That's why one should never plan.'

Seymour lets his hands drop to his lap and pulls his wedding band off his finger. He hates himself. He hates himself for this. He knew this would happen. He knew he shouldn't come here exactly because this would happen.

'Okay,' he says, 'sure.'

'Oh goody,' she says, 'I'm very thirsty.'

She waves to the bartender. He nods at her.

Seymour slips his wedding band into his waistcoat's watch pocket.

3

Leland pulls to the curb about half a block from the Pink Flamingo and watches the district attorney step from his car and head into the place. He can't believe this son of a bitch. He gets blackmailed for his whoremongering and only a week later, a week and a day later, drives to a joint whose B-girls go horizontal for ten dollars and a please. The dumb motherfucker deserves to get blackmailed – a bigshot lawyer and not enough brains in his head to keep a parrot operating at full speed.

He deserved what he got and he deserves what he's gonna get too.

And if he thinks Leland Jones will slink off with his tail between his legs, he's got another think coming.

Leland grips the steering wheel with both fists, grips it tight, and twists as if wringing out a washcloth. He clenches his teeth. He watches the door. The leather of the wheel feels grainy in his grip.

That son of a bitch. That motherfucker.

4

Seymour Markley, still fully dressed but with his belt undone and his fly open, lies on his back while the blonde woman whose name he's already forgotten, with her dress hitched up around her waist, lowers herself onto him. He grips the cot on which he lies with one hand while with the other he reaches up and strokes one of her breasts. He hates himself. He hates himself for what he's doing. Why did he let it come to this? Why did he let this whore lead him back here and push him down, reach into his pocket and pull money from his wallet, unzip his fly and stroke him? Why did he let her roll a condom onto his penis? Why did he let her lower herself onto him, wrap herself around him? Why did he allow her to make him betray his wife? He knew it would come to this. He never should have allowed it to come to this. He never should have come here. He knew better. Oh, God.

The orgasm arrives all at once, with almost no build-up.

He thrusts twice and it's finished.

The blonde woman leans down and kisses his temple, her breasts pushing against his chest. Then she pulls herself off of him, walks to a sink against the far wall, grabs a washcloth from the counter, and wets it. She wipes between her legs, the inside of her thighs, her sex. She tosses the wet washcloth into a laundry pile in the corner. Seymour tries not to wonder how many sexual partners such a pile might account for. The blonde woman lets the dress fall.

'I'm gonna head out,' she says, 'get cleaned up if you want to.'

Then she's gone.

Seymour sits up on the cot. He looks down at his now flaccid penis wrapped in a glistening condom that seems, with his erection gone, far too large for what it's wrapped around. The tip of the condom hangs down warm against his leg, filled with ejaculate. He knows he must remove it but doesn't want to touch it. What if she's diseased? He might get whatever she has on his fingers, and then, if he rubs his eyes, contract it. Can one get syphilis through the eye? He isn't certain.

He shouldn't have done this. He shouldn't have let this happen.

He peels the condom off with two fingers and throws it into a trash can, then walks to the sink, cleans himself off with a wash cloth, and scrubs his hands vigorously, scraping beneath the nails.

He feels sick.

How is he going to sit across from his wife and eat meat loaf when he's done what he's done?

He zips up his pants and fastens his belt. He wonders if his underwear might smell like sex. He'll have to throw them away. He doesn't want Margaret to find them in the laundry if they do. What if she smells it on them?

He turns around and sees a poster hanging above the cot on which he lay with the blonde woman.

BEWARE OF CHANCE ACQUAINTANCES

it says in capital letters at the top, below which is a picture of a man with a mustache hitting on a young woman. And below that:

'Pick up' acquaintances often take girls autoriding to cafes, and to theaters with the intention of leading them into sexual relations. Disease or childbirth may follow.

Avoid the man who tries to take liberties with you. He is selfishly thoughtless and inconsiderate of you.

Believe no one who says it is necessary to indulge sex desire.

Know the men you associate with!

Seymour looks at the poster for a long time. Whoever tacked it on that particular wall above that particular cot meant it as some sort of joke, but he doesn't find it the least bit amusing. It makes him feel ill.

He walks out of the back room and into the main bar, and then through the main bar to the front door. He doesn't look around. He keeps his head down. He's too embarrassed by what he's done to look anyone in the eye, even unintentionally. They would immediately know every shameful thing he's guilty of.

He cannot believe he let this happen. He cannot believe he did this.

He pushes through the door and out onto the sidewalk.

The sky overhead is dark but for the moon hanging like a paper lantern. The air is cool, but the breeze carries on it the scent of exhaust fumes.

'You son of a bitch.'

His head snaps to the right, toward the sound of the

voice. He blinks, trying to see clearly in the darkness. A hulking figure in a cowboy hat comes at him.

'You motherfucker,' the hulking figure says in a voice Seymour almost recognizes. Almost but not quite.

He takes a step back, puts up both hands.

Then the figure in the cowboy hat is upon him and the face beneath the hat is clearly visible. Leland Jones. His eyes are black with rage and glossy with drink. His fists are clenched.

Seymour takes a second step back, fear overwhelming him.

And then the violence begins.

5

Leland yanks the wheel to the right, but the goddamn pickup's going too fast to make the turn. Instead of swinging into the driveway, it jumps up the curb and comes to a skidding stop in the middle of their front yard. Leland lets it stay there. He kills the engine and steps from the vehicle. His hands are covered in blood, some of it his own from split knuckles, most of it the district attorney's. His face and shirt are speckled with more of it.

He walks to the front door and into the house. He stands by the doorway, sweaty and bloody and feeling frantic.

'Viv,' he says.

If she's left for work he doesn't know what he'll do, but she shouldn't have left quite yet. It's too early. He tries to remember whether he saw her car parked out on the street, but isn't sure. He didn't look.

He calls her name again.

She walks out of the bathroom with a towel wrapped around her torso and another on her head. 'What is it?'

'Do you love me, darlin?'

'What's wrong?'

'Do you love me?'

'Of course. What is it?'

'Would you love me even if I done something terrible?'

'Is that blood?'

'I done something terrible. I need to leave town.'

'What did you do?'

Leland licks his lips. His entire body shakes with adrenalin. He tries to calm himself, tries to think. He closes his eyes. He opens them. He can't bring himself to tell her what he did.

'You said you always wanted to see where I come from.'

Vivian, silent for a very long time, searches his face for answers.

Finally she nods.

'Okay,' she says.

FORTY

1

Candice reaches into her dress and lifts her breasts, pushing them together to create more cleavage. They're sticky with sweat and feel heavy in her hands. She leans forward slightly and looks at herself in the mirror, tries to smile but can't make it look real, can't bring light into her eyes. She hopes the makeup can at least hide their puffy redness, the fact that she's been crying.

She'll do the best she can tonight.

Maybe once the evening begins in earnest she'll forget about her real life. Maybe the music, flirtation, dancing, and drinks, watered-down though they are, will help her briefly forget everything. She doesn't think so, doesn't think anything could make her forget that her husband is dead, doesn't think anything could make her forget that her thirteen-year-old son is a murderer, or that he's missing, doesn't think even the junk Carl shoots into his veins could make her forget those things, but maybe she's wrong. Maybe there will be a moment, just one, in which she's able to feel like herself again. Maybe something will make her laugh. Or distract her enough that, for a time, she's completely free of thought and worry.

She picks up a compact and clicks it open, loads the applicator with powder, and is bringing it toward her face when a knock at the front door stops her. She sets the compact back down on the counter.

She hopes she doesn't find Carl on the other side. It'd be one thing if she didn't care for him. She could slam the door in his face and that would be that. That's the way it should be. But it was difficult to shut him out the way she did. It was difficult, and she doesn't know if she has the strength to do it again. A big part of her wants him around to lean on. But she knows, too, that he isn't really present most of the time. He's only a husk, and there's no point leaning on a husk. There's nothing solid within to support you. It could blow away in the wind. Certainly it would crumble beneath your weight. You might as well try leaning on a column of smoke.

Anyway, she hopes it isn't Carl.

She walks to the front door and looks through the peephole but sees no one and nothing but empty space. After a moment's hesitation she pulls open the door. The welcome mat is empty but for a small bundle of white flowers. Several of them still have brown clods of dirt hanging from them, held in place by thin roots.

She leans down and picks them up and smells them, earthy and pleasant with a slight pollen sharpness. It reminds her of being a teenager. When she was fifteen she was courted by an eighteen-year-old Mexican boy named Albert. He gave her flowers like this and they went for walks. Once they did more than walk. She lay back and let him take her virginity. It was sweet and awkward and brief. She wonders what happened to him, but supposes she'll never know.

She smells the flowers again. She wants to bring them into the house and put them in water, but something tells her she shouldn't. They're sure to be from Carl, she can think of no one else who'd leave flowers for her, and she doesn't want to be reminded of him every time she looks at them over the course of the next week.

He was a mistake and she doesn't want to think about it.

She tosses them aside, into the dirt to the left of the porch, looks toward them briefly with some regret, and closes the door.

Then she heads back to the bathroom. She has to finish getting ready for work.

2

Sandy watches from down the street, from behind a car. His mother opens the front door, looks around briefly, and then looks down. She picks up the flowers he left for her and smells them. It makes him smile to see her there. He misses her very much. Seeing her makes a large part of him wish that he could take it all back. If he could take it all back he could run up to her right now and hug her. He knows he's supposed to be strong now. He knows the gun tucked into his pants is supposed to make him bigger than he really is. But seeing his mother makes him feel like a little boy.

She throws the flowers to the ground, steps inside, shuts the door.

She hates him now. She must hate him now to throw his flowers away. He left them for her to let her know he was okay, to let her know he loved her, and she didn't care. She threw them to the ground and shut the door.

That's it, then. He needs to stop thinking about her. He really *is* on his own. He knew he couldn't go home, knew he couldn't talk to her no matter how much he wanted to, but he thought he still had a mother somewhere. Now he knows he doesn't. He has no one. He closes his eyes. He tells himself that men don't cry. Men are big and strong. They don't say please, they don't say thank you, and they never, ever cry.

He turns and walks away from there, walks down to Macy Street and heads west, toward Hollywood.

He never should have come here. It's getting late. It's getting dark. Unless he goes back to the house he broke into earlier he has nowhere to sleep, and it doesn't seem worth it. It's far away, and he has no car and no money. He's hungry again. He wishes he could steal a car like hoodlums in movies do, but he doesn't know how. He doesn't know how to do anything. He's just a stupid little kid and he doesn't know how to do anything and he was stupid for thinking he did. He was stupid for thinking he could do this on his own. He wishes he was tough and crazy like James Cagney, but he isn't. He's just a stupid little kid. No wonder everybody hates him. No wonder the other kids wipe boogers on his clothes and push him and punch him. He's no good. He never was any good. It was only a matter of time before his mother saw it too. No wonder she threw those flowers away. If he was her he'd have thrown them away too. And ground them into the dirt with his foot. If he was tough like James Cagney he would've pulled out his gun earlier and taken all the money from that stupid shop. He wouldn't have run. That's not what toughs do. But he isn't a tough, is he? He tries to be but he isn't.

He wipes at his eyes with the heels of his hands and tells himself to stop being a baby. He reaches into his pocket and pulls out his packet of cigarettes. He lights one. He takes a drag, inhaling the smoke, and coughs. He takes a second drag.

He can be tough like James Cagney if he wants to be. He can be crazy like him too. He knows he can. He can make it on his own.

He's a vicious dog. He's a wild horse.

He's killed people.

He doesn't need anybody.

He reaches into his pants and pulls out the gun. It feels heavy in his hand. He rubs his thumb against the hammer spur, feeling the grooves in the metal. He can see a liquor store up ahead. There are lights on. He's going to rob it.

He's going to take all their money.

And he won't say please.

And he won't say thank you.

3

Candice parks her car in the lot behind the Sugar Cube and steps into the night. She looks toward the dark sky. She likes its depth, the way it just goes on and on. She closes her eyes and experiences the same depth in the other direction. That she likes less. She opens her eyes and walks into the bar through the back door. She makes her way through the stock room, past boxes of liquor and wine and beer, into the front of the place. It's just beginning to come to life with talk and laughter.

She scans the room for Vivian, but there's no sign of her.

She does, however, see Heath sitting at a table sipping a glass of Johnnie Walker Black and watching the room.

She walks over and asks about Vivian.

'She called in.'

'She all right?'

'Didn't say.'

'How'd she sound?'

'Fine. But you don't need to worry about it. You been through too much as it is. I don't even think you should be back at work yet.'

'I don't have anything else to do.'

He doesn't respond. Eventually he looks away.

She stands there a moment, then turns toward the bar. There she sees a gentleman in a suit sitting alone, sipping his drink, looking around the room. She walks over and slides onto the stool to his right, hoping he can help her temporarily escape herself.

'You look lonely,' she says.

He turns toward her and smiles.

FORTY-ONE

Eugene twists the key, listens to the thwack of the deadbolt as it retracts, and pushes open the door. He knows the room's supposed to be empty, but his mouth is dry and his heart beats erratically in his chest. Last time he did something like this he ended up stumbling upon a couple corpses, and is still wanted by the police because of it.

He steps inside and closes the door behind him. No one else is here.

A bed fills the room, nightstands resting against the wall to its left and right. A Gold Medal paperback, something called *The Brass Cupcake* by John D. MacDonald, sits open on one of the nightstands, its narrow spine broken. A chair sits in the far right corner with a pinstriped suit coat draped over its arm. A desk and a lamp. An oak dresser with two suitcases resting on top of it, laundry piled high on the floor beside it.

A lived-in hotel room.

He pulls the switchblade knife from his pocket and walks to the nearest nightstand. He opens the drawer. But for a Gideon bible the drawer is empty. He sets the switchblade knife in the drawer beside the bible and pushes it closed. He walks to the dresser. A large leather suitcase sits on top of it beside a small square leatherette case. He begins with the large suitcase, unlatching it and looking through the contents. He finds socks, underpants, some T-shirts, half a bottle of whiskey, and a dress shirt. The dress shirt's presence in the suitcase is strange. It's the only piece of clothing which should be on a hanger. It's the only piece of clothing that looks to have been worn. He picks it up. A bit of color catches his eye, blood on the left cuff. A few drops like an ellipsis. But enough for the police to find if they search the room thoroughly.

Evelyn might be right. They might simply be able to pin those murders on Louis Lynch. They belong to him, anyway. Come here, sweetie, let Momma stick this note to your shirt so you don't lose it on the way to school.

But Eugene doesn't think a switchblade knife and a shirt with blood on it will be enough to do the job. That police detective, Bachman, saw him at the murder scene, saw him drop one of the murder weapons. A knife and a few splashes of blood won't convince him that someone else did the murders. Without a story to make them mean something, a knife and a shirt are just random items. Even if the police searched this room and found them, Eugene would remain the most likely suspect. The police have a story for him. They have motive, and they have him at the scene. They search this room, what do they have? A switchblade knife like a million other switchblade knives and a few drops of blood that could be the result of careless shaving.

He closes the suitcase. He needs more.

He looks to the small leatherette case. He unlatches it and pulls open the top, revealing a black Royal typewriter. He looks down at its QWERTY grin.

What were you expecting, the queen of England?

For some time he merely stands there unthinking. Then turns in a circle, looking around the room, not quite sure what he's looking for. Then once more looking at the typewriter it comes to him. He needs a piece of paper. He walks to the desk and finds a few sheets of hotel stationery there. He peels off the top sheet and rolls it into the typewriter. He stares down at the keys for a long time, puts his fingers against them. The gloves provide a distance he doesn't like. It makes him feel disconnected from what he's doing. He misses the feel of cool plastic against the pads of his fingers. He begins typing, simply banging out the first words that come to mind:

```
In the beginning God created the heavens
and the earth and the earth was without form
and void and darkness was upon the face of
the deep and God hovered over the surface of
the water.
```

He looks down at the words hammered into the paper. The ribbon needs replacing. The letters are light gray and difficult to read. The 't' is angled to the right, making it look like a malformed 'x'. The 'h' sits higher on the line than the other letters.

This, he can do something with. He knows it. But he needs a story and he has no idea what that story will be.

Could he simply call the police and let them know this room is here? Would they create their own story? This typewriter is the typewriter on which his blackmail note was hammered out. He left the note on his table at home, so the police are certain to have picked it up. The switchblade knife in the nightstand is of the same kind as that which was used to stab the cop who he is suspected of murdering. The blood on the shirt cuff is evidence that something happened. It is, at least, if you add in the other evidence. And the police should be able to match the blood type to one of the victims. Would a simple phone call be enough? He thinks there's a chance it would.

But there's still a problem, and not a small one. Even if Louis Lynch takes the fall for his own murders, the Man will never let Eugene live.

He needs to think of a way to finish this once and for all, but his mind is blank. There was a time when he was good at creating stories, but that time is gone.

Then something does come. It isn't a full story, but it might be enough to get him started. If it goes wrong it might end in his death, and there's a good chance it will go wrong. Unlike Evelyn's plan, this one is no hammer. But it's the only thing he can think of that might also end with him walking away free and clear, neither wanted by the police for murder nor wanted murdered by the Man.

And doesn't he deserve that?

He'll have to do some ugly things. Merely thinking about what he'll have to do makes his stomach ache. But the only people he'll be hurting are those responsible for putting him in this situation in the first place, and if anybody deserves to face harsh consequences for what's happened, it's them.

He pulls the paper from the typewriter and folds it up and puts it into his pocket. He'll burn it later. He puts the lid on the typewriter case, latching it, and pushes it back into place. He'll need to use it again, but not yet. He'll have to return once he knows more about how he's going to approach this. For now he has other things to take care of, the first of which is getting out of here.

He looks around the room, making certain everything is back the way it was when he arrived, then steps into the corridor and latches the door behind him. He walks to the elevator, takes it down to the lobby, leaves his address at the front desk with the message that Evelyn should come see him as soon as she gets in.

He heads out into the night.

He wishes he could think of another way out of this,

but he has no choice. He's been put in a corner and this is his way out.

He kicks his motorcycle to life and pulls out into the street. He heads toward his motel room, where he will await Evelyn's arrival.

THE ABANDONED WAREHOUSE

FORTY-TWO

1

In the dream, they finally catch up with him. He isn't sure how. He's been walking down and down constantly for months – years, decades – and no one went past him, but one of the cannibals managed to get below him anyway, managed to get in front of him and block his downward journey. This lone cannibal now stands in rags before Eugene, slump-shouldered but full of vitality and madness. His skin jaundiced, the color of a fading bruise. His eyes bloodshot, the eyelids red-rimmed and raw. His hands are black. His beard thick with filth and glistening with oily moisture around the mouth. He grins, revealing yellow teeth from which the white gums are receding bloody and swollen. He reaches into a leather satchel and removes a human heart. It throbs in his hand. He holds it out to Eugene. Thick strands of blood run off it, dripping from ragged meat-hoses, splashing to the concrete floor.

'It's the boy's,' the cannibal says. 'We saved it for you.'

'No,' Eugene says, shaking his head. 'Thank you, but . . . but no . . . no.'

He turns around, heading back up the stairs. He doesn't know where he'll go. He simply knows he must get away. The cannibal doesn't follow him, but as he reaches the next landing he hears the others only a floor above, and they're heading down.

They've pinned him in. Somehow they managed to pin him in. He looks to his right and sees a door. He can't go up and he can't go down, but he can go through the door. He pushes into a corridor, the door slamming shut behind him. He walks down the corridor despite the fact he knows there's nowhere to go.

The overhead lights flicker.

The door behind him opens and closes, followed by the shuffling of feet.

He looks over his shoulder.

The cannibals walk slowly after him, the one with the heart in his hand leading the way.

He looks forward once more and continues his retreat. He walks to the end of the corridor and steps into the last door on the left, the only place to go. It's an office like all the other offices. There's a desk against the wall with a typewriter and a telephone on it. A chair pushed up to the desk. A sheet of blank paper rolled into the typewriter.

He walks to the window and looks out.

The sky is gray. Lightning flashes in the distance. Sheets of clouds block his view of the ground below. He still has no idea how close he is to the bottom, no idea what floor he might be on. He wonders if he's any nearer escape than when he began. He supposes he must be. The ground is down there somewhere and he's been steadily heading toward it.

A voice behind him: 'There's only one way out.'

He turns around.

The cannibals stand in the doorway.

The one with the heart in his hand holds it out toward him. Behind the beating heart he grins with yellow teeth.

'You must be hungry.'

'No,' Eugene says, backing away. 'No.'

But then he's against the wall and can back away no further.

'You haven't eaten for months,' the cannibal says, pushing the beating heart toward his face.

It smells of iron; it smells of blood.

He turns his head away.

'It's the only way out,' the cannibal says. 'You'll see. Eat.'

Then: a strange knocking sound from within the walls. The floor drops out from under him and he's swept into a brief blackness before sitting up in bed.

Someone is knocking on the hotel-room door. It must be Evelyn.

What time is it? He picks up his glasses and puts

them on. He looks at his watch to see it's just past midnight.

He hadn't planned on falling asleep. He was only going to lie down a moment, exhale some of this tension he feels. But he did fall asleep, and he's now disoriented. He feels lost, detached from everything that's happening. He isn't ready for this. He isn't at all ready for this.

Doesn't matter what he's ready for. Evelyn is here. It's time.

He inhales, exhales.

It's time.

He gets to his feet, turns on the lamp. As well as the rest of the room it illuminates a roll of duct tape, a pair of leather gloves, and his Baby Browning. They sit beside one another on the room's rickety dining table.

How's he going to do this?

He doesn't want to hurt Evelyn but needs her immobile, and the only way he can think to get her that way is with a fight. She won't simply sit still while he tapes her up, and he can't hold a gun on her to force her to, because if he's close enough to tape her up he's close enough for her to take the gun away and turn it around on him, and she would. This is the business she's in. He's a mere tourist.

She knocks again and says his name.

'I'll be right there.'

He picks up the pistol and tucks it into his pants.

He walks to the door, pulls it open.

Evelyn stands on the other side, the black night behind

her. Her red hair frames her pale, slender, reptilian face. Her blue eyes are large and glossy with alcohol. Her red lips are moist. She smiles when she sees him.

'How'd it go?'

'Why don't you come on in?'

'You're starting to trust me.'

She steps into the room and walks to the bed and sits down. She kicks off her heels and rubs her feet against one another and splays her toes as much as her pantyhose will allow. He closes the door and puts his back to it. He stands looking at her and she looks back smiling her beautiful-ugly smile.

She pats the bed beside her with a slender-fingered hand.

'Let's talk,' she says.

He thinks of the pistol tucked into his pants.

Pull it out, Eugene, use it to smash her nose to smithereens. Tape her up while she's incapacitated. It's going to get ugly eventually, you might as well start it ugly. Do it now before she suspects anything. This is your best chance and you know it.

He walks to the bed and sits down.

She puts a hand on his thigh, rubs the flat of her palm against his leg. Even through the thick fabric of his pants her touch brings goosebumps out on his flesh.

'How'd it go?'

'He has a shirt with blood on it in his suitcase. He also still has the typewriter he typed the blackmail note on.

Typewriters have distinctive prints, same as people. And the police must've picked up the note from my table when they searched my apartment, so they're sure to put them together. And I put the knife in a drawer.'

'You wore gloves?'

Eugene nods.

'Good. Then it's all set up.'

'It is.'

'We can call the police tomorrow and end it.'

Just do it, Eugene. If you don't want to hurt her face, take the gun out and hit her in the back of the head. Hit the soft spot at the back of her skull and knock her out. Do it and get it over with. There's no sense in prolonging any of this.

He nods. 'Tomorrow.'

'Then tonight is ours,' she says. She rubs her hand up the inside of his thigh to his groin. He pulls away.

'You're drunk.'

'I want to feel close to you, Gene. We're almost on the other side of this and I want to feel close to you.'

She leans in, puts her mouth against his mouth. He can taste the whiskey she's been drinking, both sharp and earthy. At first he doesn't respond to her kiss, tells himself this can't happen, but it does happen, and he finds himself pushing his mouth against hers, biting her lip. He loves her taste and her scent. She smells of that flowery perfume of hers and beneath that sweat and salt and sex. He reaches to her neck and strokes her smooth skin. Then moves his hand down her chest, across her breasts, feeling them through the fine thin fabric of her clothes.

You're being stupid, Eugene. You need to get on with this. You let her seduce you you'll fall in love with her all over again and won't be able to follow through with it. Then where will you be? Prison, that's where. Or dead.

She reaches her hand into his pants and stops, pulls back from the kiss blinking at him in surprise. She removes her hand from his pants. In it, his pistol. She looks down at it for a time with an unreadable expression on her face, then smiles.

'You won't be needing this anymore.'

She leans over and sets it on the nightstand.

'Now where were we? Oh, that's right.'

She pushes Eugene so that he falls back on the bed. He picks up his head as he lies there and looks toward her. She gets to her feet, reaches up under her dress, and pulls down her pantyhose. She almost falls as she pulls them around her left heel and kicks them away while hopping on her right foot, but manages to catch herself on the edge of the bed before going down, and laughs at her own clumsiness. Once she regains her balance she stands and looks at him smiling.

Her eyes full of knowledge she's ready to impart.

2

Evelyn steps forward, looking at this man lying before her. He's beautiful and intelligent and mean enough that she might not destroy him as she's destroyed others who came before. She can be a hard woman and cold, has long suspected her heart dead or absent, but he's brought feeling to that previously numb part of her. She can imagine a future with him, backyard cookouts, angry fights over trivial matters, makeup sex. She can imagine bearing his children. Their boys will be hellraisers and their girl will be a heartbreaker. Like she was.

Now that this is almost finished she allows herself to believe in the possibility of that future. She knows things can still go wrong. She knows the future is unpredictable. But it seems to her things very well might work out.

She allows herself to believe in the possibility.

Her biggest concern is Daddy. If Eugene isn't wanted for those two murders, or convicted of them, Daddy will consider him a problem; he knows too much, and people who know too much about Daddy's business tend to die.

They'll have to leave before that can happen. They'll have to pack their bags and go away, take a ship across the Atlantic, live in Paris or London.

They'll think of something together.

But first they get through this. First they clear Eugene's name.

They can worry about what comes after once there is an after.

She leans forward and puts her hands on his knees and runs them up the inside of his thighs. She unbuttons his pants and pulls them down to his knees, smiling to herself as he gasps. She leans forward and kisses his slightly protruding stomach, runs her tongue along the line of hair leading to his belly button. The stink of his sweat is strong, but she likes it. He smells like man. She strokes his penis and feels it stiffen and grow in her hand and likes that feeling of power. She did that with her mere touch. She puts her mouth around him and tastes salt and teases him with her tongue.

He reaches down and runs his fingers through her hair and brushes them along the back of her neck, pushing himself deeper into her mouth. She likes his touch, and the strength of his desire, but she pushes his hand away and holds it down against the mattress. She's in charge of this and will not be led. She takes her mouth off of him. She strokes his penis slowly. Then stops. She runs her fingernails along the inside of his thighs. She smiles and crawls on top of him.

'I want you inside.'

3

Eugene lies in bed, staring at the ceiling, Evelyn asleep on her stomach beside him. His hand rests comfortably on her naked bottom. His penis lies limp and sticky against his leg. Now's the time to do this. He can take her by surprise. If he doesn't do it now he'll never do it, and he'll end up dead.

That's how he needs to think about it. He must get to Manning before Manning gets to him, and the only way he's certain he can do that is through his daughter. Otherwise he must accept that people like him, little people of no importance, are mere pawns to be moved about and sacrificed as needed, and he refuses to be a pawn. He refuses to be sacrificed. Which means he needs to stop bellyaching about what must be done and do it.

He slips out of bed and picks up his pants from the floor. He puts his legs into them, pulls them up, buttons them. He walks to the table and puts on the leather gloves. He picks up the duct tape. He looks over to the bed where Evelyn lies asleep, her face calm, a smile on her lips. Her pale back is smooth and beautiful. He'd much rather kiss the freckles down the length of her spine than do what he's about to do.

He inhales and exhales in jagged breaths. He tries to think of an alternative to what he's about to do. He could get on his motorcycle and ride away. He could simply leave all this. He could do that, but it would solve nothing. He'd still be wanted for murder. It wouldn't matter where he went or what he did, it would always hang over him. He can't live like that. These last few days during which he's been wanted for murder have been the hardest of his life. He can't imagine living in such a state for years.

But he doesn't want to do what he's about to do. He believes Evelyn's being straight with him. He believes she cares for him. He knows he cares for her. He doesn't want to destroy that. But he's afraid he must. He's certain of it.

Or they could follow through on Evelyn's plan. Afterwards maybe she could get him a meeting with her father. He could explain that all he cared about was getting his life back and now that he's got it back he wants only to live it, to live it with Evelyn. Maybe that would be enough.

No. He knows better than that.

He has only one choice. If he cares at all about his own survival he has but one choice, and it doesn't matter how much he hates it.

The alternative is death.

He looks again at Evelyn lying peacefully in bed and wants more than anything to lie beside her. To feel the warmth of her body against his body. He wants to wake beside her and look into her eyes and regret nothing.

But, so far as he can tell, that isn't possible.

He pulls the end of the duct tape, listening to it peel off the roll. Evelyn stirs but doesn't awaken. Soon she will – to an ugly surprise.

He exhales in a heavy sigh.

Then steps forward quickly, rushing toward Evelyn. He puts his knee into her neck to hold her down, pulls her arms behind her back, and wraps her wrists with tape.

She wakes with a scream and fights him, but he doesn't stop.

Not until he's finished.

FORTY-THREE

Carl sits up in bed and tries to read a story called 'I Joined a Gang of Hoods' in the most recent issue of *Stag*, but is finding it impossible to concentrate. Instead his mind turns to his last conversation with Friedman. He went to his partner's house and said we need to talk. He said you're right, I need to get this under control, but now isn't the time. We're wrapping up this case. If I try to quit now I'll get sick, I'll be useless. Let me finish this case, bring in the milkman, then I'll take time off and clean up. I have vacation days coming. I know how you feel about me using, you made that clear, but I need time. Friedman looked at him in silence, then nodded. Keep yourself as clean as possible. Use as little as you need to to keep yourself functioning, but when we wrap up this case you get yourself clean. I mean it. I won't watch you kill yourself. Okay, Carl said. Okay. And about earlier, when I said we weren't friends, I didn't mean it. Friedman nodded, said I know, I'll see you tomorrow at work, Carl, and went inside.

So he bought himself some time, which is good.

And if he finds another source he might not have to quit. It only got out because he was buying from within the department. That was a mistake. He can find another source. He can wave his badge around some jazz club and confiscate what he wants. He won't arrest anybody, he's not that big a hypocrite, just scare them a little and take their junk. Why not? There's no downside.

Except he really does need to quit. He hates that his life now revolves around using. He hates the control it has over him. He lost Candice to it already, and she was the first glimpse of light he'd seen since Naomi's death. For months he's been walking toward a dark horizon and when light finally appears there, a faint white line, he runs in the opposite direction so that he can remain in darkness.

Only a fool would do such a thing.

If he'd known at the beginning this would lead to the needle he'd never have used in the first place. He just wanted a little quiet in his mind. He wanted to get away from himself. And he got what he wanted, didn't he? For a while he got exactly what he wanted. But things have turned and he knows it, and he knows too he needs to do something about it. He needs to quit.

He'll maintain until this case is closed, and then he'll take some time off. He needs to do exactly what he told Friedman he'd do. He needs to regain control of himself and his life. He's fifty-six years old, not twenty. He shouldn't be living in some rooming house making mistakes he knows better than to make.

And what's he going to do about this case?

Neighbors and coworkers have been questioned. Evidence has been catalogued. Reports have been written. The only thing left is to find the guy and arrest him. His picture is out to the uniforms, and his apartment and the bar at which he works are being watched, so it's now nothing but a waiting game.

Part of him hopes they wait forever. Then he never has to quit. The case can remain open till the sun explodes and its fires envelop the earth. That would be good. He could use junk forever and Friedman wouldn't be able to call him a liar.

He needs to quit.

They should follow up with Darryl Castor tomorrow, find out if he learned anything about where the milkman might be.

Then something occurs to him, and he sits up in bed unable to believe a connection he's overlooked until now. They've been operating under the assumption that Eugene Dahl was working alone when he killed Theodore Stuart, but Carl now thinks that Darryl Castor might be reason to doubt that. The man is called Fingers because he has them in everything. He knows everybody. Someone has a product they don't know what to do with, Darryl Castor can find him a buyer. Someone needs something extra delivered with the morning milk, Darryl Castor knows where to get it. There's a chance he worked for James Manning at some point, peddled goods for him. He could easily be the connection between James Manning and Eugene Dahl.

But if that's true, if that's a legitimate piece of the puzzle, it means the picture he's been putting together is wrong. It means he might have to tear the whole thing apart and start again, start with this piece and work outward.

If his mind was clear he'd have thought of this much sooner. He'd have investigated it sooner. He used to be a good cop. He used to take pride in being a good cop. He can't believe he let the junk get to him in this way. It's confused his mind. He's either on the stuff or sick and in need of it.

This job was the only thing he had left that he gave a damn about after Naomi died, and he's thrown it away. He let himself stop caring. He told himself it didn't matter. But he needs to care again, and he *should* care. Despite what he sometimes tells himself, he knows it matters.

He needs to get some sleep. It's late and he needs to get some sleep. His eyes sting and he knows his mind isn't functioning at full capacity. He needs to get some sleep, and tomorrow he needs to start approaching this case like a real cop. He needs to become a real cop again. He needs to start with that new piece of the puzzle and see if he can't put together a different picture.

But not tonight. His brain is too worked over.

He needs rest.

He throws the magazine he'd been reading to the floor, then reaches to the nightstand and clicks off the lamp.

FORTY-FOUR

1

Next morning, with sunlight just beginning to seep in through the curtains, Eugene lights a cigarette and watches Evelyn as she stirs in bed, asleep on her stomach, taped up so she can move neither her arms nor her legs. Until this is finished, he's stuck in a dangerous situation with a dangerous woman. He might still feel love for her, but that's got nothing to do with anything. If they ever had a chance together, and he doesn't think they did, that chance is a thing of the past.

You should kill her. You're going have to do it eventually. You know that, right? If you're to walk away from this situation she can't live to walk away from it herself.

He closes his eyes and pinches the bridge of his nose, lifting his glasses and rubbing the skin where they usually rest.

You don't know that. I might think of a way for her to live.

God, he's tired.

No, you have to kill her. You might as well do it now.

But he can't kill her now. If his plan is going to work she can't have been dead for days when the police find her. They have ways of determining such things.

I can't think like that. She doesn't have to die. I'll think of a way around it.

It's been a long night. He hasn't slept at all.

2

Once her wrists and ankles were taped he rolled her onto her back. She glared at him with tear-filled eyes, a bubble of snot in her left nostril making her look to Eugene like a small child, and called him a motherfucker. I trusted you, you piece of shit. I was willing to give up everything for you, and you do this? She was nude. Her breasts had settled toward her armpits. Her red pubic hair glistened with sweat and flakes of his dried seed. Seeing her that way, nude and vulnerable and once-used, made him feel uncomfortably predacious, so he pulled her into a sitting position and wrapped a sheet around her shoulders.

'I'm sorry. I can't think of another way out of this.'

'Fuck you.' Rage flared in her eyes.

He looked back in silence for some time, then nodded,

resigned to what this situation had become. He turned and walked to her purse. He picked it up and dug through it, found a Berretta 418 in a thigh holster, then the message he'd left her at the front desk, which was what he'd been looking for.

He took that note and the biblical passage he typed earlier in the evening and carried them both to the bathroom sink. He set them on fire and watched them burn. He turned on the water and rinsed the ashes down the drain.

He walked back out to the main room, removed the gloves from his sweaty hands, lit a cigarette. He sat down.

'Whatever your plan is, it won't work.' She turned to look at him after she spoke, the anger now gone from her eyes.

'That so?'

'You know it is. Your hand is shaking.'

He looked at the cigarette pinched between his shivering fingers as a short piece of ash fell from it to his leg. He rubbed it into the fabric of his pants.

'It's been a long day.'

'You're scared. I understand that. But you're being stupid. We had a plan, a good plan, and we can still follow through on it. Lou will take his own fall and that'll be that. We can be together. Isn't that what you want?'

'Lou *will* take his own fall, but it can't happen like you planned.'

'Why?'

'Because of your father.'

'I don't understand.'

'I think you do.'

She looked away a moment, sighed, looked back.

'You mind sharing that cigarette?'

He got to his feet, walked to the bed, sat down beside her. He held the cigarette to her lips and let her take a drag. When he pulled the cigarette away her lipstick was smeared across the end of it. She exhaled.

'We can go away,' she said. 'Together.'

'I want to believe you.'

'But you don't.'

'I don't think you're lying.'

'What *do* you think?'

'I think if we do your plan your dad will know I know too much and want me dead. I think I'm nothing but some guy you met less than a week ago and no matter how much you protest he'll still kill me. And I think that even if your dad by some miracle does let me live you've already destroyed my life once and no matter what you say now, no matter how sincerely, if we're together for long enough you'll do it again. I can't let that happen.'

She looked at him with red eyes.

'Give me another drag.'

He held the cigarette to her lips. She inhaled.

'Is that it then?'

'I guess it is.'

'You're making a mistake.'

'I'm sorry, Evelyn.'

She opens her eyes to see a nicotine-stained wall. She smells cigarette smoke. The room is cool. Her right shoulder aches with a bone-deep pain. She's confused, doesn't know where she is. She tries to sit up, tries to reach out and push herself into a sitting position, but something holds her hands behind her back. After a moment she remembers. She rolls over and with her stomach muscles pulls herself up into a sitting position. She looks across the room. Eugene sits in a chair. A cigarette between his fingers sends smoke wafting toward the ceiling. He looks tired, haggard. She can almost feel sorry for him. She understands what he's going through. She thinks she does, anyway, to some degree. But she can't let him do what he plans to do. She isn't even certain of what it is, but she knows she needs to stop it. It was her job to come out to the West Coast and clean things up; instead she only managed to smear the mess around.

She was stupid to think she could run away from the business, stupid to think she could shack up with some milkman.

Stupid to think she might love him.

For a brief time it made her into a child again. Those fantasies of the future were childish fantasies. She'd get bored with any life other than the one she now lives. No other life suits her. She can't afford childish emotions like love.

Love? There's sex and there's marriage. She doesn't even know what love is.

So he makes her heart beat faster simply by being near her. So he makes her palms sweat. So he makes her stomach feel funny. None of that means anything. She momentarily regressed into childhood, that's all, into feeling that she needed someone other than herself to rely on. She momentarily allowed herself to go soft.

It won't happen again.

Eugene takes a drag from his cigarette, then puts it out on the bottom of his shoe and sets the butt on the edge of the table.

'Good morning.'

She doesn't respond.

'Do you need to pee or anything?'

'What?'

'Do you have to use the toilet?'

'No.'

He nods. 'Good.'

He slips a pair of leather gloves onto his hands, grabs the roll of tape from the table, gets to his feet. He picks up her panties from the floor and walks toward her. He shoves them into her mouth. They taste of laundry soap and of her sex. He shoves them down her throat, making her want to gag. She tries to spit them out, but it's difficult, the dry fabric clings to the walls of her mouth, and before she can do anything more than ineffectively cough Eugene is wrapping tape around her head. She coughs a few more times, tears streaming down her face, before she gets the fabric out of her throat. She wants to rub the moisture from her eyes but her hands are still taped behind her back. Eugene must sense it. He wipes the tears away from her cheeks himself, smearing them away with his gloved thumb.

'Sorry,' he says. 'I didn't mean to choke you. I have to take care of some business. I'll be back soon. With breakfast.'

He collects his own gun and hers, then walks to the door, grabs the doorknob, and pulls. He steps over the threshold. He closes the door behind him, leaving her alone.

Her first thought is to start banging against the walls, to get someone's attention, but she needs to think of something better than that. That will result in the police being called, which is the last thing she wants. The police will ask questions.

What are you going to do, Evelyn? Think.

She falls back in bed and kicks her legs up. Starts working her taped-together hands around her naked backside, up toward the backs of her knees, squirming through the tight loop of her arms. If she can get her legs through, if she can get her hands in front of her, well, she isn't sure what she'll do, but it'll be a start. And that's what she needs: a start. A beginning.

She'll think of something.

But first she needs to get her hands free.

4

He puts the Berretta into his motorcycle's saddlebag and his own pistol down the front of his pants, then rides to a diner. He parks at the curb and steps into the place. It smells good, of coffee and bacon. The chatter of the patrons is pleasant. He walks across the black-and-white-checkered floor to the payphone in the corner and drops a dime. He listens for a moment to the tone, then dials. It rings several times. If this call remains unanswered Eugene doesn't know what he's going to do.

'Hello?'

He exhales, relieved.

'Fingers.'

'Eugene?'

'That's right.'

'What's up, man?'

'Last time we spoke you offered to help.'

A long pause, then, finally: 'I did.'

5

Evelyn lies on her back with her feet in the air. Her right shoulder is screaming with pain. She curses into the fabric shoved down her throat. Her breathing is jagged and short. If her feet weren't taped together she could get her legs through one at a time, that would be far less painful, but her feet are taped together. That makes her task, as well as painful, nearly impossible. This is her third attempt. With her wrists at the backs of her ankles she draws her knees to her chest and tries, with a grunt, to force her hands over her heels. She feels a great tearing pain in her shoulder and screams into the wet fabric in her mouth. She rolls to her side. She closes her eyes and tears stream down her hot, sweaty face. She opens her eyes and finds herself looking, through a kaleidoscope of tears, at her hands. They're held together as if in prayer.

She laughs through her pain. She did it.

She did it.

She sits up in bed, a wet clump of hair falling into her face, and reaches to the tape covering her mouth. She pulls down, pulls the tape down over her chin, and reaches into her mouth with her searching fingers. She removes the now-sopping panties, gags, almost vomits, and throws them to the floor. She allows herself to sit motionless and catch her breath. She can't sit here doing nothing indefinitely – Eugene will return at some point, and she needs to figure out what she's going to do about him – but she allows herself a moment.

She sniffles, brings her taped-together hands to her nose, wipes at it.

Okay. What next?

She turns her wrists in opposite directions to see how much movement is available, how much give the tape has.

Not much. But, with luck, enough. With pain in her wrists she picks at the end of the tape with a fingernail, picks at the tape until almost a third of an inch has been pulled away. She brings her wrists to her mouth and bites down on the tape end, then pulls her hands away, unwinding it.

In less than five minutes her hands are free.

A minute after that her feet are free as well.

She stands and walks to her purse. She finds her cigarette case, removes a filtered Kent, and lights it. She inhales deeply, coughs, looks around the room. She has no idea how long it's been. Eugene could return at any moment. She needs to figure what she's going to do when he does.

Her first thought is to call Lou, but there's no telephone here. And anyway, she'd have a hard time explaining to him what she was doing in this room.

She could simply leave, find a phone, make an anonymous call to the police. Except she doesn't want Eugene in police custody.

He can tell them far too much, and he would.

She takes another drag from her cigarette.

He has to die. That's what Daddy would say, and Daddy'd be right. She has to kill him and get rid of the body. Drive it out to the desert, bury it. The police will still think he did the murders for which he's been framed; they'll just also think he got away with it, made it down to Tijuana where they'll never catch up with him.

Why didn't he go down to Mexico when she suggested it? She would've gotten money to him. Maybe they could have made a small life together down there. If he'd listened maybe the two of them would still have some small chance at something.

No more childish thoughts, Evelyn.

You would have gotten bored. It never could have worked out.

You have to kill him and you know it, so figure out how you're going to do it and get ready. He might show up at any moment.

She nods at that.

You're right. Of course.

It has to be something simple and brutal.

But first she has to get some clothes on. She picks her dress up from the floor and steps into it, reaching behind her to zip it up. She looks toward the panties on the floor, but refuses to put them on. This wrinkled, sweat-stinking dress alone will have to suffice.

She looks around the room for a weapon.

She has to be ready for him.

6

Eugene rides his motorcycle into the motel parking lot, steps off the bike, knocks the kickstand into place. He reaches into the saddlebag and removes a brown paper bag and, with the paper bag gripped in his fist, walks to his motel room. He keys open the door, steps inside.

First thing he notices is that the bed is empty. A wad of duct tape lies on the mattress, another wad on the floor by the foot of the bed.

His mouth goes dry. His heart knocks in his chest like a bad car engine. He reaches for the Baby Browning in his waistband, gets his hand around the cool grip, and is about to pull it out when he feels a dull thud at the back of his head and falls to his knees. He touches the back of his head and feels pain. He looks at his fingers and sees blood. He looks over his shoulder.

Evelyn stands behind him in the doorway, her red hair a wild mess, her brow furrowed, her eyes glistening. She holds in her hands a large stone with this motel room's number painted on it, a white 13. She must have been waiting outside for his return, hiding around the corner or behind a car.

She steps into the room.

He crawls backwards, away from her, until he's pressed against the bed and can crawl no further.

Then pulls the pistol from his waistband, aims it at her, gets to his feet.

'Don't take another step, Evelyn.'

She takes another step.

'You're not gonna shoot me.'

She raises the stone over her head and takes yet another step toward him.

He wills himself to shoot her. If he can't do it now he's never going to be able to do it, and it has to be done eventually. He has to do it now. If he doesn't, she'll kill him. And she won't hesitate. He can think of a new plan, a new story that makes it all make sense. The point is living, and if he's to live she must die.

The gun shakes in his hand. He looks past it to her face. He aims over her head. He pulls the trigger.

The stone splits into two big chunks, one in each hand, and rock shards and bits of lead scatter outward. Evelyn gasps and takes a staggering step backwards.

Eugene moves on her, raises the gun, and brings it down onto the side of her head.

She collapses to the floor.

He steps forward and looks out into the parking lot, sees a couple people wandering out of their rooms to find out what that noise was. Someone asks him did he hear that, too. He says, yeah, think it was only a car backfiring, and pushes the door closed. He looks down at Evelyn. She's unconscious. Blood trickles into her hair. He swallows, then reaches down to pick her up.

7

Evelyn awakens in bed. She feels slightly disoriented. She blinks at Eugene. He's once more sitting at the table. He looks at her for a long time. Then nods his head toward a paper bag sitting beside him.

'I got us some breakfast,' he says.

FORTY-FIVE

1

Carl sits in a chair in the corner of the room and stares at the wall, disoriented. He must have nodded off there for a minute. He blinks and looks down at his arm. A bead of blood rests in the crease on the inside of his elbow. He imagines a small green stem growing from it, from some subcutaneous seed, and thorns emerging from the stem, and leaves, and then a red flower, a red rose, and the red rose opening like a fist unclenching. It would be beautiful. He lazily reaches over with an arm that weighs twice what it should and smears the blood away with an index finger. He looks at the red on his fingertip and unthinkingly licks it off.

Okay. Time to get to work.

He pushes himself from the chair. He unrolls his shirt-sleeve and buttons his cuff. A dot of blood appears on his shirt. Apparently he didn't wipe all of it away. It doesn't matter. No one will see it. He slips into his coat. He picks up his fedora from the bed and sets it upon his shower-wet hair after combing his fingers through it. If his hair's still wet, thin as it is, he didn't nod off for too long. That's good.

And that's it. That's what he gets for the daylight hours. He's using no more till he gets off work. He's taking nothing with him. He doesn't want to be tempted. And he will not call his man in the hop squad because his man in the hop squad doesn't know how to keep his goddamn mouth shut. He'll be a little shaky toward the end of the day, a little sweaty, but he thinks he can make it. He made a promise.

Just enough to get him through. No more.

He steps out of his room, making sure the door is locked behind him, then walks downstairs and into the cool morning air, which wraps itself around him. He stands still on the front porch and inhales its scent.

If his wife were alive, this moment, even without her in it, would be perfect. The simple knowledge that she was alive would make it perfect.

But she isn't. And it isn't.

Still, it's pretty nice, and he stands there a moment before walking to his car.

2

He sits in a chair beside Friedman and looks across a cluttered desk to Captain Ellis. He thought he and his partner had an understanding. He thought they'd worked it out yesterday evening. They would finish this case, they'd get Eugene Dahl into custody, and then he'd take time off from work to get clean. None of the brass would have to find out about his problem. He'd get clean on his own, come back to work, and everything could go back to the way it had been before he started using.

He thought he and Friedman had an understanding, but if so why did Captain Ellis call them into his office and shut the door?

He closes his eyes a moment, preparing himself for what he fears is coming. He knows he deserves to lose his job, but he knows too it's the only thing he has left. It's an ineffective distraction, but it's something. He wants to continue this investigation. He has ideas. He has thoughts. Instead of focusing on himself, he's begun to focus on this case again. He's begun to focus on it like he used to focus on cases before Naomi died. He doesn't want to lose that now. He has a tenuous grasp on reality and he wants to use it to pull himself out of the nightmare he's been living in. Maybe he could even fix things with Candice eventually – once he gets cleaned up.

If he gets fired he doesn't know what he'll do.

'The district attorney was murdered last night,' Ellis says.

Carl opens his eyes. 'What?'

'He was beat to death in front of the Pink Flamingo.'

'Beat to death – with what?'

'Fists,' Ellis says. 'Things have really turned to shit lately.'

Friedman nods. 'Ever since that grand-jury investigation of James Manning was announced.'

'That was my thinking. But you two like Eugene Dahl as your killer.'

'We do,' Carl says, pushing thoughts of everything else out of his mind – he's not getting fired, Friedman hasn't said anything – forcing himself to focus only on the investigation. 'But I've also come to believe James Manning is involved somehow. I'm almost certain of it.'

'In what way?'

'I don't know exactly. But I was up last night thinking about it, and it seems to me he almost has to be involved. There's someone I want to talk to about it, someone in town, but I'm not sure he'll spill, so I also want to visit hotels, check hotel registries, see if any of James Manning's known associates have recently arrived in town. If we had more men at our disposal we could even check passenger lists – see who's come into town through Los Angeles Airport, Lockheed Air Terminal in Burbank, and Union Station. If we're thorough I'm almost certain we'll get something.'

'I'll get you your men. Be here at one o'clock to get them going. I'd also like you to keep Detectives Pagana and Schwartz apprised of your progress. They're investigating the district attorney's murder out of the Rampart division, and if you find a connection between your case and theirs they need to know about it.'

'Yes, sir. In the meantime is there any chance we can take the unit off Eugene Dahl's apartment?'

'Why's that?'

'I don't think he's going back and I want them to keep an eye on someone else for a little while.'

Captain Ellis nods. 'You got it.'

3

They step out of Captain Ellis's office. Carl pulls the door closed behind them, puts his back against the wall, closes his eyes. He feels a bit sick. It took all the concentration he had to carry out that conversation, to keep focused, to keep his mind from wandering. He feels sweaty and cold. He wants to lie down somewhere and sleep.

His partner puts a hand on his shoulder. 'You okay?'

'Let's go for a drive. I need some fresh air.'

FORTY-SIX

1

Fingers steps through his front door and squints at the bright morning. His head throbs with pain. He took some aspirin after he got off the phone with Eugene, but it hasn't done any good. At least not yet. This is some bad shit he's got himself stuck in, and he has no idea how to pull himself out of it.

Well, that's not entirely true. He knows one way, but he doesn't want to do it. He doesn't want to push his friend's head under as he climbs out. He has to give the police something, they made that clear, and while he could give them Eugene, he knows only a coward would do so. The man is his friend, and he's ashamed of himself already for what he's done to him, ashamed of the cowardice he's displayed. He twice betrayed the man. Eugene would never do to a friend what's been done to him.

And he doesn't even know the extent of it.

Fingers hoped he wouldn't hear from Eugene. If he didn't hear from him he'd have nothing to tell the cops, no decision to make. They might then go about dismantling his life, probably would, cops being cops, but if he really had no information there'd be nothing he could do about it.

He could take some small comfort in that knowledge. It was done to him; he didn't do it to himself.

But he did hear from Eugene. The man called him and asked for his help. So now he's got to figure out what he's going to do. The police will be back asking questions soon, and he has to know how he'll deal with that. He has to learn as little as possible about what Eugene is up to while still helping him as much as he can. He'd like to know nothing, the less he knows the less the police can get out of him, but he owes Eugene his help. He got his friend into this by talking to Louis Lynch, and he made it worse by talking to the cops. He'll be damned if he leaves him to dangle.

Then stop thinking about talking to the police at all. What you need to think about is this. Do you have it in you to do what's right even if it means the cops tear your life apart? If you do, then don't worry about anything else. Go help your friend and when the cops come back around with question marks on their faces you tell them to go fuck themselves. If that means they destroy your life, so be it. You'll be a man, and a man can build a new life. You've done it before. What the cops want is for you to be their boy. You fetch water for them once, they'll never stop coming around with their empty pails.

So, again, the question. Do you have it in you to do what's right even if it means the cops dismantle your life?

After some time he nods to himself.

Yes, I do.

He walks to his car and slips in behind the wheel. He sits there a moment, staring at the dials on his dashboard. He starts the engine. The radio comes on, playing a Cole Porter tune. He turns it up, turns it up loud.

Yes, I do.

He grabs the transmission handle on the right side of the steering column and yanks it down to drive. He pulls his foot off the brake pedal.

2

Eugene gets to his feet when he hears a car pull into the motel parking lot, its front bumper scraping against the driveway. He walks to the window, pushes the curtain aside, looks out. A cream-colored Chevrolet Bel Air convertible with whitewall tires pulls to a stop beside his motorcycle, Fingers behind the wheel. He swings open the driver's-side door and steps out. He puts his face momentarily to the sun, his eyes closed, then turns and walks toward the motel room from which Eugene stands watching him.

Eugene lets the curtain fall and turns to Evelyn. She sits silent on the edge of the bed with a sullen expression on her face. Her ankles and wrists are once more taped together. He let her eat breakfast before he did it, but watched her closely, and when she was finished he bound her. She let him do it without a fight, but he knows she's not beat. A woman like her can't be beat; she can only be killed.

Stop thinking that way, Eugene. You're going to figure a way out of that part of it. It won't come to that.

A knock at the door.

'I'll be right back.'

Eugene steps outside to greet his friend, shutting the door behind him.

'Thanks for coming.'

Fingers nods.

'Did you find a warehouse we can use?'

'My guy's gonna meet us there to hand over the keys.'

He nods his thanks. 'Now about why I need your car. I didn't want to tell you over the phone, but—'

Fingers raises a hand and shakes his head.

'Hold up,' he says. 'I need to talk to you about some things before we get into any of that. Need to be straight with you about exactly why you're in this situation.'

'What do you mean?'

He looks away from Eugene, rubs his face with both palms.

'What?' Eugene takes a step back and squints at his friend.

'The police stopped by my apartment couple days ago, about an hour after I gave you that pistol. They were asking questions about you.'

'What did you tell them?'

'You know what? That's not the right place to begin. A guy who works for James Manning named Louis Lynch called me last Wednesday asking questions about you. I answered. I didn't know what Manning had in mind, didn't know he was gonna frame you for them murders, but Lou asked questions and I answered. So I helped get you into this situation. I'm sorry for that. I wouldn't do it again. But before I let you tell me anything, I need you to know my part in what happened.'

Eugene nods but says nothing. Then turns and walks away, running his fingers through his hair. He leans against the trunk of a car, does a push up against it, exhales heavily. His one ally in all this turns out to have helped cause the trouble in the first place. Son of a bitch.

It wasn't on purpose, Eugene.

That's what he says.

He didn't have to tell you at all.

He pivots and walks back toward his friend. He stops a couple feet from him, looks him in the eye, searches his face for answers that words can't provide.

'What did you tell the police?'

'Nothing. But they pushed hard and they'll be back.'

Eugene nods again. He pinches his lower lip and pulls on it.

'Okay,' he says, thinking this through. 'Okay. This might be okay. Next time the cops come around asking you questions, I want you to talk to them. I want you to tell them a story, a mostly true story. Will you do that?'

Fingers swallows, but doesn't respond.

'I need you. I've already begun something, and I don't know how to finish it without your help.'

'What did you do, Eugene?'

'I'll explain everything, but let's take care of this warehouse business first. Back your car up to the door and pop the trunk.'

He pulls his gloves from his back pocket and slips his hands into them.

Fingers watches him put the gloves on, then looks up, looks him in the eye, and says, 'What for?'

3

Eugene walks toward Evelyn with a damp pair of panties in his hand. She backs away from him, pushing herself across the mattress with her bound legs, telling him don't you put those in my mouth, Eugene, don't do that. Please. I'll be quiet. I'll be quiet.

'I'm sorry, Evelyn,' Eugene says. 'I can't trust you.'

He shoves them into her mouth, stuffing them down with a thumb.

4

Fingers stands outside. He wants to help Eugene out of the mess he helped get him into, but feels sick about it. He's a professional middleman, and that means staying disinterested. It means not getting involved. But that's ridiculous, isn't it? He's been involved since his telephone rang last Wednesday, and on the wrong side as well. All he's doing now is regaining some of his self-respect.

He makes his own decisions, goddamn it. He doesn't let fear drive him.

The motel-room door swings open. Eugene drags a tall redheaded woman from the depths of the interior. She fights him as well as she can, but her hands and legs are bound. He picks her up as she thrashes and carries her through the door. It's what threshold crossings would look like if they were done after divorces as well as weddings. He drops her into the waiting jaw of the trunk and slams the lid down. She thrashes about inside the car, kicks at the trunk lid – and after a while stops.

'Who was that?'

'Evelyn Manning.'

For a moment Fingers cannot speak. Then: 'Jesus Christ, man.'

'What?'

'The Man is gonna kill us.'

'He was gonna kill me anyway.'

'Well, motherfucker, now he's gonna kill me, too.'

Eugene shakes his head.

'Not if this works.'

'Not if what works?'

Eugene tells him.

5

Eugene follows the Chevrolet Bel Air south through Hollywood and downtown Los Angeles to a small industrial city called Vernon, a place where children do not play on the streets, where wives do not garden in their front yards while flirting with door-to-door salesmen, and where husbands do not come home with loosened ties hanging from their necks after working comfortably in air-conditioned office buildings.

This isn't a city for living.

Foul black pillars of smoke hold up the sky. Tractor trailers backed up to docks are loaded and unloaded by sweaty-gloved men with pallet trucks. Farmers from the surrounding areas haul dead livestock toward the rendering plant. And everywhere the sounds of people getting hard, stinking work done; the kind of necessary but ugly work the rest of society would rather not know about.

Eventually they arrive at an empty warehouse.

The previous tenant's sign has been removed, but the words can still be read in relief against the filth covering the rest of the crumbling stucco facade.

B & K Lumber Co.
Construction Supplies

They drive around the corner and pull into the back lot. A few disintegrating tractor trailers sit in front of the closed and padlocked dock doors. Dead weeds jut from cracks in the asphalt. Weathered gray two-by-fours and four-by-fours are stacked willy-nilly in the parking lot like pyres awaiting sacrifices.

Near one of those piles of wood a thin blond man in a white linen suit and sunglasses leans against his Cadillac smoking a cigarette, a reddish mustache resting uncomfortably on his lip, like a rash. He raises his hand in greeting, shows his white horse teeth, and watches them park.

Eugene lights a cigarette and watches Fingers step from his vehicle.

'Wait here. I'll take care of it.'

Eugene nods, then watches as his friend struts toward the man in the white suit. The two talk a moment and make an exchange before the man in the white suit shows his horse teeth once more, gets into his Cadillac, and starts the engine. He drives out to the street and makes a left without even glancing toward Eugene.

Then he's gone.

Like that: it's finished.

Fingers walks back toward Eugene, puts a key ring into his hand.

'The square key is for the front and back doors. Round keys are for the padlocks on the roll-ups.'

Eugene nods.

6

Evelyn hears the key slide into the lock and the lock tumble.

She's covered in sweat and can smell her own stink filling the confined space in which she's trapped. She can only breathe through her nostrils – her mouth gagged, the itch of the fabric at the back of her throat making her want to cough – and doesn't think she's getting enough oxygen. She feels dizzy. She feels sick.

She can't believe she let herself go soft. Daddy would never find himself in a situation like this. Daddy doesn't let his heart tell him anything; doesn't let his heart lead him anywhere. Only a fool would do such a thing.

The trunk lid swings open.

First thing she sees is bright blue sky. It's blinding after the darkness of the trunk. Water streams from her eyes. Then a man-shaped silhouette fills the blue, darkness surrounded by a halo of light. It reaches for her.

She pulls back her legs and kicks. Her feet slam into the silhouette's chest and it stumbles backwards several steps. She slides her way out of the trunk and falls to the hard gray asphalt. She rolls onto her back and pulls herself into a sitting position. She tries to get to her feet but has no leverage with her ankles bound and her hands taped behind her back, no way to pull herself up.

She groans through the gag in her mouth.

Then Eugene reaches for her and picks her up. He drags her, struggling, toward the back door of a warehouse, up five concrete steps, through a blue door. He sets her on hard concrete.

The warehouse is hot, the sun beating down on the corrugated tin roof overhead, a few beams of light shooting through rusted-out holes, illuminating the dust floating through the air. There's a pile of wood in the far left corner, end-pieces of four to six inches in length. A table saw beside the pile. Shelves line the wall to the right, mostly empty but for a few boxes containing wood screws, finishing nails, and so on. A few pallets are scattered across the floor, and a few rusty pallet trucks.

The concrete floor is cool despite how hot the air is in here.

It feels good on her skin.

She looks at Eugene and he looks back. Neither of them makes a sound for a very long time.

Then he turns and walks away.

7

Eugene walks out to the car and collects Evelyn's purse and a roll of duct tape from the back seat, thanks Fingers for his help, he really came through, and says I'll see you later.

'I hope so,' Fingers says, and gets into his car.

He pulls his door shut.

Eugene hopes so too, but like his friend, he has his doubts. Still, he's got to do everything he can to get through this.

He has no other choice.

8

Fingers grips the steering wheel. He stares at the gray cinderblock wall in front of him for a long time. He starts the engine, backs out of the parking spot, pulls out into the street. His headache is only getting worse. The left temple throbs, feeling like someone's going at it with a tack hammer.

Eugene will be dead by the end of the day tomorrow. He's sure of it. There's simply no way he lives through what he's trying to do. A matador attempting to get two bulls to charge him from opposite directions by waving red, then stepping aside so they'll crack skulls, instead he'll end up gored. Twice.

And the worst part is, Eugene's asked Fingers to sharpen their horns.

He'll do it. He'll do what his friend has asked of him. He put the man into this situation and can't deny him his request.

But there's no way it doesn't end badly.

FORTY-SEVEN

1

Carl and Friedman sit parked at the curb in front of a pink stucco apartment building. They watch the building, but nothing happens. Carl wishes he were somewhere else. This sitting and waiting is giving him too much time to think and too little to think about. It means his mind is turning inward again, the last thing he wants or needs.

His arms itch, he's beginning to feel sweaty, he's very tired. How long has it been since he's eaten a proper meal? A couple days at least. How long has it been since he took a shit? That was only yesterday morning, and while there was no blood in his stool, he wishes there had been. That might mean he'd get to see Naomi soon. If he doesn't have the courage to tell her goodbye he might as well be with her. Living in-between as he has been isn't living at all.

'Here he comes.'

Carl looks up the street.

A cream-colored Chevrolet Bel Air rolls toward them.

Thank Christ – something outside himself to focus on.

2

Fingers knew the detectives would return at some point, and probably soon, but wasn't expecting them in front of his apartment building as he turned onto his street. He was hoping for peace, some time to relax after the stress of what he's just done and what he's agreed to do.

His mouth goes dry and his palms get sweaty.

Be cool. You deal with dangerous people all the time. Do your thing, tell your lies when you need to tell them, and be careful not to light up the tilt sign. It's that simple.

He drives his car slowly past the cops, holding a hand up at them as he does, then makes a u-turn and parks behind them.

It's true. He does deal with dangerous men all the time, but they're men he understands. He understands their motives and he knows how to handle them. He doesn't understand cops, doesn't understand what gets them out of bed. And the fact that so many of them are easily as crooked as any criminal he's dealt with makes him fear them as well. They're crooked but have the law behind them.

What's not to be afraid of?

He steps from his car and walks toward the detectives in theirs.

'How you guys doin?'

'Get in the car.'

'Is this gonna take a while? If it is I should water my plants.'

'Get in the goddamn car.'

He nods his understanding, pulls open the back door, slides into the seat.

If anybody else did this it would be kidnapping.

So what's not to be afraid of?

The cop behind the wheel, the older of the two, starts the engine.

'Where we goin?'

'Somewhere we can talk.'

'We can talk at my place.'

'No.'

The curtness of the one-word response marks it as punctuation: a period at the end of a conversation. The car pulls away from the curb.

They drive in silence for what feels like a long time, and every moment he's in the back of this silent car Fingers grows more tense. He tells himself to be cool. He tells himself not to let these guys shake him up. That's clearly what they're after, they want to get him fizzy, but he needs to remain calm. He's determined to remain calm.

You got this, man. You know what you have to do.

They stop in front of the Shenefield Hotel, rolling up to the rear bumper of an LAPD radio car. Two uniformed cops stand on the street beside it, smoking. Then one of them glances over, flicks his cigarette out to the street, and walks over.

3

Carl stands by the open door of his car and watches the two uniformed cops escort Darryl Castor into the Shenefield Hotel. One of the hotel rooms on the sixth floor has been converted into an interrogation room, which they'll be using later. For the next couple hours, however, they'll let him sit. Let him think over every reason they might be holding him. In Carl's experience, both personal and professional, the best way to get to a man is to let his mind turn on itself.

Darryl Castor steps out of sight.

Carl falls into the car and pulls the door shut behind him.

4

The hotel room is nothing like a hotel room. The bed has been removed, as has the dresser. Any painting which might once have hung on the wall is now in a storage closet somewhere. A square metal table sits in the middle of the room, four chairs surrounding it. A reel-to-reel recording device sits on the table. The windows are covered in dark curtains which allow no light to enter from outside. All clocks are absent, making it impossible to tell what time of day or night it might be.

Fingers enters the room, escorted by two uniformed officers. One of the uniformed officers pushes the door closed and locks it.

Fingers turns in a slow circle, taking in his surroundings, then looks toward the police officers, both of whom are standing silent by the door.

'What now?' he says.

'Wait.'

5

Carl looks at the twelve young detectives sitting before him. His eyes sting. His legs feel cramped. His stomach aches. He tries to ignore all of this. He needs his mind clear. He needs to be able to think.

He closes his eyes and exhales in a long sigh. He tries to think about nothing but the case at hand. He needs to get these guys on the street. There's someone in this city doing James Manning's bidding and they need to find him.

He opens his eyes.

'All right,' he says. 'Let me tell you why you're here.'

FORTY-EIGHT

1

Eugene stands in the lobby of the Fairmont Hotel with a ringing telephone pressed against his ear. With each ring he dreads the answer more. From now on everything will have to line up or he's dead. Yet he knows if he does nothing he's also dead, so he must try. He doesn't feel up to this. He isn't the type of person who does what he'll have to do if he's to make it out of this alive. He isn't the type of person who does much. He likes simplicity in his life, calm, which is perhaps the reason he was never in a serious relationship, and the reason he was happy working as a milkman. He had a simple life and a simple job with a simple routine. He liked the job and he liked the routine. And he liked having a dream – a perpetually unrealized dream. But now all that's gone and he's being forced to make decisions a man like him was never meant to make.

'Hello?'

He swallows. This is it.

'I have Evelyn Manning.'

'Who is this?'

'The person who has Evelyn Manning.'

A long pause, then: 'I don't believe you.'

Eugene swallows. His mouth is dry.

'Open your hotel-room door,' he says. 'I'll wait.'

2

Lou sets the telephone down on the table and walks to the door. He unchains the door and retracts the deadbolt. He wraps his hand around the knob and turns it and pulls. He looks out into the corridor. It's empty. He's about to close the door and tell the man on the phone to go screw when he sees something hanging from the outside door-knob. He looks down and sees a small locket. He pulls the locket from the doorknob and clicks it open. He finds himself looking at a picture of the Man with his arm wrapped around the shoulders of his smiling teenage daughter. He steps back into his hotel room and closes the door. He walks to the telephone and picks it up.

'Who is this?'

'I've already given you the only answer you're gonna get.'

'What do you want?'

'I want the Man on a plane. He leaves for Los Angeles today with ten thousand dollars in cash. I've made a reservation for him at the same hotel you're staying in. The reservation is in the name of Humphrey Smith. When he checks in, there will be a note at the front desk for him. It will contain further instructions. This isn't a negotiation. This isn't even a conversation. This is me telling you how it's gonna be. I hope you have a good memory because I'm not repeating myself. I suggest you call him as soon as I hang up and tell him what I've told you.'

Click.

Lou pulls the phone away from his ear and looks at it for a moment before setting it into its cradle.

He's been wondering all morning what happened to Evelyn. Now he knows.

This is turning into a nightmare job.

He walks to his suitcase and pulls out a bottle of whiskey. He uncorks it, takes a swallow. It's harsh and warm. As soon as he swallows he can feel acid boiling at the back of his throat and taste bile. He replaces the cork and tosses the bottle into the suitcase. He finds a calcium antacid and chews it. He walks to the telephone. He picks it up. He doesn't want to make this phone call but knows he must.

An operator answers.

He tells her, 'I'd like to place a long-distance phone call.'

3

Eugene sits on a couch in the lobby, the same couch on which he sat while waiting for Evelyn on the night of their date. He hides his face behind a newspaper and watches the elevator. He tries not to think about Evelyn. There never could have been anything serious between them. He was deluding himself. He knows that.

He tries to read the paper but can't process even so much as a single sentence. His mind won't let him focus. Each word sits on the page alone, unconnected to any other by either logic or grammar.

The elevator doors open. A pale, thin man with slicked-back black hair steps from within. He wears a pin-striped suit. His back is very straight. He walks to the front desk and speaks with the gentleman there.

Eugene watches their exchange, and waits.

4

Lou hangs up the telephone, walks to his bed, sits down. He puts his hands on his knees and stares straight ahead, thinking about his conversation with the Man. It didn't go well. It didn't go well at all. There was never any chance that it would, but it went worse even than he'd expected.

How could you let this happen? How in the name of an

ever-loving Christ could you let this happen, Lou? I swear to you here and now if her fingernail polish is so much as chipped you're a dead man. You think I don't mean it you just wait and see. I don't care how long you've worked for me. If she's hurt in any way I will nail you to the floor, pour gasoline down your throat, and let you dehydrate until you're dead. I will dance to the tune of your screams. I'm on my way.

Lou asks himself who might have done this and thinks only one name. But is it really possible that the frightened-looking man he saw in the corridor at the Shenefield Hotel did this? He thinks it is possible. He thinks it must have been him. Nobody else would be desperate enough to do something like this.

Nobody else would be stupid enough.

Lou gets to his feet. He has to do something. He can't simply sit here and wait. He can't. He has to do something. But at first he doesn't know what, knows only that he can't sit still, so he paces the floor. He thinks better when he's moving anyway. When he sits still too long his blood turns to sludge and his brain stops functioning.

What is he going to do?

What the fuck is he going to do?

Eugene Dahl might have already left the note for the Man at the front desk. If he did, and if there's an address on the note, maybe he can take care of this himself. He can't imagine the milkman being much trouble. The guy's got fight in him, and Lou can respect him for that if nothing else, but he's still in over his head, and this is the kind of thing Lou handles for a living.

Lou steps out into the corridor, closing the door behind him.

He takes the elevator down to the lobby.

He walks to the front desk.

A gentleman in a crisp uniform says, 'How can I help you, sir?'

'Someone left a letter for my boss. He's asked me to retrieve it for him.'

5

Eugene doesn't follow Lou's car for long. He knows where it's going and wants to get there first, which he can't do from behind, so after a few blocks he passes it on the left and twists the throttle, glancing in his mirror to see it shrinking into the background. The wind blows through his hair, and the sun shines down on him from a cloudless blue sky hot against the bare skin on his arms and face, and he could almost enjoy the moment but for a single nagging question.

What exactly is going to happen in that warehouse? He doesn't know. He knows what needs to happen, but he doesn't know that it will. Now that he's in the midst of this it feels very messy. It's too complicated. When he thought about it last night, before it was something he had to implement, when he thought of it in the abstract, it seemed like something that might work. But no sane person could have conjured this plan. Now that he's in the middle of it he sees it for what it is, madness, because what will happen in that warehouse is only one uncertainty of many, the first of many, and if any of them goes badly it's finished. He's finished.

And even if everything goes the way he needs it to, he will walk away from this a murderer. He's asked himself more than once if he could kill a person. He believes he could do it in self-defense, but for this to work he'll have to murder in cold blood. He must be careful about how and when he does it. It needs to look a certain way. The question is, can cold-blooded murder also be self-defense? And is he capable of it?

He doesn't know. He thinks of killing Evelyn and his chest feels tight and still, his lungs breathless; she's the only woman he's ever come close to loving; but he'll try all the same, because either he can do this or he's dead, and he doesn't want to die.

He brings the motorcycle to a stop in the parking lot behind the warehouse. He steps off it and lights a cigarette. He takes a drag. His exhalation is nervous and shaky. He walks up a set of concrete steps, into the warehouse, to dock number three. The roll-up door is opened, revealing a tractor trailer which is parked against the rubber bumper bolted to the concrete edge of the dock. The trailer's back doors are closed and latched. A padlock hangs from the staple but isn't fastened. There's a triangular hole in the left door. It looks to have been made by the corner of something heavy falling against it. Eugene picks the splinters away from the hole and puts his eye to it. The inside of the trailer is very dark, only a small amount of light splashing into it through a rot-hole in the roof.

Evelyn is sitting on the floor against the far wall, exactly where she's supposed to be. She must have either heard him or noticed the bright spot in the door go dark because she looks up. She makes a sound through the gag in her mouth.

Eugene doesn't answer. He drops his cigarette to the floor and smears it out with the ball of his foot.

Louis Lynch will be arriving soon. He'd better be ready for him.

6

Lou parks on the street in front of an old warehouse. The stucco siding is crumbling, revealing rusted wire beneath. Several of the narrow ventilation windows have been shattered. Weeds grow thick around the base of the building and from cracks in the asphalt parking lot. It looks to have been abandoned some time ago.

This is the place, no question.

He steps from the car and removes his automatic pistol from its holster. He walks toward the building slowly, deliberately, his eyes taking in everything: the ancient piles of weathered gray wood, the birds nesting in the rusted tin roof, the three abandoned trailers parked at the docks, the motorcycle sitting near the back door.

He walks the perimeter of the building, hoping he might be able to see inside, but ends up circling the entire place without learning anything. Then he sees that one of the roll-up doors is opened. There's a trailer parked in front of it, but even so he should be able to see something. He walks to it. There's a six-inch gap between the edge of the door and the trailer. He looks through the gap. The place appears to be empty of life. He sees neither Evelyn nor the milkman, just the dusty interior of an out-of-use warehouse. He knows they must both be here, but he can't see them.

He doesn't want to go into the place blind, but supposes he has no choice.

He walks up a set of concrete steps which lead to the back door. On the landing at the top of the steps he kicks off his shoes, revealing plaid socks. He grabs the doorknob and turns it slowly. He pulls open the door, hoping for silence and getting it. He steps into the place and eases the door shut behind him. It latches quietly. He looks left, then right. He sees no one. He thumbs back his revolver's hammer and pads in stocking feet around the edge of the large warehouse, keeping his back to the wall. He can smell cigarette smoke on the air. It's a large space and mostly empty. There aren't many places to hide.

So where are they?

He walks along a wall of mostly empty shelves, keeping his back to them, eyes looking for movement in the room spread out before him. He reaches the front wall and continues along it. The only sound he hears is the sound of his own breathing. He reaches the next corner, where a table saw sits beside a pile of throw-away lumber.

He carefully looks behind the lumber but finds no one and nothing.

He glances toward the docks, toward the rolled-up door at dock number three. He wonders if Evelyn is inside the trailer parked there.

She might be, but Eugene Dahl isn't.

So where is he?

The motorcycle outside means he must be here, but he isn't here.

Lou licks his lips.

Maybe he stepped out for a few minutes. He could have walked somewhere to get a packet of cigarettes or a bite to eat.

Lou walks to the trailer, holsters his pistol, and pulls the padlock from the staple. Someone within the trailer begins to moan loudly. He yanks up on the large metal handle, which causes two bolts attached to it to retract, sliding out of their slots in the floor and ceiling of the trailer. The doors swing open, revealing Evelyn. She sits on the rotting wood floor of the trailer in a puddle of liquid. The liquid runs down the slant of the floor and splashes to the ground below. The smell of urine is strong. Her mouth is gagged but she tries to speak anyway, and shakes her head violently.

He walks to her and pulls the duct tape from her face and the wadded fabric from her mouth. Her lips are red and raw.

'Where is he?'

But before Evelyn can speak he has his answer.

7

Eugene lies prone on the filthy roof of the tractor trailer parked at dock number three. He doesn't move. His head is turned to the right, to the two other trailers parked at the docks and past them to the street. The street is empty. He breathes in through his nose and out through his mouth. When he exhales he sees the dust on the white roof of the trailer blow away on the wave of his breath. He tries to listen to what Lou's doing inside the warehouse but hears nothing. The man moves in silence.

Then finally Eugene hears something at the back of the trailer, metal sliding against metal. Evelyn starts to make noises through the gag in her mouth. Eugene's certain she's trying to warn Lou of his presence. The trailer doors swing open. Eugene slides across the roof as quietly as possible and peers down through the space between the top of the trailer and the bottom of the roll-up door. He can see Lou's head, his greasy slicked-back hair. Then the man disappears into the trailer.

Eugene pushes up on the roll-up door, creating another six inches of space. He reaches out, grabbing the doors, and swings them closed. They slam into place and the handle falls about six inches, ejecting the bolts into their holds.

Lou curses and bangs against the doors. They want to give and almost do, must be hanging onto their holds only by mere millimeters.

Eugene drops to the concrete, spraining his ankle, and slams the handle down into place, sending the bolts fully into their holds.

A gunshot goes off and a black dot appears in one of the doors, surrounded by splinters and a star of fresh wood revealed where the splinters once held.

Eugene drops to the concrete. A second shot goes off.

'If you kill me,' he says, 'you'll die in there.'

FORTY-NINE

Fingers sits in silence. The uniformed officers stand by the door. He's tried to speak with them two or three times now, empty chatter to fill the empty minutes, but they responded only with one-word answers to his queries, which filled no time at all. He's been here at least two hours. Even without a clock or a watch available he knows he's been here that long, and maybe longer. He briefly wishes he'd remembered to put on his watch when he left the apartment this morning, but supposes the cops probably would have taken it, anyway.

He wonders if Eugene's still alive. He might already have gotten himself killed. Lou might have already put a bullet into him – or six. He wishes Eugene hadn't told him what he was attempting. It's insane, will never work. He's tempted to tell the police everything, the truth beginning to end, simply to save his friend's life, but he won't. He tells himself he won't. He'll tell them the story he's supposed to tell them and no other. That may mean he's helping to kill Eugene, he's almost certain that's exactly what it means, but he'll not betray his friend's trust a third time. And maybe Eugene will even pull it off. Maybe he'll manage it and walk away unscathed.

Don't kid yourself, man, you know better than that.

He supposes the chances are small.

The chances are nonexistent. Eugene might come across as cool, but he's square and you know it. He can't kill nobody. Man gets nervous in the presence of a few reefers. You let your friend surround himself with criminals and cops, you're letting him kill himself. He don't have it in him to do what he's planning to do, and when the time comes, he'll find he's nothing but a mouse in a snake pit. They'll eat him alive and you'll be the one who let it happen, because you're the only one in a position to stop it.

So ask yourself this. Is it a betrayal to save your friend's life?

Three knocks at the door. One of the uniformed cops pulls it open. The older detective steps into the room. His face is beaded with sweat. A uniformed cop pushes the door closed and locks it. The detective carries in his hand a white paper bag. He walks to the table and sets it in front of Fingers. The bottom is translucent with grease.

'Got you some food. Eat up, then we'll talk.'

The detective pulls out a chair and sits across from him.

FIFTY

1

Eugene carries Evelyn's purse to Louis Lynch's rented car, opens the door with a gloved hand, tosses the purse into the back seat. It falls to the floorboard, where its contents spill out across the carpet.

He slams shut the door.

2

He grabs his motorcycle by the handlebars and pushes it out to the street and along the sun-faded asphalt, rolling it away from the building silently. Once he's put some distance between himself and the warehouse, he kicks the machine to life and rides north, feeling shaky now that the adrenalin within him has been spent. The front of his shirt is filthy from lying on top of the trailer. His face is grimy. He feels sticky with nervous sweat now dried. He doesn't care. He managed to make it through the first part of this madness, and that's something. He wasn't sure he would, but he did, and without any trouble at all. It gives him hope he might actually pull it off. He'll know for certain by tomorrow afternoon – if he's still alive to know anything.

There's more than a small chance it'll turn out to be his last tomorrow.

For now, though, he must finish with today.

3

He pushes into Louis Lynch's hotel room and closes the door behind him. He walks to the small leatherette hardcase on the dresser and opens it, squeezing the latch with thumb and index, flipping the body of the case up. He looks down at the black Royal typewriter revealed. Then, after a moment, he rolls a sheet of hotel stationery into the machine. He looks down at the blank cream-colored paper. His mouth goes dry. He licks his lips. He swallows. Finally he types:

2294 E. 37th St.

Vernon, CA.

1:30 p.m.

Come alone or she dies.

He stops typing, pulls his gloved fingers off the round keys. His hands hover over the typewriter. He reads the note and, satisfied, removes it from the machine. It says everything he needs it to say, and most of what he needs it to say has nothing to do with the words on the page or what order they're in. He carefully folds the paper into thirds, making certain the creases are straight – Louis Lynch seems like a straight-crease kind of guy – then stuffs the folded paper into a hotel envelope and seals it. He types a name on the front of the envelope and with it in his hand steps out of the hotel room. He takes the elevator down to the lobby, slides the envelope across the front desk, tells the gentleman who picks it up it's for Humphrey Smith, I understand he's expected to check in late tonight or early tomorrow morning. He must receive it as soon as he arrives. The gentleman tells him yes, sir, not a problem. Eugene says thank you, then turns and walks out of the hotel. As he makes his way toward the street he asks himself what else he needs to do, what else he needs to take care of.

A few things yet.

4

He stops at a liquor store and buys himself a bottle of Old Grand-Dad. He knows there's a good chance he'll get sloppy if he works drunk, make mistakes that might kill him or put him in prison, but he doesn't think he can remain sober and still do what needs to be done. He knows he can't. Tomorrow will be a day filled with ugliness and he can't face it straight. Every time he thinks about it he feels sick to his stomach. But it has to happen. If he's going to walk away from this, it simply must happen, and that's all there is to it. So he'll do what he needs to do to make sure it does. He'll try not to get drunk, he'll try to consume only enough so he can face the day, but he needs his medicine.

With the bottle purchased he steps back into the daylight. As he does he throws Louis Lynch's room key into a trash can by the door.

He won't be needing it again and doesn't want it on him.

5

He makes one last stop before heading back to the warehouse. He parks in front of a hamburger joint, steps inside, and walks to the cash register, behind which a pimple-faced young man in a white hat stands waiting. He orders six hamburgers for take-out. He pays and walks to a red vinyl stool. He sits down and leans forward with his arms on the counter and glances around the room, checking out the few other patrons. To his right a woman sips an ice-cream soda through a straw, and a teenage boy drags French fries through a smear of ketchup. Then he looks left. The detective he ran into at the Shenefield Hotel, the one who saw him drop the murder weapon, sits not twenty feet away in a booth in the corner. A greasy white take-out bag sits on the table to his left, presumably lunch for someone who couldn't make it to the diner. Eugene turns quickly away, head snapping forward. He looks straight ahead at the wall behind the counter, at shelves of ketchup and mustard and various flavors of syrup for sodas and fresh fruit in baskets. He wants to glance over his shoulder again, to see if the detective noticed him, but doesn't. He must simply sit here and look normal and wait for his food. He wants to leave immediately, but doesn't do that either. If he leaves the counter boy might call after him, hey, mister, you forgot your food, and this would bring him attention he doesn't want. No, he must sit and wait. He must not look around nervously. He must act normal. He closes his eyes and swallows. He opens his eyes and looks at the clock on the wall.

After what feels like an hour a white paper bag is set in front of him.

He says thanks, picks up the bag, turns around. He doesn't glance toward the table at which the detective sits. Only an asshole would do that. He walks straight for the door. He feels stiff and awkward in his movements, as if he were drunk and trying not to reveal the fact. He pushes his way outside. He walks to his motorcycle.

No one tries to stop him. No one says a word.

6

He steps into the warehouse and walks to the tractor trailer parked at dock number three. He looks into it through a hole in one of the doors. Evelyn and Louis Lynch are sitting across from one another, silent and motionless. Evelyn's arms and legs have been freed, the gag removed from her mouth. At this point it doesn't matter. She'll be locked in the trailer until it's finished and it'll be finished tomorrow afternoon.

Besides, she needs to eat.

'I got you food.'

Neither Evelyn nor Louis Lynch says anything.

'Stand up.'

They both get to their feet.

Louis Lynch glances toward him. 'Do you really think you have any chance of walking away from this?'

'Toss your gun toward the door.'

He removes a revolver from its holster and throws it toward Eugene. It thuds against the wood paneling and slides to the door, which brings it to a stop.

'You're already dead,' Louis Lynch says, 'you just don't know it yet.'

'Turn around and put your hands to the wall, both of you.'

They both turn their backs to him. They both walk to

the opposite end of the trailer. They press their palms against the wall.

'Don't move.'

Eugene pulls up on the handle, the bolts retract, and the doors swing open. He removes two burgers wrapped in greasy white paper, then tosses the bag containing the four remaining hamburgers into the trailer. It lands with a heavy thud against the floor. He picks up Louis Lynch's revolver and tucks it into the back of his pants. He shuts the trailer doors and brings the handle down, sliding the bolts back into their holds. He puts the padlock into place.

Then he walks to a stack of pallets in the middle of the floor and sits down. He takes off his gloves. He unwraps one of his burgers. The smell makes his stomach turn. He knows he should eat, but he isn't at all hungry. He feels sick. He brings the burger to his mouth and takes a bite. It's very salty. He chews slowly and forces himself to swallow.

This is it, then.

There's nothing left to do until tomorrow – when it all happens.

THE CANNIBALS

FIFTY-ONE

At nine twenty, with the Lazarus sun drowned once more in the western sea, a heavy-set man in a gray suit with a blue silk tie wrapped around his neck and a matching handkerchief poking from his breast pocket steps from a DC-6, descends a set of rolling steps, and, trailed by three men, makes his way across the tarmac, through Los Angeles Airport, and out the front doors. Crowds, without realizing they're doing it, part for him as he walks. People simply glance in his direction as he cuts through space with the ease of a sharp knife and step out of his way. They do it as a unit, a group of people suddenly moving as one, like a sheet of paper unfolding.

He carries in his right hand a black leather briefcase.

FIFTY-TWO

1

Next morning, the sixteenth of April, the sun breaks past the horizon at five twenty-one. The temperature is fifty-two degrees Fahrenheit, though it will increase to sixty-eight before the day is finished. The air is clear enough to see Mount Wilson to the north through the morning haze and to the northwest the Santa Monica Mountains. The wind speed is a little over five miles per hour. The sky is cloudless and when the sun rises fully will be a one-color canvas – solid blue. In other words, it's a beautiful spring day, last weekend's rainstorm nothing but a distant memory.

2

At seven thirty Carl steps into the cool spring morning.

He hopes they catch a break on this investigation

today. They need to catch a break on this investigation. They have too many man-hours put into it to come up with nothing. And Carl feels they're close.

He can sense it. They're close.

To what, though, he doesn't know.

3

Eugene opens his eyes at seven forty-five to find himself looking at pin-dots of morning light shining through holes in the corrugated tin roof overhead like stars in a makeshift sky. His night was long and restless and cold, and what little sleep he had was unpleasant. His head aches and he feels sick to his stomach.

The best outcome today is still something to dread.

Today will be a day filled with ugliness and horror.

He wishes it were otherwise, but it isn't.

He wishes he could take Evelyn out of that trailer and scrub her body clean and give her a fresh set of clothes. He wishes he could apologize and wrap her in his arms and forget any of this ever happened. But he can't do any of that. He can't even allow himself to *feel* any of that.

Much worse is yet to come.

4

They didn't let Fingers leave last night. They led him instead to a hotel room with a bed and told him to get comfortable, we're not letting you leave till you talk. He thinks they're getting desperate, or else they sense something approaching. He certainly does.

But then he knows Eugene has summoned the Man.

He gets to his feet and walks to the window. He pulls open the curtains and looks out at the day. Cars roll by on the street six floors below. People walk on the sidewalk.

Someone knocks.

He turns around. A uniformed officer pushes open the door and says, 'Get dressed. They want you in the interrogation room.'

He nods.

'Okay.'

5

Louis Lynch paces the floor of this tiny fucking prison while Evelyn sits expressionless with her knees drawn up to her chest. He wants to yell at her, to shout in her face, where's your fucking heart? We need to get out of here! We need to *do* something! But he doesn't shout at her. This is at least partly his fault. He should have listened to her worries day before yesterday. If he'd listened to her worries this never would have happened. She knew it was coming and he ignored her.

He can't believe he allowed himself to walk into a trap.

It was a big mistake, but the milkman made a mistake of his own.

Because Lou isn't someone who walks through strange doors with only one weapon. Even now he can feel the weight of the small six-shot Colt Vest Pocket fitted snugly into its custom holster on the inside of his left wrist.

Even now he has plans for it.

6

Carl and Friedman step into the interrogation room at ten to nine.

Darryl Castor is already inside, facing the reel-to-reel magnetic tape recorder on the table before him. He looks bored, his shoulders slumped, his eyes distant.

Carl hands him a cup of hot coffee.

'Thanks.'

He nods, then takes a seat. Friedman takes another.

'Sleep all right?'

'I don't like being held captive.'

'You can walk out that door as soon as you tell us what we need to know.'

He lights a cigarette and inhales deeply. The dry tobacco crackles as it burns. He looks toward the ceiling and exhales. He thinks for a moment about his house. He thinks about his front door and walking through it. He thinks about the years stolen from Naomi and what they might have been like if she were allowed to live them. He thinks about her laugh, wonderful and loud and infectious. He misses sitting on the couch with her. He misses holding her hand while they watched television. He misses the way she would lean over and kiss the corner of his mouth for no reason at all. He misses her scent.

He glances toward Darryl Castor.

'Cigarette?'

'No, thanks.'

'Then let's get started.'

'Like I said yesterday, I don't have anything to tell you.'

'I'm hoping to change your mind.'

'It's not a decision, man. I'd cooperate if I knew anything, but I don't.'

'You know plenty.'

7

Eugene opens his bottle of Old Grand-Dad at half past ten. He holds it to his nose and inhales its scent. He takes a swallow. It burns going down. He doesn't know if he can bring himself to do what he needs to do. He doesn't want to do it. He can't do it. He feels sick when he thinks about it. But he has to do it. He takes a second swallow of whiskey and looks at the day-old hamburger on the pallet beside him. He should eat it. He doesn't want to. He's both hungry and sick to his stomach simultaneously. He should try to eat. He picks up the hamburger and unwraps it. He brings it to his mouth and takes a bite. It's cold and the fat in the burger has congealed. The tomato is grainy and flavorless. He chews slowly, tasting nothing. He wants to be sick. He swallows. It goes down like a lump of lead. He washes the bite down with yet another swig of whiskey. He tells himself he needs to be careful about the drinking. He tells himself he can't get drunk. He takes another bite of hamburger. He wonders how he ended up in this mess. He's always tried to be a decent human being. He's always minded his own business. He had his simple life and his small ambitions unfulfilled, his small dreams, and the occasional woman to keep him warm on the occasional cold night, but that's all, and that's all he needed, all he wanted if he's honest with himself. So how did he end up here?

Stop it, Eugene. How you ended up here is irrelevant. You're here. You're in the situation you're in. You have to deal with it. Bellyaching accomplishes nothing. You know it accomplishes nothing. Just eat your goddamn hamburger and wait. At one o'clock you get up and you walk to that trailer and you begin. Don't get drunk. Have enough whiskey that you can do what you need to and not a drop more. You can get through this. In three hours it'll be over.

You can handle that. Three hours is no time at all. So no more feeling sorry for yourself. No more bellyaching. You wait till one o'clock and you do what you need to do. Okay?

He nods to himself.

Okay.

He takes another swallow from his bottle.

8

Fingers scratches his cheek and looks down at the older detective's left wrist, but the man's watch is covered by the cuff of his shirt. He thinks it might be time to start talking, but he's not certain. He could be kidding himself, but it feels right, and he has nothing else to go on. He exhales in a sigh and looks toward the reels of magnetic tape waiting to record. Then he looks from one detective to the other. He hopes to God he isn't making a mistake.

'Okay.'

'Okay what?'

'I'm tired of being locked in this fucking room.'

'You and me both.'

'Then let's get this over with.'

But before they can even begin the telephone rings.

The younger detective gets to his feet and picks it up.

'Hello?' He listens for a moment, then says, 'Okay. We're on our way.'

He hangs up.

'What is it?'

'We got a match at The Fairmont on Wilshire.'

'Who?'

'Louis Lynch.'

'We sure?'

'It's an also-known-as, could be someone who really is named Leopold Jones, but the check-in date is right.'

'Okay.' The older detective gets to his feet.

Fingers looks up at him and says, 'He's not there.'

'How do you know?'

'Because I know where he is.'

The older detective looks to his partner. 'You go.'

'You sure?'

He nods.

'Okay.'

The younger detective heads out the door.

'You better start talking.'

9

At a little past noon a heavy-set man in a gray suit with a red silk tie wrapped around his neck and a matching hand-kerchief poking from his breast pocket steps from the elevator at the Fairmont Hotel and, trailed by three men, heads through the lobby toward the bright midday sun-shine, and then into it, breathing in the fresh Pacific air. He pauses a moment and puts his face toward the sun before continuing toward a black rental car parked on the street. First he needs to pick up a few weapons, then he'll head to an important appointment – at which he fully intends to kill a motherfucker.

10

Fingers watches the reels spin as he speaks, watches the magnetic tape transfer from one to the other. There's something hypnotic about it. The tape rolls while he thinks of nothing at all, and the words come easily, as if the tape were simply pulling them from his mouth. If he were to look at the detective instead he might start wondering whether the man could see his lies; he'd stumble mid-sentence, forget what he was saying, and contradict himself. It's best to simply watch the reels spin. So that's what he does.

He watches them spin and tells the detective he got a call from Louis Lynch last week, during which he was asked several questions about Eugene Dahl. He thought it odd, Eugene isn't part of that world, but he answered the questions all the same. Lou was asking for the Man and when the Man wants to know something you tell him. It's just that simple. Or it was until he learned he'd inadvertently helped to frame his friend for the murder of Theodore

Stuart. It made him sick. He doesn't get involved in that ugly sort of business even when it means sinking a stranger. It fucks with his sleep, and he's a man who likes his sleep. To mitigate his guilt he tried to help Eugene. He gave him a gun, offered him money. He didn't want to put himself at risk, but he wanted to do something.

Unfortunately, he believes he made it worse for Eugene rather than better. He believes he might even have sent him to his death.

That is, unless someone stops it, and he doesn't even know if that's possible at this point. The situation's a mess.

In addition to everything else that's happening, maybe even because of everything else that's happening – there's no better time than in the midst of confusion to attempt such a thing – Louis Lynch is planning to eliminate the Man and take over his organization. He believes so, anyway.

Up until six years ago everybody with an opinion on the matter believed Lou would end up running it anyway, but when Evelyn Manning turned twenty-one she began working for her father, learning how things operated, preparing to take over herself once her father retired. That didn't sit well with Lou. He wasn't going to take orders from a woman. He wasn't going to take orders from anybody. He'd worked for the Man for twenty years, helped to build an underground empire, and he was its rightful inheritor. For six years he's been growing increasingly unhappy, and now it looks like he's using this time on the

West Coast to seize the organization and bury anyone who might stand in his way.

Two days ago Lou came to him and asked if he had access to a warehouse. He needed an isolated place where loud noises wouldn't raise any eyebrows. He said he knew about a place in Vernon that a real-estate investor used as a tax loss. He said he could have the keys in Lou's hand within an hour. Lou said that sounded fine, so he took care of it.

Next thing he knows Evelyn Manning's been kidnapped, and rumor has it the Man has flown to the West Coast to get her back. He thinks Lou is trying to lure his boss to the warehouse in order to kill him. He thinks Evelyn Manning might already be dead. He thinks it's all happening today.

And he thinks Eugene is walking into the middle of it.

He met with Eugene yesterday morning, just before getting picked up by the cops, tried once more to give him money and talk him into leaving the country, but he refused. He said he had to find evidence that would prove his innocence. He said he couldn't live the rest of his life on the lam. The last couple days had been the worst days of his life and he couldn't live this way for years. He'd rather died than live this way.

The desperation in Eugene's voice got to him. He told his friend about the warehouse. He told him he might find evidence there. He also told him not to go, told him it was far too dangerous. But first he told him where it was.

And he's afraid he sent him to his death.

He shakes his head and looks down at his hands. He hopes he's done the right thing, but is almost certain he hasn't.

The detective leans forward and asks him, where's this warehouse at?

Fingers tells him.

11

The police search Louis Lynch's hotel room.

12

Eugene takes one last swig from his bottle of whiskey, wipes it down with a rag, sets it on a stack of pallets. He slips his hands into a pair of gloves and picks up Evelyn's Berretta, wiping his prints from that as well before gripping it for use in his gloved fist. He looks at the trailer parked at dock number three.

He works himself up, breathing heavily, rocking back and forth on the balls of his feet. He can do this. He can do this. He has to do this, so he can.

He tries to envision the scene the police must come upon. He plays it out in his mind. He nods. There are holes. It isn't perfect. But it's all he's got, so it'll have to do. If the police don't buy it immediately, he's finished. If they do buy it, he might be okay. They can't look too close, that's all.

It's the small details that kill an illusion.

Don't worry about that. It's too late to worry about that. It's time to get on with it. The time for thinking is finished, the time for doing has arrived. Time to get on with it.

He walks to the trailer and grabs the handle.

13

Lou stands in the trailer with his hands raised. He faces the open doors, looking to the milkman on the other side. The milkman stands with a gun in his hand, stands as if rooted to the ground. The gun is aimed at Lou's face and his eyes are alive with terror and determination. He means to kill Lou. Whether he'll be able to do it is an open question, but it's clear from his eyes that he means to do it and no maybes.

He tells Lou to step from the trailer. His voice is shaky with emotion.

Lou walks slowly toward him, thinking about the Colt Vest Pocket in its custom holster. Nothing up my sleeve but six doses of death. He thinks about punching a hole in the milkman's forehead. He steps from the forgiving wood-paneled floor of the trailer, which bows with each step, to the hard concrete floor of the warehouse. He swallows.

'Turn around.'

He turns around. He looks at Evelyn, who stands at the other end of the trailer with her hands raised. He smiles at her and winks; don't worry, I'll get us out of this.

'Shut the trailer. Lock the doors.'

This is his opportunity, probably his only opportunity, so he'd better use it wisely. He'd better be fast and sure and do what needs to be done.

He reaches left and right, grabbing the trailer doors. He brings them together, closing Evelyn inside. He reaches up and swings the handle down, locking the doors. Then with his right hand he grabs for his left wrist, feels cool metal against his palm, thumbs away the holster's snap.

A quick turn and he should have a shot. Hopefully he can get it off before the milkman even realizes he has a gun in his hand.

He pivots left.

14

Eugene watches Louis Lynch close the trailer doors and thinks about putting a bullet in his head. He needs it to look like Evelyn pulled the trigger. For this to work, it must look like Evelyn shot him from the trailer, where she was being held. Which means Eugene must shoot him from that direction. Which means he and Louis Lynch must trade positions.

He can't believe he has to do this, can't believe he's been put in this position. When he finds spiders in his apartment he carries them outside rather than kill them, but he's going to kill a man, and not in self-defense. He's simply going to aim and pull his trigger. He's going to shoot an unarmed man in the head. First he'll shoot him in the leg, then he'll shoot him in the head.

It has to look right.

Louis Lynch reaches up and grabs the handle and pulls it down, locking the trailer doors into place. Then he pauses and pivots left, turning quickly with something in his right hand. Light reflects off it. He has a gun in his hand. Eugene doesn't know where it came from, but he has a gun in his hand.

Eugene drops to the concrete and pulls his trigger.

Then Louis Lynch's gun fires.

Eugene doesn't know if he's been hit, he doesn't feel any pain, but he knows Louis Lynch has been. Blood spreads on his shirt.

Eugene fires again, aiming for the face. A black dot appears above the right eyebrow and a door opens in the back-left side of his head, a flap of skin and hair hinging the bone as it dangles there, and the contents of his head splatter the white trailer doors behind him. He falls to his knees, then onto his side, and slowly rolls supine, his right arm flopping out. Then he stops moving and is completely still.

Eugene gets to his feet and examines himself. He's not been shot.

He looks to the corpse on the concrete floor across from him. He killed a man. Louis Lynch did him a favor and made it self-defense but still he wants to be sick. He tells himself he can't be sick, can't vomit, because he doesn't have time to clean it up, and it can't be here when the police arrive. He leans down and rests his hands on his knees and stares at his feet. He tells himself he cannot be sick, goddamn it, get your shit together, Eugene.

The nausea passes.

He stands up and again looks to the corpse and feels a second wave of nausea, not because he's killed a man but because the scene he wanted the police to stumble upon has been ruined. Louis Lynch was not supposed to die there, and Eugene can't move the body. He knows he can't. The police would easily be able to see it had been moved, and that would ruin the illusion. He needs to work with what's happened. He can do that.

Jesus Christ, he killed a man.

A wave of dizziness envelopes him and all at once he sits down on the concrete. He sits down hard. He thinks of nothing for a long time. His face feels numb.

He looks at his watch.

He needs to figure out what he's going to do. He doesn't have much time.

15

Carl drives south with his gas-foot heavy on the pedal and the pedal pushed to the floorboard. If there's an itch at the back of his brain he isn't aware of it. All he's thinking of as he drives is the situation at hand. He spoke with Captain Ellis who spoke with someone else, and now the Newton Division is providing half a dozen six- and eight-dollar shooters for the warehouse raid. If what Darryl Castor told him is true, it's going to get ugly in there. James Manning won't walk into such a situation alone, and chances are Louis Lynch knows that, which means he probably isn't working on his own either. There could be eight or ten armed men in there, not counting cops. Add to that situation a kidnapped woman and a milkman in the wrong place at the wrong time (based on what Friedman found in Louis Lynch's hotel room – a switchblade knife like the one used to murder the police officer, a shirt with blood on it, a locket containing a picture of James Manning and his daughter, a typewriter that may have been used to type up a blackmail note – that's all Eugene Dahl is: one unlucky son of a bitch), and you've got yourself a recipe for chaos.

He leans into the steering wheel, telling the car to go faster, you piece of shit.

But it doesn't go faster.

He hopes he isn't too late. He's afraid he is.

16

Evelyn sits in darkness. She heard three gunshots several minutes ago and has heard nothing since. One of them is dead, she's certain of it, and she thinks it must be Lou or he would have let her out of here by now.

The doors swing open, letting light in.

She squints, unable at first to see who's on the other side. Then her eyes adjust, slowly and by degrees. Eugene stands at the opposite end of the trailer with a pistol – with what looks like Lou's Colt Vest Pocket – hanging from his fist. Behind him she can see one of Lou's arms stretched across the concrete. The fingers are curled around nothing.

'Stand up.'

Evelyn gets to her feet.

'You don't have to do this, Gene.'

'I wish that were true.'

'It *is* true. You don't have to do this.'

'Come on out of the trailer, Evelyn.'

For a moment she doesn't move. She can stay in here. If she doesn't leave the trailer, she can stop time. Time will stop right here and nothing more will happen. She should have hit him harder when she had the chance. She should have bashed his fucking brains out. Why does she still feel love for him – or something like it? Maybe he won't do it. He didn't do it in the motel room. He had every reason to shoot her then, and he had the opportunity, but he didn't do it, so maybe he won't do it now.

'Evelyn.'

She nods. 'Okay.'

She walks toward the light. Her feet are bare and the cool wood feels good against them – rough and organic and good. A breeze blows through the warehouse and into the trailer. It cools the sticky sweat on her skin. These could be her last moments. She tells herself that's impossible, it's impossible for her to die, she's only twenty-seven, but she knows it *is* possible. Maybe she even has it coming. In the last six years she's brought death to others, and she's done it without remorse, so maybe she has it coming.

Eugene can't kill her. She knows he can't. She can see in his eyes as she walks toward him that he still has feelings for her, and you don't kill something you love.

She steps from the trailer.

17

Eugene looks at Evelyn. Her red hair's a tangled mess. She has mascara smeared around her eyes and running down her cheeks. The skin around her mouth is red and raw from the duct tape which covered it. There's a bruise on her left shoulder, purple in the middle but fading to yellow-green around the edges. Her blue eyes are bloodshot. She swallows and frowns and looks at him pleadingly. Once more he feels the urge to take her in his arms and tell her he's sorry. He's sorry for everything. The urge is great, but he knows he can't do it. Her eyes can't be trusted. She's a serpent; she'll only tempt him with doom disguised as something lovely.

He motions with the pistol in his hand.

'Over there.'

'I can get you money.'

'Move, Evelyn.'

'I can—'

'Move.'

She walks slowly.

He watches her, following her with the gun.

'Stop.'

She stops, stands there, looks at him. Her arms hang limp at her sides. Her shoulders are slumped. She looks sad and defeated. He tells himself it's an act. He tells himself she's trying to get him to drop his guard so she can attack. He tells himself she'd kill him if she had the chance, if she had even the slightest opportunity. He even believes most of those things. But he looks at her and he wants to be near her. There was a time when he believed they could have a life together, a quiet life in the suburbs somewhere, and he wants that still. Looking at her he wants that more than he's ever wanted anything.

But he's awake now, and there's no time for dreaming.

He takes several steps back toward the trailer and raises the gun in his hand. He looks across the sights to Evelyn's sad face and tells himself he has to do this. He doesn't have a choice. He simply doesn't have a choice. He'll never be safe until they're dead. These people eat people like him for lunch; they're cannibals. Evelyn would kill him without hesitation and her father would kill him quicker still. If he's to get his life back he has to end theirs. That's all there is to it. Otherwise the threat will always be there. Every time he turns a corner he'll know death might be waiting on the other side. He couldn't live like that. There's simply no way he—

'Gene.'

'No.'

He pulls the trigger. The gun explodes in his hand, kicking his arm back.

A moment later, Evelyn collapses to the floor.

18

At one twenty-five a black car pulls to a stop across the street from a dilapidated warehouse which once, long ago, was occupied by a construction-supply company. A heavy-set man in a gray suit with a red silk tie wrapped around his neck and a matching handkerchief poking from his breast pocket sits in the back of the car with a black briefcase resting on his knees. Two men sit in the back seat with him while another occupies the spot behind the steering wheel. The heavy-set man looks through a tinted window to the warehouse in which his daughter's being held.

'Whatever else happens, Evelyn's kidnapper dies in

there. That warehouse is his fucking coffin, right? So ready yourselves.'

'Yes, sir.'

'And if you hear any gunfire while I'm inside, don't wait. Something's gone wrong. I intend to get Evelyn out of there quietly.'

'Yes, sir.'

'What time is it?'

'One twenty-eight.'

The heavy-set man nods to himself, then pushes out of the car.

19

Eugene walks to Evelyn and looks down at her. She lies on her back with her legs folded under her body, her right arm bent over her chest, her left arm extended across the smooth concrete, as if she'd been reaching for something. Her eyes stare blank at the tin-roof sky.

His chest feels tight when he looks at her. He can't believe what he's done. He planned to do it, he knows he had to do it, but still he looks at her inanimate and can't believe it. This isn't what's supposed to happen when you meet a woman you could love; this simply isn't the way it's supposed to go.

He closes his eyes. He tells himself to be calm, to be focused. He's almost at the end of this. It's almost over.

He opens his eyes.

He pushes up her dress, revealing her sex, her red pubic hair, and straps her holster around the inside of her thigh, then pulls the dress back down, covering her once more. She deserves that at least. He tapes her ankles and wrists, being careful not to step in the puddle of blood forming beneath her body. He removes Evelyn's gun from his pocket and puts it into her hands. With her hands wrapped around it, he fires the gun toward Lou so that if the police check her for gunpowder residue they'll find it. He gets to his feet. He looks down at her yet again. He looks at her mouth. He wants to kiss it and say goodbye, but he doesn't. He doesn't deserve it. And, anyway, he's already told her goodbye in the most definitive way possible.

Kissing her would be a lie; he did this and must own it.

He takes a step back, away from the body, and tries to think about what to do next. It's difficult to think at all, let alone clearly.

He glances at his watch to see how much time he has before the Man arrives.

The second hand glides past the twelve. The minute hand moves forward a notch.

He has no time at all.

The blue door squeaks open.

He looks up to see a heavy-set man in a gray suit walk into the warehouse. He carries in his right hand a black briefcase.

Eugene looks at him across the empty room. There he

is, James 'the Man' Manning, that mythological figure he's heard about for as long as he can remember. If you were to judge only by outward appearances you'd think he might be a bank manager in a small town somewhere; an unhappy bank manager with a drinking problem. But there's something within him which belies that outward appearance, some cold black malevolence. Eugene knows the exterior is a lie, a facade which means nothing.

He stands fifty feet from Eugene and looks at him while Eugene looks back.

'Where's my daughter?'

His voice echoes in the empty room.

Eugene glances briefly to his left.

'Your daughter's dead. So are you.'

Eugene raises Louis Lynch's pistol while taking several running steps to his right, toward the back of the trailer at dock number three.

The Man drops his briefcase and reaches into his coat. The briefcase hits concrete and breaks open, revealing thousands of dollars in twenties. A breeze blows through the warehouse. Paper money flutters through the room.

The Man comes out with a rifle of some kind, swings it up, pumps it, and fires. The muzzle flashes and the gun kicks, but Eugene feels no pain. The round flies instead through the air where he once stood and slaps into the wall behind him. The echo of the report bounces around the warehouse, sounding like a series of hands clapping – softer, softer.

Eugene gets off three shots himself but because he's running to the right while firing he misses with all three.

The Man pumps the rifle, sending an empty brass shell arcing through the air, clinking to the concrete floor. He walks slowly toward Eugene, cool and calm. His daughter's dead, he's in the middle of a shootout, and but for the rifle jutting from his right hip he looks as though he's simply gone for an evening stroll, his face placid and emotionless.

Eugene slides to a stop, hunching behind one of the trailer's doors at dock number three, his heart pounding in his chest. If he panics he'll miss and he can't miss. This is his last round. He glances toward the pallets where he set Louis Lynch's revolver last night and wishes he'd thought to pick it up; but he didn't, so this is his situation. He empties his lungs, blowing out a long stream of air. Then he inhales, gets to his feet, and steps from behind the trailer door.

The Man continues toward him, face stoic, gun raised.

Both men aim as the distance between them shrinks.

They fire simultaneously.

20

Three men in suits push out of a black car and step into daylight. They walk to the trunk, on the floor of which lie three Thompson submachine guns with fifty-round drum magazines already locked in place. They pick them up, each man yanking back the bolt on his machine, readying it for fire.

They walk across the street, moving in on the warehouse.

21

The police come screeching around the corner, a radio car with its lights flashing followed by a black van. They slide along the asphalt, leaving dark trails of burned rubber as they come to a stop in the street one in front of the other. The van's back doors swing open and several uniformed cops, half a dozen armed six- and eight-dollar shooters, step from within, rifles gripped in their fists.

Carl follows them out, frantic-eyed and sweat-drenched. He blinks, pulls off his fedora, wipes his forehead with an arm.

Then looks toward the warehouse on the south side of the street. There he sees three men standing on the sidewalk with submachine guns hanging from their arms. The three men are looking in his direction.

For a moment nobody moves. Then the three gangsters lift their Tommy guns.

'Oh, shit.'

Eugene stands motionless, smoke wafting from the pistol in his gloved fist as smoke also wafts from the barrel of his enemy's rifle only ten feet away. He looks across those ten feet to a heavy-set man in an impeccable gray suit, his white shirt bright and starched crisp, his tie in place, the corner of his handkerchief poking neatly from his breast pocket. His hair is parted razor-straight on the left and combed into place but for a single gray strand hanging over his brow. He doesn't move. When the guns went off he stopped, wobbled a moment, and now he simply stands there, the barrel of his rifle slowly dropping toward the floor. Eugene sees no wound.

But behind him, a long smear of blood on the concrete floor. He opens his mouth to speak to Eugene, but no words pass his lips. Only a low groan and bits of bloody teeth which fall to the concrete like shattered porcelain.

Eugene watches as he falls sidewise, and it's a strange thing to see. He goes down stiff and doesn't try to catch himself, simply falls to his side like a felled tree and rolls prostrate, bloody drool and bits of teeth leaking from his mouth to the concrete floor. The back of his head is an inverted cone and his suit coat is dotted with gray pieces of brain and flecks of skull.

For a moment Eugene just stares.

Then he blinks and his mind begins working once more.

The police could be here at any moment. He doesn't have time to stand around.

He walks to Louis Lynch's body and puts the pistol into his hand before searching his pockets for a piece of paper. He finds the paper in a hip pocket: the bait with which Eugene lured him here. He folds it up and pockets it.

He tries to think of what he's done. Has he forgotten anything? The revolver. He walks to the stack of pallets on which it lies and picks it up. He doesn't know what to do with it. After a moment's thought he simply slides it across the concrete floor toward the blue door, as if the Man had told Louis Lynch to lose his weapon before they carried out the trade. Then he glances around the room to see if he missed anything else. He doesn't think so.

He's done the best he could.

He looks toward Evelyn.

And he's done the worst he could.

He hears gunfire from right outside. That's it. He's out of time.

He steps into the trailer and pulls the doors shut. He has to slam the second door three times before he gets the outside handle to fall and lock him inside.

Once in darkness, he removes his gloves.

23

Carl dives for cover behind the police van as gunshots ring out. He hits asphalt and draws his weapon. He hears cops shouting all around him, and explosions of gunfire, and bullets hitting metal and glass.

He ignores all of this. He takes aim.

He squeezes his trigger.

A moment later a man collapses to the sidewalk, suddenly vacant of life – an empty nest from which the birds have flown.

The two remaining gangsters continue their retreat.

24

Eugene sits in the trailer. The air is hot and nearly without oxygen. His lungs hurt. He's covered in sweat. He thinks about how he kept Evelyn in here for hours. He thinks about how he killed her.

Outside the gunfire stops.

The warehouse door opens and closes.

He gets to his feet and walks to the back of the trailer. He looks out to see two men in black suits with Tommy guns hanging from their fists. They look around the warehouse with their weapons ready, but only silence greets them, and the dead, whom they see and approach without speaking. They stand before the carnage like children awed, their faces pale. For a long time they neither move nor say a word.

Then, from outside, tinny through a bullhorn: 'You have ten seconds to come out with your hands up.'

Without looking away from the dead, the two men speak in soft tones. Eugene is only ten feet away, but cannot hear their words. When the speaking is done they turn toward the blue door and raise their weapons to await the police.

'Ten,' through the bullhorn. 'Nine.'

25

But when the police count their last nobody rushes into the warehouse.

From a rooftop across the street one of the LAPD shooters squeezes his trigger twice. A ventilation window shatters. He looks down to the street.

He gives a thumbs-up.

26

One moment the two men are simply standing there with their weapons raised at the ready; the next their heads are replaced by red mist. They collapse to the warehouse floor, one after the other. Their weapons fall from their hands.

Eugene backs away from the trailer door. The shooting is finished.

He sits down, pulls his knees up to his chest, wraps his arms around them. He closes his eyes. He hears police push into the warehouse. He hears their feet stomping. He hears their talk. He hears their exclamations.

He puts his hands over his ears.

He knows the police will soon discover him. They'll pull him from this trailer, put him in handcuffs, and haul him away. He knows that, and he knows he deserves it.

But for a few minutes he can have this quiet.

27

Carl stands watching while around him other men work. Bodies are bagged. Evidence is collected and numbered. Flashbulbs explode. The case is wrapping up. It's almost finished. He wonders if he has it in him to get clean, but he doesn't want to think about that just yet. He doesn't want to think about that at all.

Someone says his name. He looks up. One of the men from the crime lab stands by the back of a trailer looking at him.

'What is it?'

The man points.

He walks over and looks into the trailer. Eugene Dahl

sits on the floor inside with his legs pulled up to his chest. He looks at them, his face pale and drawn. Blood drips from his left ear.

'He was locked inside.'

28

Eugene steps from the trailer. Detective Bachman leads him to a quiet corner of the warehouse, somewhere we can talk for a few minutes, and hands him a handkerchief.

He holds it in his hand and looks at it, confused.

'Your ear,' Detective Bachman says, pointing.

He touches it and is surprised by the sharp sting of pain. He hadn't realized he'd been injured. He felt nothing when it happened, but he feels it now. The last rifle shot must have come within mere inches of killing him.

'Looks like the lobe is gone. Stray bullet must have gone into the trailer. Lucky you aren't dead. Need a few stitches but that's all.'

Eugene nods and puts the handkerchief to his ear. He doesn't know how much longer he can do this. He needs answers. He needs finality. He doesn't even care what the answers are so long as he understands what's happening.

A man can warm himself even beneath the blanket of certain doom.

He looks at the detective.

'Are you going to arrest me?'

FIFTY-THREE

1

Nobody arrests him. It's almost impossible to believe. He should be arrested. He should be tried and convicted and electrocuted till he's dead, but nobody arrests him. The detective takes his statement, and when he's finished talking simply nods and says yeah, that's about what I thought. He asks if he can go home. The detective says he can, but in the next couple days we'll need you around to answer any questions might come up. He says okay and walks out of there.

The daylight is very bright.

He supposes they might arrest him later, but he doesn't think so. The police like his story. And who gives a shit about a few dead lowlifes, anyway?

He rides his motorcycle to his apartment. He'll have to stop by the motel room on Whitley and collect his things at some point, but not today. Today he wants to lock himself in a small room and not come out again. He wants silence and darkness.

Everything seems alien to him now and oddly flat. His street doesn't feel like his street. His stairs don't feel like his stairs. Standing before his front door he's sure it isn't really his front door at all, and there's no chance that his apartment is on the other side of it. He unlocks the door and pulls the police tape away and steps inside. While it looks like his apartment, he knows it isn't. It feels wrong. It feels like nothing. The world has somehow become two-dimensional, a stagecraft version of itself.

There's no depth to it, nor is there feeling.

He closes his door and locks it.

He walks to his bedroom and grabs a blanket from the bed and carries it into the bathroom. He lies in his bathtub and covers himself with the blanket and closes his eyes.

This is what he needs. Darkness and silence.

But there's neither darkness nor silence to be found, not for long, because the darkness isn't empty. It never was.

2

Carl packs his suitcase and leaves the boarding house. He drives home, parks in front of his house. He walks to the front door and stands facing it for a long time. He doesn't know if he can do this. He doesn't think he can.

He reaches forward with a shaking hand, key extended. He pauses. He puts the key into the lock and turns it. He pushes the door open. It swings wide. He looks into his living room without stepping inside. He can see Naomi everywhere. Pictures of her rest on end-tables, the curtains she bought cover the windows, the couch they shared sits in the middle of the room.

He looks down at the metal threshold, afraid to pass over it. He considers pulling the door closed and walking away. He doesn't think he's ready for this.

He steps forward – for the first time in months he steps into his home. Then he closes the door behind him and locks it.

He sets down the suitcase.

He already feels sick, and knows over the course of the next week it'll only get worse. Much worse. There will be vomiting and diarrhea and tremendous leg cramps and probably he won't be able to sleep through any of it. There will come a time, he knows, when he thinks he might die and hopes he does. He will want to use so that he doesn't die, but he won't use, and he won't die either.

He's determined to reach the other side of this.

He will.

And he'll do it here, in his home, where almost every beautiful moment he ever experienced still lives.

He picks up a picture of Naomi. He looks at her beautiful heart-shaped face and her kind eyes. He loved her very much and he loves her still. He misses her and knows he won't ever stop missing her, not completely, and it hurts, but he knows that's okay. It's how you hold onto a memory; you accept the pain so you can keep the memory alive. You move on not by ignoring pain, but by accepting it and carrying it with you to the new places you go.

He'll get through this week because Naomi would want him to. She'd not want him to leap into the abyss after her. She'd not accept that. So he can't either.

This week will be the most difficult week of his life. He knows that.

But it's time.

Looking at his picture of Naomi, and thinking of his loss, he begins to cry. He gasps as the hurt washes over him. He tries to speak to her, to the photograph, but he's incapable of words. Words are insufficient. Words are for everyday experiences. Only childish grunts can properly express what he's feeling – this raw loneliness and pain. But he lets himself feel it. He lets himself cry.

It's time.

3

Eugene sits up alone in the gray early morning. He looks around the bathroom, feeling confused and sick. His neck is sore from sleeping in the bathtub. He pushes his way out from under his blanket and gets to his feet. He lights a cigarette and inhales deeply. He looks at himself in the bathroom mirror for a long time without knowing exactly what it is he's trying to catch a glimpse of, but he knows he isn't seeing it and suspects it isn't there. Whatever it is. He walks out to the living room, and through it to the balcony. He looks at the shallow world he now inhabits, drained of color and life. He thinks of the dream he just awakened from, the nightmare. He thinks of the cannibals. He thinks of that small boy they murdered, and the part they saved for him. He takes a drag from his cigarette. He knows who the boy was now, and supposes he always did.

But the boy is gone, even to the last part.

He flicks what remains of his cigarette out to the street. This is what he's left with.

EPILOGUE

Carl steps from the shower and dries off. He puts on slacks, a clean white shirt, and a coat. He combs his hair and looks at himself in the mirror. His cheeks are hollow, and his eyes tired, but he's healthy and his mind is clear.

He almost never thinks of junk these days, and when he does he finds he can push the thought aside. Sometimes it's difficult, but he can do it – and every day it's easier than the last. He relapsed once, four months ago, but it won't happen again. He won't *let* it happen again.

He puts on a hat and steps into the October evening. It's cool and crisp and wonderful. He inhales its scent and walks to his car. He gets inside and starts the engine. He drives toward Bunker Hill with his window down, the chill autumn air blowing against his face.

He parks in front of a small house where a blonde woman in her thirties lives alone. She's had husbands, but her first left and her second was murdered. She's given birth, but her son is missing and has been for months. She still reads the newspaper daily hoping to find him lurking between the lines in stories of burglary, armed robbery, and car theft. Sometimes she thinks she sees evidence that he was there.

On Saturday nights Carl drives to her house, picks her up, and they roll through the streets while she looks for him. Probably she'll never find him, he's just one small boy in a city of two million, but there's a kind of bravery in her refusal to give up despite the odds, and there's hope.

He's learned a lot about that from her.

He steps from his car and walks up the path to her front door. He raises his fist, hesitates a moment, and knocks. After a while Candice pulls open the door. She smiles at him. He smiles back, kisses the corner of her mouth.

'Are you ready?'

She says she is, and steps outside.